The
Dreamseller
COLLECTED

The
Dreamseller
COLLECTED

THE CALLING AND *THE REVOLUTION*

AUGUSTO CURY

ATRIA PAPERBACK

New York   London   Toronto   Sydney   New Delhi

ATRIA
PAPERBACK

An Imprint of Simon & Schuster, Inc.
1230 Avenue of the Americas
New York, NY 10020

First Atria Paperback edition May 2021

ATRIA PAPERBACK and colophon are trademarks of Simon & Schuster, Inc.

For information about special discounts for bulk purchases, please contact Simon & Schuster Special Sales at 1-866-506-1949 or business@simonandschuster.com.

The Simon & Schuster Speakers Bureau can bring authors to your live event. For more information or to book an event, contact the Simon & Schuster Speakers Bureau at 1-866-248-3049 or visit our website at www.simonspeakers.com.

Manufactured in the United States of America

1   3   5   7   9   10   8   6   4   2

Library of Congress Control Number: 2021934595

ISBN 978-1-9821-7985-4
ISBN 978-1-9821-8513-8 (ebook)

The Dreamseller

THE CALLING

A Novel

I dedicate this novel to the readers in every country where my books have been published. Especially to those who in one way or another sell dreams through their intelligence, critical approach, sensibility, generosity and kindness. Dreamsellers are often outsiders in the social nest. They are abnormal. For what is normal is to wallow in the mud of individuality, egocentrism and personalism. Their legacy will be unforgettable.

Preface

THIS IS MY FOURTH WORK OF FICTION AND MY TWENTY-SECOND book. My novels do not have as their goal plots that merely entertain, amuse or arouse emotion. They all involve theses, whether psychological, psychiatric, sociological or philosophical. Their intent is to foment debate, to journey into the world of ideas and go beyond the borders of prejudice.

I have been writing continuously for over twenty-five years and publishing for slightly over eight years. Perhaps it is because of the voyages into the territory of the unfathomable world of the human mind. Sincerely, I do not merit this success. I am not an author who can produce texts easily. Striving to be an artisan of words, I continually write and rewrite every paragraph, day and night, as if I were a compulsive sculptor. You will find in this novel thoughts that were sculpted after having been rewritten ten or twenty times in my mind.

Some books come from the core of the intellect; others come from the viscera of emotion. *The Dreamseller* came from the depths of both. While writing it, I was bombarded with countless questions, I smiled a lot, and at the same time reconsidered our follies, or at least my own. This novel journeys through the realms of drama and satire, through the tragedy of those who have experienced loss and the ingenuousness of those who treat existence like a circus.

The main character is endowed with unprecedented daring. Nothing or no one succeeds in controlling his acts and his words, except his own conscience. He shouts to the four winds that modern society has become a vast global madhouse in which it is normal to be anxious and stressed, and abnormal to be healthy, at peace, serene. With his Socratic method he challenges the thoughts of all who meet him. He bombards his listeners with countless questions.

My dream is that this book will be read not only by adults but by young people as well, many of whom are becoming passive servants to the social system. Unenraptured by dreams and adventures, they have become, despite some exceptions, consumers of products and services, not of ideas. Nevertheless, consciously or unconsciously, they all want a life peppered with effervescent emotions, even as babies when they risk leaving the crib. But where in society can such emotions be found in abundance? Some pay large amounts of money to achieve them and yet live in anguish. Others desperately seek fame and renown but die in boredom. The characters in this novel reject the crushing social routine, yet experience high doses of adrenaline daily. Still, the "business" of selling dreams comes with a high price. That is why risks and windstorms are their companions.

CHAPTER 1

The Encounter

O N THAT MOST INSPIRING OF DAYS, A FRIDAY, AT FIVE PM, people usually in a hurry stopped and congregated at a downtown intersection of the great city. They stared upward, frozen at a corner of the Avenue of the Americas. A fire truck's ear-splitting siren announced danger. An ambulance attempted to break through the jammed traffic to reach the building.

Firemen arrived quickly and cordoned off the area, keeping any onlookers from approaching the imposing San Pablo Building, which belonged to the Megasoft Group, one of the largest companies in the world. Curious pedestrians lined the streets and soon the area was buzzing with questions: *What's going on? Why all the commotion?* Others simply pointed upward. On the twentieth floor, on the ledge of the stunning mirrored-glass building, stood a man ready to jump.

One more person hoped to cut short his brief existence. In a time steeped in sadness, more people died at their own hands than through war or murder. The numbers were astonishing to anyone who thought about them. Pleasure had become as wide as an ocean but as shallow as a pond. Many of the financially and intellectually privileged lived dull, empty lives, isolated in their world. Society afflicted the poor and the well-to-do equally.

The San Pablo jumper was a forty-year-old man with a

well-chiseled face, strong eyebrows, taut skin and overgrown well-kept salt-and-pepper hair. His air of sophistication, though, sculpted through long years of study, was now reduced to dust. Of the five languages he spoke, none had helped him understand the language of his internal demons. Drowning in depression, he lived a meaningless life where nothing moved his spirit.

At that moment, only the end of his life seemed to matter. The monstrous phenomenon called death, which seemed so terrifying, was also a magical solution to his tortured soul. He looked upward, as if wishing to redeem himself for his last act, looked at the chasm below and took two quick, careless steps forward. The crowd gasped, fearing he was about to jump.

Some of the onlookers bit their fingernails under the mounting stress. Others didn't dare blink for fear of missing a single detail. Human beings hate pain but have an extreme attraction to it; they detest misfortune and poverty, but such things seduce the eye. Even knowing that watching the outcome of that tragedy could cost them countless sleepless nights, they still could not look away. Meanwhile, drivers caught in the snarling traffic could not care less about the impending doom above, and leaned impatiently on their horns. Some stuck their heads out the windows and bellowed, "Jump and get it over with!"

The chief of police followed the firemen to the top of the building, each trying and failing to reason with the would-be jumper. Defeated, the authorities reached out to a renowned psychiatrist, who was hastily called to the scene. The doctor, too, attempted to gain the man's trust, trying to make him see the consequences of his actions—but he couldn't even get close. "One more step and I'll jump!" the man shouted. He seemed certain that only death would finally silence his thoughts. Audience or no, his decision was made. His mind replayed his misfortunes, his frustrations, feeding the fever of his grief.

Meanwhile, down on the street below, a man tried to make his way through the crowd toward the building. He looked like just another curious on-looker, only more poorly dressed. He wore a wrinkled black blazer over a faded blue shirt, long-sleeved and stained in places. He wasn't wearing a tie. And his wrinkled black pants looked like they hadn't been washed in a week. His longish, uncombed hair was graying at the temples. His full beard had gone untrimmed for some time. Dry skin with prominent wrinkles around his eyes and in the folds of his face showed he sometimes slept out in the open. He was between thirty and forty, but seemed aged beyond his years.

His unstructured appearance contrasted with the delicacy of his gestures. He gently touched people's shoulders, smiling as he passed. They couldn't describe the sensation of being touched by him, but they quickly made room for him.

He approached the crime scene tape but was stopped from going any further. Disregarding the barrier, he stared into the eyes of those blocking his way and said flatly, "I need to go in. He's waiting for me."

The firemen looked him up and down and shook their heads. He looked more like someone who needed help rather than someone who could provide it.

"What's your name?" they asked, without blinking.

"That doesn't matter at a time like this," the mysterious man answered firmly.

"Who called you here?" the firemen asked.

"You'll find out. But if you keep me here any longer, you'll have to prepare for another funeral," he said, raising his eyes toward the top of the building.

The firemen were starting to get nervous and the mysterious man's last phrase shook them. He hurried past them. "After all," they thought, "maybe he's an eccentric psychiatrist or a relative of the jumper."

When he got to the top of the building, the stranger was stopped again, this time by the police chief.

"Hold it right there. You can't be here," adding that he should go back down at once.

But the man stared at them for a moment and answered calmly, "What do you mean I can't be here? You were the ones who called me."

The police chief looked at the psychiatrist who looked at the fire chief. They gestured to one another to find out who might have called this man. In that moment of confusion, the stranger hurried past the officer. There was no time to stop him. Any commotion could spook the jumper into carrying out his plan. They bit their lips and waited to see what happened.

This man who had come out of nowhere, uninvited and apparently unshaken by the possibility of this jumper plunging to his death, moved toward the ledge until he was dangerously close, about three feet away. Surprised, the jumper stammered, "Get away from me or I'll kill myself!"

The stranger didn't flinch. Nonchalantly, he sat down on the ledge, took a sandwich from his coat pocket, and started eating it with gusto. Between bites, he whistled a cheery tune.

The jumper didn't know what to think. He took it as an insult and shouted:

"Stop that whistling! I'm going to jump."

Annoyed, the stranger turned from his sandwich. "Could you not interrupt my dinner?" he said and took several more healthy bites of his meal, swinging his legs over the ledge. He then looked at the confused jumper and offered him a bite.

Looking on, the officials were stunned. The police chief's lips trembled, the psychiatrist's eyes widened and the fire chief could only furrow his brow.

The jumper just stared and thought, "This guy's crazier than me."

CHAPTER 2

The Introduction

To watch someone enjoy eating a sandwich just inches from a man about to jump to his death was surreal, like something out of a movie. The would-be jumper narrowed his eyes, tightened every muscle in his face and breathed fiercely, not knowing whether to jump, scream or pummel this stranger. Panting, he yelled at the top of his lungs, "Get out of here, already! I'm going to jump."

And he came within a hair of falling. This time, to those down below, it seemed, he really would smash into the ground. The crowd buzzed in horror and the police chief covered his eyes, not bearing to watch.

Everyone expected the stranger to pull away. He could have said, as the psychiatrist and the policeman had, "No, don't do it! I'm leaving," or simply offered advice like, "Life is beautiful. You can overcome your problems. You have your whole life ahead of you." But, to everyone's surprise, especially the man on the ledge, he hopped to his feet and began reciting a poem at the top of his lungs. He spoke toward the sky and pointed at the would-be jumper:

Let the day this man was born be struck from the record
of time!

Let the dew from the grass of that morning evaporate!
Let the clear blue sky that brought joy to strollers that
*   afternoon be withheld!*
Let the night when this man was conceived be stolen by
*   suffering!*
Reclaim from that night the glowing stars that dotted the
*   heavens!*
Erase from his infancy all his smiles and his fears!
Strike from his childhood his frolicking and his
*   adventures!*
Steal from him his dreams and his nightmares, his sanity
*   and his madness!*

When he was done, the stranger let a sadness wash over him. He dropped his voice and his gaze and said softly, "one," offering no further explanation. The crowd, amazed, wondered whether it might all be some sort of street theater. Neither did the police officer know how to react: Would it be better to interfere or wait to see where this all led? Hoping for an explanation himself, the fire chief looked at the psychiatrist, who said, confused:

"I don't know a thing about . . . He must be just another nut."

The jumper was stunned. The stranger's words echoed in his mind. Trying to make sense of it, he lashed out: "Who are you to try to assassinate my past? What right do you have to destroy my childhood? What gives you the right?"

Even as he said it, the jumper thought, "Can it be that I'm the one committing this murder?" But he tried to shrug off the thought.

Catching the jumper deep in thought, the stranger provoked him further.

"Be careful. Thinking is dangerous, especially for someone who wants to die. If you want to kill yourself, don't think."

The man was dumbfounded; the stranger seemed to read

his mind. He thought: "Is this man encouraging me to jump? Is he some kind of sadist? Does he want to see blood?" He shook his head as if to cut short his trance, but thoughts always undermine impulsive desires. Seeing the jumper's mental confusion, the stranger spoke softly, to drive home his point.

"Don't think. Because if you do, you'll realize that whoever kills himself commits multiple homicides: First, he kills himself and then, slowly, he kills those left behind. If he thinks, he'll understand that guilt, mistakes, disappointments and misfortune are the privileges of living. Death has no privileges." The stranger's personality shifted from confidence to sorrow. He said the word "four" and shook his head indignantly.

The jumper was paralyzed. He wanted to disregard this stranger's ideas, but they were like a virus infecting his mind. Trying to resist the temptation to think, he instead challenged the stranger.

"And who are you to try antagonizing me instead of saving me? Why don't you treat me like what I am: a sick, pitiful mental case?" He raised his voice. "Leave me alone! I have nothing left to live for."

Undaunted, the stranger lost his patience and pressed forward.

"Who says you're this wilting flower? A man who has lost his love of life? Some poor, underprivileged soul who can't bear the weight of his past? To me, you're none of that. To me, you're just a man too proud to be affected by misery greater than your own, a man who has locked his feelings away deep inside."

The man on the ledge felt as if he had been struck in the chest, unable to breathe. Angrily, he growled, "Who are *you* to judge me?"

The stranger had pegged him perfectly. Like a bolt of lightning, his words had pierced the deepest reaches of his memory.

At that moment, the man on the ledge thought about his father, who had crushed his childhood and caused him so much pain—his emotionally distant father, who would never let anyone in. It was extremely difficult for the man to deal with the scars from the past. Rattled by those haunting memories, he said in a softer tone, now with tears in his eyes:

"Shut up! Don't say another word. Let me die in peace."

Seeing that he had touched a deep wound, the stranger also softened his tone. "I respect your pain and cannot judge it. Your pain is unique, and you are the only one who can truly feel it. It belongs to you and to no one else."

These words nearly brought the man to tears. He understood that no one can judge another's suffering. His father's pain was unique and therefore could not be felt or judged by anyone other than his father. He had always blamed his father, but for the first time he began to see him through different eyes. At that moment, to his surprise, the stranger said something that could have been taken as praise or criticism.

"And in my eyes, you're also something else: courageous. Because you're willing to smash your body in exchange for a restful sleep, even if it is inside of a tomb. That is, without a doubt, a beautiful illusion . . ." And he paused so the man could fully realize the consequences of his actions.

Again, the man wondered about this stranger who showed up just in time with words that cut to the quick. A night of eternal sleep in a tomb? The idea suddenly sickened him. Still, insistent on carrying out his plan, he fought back:

"I don't see any reason to go on with this worthless life," he argued, vehemently, furrowing his brow, tormented by the thoughts that ran uninvited into his head. The stranger confronted him poignantly:

"Worthless life? You ingrate! Your heart, at this very moment, must be trying to burst from your chest to save itself from being killed." He pleaded, in the voice of the man's own heart: "No! No! Have pity on me! I pumped your blood tirelessly, millions of times. I lived only for you. And now you want to silence me, without even giving me the right to defend myself? I was the most faithful of servants. And what is my reward? A ridiculous death! You want to stop my beating only to end your suffering. How can you be this selfish? If only I could pump courage into your selfish veins." Challenging the man further, he asked, "Why don't you pay attention to your chest and hear the desperation of your heart?"

The man felt his shirt vibrate. He hadn't noticed that his heart was about to explode. It did in fact seem to be screaming inside his chest. But, just when the man appeared convinced, he mustered one last defense.

"I've already sentenced myself to death. There's no hope."

"You've sentenced yourself?" the stranger asked. "Did you know that suicide is the most unjust judgment? Why condemn yourself without defending yourself? Why not give yourself the right to argue with your ghosts, to face your losses? It's much easier to say life isn't worth living . . . You're not being fair to yourself."

The stranger knew in masterly fashion that those who take their own lives, even those who plan their deaths, can't understand the depth of the pain they cause. He knew that if they could see the despair of their loved ones and the inexplicable consequences of suicide, they would draw back and fight for their lives. He knew that no letter or note could serve as a defense. The man on top of the San Pablo Building had left a message for his only child, trying to explain the unexplainable.

He had also spoken with his psychiatrists and psychologists about his ideas on suicide. He had been analyzed, interpreted, diagnosed, and had listened to countless theories about his metabolic and cerebral deficiencies. And he had been encouraged to overcome his problems by seeing them from a different perspective. But none of it made sense to that rigid intellectual. None of those interventions or explanations could lift him from his emotional quagmire.

The man was inaccessible. But for the first time someone, this stranger at the top of a building, challenged his thinking. The stranger was a specialist in piercing impenetrable minds. His words evoked more noise than tranquillity. He knew that without that noise there is no questioning, and without questioning the gamut of possibilities goes undiscovered. The jumper couldn't stand it any longer, and decided to ask the stranger a question; he had strongly resisted doing so, as he had assumed that he would be entering a minefield. But he stepped into it, regardless.

"Who are you?"

The man was hoping for a short, clear answer, but none was forthcoming. Instead, he fielded another burst of questions.

"Who am I? How can you ask who I am if you don't know who *you* are? Who are you, who would seek to silence your existence in front of a terrified audience?"

The man answered sarcastically, "Me? Who am *I*? I'm a man who in a few short moments will cease to exist. Then I won't know who I am or what I was."

"Well, I'm different from you. Because you've stopped looking for answers. You've become a god, while every day I ask myself 'Who am I?'" The stranger paused, then asked another question: "Would you like to know the answer I found?"

Reluctantly, the man nodded.

"I'll answer you if you answer me first," the stranger said. "From what philosophical, religious or scientific fountain did you drink to believe that death is the end of existence? Are we living atoms that disintegrate, never again to regain their structure? Are we merely an organized brain or do we have a mind that coexists with the brain and transcends its limits? Does any person know? Do you? What believer can defend his thought without the element of faith? What neuroscientist can defend his arguments without making use of the phenomenon of speculation? What atheist or agnostic can categorically defend his ideas free of uncertainty?"

The stranger seemed to press on with this Socratic method, asking endless questions, challenging every answer, trying to stimulate critical thinking. The man grew dizzy from that explosion of inquiries. He considered himself an atheist, but he discovered that his atheism sprang from a fountain of speculation. Like many "normal" people, he pontificated about these phenomena without once debating them removed from passion and ideology.

The stranger had turned the questions on himself. But before the man on the ledge could answer, he offered his own response:

"We're both ignorant. The difference between us is that I recognize my ignorance."

CHAPTER 3

Shaking the Foundation of Faith

WHILE GRAND IDEAS WERE BEING DEBATED AT THE TOP OF the building, a few people below walked away without ever knowing what happened. Some couldn't stand to wait to know another man's misfortune. But most remained, eager to see the result.

From the crowd emerged a man named Bartholomew, who was marinated in whiskey and vodka. He, too, was an ordinary man with hidden scars, despite being extremely good-natured—and from time to time brazen. His short, unruly black hair had gone weeks without touching a comb or water. He was over thirty. Clear skin, high eyebrows. A slightly swollen face concealed the scars of his battered existence. He was so drunk that his legs wobbled as he walked. When he bumped into people, instead of thanking them for keeping him on his feet, he complained in a slurred and tongue-tied voice.

"Hey, you knocked me down," or "Let me through, pal, I'm in a hurry."

Bartholomew took a few more steps before tripping against the curb. To avoid crashing into the ground, he grabbed onto an old lady and fell on top of her. The poor woman almost suffered a broken back. She cracked him on the head with her cane as she tried to disentangle herself, yelling, "Get off me, you pervert!"

He didn't have the strength to move. But hearing the old woman scream, he wouldn't be outdone.

"Help! Somebody help me! This old lady is attacking me."

People nearby shifted their gaze from the sky to the ground. They pulled the dizzy drunk off the old woman and gave him a hard shove. "Get moving, you bum."

Bewildered but petulant Bartholomew stammered, "Thank you, folks, for the ha . . . the ha . . ." He was so drunk it took him three tries to thank them for the "hand." He tried to brush the dust from his pants and almost fell again.

"You saved me from that—" he said, pointing at the old woman.

She lifted her cane, menacingly, and he caught himself in time.

"—from that lovely lady."

He retreated and began to walk away. As he was making his way through the crowd, he asked himself why everyone seemed so intent on staring into the sky. He thought maybe someone had seen a UFO. As if the scene wasn't chaotic enough, he struggled to stare up at the building and started to shout.

"I see him! I see the E.T. Careful, people! He's yellow with awful horns. And he's holding a weapon!"

Bartholomew's drunken mind was hallucinating again. This was not your run-of-the-mill alcoholic. He loved egging people on and making a scene. That's why he called himself Honey-mouth. The only thing he loved more than drinking was hearing the sound of his own voice. His closest friends joked that he had CSS—compulsive speech syndrome.

He grabbed those next to him, urging them to see the alien only he could see. But they shoved him aside.

"Man, how rude! Just because I saw the E.T. first they're green with envy," he slurred.

Meanwhile, atop the San Pablo, the man on the ledge was deep in thought. Maybe what he needed, he thought, was a clear mind. His was a jumble of empty ideas and superficial concepts about life and death. Maybe what he needed was to encourage his ignorance—quite a change for a man who always considered himself an intellectual.

He felt a sudden calm wash over him. And the stranger used that moment to tell the story of a great thinker:

"Why did Darwin, in the waning moments of his life, when he was suffering unbearable fits of vomiting, cry out 'my God'? Was he weak to call on God when faced with his draining strength? Was he a coward in the face of death? Did he consider it an unnatural phenomenon even though his theory was based on the natural processes of the selection of species? Why was there such a chasm between his existence and his theory? Is death the end or the beginning? In it, do we lose ourselves or find ourselves? Can it be that when we die we are erased from history like actors who never again perform?"

The man swallowed hard. He had never thought about these questions. Though he accepted the theory of evolution, he knew nothing of Darwin the man and his internal conflict. But could Darwin have been weak and confused? "Could Darwin have ever given up on life? No. It's not possible. He surely was much too much in love with life, more so than I am," he thought.

This stranger, with his endless piercing questions, had stripped the man bare. His heart quieted and he tried to catch his breath before replying, "I don't know. I've never thought about those questions."

The stranger went on:

"We work, we buy, we sell and we build friendships. We

discuss politics, economics and science, but deep down we're simply children joking at the dinner table, unable to fathom life's complexities. We write millions of books and store them in immense libraries, but we're still mere infants. We know almost nothing about what we are. We're billions of little children, thoughtlessly at play, on this dazzling planet."

The man's breathing slowed. And soon, he began to recover who he was. Julio Lambert—that was his name—was the bearer of a sharp, quick, privileged mind. In his promising academic career, he had earned doctoral degrees and become an expert in his field. He reveled in grilling aspiring young graduate students presenting their theses with his incisive, biting critiques. He had always been self-centered, and expected that others would orbit around his brilliance. Now, however, his theories were being picked apart—by a man in rags. He felt like a helpless child realizing his own fears and ignorance. He was being called a boy and didn't react with rage. Instead, for the first time, he took pleasure in recognizing his smallness. He no longer felt like a man reaching the end, but one starting anew.

CHAPTER 4

The Losses

INSANITY CAN ONLY BE TREATED WHEN IT DROPS ITS DISGUISE. And Julio, who hid behind his eloquence, culture and academic status, was now beginning to remove his mask. But there would be a long road ahead of him.

The sun was low on the horizon. And thoughts of suicide were dissipating atop the San Pablo Building. At that moment, the stranger said the number twenty, and a rush of sadness consumed him momentarily.

"Why do you call out numbers while you talk?" Julio asked.

The stranger did not reply immediately. He stared at the horizon, saw several lights across the city being turned on, others extinguished. He breathed slowly, as if wishing to be able to relight them all. He turned to Julio, looked intently into his eyes and spoke:

"Why do I count numbers? Because in the brief time we've been on the top of this building, twenty people closed their eyes forever. Twenty healthy but desperate people gave up on life. Twenty did not give themselves a chance. People who once played and loved, wept and battled, felt completely defeated . . . Now, they leave a trail of pain for their loved ones in their wake."

Julio could not understand why this man was so attuned to others' feelings. Who was he? What had he experienced to have these deep sentiments? That's when he noticed the stranger was weeping. It was as if this man were feeling the indescribable pain of children who have lost their parents to suicide and grow up wondering, "Why didn't they think of me?" Or it was as if he were reading the minds of parents who, having lost their children to suicide, are wracked with guilt and wonder endlessly: "What more could I have done?" Or perhaps the stranger was simply remembering his own unknown losses.

The fact was that both the stranger's words and his tears completely disarmed Julio. The intellectual began a journey along the path of his own childhood and could not bear it. He allowed himself to break into tears without caring who was watching him. This man who rarely showed his pain was deeply scarred.

"My father used to play with me, kiss me, and call me 'my dear son . . .'"

And, taking a deep breath, he said something he had always thought forbidden to say aloud, something which even his closest colleagues didn't know, something which, though buried deep within his heart, continued to shape his life.

". . . but he abandoned me when I was a child, without any explanation." He paused, then added, "I was watching cartoons in the living room when I heard a loud bang from his bedroom. I rushed in and found him on the floor, bleeding. I was only six years old. I screamed and screamed, begging for help. My mother wasn't home. I ran to the neighbors, but I was so despondent that for a few minutes they couldn't understand what I was saying. I had barely begun my life and had lost my childhood, my innocence. My world collapsed. I came to hate cartoons. I had no brothers or sisters. My mother, a poor widow, had to go back to work and struggled to support me. But she got cancer and died when I was twelve. Relatives raised me. I moved from house to house, always feeling like a stranger. I was a difficult teenager, and hated family gatherings. Sometimes I was treated like a servant and had to keep my mouth shut."

Julio had developed a rough exterior. He was distant, shy, unyielding. He felt ugly and unloved. He buried himself in his studies, and with little help, got himself into college and became a brilliant student. He worked during the day and went to school at night, studying in the late hours and on weekends. And, now, he vented aloud a deep-seated anger he had never overcome:

"But I showed them. I became more cultured and successful than all those who had ridiculed me. I was an exemplary college student and became a highly respected professor, envied by some and hated by others. I was admired. I married and had a son, John Marcus. I don't think I was either a good husband or a good father. Time went by, and a year ago I fell in love with a student who was fifteen years younger than I. I tried to seduce her, buy her, I took on debts. I ruined my credit, lost everything . . . and in the end she left me. It was as if the earth had opened up and swallowed me whole. My wife discovered the affair and left me, too. When she left, I realized that I still loved her; I couldn't lose her! I tried to win her back, but she was tired of the cold intellectual who had never been affectionate, who was a pessimist, depressed and, on top of everything else, bankrupt. She left me for good."

At that moment, he allowed himself to cry. He hadn't cried this much since losing his mother. He sobbed and wiped his eyes. Whoever looked at him and saw a rigid professor knew nothing of his scars.

"John Marcus, my son, started using drugs. He was always angry and accused me of being a distant father. He went to rehab several times. Today, he lives in another state and refuses to speak to me. Ever since I was five years old people have been abandoning me. Some through the fault of others, some through my fault," he said, learning for the first time how to remove his mask.

Pictures of his childhood ran quickly through his head and he remembered the final images of his father, images he had blocked out. He remembered that he had called out to him day and night for weeks after his loss. Julio grew up angry with his father and was convinced he had locked away those injured feelings deep inside.

Now he was reliving all those painful emotions. His notable education was no match for the pain that had been formed in his past. His learning and sophistication could not help him to be flexible and relaxed. He was an intense, rigid man. He never let down his guard before his psychiatrists and psychologists. Instead, he criticized them because he thought their evaluations of him were childish for someone of his intellectual level. Helping this man was a daunting task.

After telling his story openly for the first time, Julio fell silent again, fearing the stranger would offer more of the same glib, useless advice he had often heard before. Instead, the stranger found a way to joke.

"My friend, you're in a real bind," the stranger said.

Julio gave a wan smile. He wasn't expecting that response. And the stranger offered none of the empty advice. He couldn't feel Julio's pain, but the stranger was familiar with abandonment.

"I know what loss is. There are moments when our world seems to come crashing down around us and no one else can understand it."

The stranger wiped tears from his eyes as he spoke. Perhaps his scars were as deep or deeper than Julio's.

Julio, once again moved, said, "Tell me, who are you."

The stranger responded with a warm silence.

"Are you a psychiatrist or psychologist?" he asked, believing himself in the presence of an extraordinary professional.

"No, I'm not," the stranger affirmed with assurance.

"A philosopher?"

"I appreciate the world of ideas, but I'm not a philosopher."

"Are you the head of some church?" he asked.

"No," the man replied firmly.

Julio asked impatiently, "Are you crazy?"

The stranger replied with a slight smile. "Now, that's more likely," he said, and Julio couldn't have been more confused.

"Who are you? Tell me."

He pressed the stranger who was now being watched from below by a confused crowd. The psychiatrist, the fire chief and the police chief strained to hear the conversation, but could only hear murmurs. Seeing that Julio was not going to back down, the stranger spread his arms, raised them to the sky, and said:

"When I think about how briefly our lives pass, about all that has come before me and all that remains to come, that's when I see how truly small I am in the grand scheme of things. When I consider that one day I will fall into eternal silence, swallowed by the passing of time, I realize my limitations. And when I see those limits, I stop trying to be a god and simply see myself as what I am: a mere human being. I go from being the center of the universe to simply a wanderer searching for answers . . ."

The stranger didn't answer the question, but Julio drank in the words. His answer made Julio wonder the same thing as so many who would encounter the stranger: "Is this man a lunatic or a genius? Or both?" He tried to fathom the depths of the stranger's words, but it was no easy task.

The stranger again looked toward the heavens and began to question God in a way Julio had never heard:

"God, who are you? Why do you remain silent before the insanity of some believers and do nothing to calm the doubts of skeptics? Why do you disguise your will as the laws of physics and conceal your designs as simply random events? Your silence unnerves me."

Julio was an expert in religion—Christianity, Islam, Buddhism and others—but none of it helped him understand the stranger's mind. He didn't know whether these were the ramblings of a bald-faced atheist or someone who was close friends with God himself. The renowned professor again wondered: What kind of man is this? And where did he come from?

CHAPTER 5

The Calling

PEOPLE ARE PREDICTABLE. LEADERS, TOO. IN MODERN society, most people don't inspire emotion or imagination. But what was lacking in "normal" people abounded in the mysterious stranger. Julio was so curious about this man's identity that he asked again he who was. Though, this time, he asked knowing full well that he didn't know much about himself, either.

"I don't know who I am. I need to find myself, I know. But please, grant me just this. Who are you?"

The man flashed a thin smile; Julio was finally beginning to speak his language. And feeling that rush of inspiration, the stranger stood up and faced the horizon, spreading his arms to the fading sun, and said confidently, "I'm a dreamseller."

Julio was even more confused. The stranger seemed to have plunged from lucidity into lunacy. None of this made any sense to Julio, but it seemed to mean everything to the stranger.

On the street below, Bartholomew's ramblings reached a fever pitch: "Look, it's the alien leader! He spread his arms and changed colors."

The dreamseller looked down on the eager masses below and felt a deep, abiding pity for them.

Julio rubbed his face. He couldn't believe his ears.

"A dreamseller? What . . . What is that?" he asked, totally lost for words.

The stranger had seemed so intelligent. He had shown such intrepid thinking, had shattered Julio's preconceptions and helped organize his cluttered mind. And just when he had Julio convinced, this dreamseller had shattered the image with a single word.

The psychiatrist, who was standing about twenty-five yards away, heard the stranger identify himself and quickly sized him up for the police and fire chiefs: "I knew it. They're both crazy."

Just then the dreamseller looked to his right and saw a sniper in a nearby building, about a hundred and fifty yards away, aiming a rifle with a silencer at him. The dreamseller quickly pushed Julio to the side and the two fell next to each other on the ledge. Julio had no idea what was going on, and rather than scare him, the dreamseller just said:

"If that fall bothered you, just imagine what would happen when you hit the ground from this building."

The crowd below thought the stranger had held the jumper back, but they all misunderstood what had happened. The dreamseller looked toward the horizon and saw that the sniper had left. Was he hallucinating? Who could want such a simple man dead? Then they both stood back up on the ledge and the stranger repeated himself, "Yes, I'm a dreamseller."

Julio was still confused and thought maybe the stranger meant he was some kind of traveling salesman.

"Wait, what do you mean? What *products* do you sell?"

"I try to sell courage to the insecure, daring to the timid, joy to those who have lost their zest for life, sense to the reckless, ideas to the thinkers."

Julio falling back into his staid thinking, told himself, "This isn't happening. I'm having a nightmare. I must have died and didn't realize it. A while ago, I was ready to kill myself because

I couldn't understand the source of my pain. Now I'm even more confused because the man who rescued me claims he sells what can't be sold." And to his surprise, the stranger added:

"And for those who think of putting a period to life, I try to sell a comma, just a comma."

"A comma?" asked Julio.

"Yes, a comma. One small comma, so they can continue to write their story."

Julio began to sweat. In a kind of sudden enlightenment, he realized that the dreamseller had just sold him a comma, and he had bought it without realizing it. No price, no pressure, no tricks, no haggling. He placed his hands on his head to see if everything that was happening to him was real.

The professor was starting to understand. He looked down and saw the crowd awaiting his decision. Down deep, those people were as lost as he was. They were free to come and go, but they were missing out on the sweetness of life. They didn't feel free to express their own personality.

Julio felt like he was trapped in a movie, floating between the surreal and the concrete. "Is this guy real, or is my mind playing tricks on me?" he wondered, in a haze of fascination and uncertainty. No one had ever cast a spell on him like this.

Then this stranger made him a very real offer.

"Come, follow me and I will make you a dreamseller."

Julio's mind was racing, but he was frozen. His voice was stuck in his throat. He was physically paralyzed, but deep in thought: "How can I follow a man I've known for less than an hour?" he thought. But at the same time, he was drawn to this calling.

He was tired of academic debates. He was one of the most eloquent intellectuals among his peers, but many of his colleagues, and he himself, lived mired in the mud of envy and endless vanity. He felt that the university where he taught—

this temple of learning—lacked the tolerance and creativity to unleash fresh thinking. Some temples of learning had become as inflexible as the most rigid religions. Professors, scientists and thinkers weren't free to explore. They had to conform to their departments' thinking.

Now he stood before a shabbily dressed man with unkempt hair and no social standing, but one who was a thought-provoking adventurer, a dissenter from conventional wisdom, free to chase new thoughts. And this man had made him the craziest and most exciting of proposals: to sell dreams. "How? To whom? To what end? Will I be praised or mocked?" the intellectual wondered. He also knew that all great thinkers must travel unexplored paths.

Julio had always been sensible and had never made a scene in public—not until he climbed to the top of this building. He knew this time he had caused an uproar. It hadn't been for show; he really was going to end his life. He was afraid of using a gun or taking pills, so he'd come to the top of the San Pablo Building.

But the dreamseller's invitation continued to echo in his mind like a grenade blowing apart all the concepts he held true. A long minute passed. Conflicted, he thought, "I've tried to live my life sheltered in the life of academia, but it failed me. I tried to challenge my students to think for themselves but instead taught them only to regurgitate information. I tried to contribute to society, but sealed myself off from it. If I manage to sell dreams to a few people, as this stranger has sold to me, maybe my life will have more meaning than it has had until now."

And so I decided to follow him. I am Julio, this extraordinary stranger's first disciple.

He became my teacher. And I, the first to agree to this unpredictable journey with no set course or destination. Crazy? Maybe. But no crazier than the life I had been living.

CHAPTER 6

The First Step

A S SOON AS WE LEFT THE SCENE WE WERE STOPPED BY ONE of those closely watching us at the top of the building, the police chief. He was a tall man, about six-foot-three, and slightly overweight, impeccably dressed, graying hair, smooth skin and exuded the air of a man who loved power.

When we stopped in front of him he barely noticed me. He was used to dealing with suicides and considered them weak and damaged. To him, I was just another statistic. I could taste his bitter prejudice and I hated it. After all, I was much more learned than this gun-toting buffoon. My weapons were ideas, which were more powerful and more effective. But I didn't have the strength to defend myself. And I didn't have to. I had a torpedo at my side, the man who had saved me.

The policeman was really interested in grilling the dreamseller. He wanted to know more about this character who fell outside of his statistics. He hadn't been able to hear much of what we said, but the little he heard had amazed him. He studied the dreamseller from head to toe, unable to reconcile the image. The stranger seemed alien to his surroundings. Uneasy, he began his interrogation. I guessed that, like me, the policeman was about to step into a hornet's nest. And he did.

"What's your name?" he asked in an arrogant tone.

The dreamseller studied him for just a second, then said:

"Aren't you happy this man changed his mind? Aren't you simply overwhelmed with joy at knowing this man's life has been saved?" And he gazed at me.

The policeman lost his footing on his pedestal. He hadn't expected his insensitivity to be laid bare in a few short seconds. He stammered, then said in a formal tone, "Yes, of course I'm happy for him."

The dreamseller had a way of making any man realize his insensitivity. He made them see how foolish they were acting. And then he launched another torpedo:

"If you're happy, why don't you show your happiness? Why don't you ask him his name and tell him how glad you are? After all, isn't a human life worth more than this building?"

The police chief was stripped naked more quickly than I was, and it was perfect. The dreamseller won back my self-esteem. He was a thought-provoking expert. Watching him rattle the police chief, I started to understand: It's impossible to follow a leader like this man without admiring him. Admiration is stronger than power, charisma more intense than intimidation. And I had begun to greatly admire the charismatic dreamseller.

It made me think about my relationship with my students. I was a vault of information but had never understood that charisma is fundamental to teaching. First you fell in love with the dreamseller's charisma, then you opened to his teachings. I was afflicted with the same disease of most intellectuals: I was boring. I had been dull, critical, demanding. Even I couldn't stand myself.

The police chief, now shamed by the dreamseller, turned quickly to me and, like a child who has been told to apologize, said, "I'm happy for you, sir."

In a softer tone, the officer asked for the dreamseller's identification.

The reply was simple: "I don't have any ID."

"How can that be? Everybody needs some kind of identification. Without it, you have no . . . identity."

"My identity is what I am," the dreamseller said.

"You can be arrested if you don't identify yourself. You could be a terrorist, a public threat, a psychopath. Who are you?" the policeman asked, slipping back into an aggressive tone.

I saw where this was headed. The dreamseller replied:

"I'll answer you if you answer me first. On whose authority should you be able to know my most intimate secrets? What are your credentials for plumbing the depths of my mind?" he said flatly.

The policeman took the bait. He started to raise his voice, not knowing he'd be trapped by his own wit.

"I'm Pedro Alcantara, chief of police of this district," he said, radiating a proud and self-confident air.

Annoyed, the dreamseller said, "I didn't ask about your profession, your social status or your activities. I want to know about your essence. Who is the human being beneath that uniform?"

The police officer quickly scratched an eyebrow, revealing a nervous tick he'd hidden away, not knowing how to respond. Lowering his voice, the dreamseller asked another question: "What is your greatest dream?"

"My greatest dream? Well, I, I . . ." he stammered, again not knowing how to reply.

Never had anyone using so few words confronted this pillar of authority. He remained motionless. I could look into the dreamseller's eyes and see what he was thinking. The police chief protected "normal" people but couldn't protect his own emotions.

That's when I began to see myself in him. And what I saw bothered me. How could a person without dreams protect society, unless he was a robot whose sole function was to make arrests? How could someone without dreams mold citizens who dream of being free and united?

Then the dreamseller added, "Careful. You fight for public safety, but fear and loneliness are the thieves that steal our emotions, and they can be more dangerous than common criminals. Your son doesn't need a chief of police. He needs a shoulder to cry on, a friend with whom he can share secret feelings and who teaches him to think. Live that dream."

The police chief was speechless. He had been trained to deal with criminals, to arrest them, and had never heard of thieves who invade the mind. He didn't know what to do without his weapon and his badge. Like most "normal" people, including me, he defined himself through his profession. At home, he didn't know how to be a father, only a police officer. He was unable to separate the two roles. He won medals for bravery, but was wasting away as a human being.

I wondered how the dreamseller knew the chief had a son, or whether he had made a lucky guess. But I saw the police chief squirming, as if handcuffed inside his mind, trying to escape from a prison years in the making.

The psychiatrist couldn't hold back any longer. Seeing the police chief at a loss, he tried to trip up the dreamseller. Using psychiatry, he tried to rattle the dreamseller, saying, "Anyone who won't reveal his identity is hiding his own frailty."

"Do you think I'm frail?" asked the dreamseller.

"I don't know," replied the psychiatrist, hesitating.

"Well, you're right. I *am* frail. I've learned that no one is worthy of being called an expert, including a scientist, especially if he doesn't recognize his own limits, his own frailties. Are you frail?" he shot back. "Well?"

Seeing the psychiatrist hesitate, the dreamseller asked, "Which discipline of psychotherapy do you subscribe to?"

That question came as a surprise. I didn't understand where

the dreamseller was going with this. But the psychiatrist, who was also a psychotherapist, said proudly, "I'm a Freudian."

"Very well. Then answer me this: Which is more complex, a psychological theory, whatever it is, or the mind of a human being?"

The psychiatrist, fearing a trap, didn't answer for a moment. Then he replied indirectly. "We use theories to decipher the human mind."

"Fine. Then allow me one more question: You can map out a theory and read every last text on the subject. But can you exhaust the understanding of the human mind?"

"No. But I'm not here to be questioned by you," he said dismissively, not realizing what the dreamseller was driving at. "Besides, I'm an expert in the human mind."

The dreamseller took that opening:

"Mental health professionals are poets of existence, they have a grand mission. However, they can't put a patient into a theoretical text, yet try desperately to put a theoretical text inside of a person. Don't trap your patients between the walls of a theory, or you'll reduce their abilities to grow. Each sickness is unique to the one who's sick. Every sick person has a mind. And every mind is an infinite universe."

I understood what he was telling the psychiatrist, for I felt in my own skin what he meant. When the psychiatrist approached me, he used techniques and interpretations that I immediately rejected. He dealt with the act of suicide, but not with the ravaged human being inside me. His theory might be useful in predictable situations, especially when the patient seeks help, but not in situations where the patient rejects help or has lost hope. I was resistant. First, I needed to be touched by the psychiatrist the man. And later, by the psychiatrist the professional. Because he had approached me as an illness, and not as a person, I perceived him as an invader and withdrew.

The dreamseller took the opposite approach. He started with the sandwich; he asked me deep questions to know more about who I was, like nourishment that reached down into my bones. Only then did he deal with the act of suicide.

The psychiatrist, though he had been called a poet of existence, didn't like being called out by some shabbily dressed stranger with no credentials. He didn't seem happy at all that I no longer wanted to commit suicide. Damn his envy! I wanted to make him see that he was missing the bigger picture. But then again, I'd done the same thing inside the sacred temple of my classroom.

Then, the dreamseller placed a hand on the shoulder of the young fire chief and told him, "Thank you, son, for the risks you have taken to save people you don't know. You *are* a dreamseller."

The dreamseller turned and headed toward the elevator, and I followed him. The psychiatrist turned to the police chief to speak just as the dreamseller turned around to say something himself, and, amazingly, they said the same thing:

"Crazy people understand each other."

The psychiatrist turned red. He must have asked himself, as I did, "How could they have been thinking the same thing?"

The dreamseller saw there was time for one final and unforgettable lesson at the top of that building. He told the psychiatrist, "Some people's craziness is obvious. For others, it's hidden. Which type is yours?"

"Not me, I'm normal!" the psychiatrist snapped.

"Well, mine is visible," the dreamseller said.

He then turned his back and began to walk, his hands on my shoulders. After three steps, he looked toward the sky and said, "God save me from 'normal' people!"

CHAPTER 7

Exorcising the Demons

W E RODE DOWN THE ELEVATOR SILENTLY. I WAS LOST IN thought, the dreamseller calmly whistling and staring ahead. We passed through the immense lobby, richly decorated with chandeliers, antique furniture and an enormous reception desk of dark mahogany. Only then did I realize their beauty. Before, my world was colored by my own dark emotions.

Outside, the lights shone brightly, lighting the crowd that was anxiously awaiting news from the top of the building. News that I would do my best not to provide. Truth be told, I wanted to hide, forget the commotion, turn the page and not think about my pain for a second longer. I was ashamed and shrank from the attention. But I couldn't teleport myself out of there. I had to face the stares of my audience. For a brief moment I was angry with myself. I thought, "There were other ways I could have faced my demons. Why didn't I choose one of them?" But pain blinds us, and frustration clouds our thinking.

When we left the San Pablo Building and broke through the police tape, I wanted to cover my face and leave quickly, but the huge crowd made it impossible; there was no room to run. The media wanted information. I made my way through this Trail of Tears, eyes downcast.

The dreamseller kept my secret. No one knew what had really happened atop the building; the rich exchange I had with that mystery man remained lodged in my head alone.

As we escaped the media and began walking among the crowd, I was startled. We were treated like celebrities. I was famous, but not in the way I had hoped.

To the dreamseller, society's obsession with worshipping celebrities was the clearest sign that we were losing our minds. As we walked, he asked aloud:

"After all, who deserves more applause, an unknown garbageman or a Hollywood actor? Whose mind is more complex? Whose story is more complex? There is no difference. But 'normals' think this heresy."

As the crowd kept prodding to know what had happened on top of the building, the dreamseller, seeing me withdraw, changed the topic. Instead of trying to discreetly shift the focus, he raised his arms calling for silence, which came only after a prolonged moment.

I thought: "Here comes another speech." But the dreamseller was more eccentric than I imagined. He asked everyone to form a large circle, which was difficult given the tightly packed crowd. And to everyone's surprise, he went to the center and began dancing an Irish jig. He crouched, kicking his legs into the air and sang euphorically.

I couldn't stop thinking: "An intellectual wouldn't act like this, and even if he felt the inspiration, he wouldn't have the courage to do it." Damn my prejudice. A little while ago, I had almost killed myself, but prejudice was still alive and well. I was a "normal" in disguise.

No one really understood the dreamseller's actions, least of all me, but some started to join in. They couldn't believe that just a few minutes ago they had nearly witnessed a tragedy, and now they were dancing with joy. Joy is contagious, and they had been infected with the dreamseller's euphoria.

The circle widened. Those who knew the dance or those who risked dancing it without knowing the steps began hooking arms and whirling in circles. Those at the edge of the circle eventually got into the spirit and started clapping to the rhythm. But many remained farther away, among them several well-dressed executives. They didn't want to be anywhere near that band of maniacs. Like me, they preferred to hide their madness.

People kept jumping in and out of the circle to show off their dance skills, each one leaving to wild applause. I felt just fine on the outside of the circle, protected. But suddenly the dreamseller grabbed my arms and thrust me into the center of the circle.

I was embarrassed and just stood there. The others went on dancing around me and urging me on, but I was paralyzed. A few minutes earlier I was the center of attention, and now I just hoped no one would recognize me—certainly not a colleague or student from the university. I didn't fear death, but I was deathly afraid of being embarrassed. God, I was sicker than I thought.

I was usually discreet, reserved and spoke in measured tones, at least when I wasn't annoyed. I never showed joy in public. I was infected with the virus of most intellectuals: a stiff formality. The crowd waited for me to let loose, but I was paralyzed by my shyness. Suddenly, another surprise. The penniless drunk, Bartholomew, hooked his arm in mine and spun me into a dance.

The man had awful breath and, still drunk, he could barely stay on his feet, much less dance. I had to hold him up. Seeing how stiff I was, he stopped dancing, looked at me—and planted a kiss on my left cheek. "Lighten up, man. The leader of the E.T.s saved you. This party's for you!"

My pridefulness took a direct hit. Seldom had I seen or

heard so much liveliness and spontaneity in so few words. And I started to understand. I thought of the parable of Jesus Christ and the lost sheep. I had read it once, years ago, through the eyes of a scientist and thought it ridiculous to abandon ninety-nine sheep to go looking for a lost one. Socialists sacrificed millions of people for an ideal, but Christ took it a step further. He was wild with grief at losing one soul, and wild with joy when he found it.

I had criticized how Christ romanticized that moment, but now the dreamseller was showing the same joy. Only after the loopy drunk kissed me did I realize the dreamseller was celebrating for me. The drunk was more sober than I was. I was thunderstruck; I had never thought it possible for a stranger to place so much importance on someone he didn't know. I was lost then found, "dead" then brought back to life. What more could I want? Shouldn't I celebrate, too? I tossed aside my status as an "intellectual."

I was "normal," and like many normals my madness was hidden, disguised; I needed to be spontaneous. I let go. The dreamseller had emphasized that the heart needs no reason to beat. The greatest reason for staying alive is life itself. At the university, I had forgotten that the great philosophers often discussed the meaning of life, the pursuit of happiness and the art of beauty. It was the first time I had ever danced without a head full of whiskey. It had been years since I'd felt this good.

The "normals" were so starved for joy that when this dreamseller gave them permission, they frolicked like children. Everyone was dancing. Men in ties. Women in long dresses and miniskirts. Children and teenagers joined in.

A little old lady danced by with her cane. It was the same woman Bartholomew had fallen on. Her name was Jurema. She had lived eighty good years. Anyone who thought she should be hobbling around at her age was in for a surprise. She was in better shape than me, though she showed a slight shiver of Parkinson's. But she could dance like a star. The dreamseller liked her immediately. They danced together, and I rubbed my eyes to see if it was all real.

Suddenly, she broke loose from the dreamseller's arms and bumped into Bartholomew at the center of the circle. She tapped him on the head with her cane, and joked sweetly, "You pervert." I couldn't hold back. I rolled on the ground with laughter. She did what I'd have liked to do when he gave me that smelly kiss on the cheek.

The dreamseller turned to the old woman and said, "You're a thing of beauty." Then, taking her by the waist, he spun her around and she danced like a twenty-year-old.

For a moment, I thought the dreamseller had been patronizing here. But then I thought, "Who's to say she isn't beautiful? What does it really mean to be beautiful, anyway?" Just then, Bartholomew sidled up to the woman and started pouring on the flattery: "Yes, beautiful! Wonderful! Delightful! Marvelous!"

Then the old woman whacked him with the cane.

"You hopeless pervert! Cheap Don Juan!" she said, feigning anger. Bartholomew ran for cover before he saw she was joking. Her heart melted. It had been fifty years since anyone had called her beautiful or anything of the sort. She took the dizzy drunk by the arms and danced with him, happy as could be. I was in awe. I had known the power of criticism but was new to the power of praise. Could it be that those who use that power could live longer and better lives? My head was spinning. I had never witnessed so much craziness in a single day.

During this short time, the dreamseller had taught me that small gestures can have more impact than great speeches, that our actions and moments of silence can be more effective than all the world's PowerPoint presentations. I knew he had a great many secrets. But I didn't dare ask, worried that he'd again strip me bare with his Socratic method. He had become an expert in making life a celebration, even when there were ample reasons to weep with sorrow.

He would always tell us, "Those who can laugh at their foolishness have found their fountain of youth."

I detested fools who gave simple answers, but deep down, wasn't I a fool myself? I had so much to learn about laughing at myself. I had so much to learn about simplifying my life—an unknown art in any university.

How many students had I sent to commencement without teaching them to look at themselves, to detect their own stupidity, to let go, to cry and to love, to take risks and escape the prison of routine? And to dream. I was the most feared of professors. I drowned my students in criticism, but had never taught them to enjoy life. But how could I? No one can teach what he doesn't know himself. My life, to this point, had been worthless.

I was proud of being just and honest, but I realized I had failed to be just and honest with myself. Fortunately, I was beginning to learn how to exorcise the demons that had made me into an unbearable human being.

CHAPTER 8

Strengthened by Challenges

A FTER TWENTY MINUTES DANCING AT THE BASE OF THE SAN
Pablo Building, the dreamseller again asked for silence. The
euphoric crowd eventually calmed down. To our surprise, he
recited a poem aloud, as if he were on a mountain top:

> *Many dance on the ground,*
> *But not on the path to self-knowledge.*
> *They are gods who do not recognize their limits.*
> *How can they find themselves if they've never been lost?*
> *How can they be human if they've never known their own*
>   *humanity?*
> *Who are you? Yes, tell me, who are you?*

The people stared, wide-eyed. After their street fair, the emcee
was now asking them whether they were human or divine.
Several men in suits, particularly those who hadn't danced and
were ready to criticize, were stunned. Every day they were
fixated on the exchange rate of the dollar, the stock market index, management techniques, fancy cars and luxurious hotels,
but none had traveled the path to self-knowledge.

They led bored, empty lives, clouded in tranquilizers. They
would not let themselves be human first. They were gods who

died a little every day, gods who denied the internal conflicts that made them human.

Seeing the crowd fall silent, he continued:

"Without thinking in depth about life, they will forever live superficially. They will never perceive that existence is like the sunlight that comes with the dawn and will inevitably disappear with the sunset." Some applauded without understanding or realizing that their nightfall was fast approaching.

Moments later, to my surprise, he went around greeting people, asking, "Who are you? What's your great dream?"

Many were confused at first. They didn't know how to answer who they were or what their great dream was. Some, more uninhibited and open, said, "I don't have any dreams. My life is shit." Others said, "I'm swamped with debt. How can I dream?" and still others stated, "My work is an endless source of stress. My whole body aches. All I ever do is work." I was impressed with the responses. I realized that the audience watching me on the ledge wasn't that far removed from my own misery. The audience and actor were living the same play.

The dreamseller had no magical solutions for them. What he wanted was for them to rethink their lives. Seeing their desperation, he called out:

"Without dreams, whatever beast it is that chases us, whether in our minds or in society, will eventually catch us. The fundamental purpose of dreams isn't success but to free us from conformity."

An obese young woman, five-foot-ten and weighing nearly three hundred pounds, was moved by these words. She felt doomed to a life of rejection and unhappiness. She had been taking antidepressants for years. She was negative and overly self-critical. She always put herself down in the presence of other women. She approached the dreamseller and gathered the courage to open up in a voice that only some of us could hear.

"I'm so deeply sad and lonely. Can someone who's unattractive be loved one day? Can someone who's never even been asked out have a chance of finding true love?" She dreamed of being kissed, held, loved, admired, but you could see she had been ridiculed, rejected, called names. Her self-esteem, like mine, had been killed in childhood.

Bartholomew, reeking of alcohol, called out:

"Sexy! Beautiful! If you're looking for your prince, you've found him. Wanna go out with me?" And he spread his arms. I had to hold him to keep him from falling over. She smiled, but the advances of a shameless drunk were not what she had in mind.

The dreamseller looked into her eyes. Moved, he answered:

"It is possible to find true love. But even with true love at your side, you can never be happy if you cannot learn to love yourself." And he told her: "Still, to find true love, you must stop being a slave."

"A slave to what?" she asked, surprised.

"To society's standards for beauty," he answered.

Some of those listening were encouraged by his words and commented that they dreamed about overcoming their shyness, loneliness, fears. Others yearned to make friends or change jobs because the money they made was never enough to pay their bills. Others said they dreamed of going to college but lacked the resources to do so.

They were hoping for a miracle, but the dreamseller was a vendor of ideas, a merchant of knowledge. Knowledge was better than gold and silver, more enchanting than diamonds and pearls. That's why he didn't endorse success for its own sake. To him, there were no paths without obstacles, no seas without storms. Looking people in the eye, he said with certainty:

"If your dreams are desires and not plans for living, you will surely take your problems to the grave. Dreams without plans produce frustrated people, servants of the system."

He fell silent and let us reflect on his words. In a world consumed with wants, no one plans to have friends, no one plans to be tolerant, to conquer phobias, to have a great love.

"If chance is our god and accidents our demons, we will be as children," he said finally.

I was startled to look around me and realize how society had damaged all of us. Quite a few people consumed a lot but were like robots, living without purpose, without meaning, without goals. They were experts at following orders and not at thinking. I asked myself, as an educator, "Had I trained servants or leaders at the university? Robots or thinkers?" But before answering these questions, I started to feel uneasy about my own situation. I wondered, "Does being critical free me of servitude?" I knew it didn't. I was a servant to my negativity, to my false independence. Unless I changed, I would take my troubles to my grave.

"Victory without risk is a dream without value. Our defeats, our challenges help nurture our dreams."

In studying the history of the wealth of nations, I understood the sociological meaning of this latest thought. Many who received inheritances without working for their success could not value their parents' struggles. They squandered their family fortunes as if the money were unlimited. Inheritance bred empty, superficial lives. They were people who lived for the moment, trying to suck the maximum pleasure from the present with no regard for the future.

While I criticized people for not being masters of their own destinies, I suddenly realized I was no different from them. I didn't understand why such simple thoughts were so true. I dreamed of being a happy person but became miserable. I dreamed of living a better life than my father but replicated what I most despised in him. I dreamed of being more sociable than my mother but inherited her bitterness.

I hadn't learned what my struggles had to teach about reaching my dreams. I hadn't dared reach for my dreams if it ever meant risking my reputation, my so-called brilliant academic career. I was barren inside and gave birth to no new ideas. I forgot that great thinkers were also risk-takers. They were called lunatics and heretics, and often became the subject of public scorn.

Even students defending their masters and doctoral theses weren't encouraged to take risks. Some of my colleagues tried to encourage them, but I held them back. Only after meeting the dreamseller did I come to understand that it was often our youth who brought about our greatest discoveries.

CHAPTER 9

Bartholomew's Dream

——————

A MAN ABOUT THIRTY-FIVE YEARS OLD, WEARING A BEIGE polo shirt, with well-trimmed black hair and a frown, bluntly told the dreamseller, "My great dream is to strangle my wife."

He wasn't joking. He actually seemed ready to kill. The dreamseller didn't answer right away, waiting for the man to continue venting his anger. "Who deserves a wife who betrays her husband?" the man said.

Instead of calming the man down, the dreamseller added fuel to the fire. "Are you a betrayer, too?"

The man reared back and hit the dreamseller so hard that he knocked him to the ground and bloodied his lip.

Several onlookers came at the man, but the dreamseller quickly calmed them: "No, don't hurt him!"

The dreamseller dusted himself off and explained to the man, "We may not betray with our sexual organs, but we betray in thought, in action. If we don't betray those we love, we betray ourselves. We betray our health, our dreams, our peace of mind. You mean to say you've never betrayed another or betrayed yourself?"

The man silently nodded his head, confirming that, yes, he, too, was a betrayer. He betrayed himself daily with thousands

of morbid thoughts. His aggressive nature was only the tip of
the iceberg. The dreamseller continued:

"Is your wife your property? If not, why do you want to
destroy her or destroy yourself because of her? Who said that
because she betrayed you she is no longer a human being, a
person who has cried, loved, been angered, known frustration?
If you're incapable of forgiving her and winning her back, why
don't you simply say, 'I'm sorry, it's over'?"

The man walked away dazed. It was hard to tell if he would
manage to win his wife back or allow himself to be won back
by her, but he would no longer kill her. I was impressed by the
dreamseller's approach. It seemed like he provoked the man, so,
in hitting the dreamseller, the man would get just a glimpse of
what his murderous rage could do. And maybe that opened the
man up to considering another alternative. The people nearby
stared at the dreamseller as if watching an action film.

As if that incident weren't enough, the dreamseller turned
to Bartholomew and asked him what his greatest dream was. I
thought it was a bad time to open up such a question. Honeymouth had a way of turning any serious situation into a joke.

He looked at the dreamseller and spoke so enthusiastically
that he almost fell to the ground:

"My great dream, chief? Russian vodka! Oh, oh, and to take
a bath—" Everyone appeared heartened at this desire, because
he certainly needed it. That is, until he finished. "—to take a
bath in a vat of Scotch whiskey." Then he fell into a sitting position. He was penniless and seemed in ecstasy at the thought
of that singular bath.

I couldn't hold back. I started laughing at the sight of that
poor clown and the dreamseller. But I was surprised at my sar-
casm, and that deep down, I found pleasure in another's misfortune. I thought to myself, "Let's see how the dreamseller
handles this one."

Before the dreamseller could answer, Jurema appeared with her cane and threatened to give Bartholomew another whack. She had overheard his dream and was indignant. This time she didn't call him a pervert but a host of other names. "You inveterate alcoholic! Dreg of society! Insolent wastrel!"

Honeymouth, who apparently had little schooling, thought they were compliments. "Thanks for the kind words, but a barrel of Brazilian rum or Mexican tequila would also be fine," he said.

The man was incorrigible. His drinking had been out of control for twenty years. For the last ten he had wandered from bar to bar, street to street, lost in the drink. I was certain that the dreamseller would never be able to teach that drunk anything. I was sure the dreamseller would dismiss him and quickly be done with him. But, to my surprise, he praised the man's sincerity.

"Well, congratulations on your honesty."

I cleared my ears to make sure I was hearing right. There's no way the dreamseller was praising this drunk. Between the alcohol swimming in Bartholomew's brain and the dreamseller's praise, the man was euphoric. Feeling a self-esteem that he hadn't known in years, he looked around at the mob that was jeering him just minutes earlier and yelled, "Aha! You see! I'm environmentally friendly. I run on alcohol."

Then he crossed his fingers and said, "I'm like *that* with this guy. He's *the man*. Hey, can I take a ride in your spaceship, E.T.?" Then he tripped against a couple of people and almost fell again.

I, who had always been intolerant, thought, "Ship the guy off to the loony bin." The dreamseller looked at me, and for a second, I thought he was reading my mind and taking my advice. But, to my amazement, he said something that almost made me fall over. He touched Bartholomew's shoulder and told him in a firm voice, "Come, follow me. And I'll inebriate you with a drink unlike any you have ever known."

I was horrified. I shook my head to see if I understood what I'd heard. The drunk, who was weak both from dancing and from years of running on alcohol, immediately replied, "You say there's a drink I don't know about? I doubt it. Is it high-proof vodka?"

I was embarrassed by the alcoholic's naïve irreverence. But the dreamseller, finding it humorous, smiled. He was always able to relax in these tense situations. He looked at me and said, "Don't worry, I specialize in the complicated ones."

I thought about running right then and there. Following this social outcast was one thing. Following him side by side with a witless drunk was too much. Who knew what risks lay ahead?

CHAPTER 10

The World Is My Home

THE DREAMSELLER, BARTHOLOMEW AND I TURNED TO BEGIN our journey. As we were leaving, the crowd applauded. Some people even took photos. I had hoped for a discreet escape, but that idiot Honeymouth posed for pictures. I tried to lead him away without causing more of a scene. The last thing I wanted was to babysit a drunk. A few nearby reporters looked on and took notes.

We hadn't walked three blocks before I started wondering, "What am I doing here? Where are we going?" But my new companion wasn't thinking at all. He was just happy to be part of our merry band of men. Me? I was worried.

I looked ahead and tried to relax. The dreamseller watched me with a half-smile; he seemed to hear my doubts. I imagined we were heading to his humble home. Judging by his clothes, he seemed to be poor, but surely he must have a rented house or apartment. Maybe it wasn't much to look at, but he was so insistent that we join him, I figured there must be enough room for his guests, Bartholomew and me. The thought of sleeping in the same room with that drunkard turned my stomach.

Maybe the room where I'd sleep would be simple but comfortable. Maybe the mattress would be worn but decent. Maybe the sheets would be old, but at least they'd be clean.

Maybe his refrigerator wasn't packed, but I imagined there would be something healthy to eat. After all, I was hungry and exhausted. Maybe, maybe, maybe . . . I thought, but I wasn't sure of anything.

Along the way, he waved at children and adults, helped a few people carry heavy bags. Bartholomew said hi to everyone, even trees and lampposts. I waved, too, but only not to seem out of place.

Most people responded with a smile. I wondered how the dreamseller knew all of them. But, of course, he didn't know them. It was just his way. He treated any stranger as an equal. And, in fact, to him, no person was a stranger. He greeted them because it made him happy. I had never seen such a lively, good-natured, sociable person. He didn't just sell dreams, he lived them.

We walked for blocks, then for miles, but never seemed to be any closer to his home. A long while later, when I couldn't walk any further, he stopped at an intersection and I let out a sigh of relief. We're here, I thought to myself. Yes, he said, we had arrived.

I looked to the left and saw a row of identical, white, low-income homes with small porches. I scratched my head and thought, "The houses look really small. They can't have three bedrooms."

Then the dreamseller looked down the other street. Behind a bridge was a tall apartment building that looked to have about eight rooms per floor, like a pigeon coop for people. It looked even more cramped than the row houses.

Remembering my own students, I said to myself, "I'm not going to complain. It'll just be a tough night and that's that." The dreamseller saw the look on my face and said, "Don't worry. There's plenty of room."

Trying to disguise my worry, I asked calmly, "So what floor is your apartment on?"

"My apartment? My apartment is the world," he said calmly.

"I like that apartment," Bartholomew said.

Confused, I asked, "What do you mean?"

He explained:

"Foxes have their dens, the birds of the sky their nests, but the dreamseller has no fixed address to lay his head."

If I was nervous before, I really worried when he started quoting Jesus Christ. Did this man think he was the Messiah? Could he be having a psychotic break? Or would he have one later? I mean, he seemed highly intelligent. And he speaks of God in a secular way. But I couldn't help wonder who this man was. And what I was getting myself into.

"Don't worry," the dreamseller said, "I'm not Him. I only try to understand Him."

"You're not who?" I asked, not following.

"I'm not Jesus Christ. Like I said, I'm just the least of his brethren. I just try to understand him," he replied calmly.

"But who are you?" I repeated anxiously, seeking a fuller explanation that never seemed to come.

He said emphatically, "I've already told you who I am. Don't you believe in me?"

Bartholomew should have kept quiet just then, but he didn't have it in him. He tried to correct me by saying, "You don't believe he's the alien commander."

This time I couldn't hold back.

"Shut up, *Trashmouth*," I shouted.

"Trashmouth? You second-rate snob!" he shouted and struck a karate pose. This would be the first of many arguments among the dreamseller's ragtag band of disciples.

The dreamseller gently corrected me, that warm smile and calm demeanor more effective than any physical punishment.

"Julio, you're a smart man, so you know that no artist owns his work. It's he who interprets the art who gives it meaning. If

Bartholomew thinks I'm the leader of an alien race, so be it. You shouldn't worry. Generosity, not obedience, is what I want. Be generous to yourself."

Back then, I thought he misspoke and meant that I should be generous to Bartholomew. But during this journey I would discover that a man who isn't generous to himself can never be generous to others. One who demands much of himself is a tyrant to others.

Generosity was one of the most important dreams that he wanted to share with the world. The "normals" living in their cages, isolated in their own little worlds, had lost the indescribable joy that comes from giving, embracing, offering a second chance. Generosity was a word found in dictionaries but rarely in mankind. I knew how to compete but not how to be generous. I knew how to point out the ignorance and shortcomings of others, but not how to accept them. Seeing others fail pleased me more than my own successes. I was no different from politician who wanted to see the ruling party fail.

After that careful lesson, I calmed down. But there was still the question of where we would be staying. Then the dreamseller pointed to the shade beneath the bridge and said, "This is our home."

I felt dizzy. Suddenly I began to miss the San Pablo Building. There were several torn mattresses strewn under the overpass and only filthy rags to cover us. There was one jug of water and we all would have to drink straight from the bottle. I had never seen such poverty. I thought, "This is the man who saved me?"

It all looked so destitute that even Bartholomew protested. Now I was starting to like the guy. He scratched his head, rubbed his eyes to make sure he wasn't hallucinating and said, "Chief, you sure this is your house?"

The alcohol was wearing off and Bartholomew had begun to see reality. Even he had slept in better places. He slept in a

friend's tiny efficiency, in the back of bars and even in homeless shelters, but never under a bridge.

"Yes, Bartholomew, this is my house. And we have a long
night ahead of us."

Because everything the dreamseller said had another meaning, he wasn't predicting a bad night's sleep. We were in for
more of the dreamseller's eye-opening world.

For dinner there was some stale bread and old crackers. I
had hated fast-food hamburgers, but now I started to fantasize
about them. After taking a few bites of the crackers, I decided
to lie down. Maybe tomorrow I would wake up and find it was
all a nightmare. I lay down on the lumpy mattress, rolled a
piece of cardboard into a pillow, and rested my head—but not
my racing mind.

Trying to relax, I told myself, "OK, stay calm. You're a sociologist. You *like* to study eccentric groups, don't you? Now
you're part of one. It'll be good for your academic career. At
the very least, you'll have one hell of a story to tell. Remember,
'Victory without risk is a dream without value.'"

Still, I couldn't imagine what I was getting myself into.
I had left the safe microcosm of a college classroom to live
in the underbelly of society, a place completely foreign to a
theoretical sociologist like me. My spinning mind wouldn't
let me sleep.

But then I tried something else. I started remembering all
the lessons I had learned next to the dreamseller, reliving each
experience. I tried to think about everything that had happened hours earlier. The experience of following this stranger
was so powerful that I thought less about the top of the building and more about my home under the bridge, less about suicide and more about my journey.

And then it hit me. Everyone should set out like this, without a goal or a destination, at least for a day, searching for the

lost pieces of themselves. These thoughts relaxed me, the anxiety passed and sleep approached.

I learned that night that what determines how soft a bed feels depends on the anxiety inside our heads. One only sleeps well when he can find peace within. I was beginning to think like the dreamseller. I ignored whatever worry lay ahead. For the moment, that tattered lump became the most comfortable of mattresses.

CHAPTER 11

A Band of Misfits

I_T WAS FOUR IN THE MORNING, COLD AND WINDY, WHEN I awoke to a desperate cry.

"The bridge is gonna collapse! It's gonna collapse!" Bartholomew screamed. He was panting, terrified.

My heart was racing. I had never been so afraid. I leaped up, trying to run.

But the dreamseller took my arm and urged me to stay calm.

"Calm, how? We could die!" I said, looking at the construction and seeing old cracks, in the darkness, as if they were new.

Calmly, he told me, "Bartholomew is going through alcohol withdrawal."

My survival instinct had kicked in, even though a few hours earlier I had wanted to end my life. My drunken companion had led me to one of the greatest discoveries of my life: Even those who plan their death don't want to die; they want to kill their pain. I took a deep breath, tried to relax, but my heart was racing. I looked at Bartholomew, who was in a state of terror.

He was in a state of delirium tremens. Because he was addicted, and his body craved alcohol, he was suffering shortness of breath, accelerated heart rate and excessive sweating. The worst part was that his already confused mind shut down, and he was starting to hallucinate.

After imagining that the bridge was falling, he started having other wild visions. He saw spiders and rats the size of automobiles scurrying along the ground, threatening to devour him. His face was dripping with sweat, his hands shaking. His entire body was hot with fever. As the dreamseller always said, you can run from the monsters outside but not those within. And it's incredible how the human mind tries to create phantoms to frighten away those demons. Even in our digital world, these primitive feelings still exist.

Bartholomew tried to fight the beasts attacking him from within. He screamed in agony, "Chief, help me! Help me!"

We tried to calm him and sat him down on an old crate. But he jumped to his feet with a new nightmare, and, another time, he ran down the street in fear. There were millions of alcoholics in this country, but I never imagined how much they suffered. I just thought they were happy drunks. Fearing Bartholomew would be run over, the dreamseller suggested we take him to a public hospital three blocks away.

That's the day I began to give a little of myself to others without asking anything in return. Of course, there's always self-interest in the things we do, but as the dreamseller said, there are interests that go beyond financial gain and public recognition, such as those linked to the fulfillment of contributing to the well-being of others. It was a system of trade unforeseen by capitalism or socialism, a world alien to me.

I began to understand that selfish people live in a prison of their worries. But those who work to ease the pain of others ease their own pain. I don't know if I'll regret taking this path, I don't know what awaits me, but selling dreams, even with its risks, is an excellent "business" in the marketplace of emotion. Bartholomew's suffering was so great that, at least for the time being, it made the countless issues in my life, the worry in my mind, seem smaller.

I thought of all the trouble the dreamseller went through to rescue me. He hadn't asked for money, recognition or praise, afterward. But what he received was an immeasurable dose of joy. He was so happy that he danced in public. All he asked of me was that I do the same.

Helping Bartholomew was my first experience in contributing humbly to someone's wellness. A difficult task for a selfish intellectual.

Getting Bartholomew admitted into the hospital was a struggle. We had to convince the night crew that our friend was in mortal danger. His raving alcohol-induced madness wasn't enough to convince them immediately. General hospitals weren't prepared for accidents involving the human psyche. The body they could deal with. But they either didn't know or didn't care about how to deal with an injured mind. By the time we succeeded in getting him admitted, Bartholomew was less agitated. They gave him a strong sedative and carried him, asleep, to his room.

We went to visit him in the afternoon. Bartholomew was much better. He was no longer having hallucinations and was released. He asked us to tell him everything that had happened and how we'd met. His memory was cloudy. The dreamseller signaled to me. I tried to explain the incomprehensible. When I began to speak, the dreamseller left. He didn't like to be praised.

I spoke about the dreamseller, how I'd met him, how he'd helped save me, how we met at the foot of the building, the dancing, the question about Bartholomew's great dream, how he'd called him, the bridge, the night terrors, everything. Bartholomew paid close attention and nodded his head, muttering, "hmm." Everything seemed so unreal that I felt like a fool explaining something I didn't even understand. The poor man was as good-natured as the dreamseller.

"You don't know who he is or what his name is? Buddy, I think I need a drink to figure this all out," he joked. "I've always wanted to follow somebody crazier than me."

And that's how I became part of this band of misfits. My sociological experiment was widening. I only hoped I wouldn't run into anyone I knew. I'd rather anyone from my former life think I was dead or had left the country. Bartholomew whistled in a carefree manner. The dreamseller walked beside us with unabashed joy. Suddenly, he started singing a beautiful and rousing song he had composed, with lyrics that portrayed the story of his life. Little by little, the song became the central theme of our journey.

> *I'm just a wanderer*
> *Who lost the fear of getting lost*
> *I'm certain of my own imperfection*
> *You may say I'm crazy*
> *You may mock my ideas*
> *It doesn't matter!*
> *What matters is I'm a wanderer*
> *Who sells dreams to passersby*
> *I've no compass or appointment book*
> *I have nothing, yet I have everything*
> *I'm just a wanderer*
> *In search of myself.*

On the walk home, or rather, to the bridge, we ran into another strange character. His name was Dimas de Melo, nicknamed "Angel Hand." His nickname should have been "Devil Hand," because he was a con man and a thief. He was twenty-eight with blond hair that fell over his brow, a long, pointed nose and Asian features.

Angel Hand was caught stealing a portable DVD player

from a department store. He had already stolen countless other more valuable things without getting caught. But this time a camera had filmed him in the act. Of course he had slyly checked out all the cameras when he placed the machine in his large bag, but hadn't seen there was a hidden one, and he landed in jail.

At the police station, he asked for a lawyer before detectives could question him. He told his lawyer he didn't have money for bail. The lawyer said, "No money; no freedom."

Whenever the thief felt nervous, he began to stutter badly. He argued, "Hold on a minute . . . I'm, I'm gonna get out of this without pa . . . paying a thing. Just f . . . follow my lead." The lawyer didn't understand what he had in mind. They went into the office of the impatient police chief.

When the chief asked the prisoner's name, Dimas, acting like he had mental problems, twiddled his lips with his index finger and smacked his forehead three times. The chief got mad and again asked his name. And Dimas repeated the gesture.

"Are you playing with me, son? Because I'll lock you in that holding cell and throw away the key."

The chief tried asking for Dimas's address and employer, but Dimas just repeated the same gesture, twiddling his lips like a monkey and slapping his forehead three times. He wanted to look like someone out of his mind, someone who couldn't possibly have known what he was doing when he put that DVD player into his bag. The chief insisted on asking more questions and Dimas just deflected them like an imbecile. The chief cursed, banged the table, threatened, but Dimas wouldn't break. He should've won an Academy Award for his acting. The lawyer was enjoying his client's cleverness.

"There's no use. This guy's nuts!" the chief shouted.

The lawyer took over and told him, "Sir, I didn't say anything about my client's mental handicap because I knew you wouldn't believe me. But you can see for yourself he has no idea what he's doing."

Not wanting to waste any more time, the chief let the crook go. Outside, the lawyer shook Angel Hand's hand and praised his cunning.

"That was unbelievable! I've never seen such a clever con man," the lawyer said, congratulating him. He quickly asked for his fee so he could be on his way to see another client.

Angel Hand stared blankly into the lawyer's eyes and twiddled his lips, slapping his forehead three times. The lawyer laughed out loud, but said he didn't have time to joke around. Dimas repeated the gesture. We were on the other side of the street, watching this all go on.

"OK, enough! Let's settle up," shouted the lawyer.

Angel Hand repeated his ritual once again. The lawyer became irritated, but Dimas just repeated his act. Nothing could dissuade that scoundrel. The lawyer threatened him in every possible way. He even threatened to call the cops. But how could he? He had told the police chief that his client was mentally ill; if he recanted, it could cause him problems with the bar. It was the first time in the history of jurisprudence that a con artist had tricked the police and his lawyer in the space of fifteen minutes.

The lawyer left fuming and Angel Hand said aloud, "One more sucker."

The dreamseller was paying close attention to the thief. I couldn't really understand why. But I thought maybe he wanted to sell him the dream of honesty. Maybe he wanted to reprimand him, deliver one of his sermons. Maybe he wanted to tell us to have nothing to do with a guy like this, who could ruin our path to self-discovery.

He crossed the street and approached the thief. We followed apprehensively, worried that this crook might be armed. Dimas saw him coming and immediately asked who he was and what he wanted. To our surprise, the dreamseller pulled no punches.

"Your dream is to get rich and you don't care how you have to do it," the dreamseller said.

I liked how the dreamseller put him in his place. But what he said next took me by surprise and sent Bartholomew's head spinning—without vodka. He told Angel Hand, "Those who steal for a living are terrible money managers. They run from poverty, but it always catches up with them."

The con man was taken aback. He didn't know how to invest what he stole and lived in poverty. He detested it, begged for the scarcity to go away, but like a faithful companion it insisted on staying. And then, the dreamseller brought the crook's world crashing down: "The worst swindler isn't he who deceives others but he who deceives himself."

Angel Hand took two steps back. He wasn't much for thinking, but what he heard rocked his mind. He began to ask himself: "Am I maybe the world's worst swindler? I'm a pro at cheating people, but maybe I've cheated myself. Who is this character who's stealing my peace of mind?"

Then the dreamseller did what we never expected.

"Come, follow me and I will show you a treasure called knowledge, much more valuable than silver and gold," he said. The dreamseller had a pointed, seductive way of selling his dreams.

But the con man looked the dreamseller from head to toe, saw his ragged clothes and empty pockets and snickered. He thought about that treasure of knowledge and understood nothing. And he started to stutter again.

"What . . . tre . . . treasure do you mean? What mo . . . money?" he asked suspiciously.

Without offering an explanation, the dreamseller merely stated confidently, "You'll find out."

And he walked away without saying another word. The crook followed us. Initially, he followed out of curiosity. Maybe he thought the dreamseller was an eccentric millionaire. The fact is that the dreamseller's ideas attracted people, especially those on the edge of society, like a moth to a flame.

Bartholomew, many years ago when he had money, had undergone psychotherapy, but it didn't work. In fact, it had left him worse off. He had driven some of his therapists crazy, and they needed therapy themselves after they began to treat him. The guy was hopeless but brilliant. He discovered that pridefulness was my weakness. When we made our first trek toward the bridge, after the San Pablo dance, he nicknamed me Superego, unknowingly misusing Freud's term. He now called me aside and whispered in my ear:

"Superego, putting up with you isn't easy, but having to deal with this crook is impossible."

"Look who's talking," I started to say, but then I thought he might be right. This new member of our family could be dangerous. I had never imagined myself associating with a common criminal.

Even more quietly, I told Bartholomew, "Putting up with an alcoholic like you is complicated, but that crook's too much. Count me out of this."

I thought about abandoning the sociological experiment for the second time. But then I remembered that I, too, had been lost and was found. I looked at the dreamseller's calm expression and decided to hold out a while longer. I, too, was curious about where this journey would lead me. It could surely be the subject of many future theses.

The dreamseller's new disciple had a disarming voice, but he was an expert in taking advantage of others. He sold counterfeit winning lottery tickets. He stole women's credit cards and snatched purses from little old ladies after graciously helping them cross the street. The problem is that every schemer is overconfident. Dimas thought he could never be caught—until he encountered someone wilier than him. He didn't realize that by accompanying the dreamseller he would be entering the biggest ambush of his life.

We sat down on a bench in the square to rest. The dreamseller suggested that Bartholomew and I explain the project to Dimas. Not an easy task. The young man didn't look very smart and I thought it might be just the right time to scare him off. Bartholomew exaggerated everything that had happened to us.

"Dude, the chief is a genius. I think he's from another planet. He hypnotizes people. He's called on us to set people on fire with dreams."

Drunk, Bartholomew hallucinated about monsters; sober, he had delusions of grandeur. Unfortunately Dimas liked what he was hearing. These two, living at the edge of society, they spoke the same language. I thought to myself, "Now I'm living at the edge of society *and* I'm alone. I'm worse off than both of these wretches."

We knew whatever explanation we gave Dimas about this journey wouldn't satisfy him—we were as confused as he was. But to someone lost in the desert, a mirage of an oasis brings hope. I was hoping to scare off this con man, but he was now determined to follow us. Thus, our band of misfits was born.

CHAPTER 12

The Brave Little Swallows

L ATER THAT DAY, WE PASSED BY A NEWSSTAND IN THE square and saw our photo on the front page of the newspaper under the headline "A Small Band of Misfits Stirs Up the City." In the foreground was the dreamseller with Bartholomew and me at his side. I bought the paper with the few coins in my pocket.

I was shaken, perplexed. I knew I had caused a scene when I tried to kill myself, but I had hoped it was buried. I just wanted to forget the matter and return to my quiet life in academia. Now my name was on everyone's tongue. The article described my suicide attempt and my rescue by a stranger whose name no one knew.

Dimas and Bartholomew saw one out-of-control intellectual reading that paper. They were accustomed to being insulted. I wasn't. My social image was carefully protected. "I'll be a laughingstock, especially to my enemies at the university," I thought.

What a fool I'd been. I wanted to die without attracting attention, but I went about it all wrong. Instead, I had become infamous. I wanted to grab all the papers and burn them. I wanted to protest the unauthorized use of my photograph. I wanted to sue the journalist for that slanderous reporting. The article called me an attention-seeking mental case. And it also said that the psychiatrist who'd been at the top of the building diagnosed the dreamseller as a dangerous psychopath who could be a public hazard. The way the article read, I hadn't been rescued by a hero; rather, we had been the villains in a Hollywood film.

The dreamseller sat on a nearby bench along with his other followers. Respecting my pain, he merely observed me. He was waiting for my temper to subside before he intervened. But it didn't diminish. My mind raced out of control. I imagined all my colleagues and students reading the story. I was the chairman of a sociology department and had never bowed to any professor or student. I appeared unbeatable, detested stupid minds, but never saw my own stupidity. I had always been skilled at cultivating enemies and rotten at making friends.

"And what will they think of me now?" I thought. "What will they think of a jumper saved by a crazy man? And what's worse, what will they think of that jumper who, after being rescued, danced merrily in a crowd of strangers? Obviously, they'll say I've gone stark raving mad. They'll say I have an advanced degree in insanity."

It was everything that Mario Vargas, Antonio Freitas and other malcontents dreamed of, sullying my image. Without realizing it, I sold the dream they most desired, the dream of stomping on my image. Defeated, I concluded that I was through in the academic world, done at the university. Never again would I face the same silence when I wove social criticism, or respect when I debated ideas or corrected someone.

I began to feel angry toward the journalist who had written the article. I fumed, "Why don't journalists, as part of their training, take a workshop simulating the public destruction of their reputation? Maybe then they'd learn to investigate all the facts and put themselves in other people's shoes before trashing someone else's name."

To the journalist I was just another story. But to me it was my personal struggle: everything that I have and am, even if it is a twisted, troubling tale. A few minutes can change a life story. How could I go back to my old life? If I returned, I'd never be the same to the others. All I had left was to follow a man who proposes a revolutionary plan without the slightest intellectual, social or financial basis. And, moreover, he calls as his followers people who I normally would never associate with.

I had been protected inside the university for many years. And now, the first time I had left the protection of my notable degrees and become a simple mortal, I had been tossed about. I was outraged.

But just as my anger had reached a fever pitch, my mind suddenly shifted and I saw things from a different point of view.

I glanced at the dreamseller and realized that the "comma" he had sold me allowed me to feel all of this, even though it was unpleasant. Whatever negative effects that article might have brought, it also came with something positive: The living *feel* frustration. The dead feel nothing. And I was alive.

I had almost died that day. I should be celebrating life. But the conflicts wedged deep in my unconscious, though weakened, were not dead. I wanted to live a simple, calm life, instead of worrying about my public reputation. But I was a man ruled by anxiety.

Now I understand why the father of a colleague of mine, a seventy-year-old man, arrogant, aggressive, prejudiced, who had been kidnapped for six months, hadn't changed at all after his long captivity. When he was released, everyone thought he would be a gentle, generous, altruistic individual, but after his rescue he was more unbearable than ever.

My love of power had always been hidden beneath the cloak of my intellect. It was not eradicated, even by the threat of suicide. I thought this business of selling dreams wouldn't easily change a selfish man like me. It isn't pain that changes us, but the intellect to use that pain. I realized that if I didn't use that pain, I would continue being simply a hollow human being with a vast intellect but stunted emotions.

As I wrestled with these thoughts, I sensed the dreamseller at my side. He seemed to have entered the whirlwind of my ideas. I could see the concern on his face. He seemed to read my thoughts. In an effort to calm the turbulent waters of my emotions, he said:

"Don't fear criticism from the outside. Fear your own thoughts, for only they can penetrate into your essence and destroy it."

As I pondered his words, he continued:

"Someone can bruise your body without your permission, but he can never invade your mind unless you allow it. Don't let yourself be invaded. We are what we are." Then he challenged me more than I could have imagined: "The cost of selling dreams is high, but you're under no obligation to pay. You're always free to leave."

The dreamseller had dragged me to a crossroads. I had the chance to turn my back and go anywhere in the world. But to quit now? Me? I had always been stubborn, fighting for what I wanted. I was wracked with doubt in a way I never had been before. I recalled a sociological study I had read about the relationship between Jesus and his disciples, and I began to understand psychological and social truths that I had never analyzed.

I began to think about the indescribable power of Jesus' words and actions. They were enough to convince young Jews, in the flower of youth, wild for adventure, some even with established families and businesses, to abandon everything and follow him. What madness! They blindly followed a man with no known political power and no visible identity. He didn't promise them money or riches or an earthly kingdom. What a risk they took! What internal turmoil they must have felt!

They lost everything, and in the end, lost the man who taught them to love, crucified on a wooden cross. He died humbly, loving as he breathed his last, forgiving as he perished. After his death, the group might have faded away, but they had been invaded by an indescribable force. They became stronger after that chaos. They spread His message throughout the world.

They gave their tears, their health, their lives—everything they had—to humanity. They loved strangers and devoted themselves to others. Countless societies across the world, from Europe to Africa to Asia to the Americas, were founded on these very principles, as well as the basis for basic human rights.

Centuries passed and that life became "normal." Churches became excellent temples to conformity. These days, hundreds of millions of people across the world enter these temples to recall a sanitized version of Christmas, the Passion, and other milestones of Christ's life without ever imagining what it's like to sleep out in the open, to be branded a lunatic, and to feel society's scorn. Over the millennia, they have lost the ability to imagine the intense pressure those young men endured to follow that enigmatic master, Jesus.

I imagined the lumpy straw beds they slept on under the open sky. I reflected on the pain they suffered in trying to explain the unexplainable to family and friends in Galilee. They couldn't say they had learned to love a man, lest they be stoned. They couldn't point to this master plan they were helping unfold because the plan was intangible. They couldn't say they were following a powerful man, the Messiah, for he demanded anonymity. What courage they must have had to summon to answer his call. And just like that, Bartholomew brought me back from my deepest of thoughts with a shot. I don't know whether he was praising me or attacking me.

"Hey, Superego, if you're too scared to stick around, we'll still respect you. But you're important to the team."

I took a deep breath. I thought about the man who had stopped my suicide and brought me to sleep under a bridge. He's not Christ, he has no messianic calling. He doesn't perform miracles. He doesn't promise the kingdom of heaven, or an earthly realm, and he doesn't even provide us safety in society. He had nowhere to live, he's broke, had no car, no health insurance. But he had an incredibly magnetic personality. He was the definition of solidarity, he dreamed of opening people's minds, of fighting the system and confronting selfishness.

Wouldn't it be less dangerous to just let society go on being an insanity factory? Wouldn't it be better to let people wallow in their own selfishness? Wouldn't it be easier to let obtuse minds go on thinking only about the superficial mysteries of shopping centers, computers and fashion instead of the mysteries of existence? We're too small to do anything against the powerful system, anyway. We could be arrested, injured and continue to have our names dragged through the mud.

While this circus was playing in my mind, the dreamseller was still in the center ring performing wondrous feats. Patience was his number one virtue. Seeing my worry, he called the three of us together and told us a simple parable that touched the depths of my fears.

"There was once a flood in an immense forest. The weeping clouds that should have promoted life this time predicted death. The larger animals fled, leaving even their offspring behind. In their stampede, they devastated everything in their path. The smaller animals followed their steps. Suddenly, a small swallow, completely soaked, flew in the opposite direction, looking for someone to save.

"The hyenas, seeing this, were astonished. They said, 'You're insane. What can you possibly do with that fragile little body?'

The vultures groused, 'Just look at how tiny you are.' Wherever the fragile swallow flew, it was ridiculed. But it continued seeking someone to rescue. Its wings were fluttering wearily when it spied a baby hummingbird thrashing in the water, ready to give up. Despite never having learned to swim, the swallow plunged into the water and, struggling terribly, grabbed the tiny bird by its left wing. It flew off, carrying the infant in its beak.

"When it returned, it encountered other hyenas, who quickly declared, 'This is crazy! You're just trying to be a hero!' But the swallow didn't stop, despite its fatigue, until it had deposited the little hummingbird in a safe place. Hours later, it found the hyenas in a shady spot. Looking them in the eyes, it told them, 'I only feel worthy of my wings if I make use of them so others can fly.'"

The dreamseller let this story marinate in our minds, then told us:

"There are many hyenas and vultures in society. Don't expect much from the large animals. Rather, expect a lack of understanding, rejection, ridicule and a sick need for power. I don't call you to be great heroes, to have your feats recorded in the annals of history, but to be small swallows who fly anonymously throughout society, loving strangers and doing for them whatever you can. Be worthy of your wings. It is in insignificance that great significance is achieved, and in smallness that great acts are realized."

The dreamseller's parable at once moved me and wounded me deeply. I thought, "I have to admit I've acted like a hyena or a vulture on many occasions in my life; now I need to learn how to act like a brave little swallow."

CHAPTER 13

The Most Lucid Place in Society

"NORMALS" ALWAYS GET OUT OF BED THE SAME WAY. THEY complain the same way. Get irritated the same way. They curse using the same words. They greet their friends in the same fashion. Give the same answers to the same problems. They express the same humor at home and at work. They have the same reactions to the same circumstances. Give presents on the same days. In short, they have a tiring and predictable routine, which becomes an excellent source of anxiety, anguish, emptiness and boredom.

The system has blocked people's imagination, corroded their creativity. They rarely give presents on unexpected days. Rarely react differently in tense situations. They are prisoners and don't know it.

"Normal" parents, when they correct or advise their children, are interrupted midway through. Their children can't stand hearing the same arguments anymore. They say, "I know that already . . ." And they really do. "Normals" don't know how to relate their own experiences in order to stimulate the thinking of others.

I was always predictable in my relationship with students, and I only discovered this when I began my journey with the dreamseller. I taught class in a single tone of voice. I criticized and admonished in the same manner. I varied the verbs and nouns, but not the form or the content. The students were fed up with a professor who seemed more like an Egyptian mummy than a human being. They couldn't stand hearing over and over that they'd be losers in life if they didn't study.

On the other hand, the dreamseller continually sold the dream of enchantment. How can someone who has nothing on the exterior be so captivating? How can a man without any kind of teaching background so effectively engage our imagination? Walking with him was an invitation to innovative thinking. He saw ordinary situations from different angles. We seemed to travel without a destination or purpose. But deep down, he knew very well what he wanted and where he wanted to go. He was training us to find an unimaginable freedom. Each day was like a garden full of surprises, some of them pleasant, others not.

The next morning, after meditating silently on his own worries, the dreamseller rose, took several deep breaths of the polluted city air from under the bridge and gave thanks to God in an unusual way.

"God, you exist in every space in time. You are infinitely distant and infinitely near, but I know that your eyes are upon me. Let me capture your feelings. Thank you for granting us one more show in this surprising existence."

Honeymouth, who loved country music, said, "What show are we gonna see, chief?" And he expressed an early-morning enthusiasm that I had seldom seen.

"Show? Each day is a show, each day is a spectacle," the dreamseller answered, roused with excitement. "Only he who's mortally wounded by tedium doesn't discover it. Drama and comedy are in our minds. All we need to do is decide to release them."

Bartholomew had to be drunk to free himself of his sorrow,

to rid himself of his boredom. Now he, as well as Dimas and I, were discovering another world, another stage. The dreamseller set off, and we followed. We climbed a hill, walked three blocks, turned to the right, then walked four more blocks. We exchanged glances, questioning one another, trying to guess where the dreamseller was headed.

After walking for forty minutes, Dimas, who still had not been sufficiently astonished by the dreamseller's words, asked, "Where are we going?"

The dreamseller stopped, looked him in the eye and said, "Those who sell dreams are like the wind: You hear your voice but don't know where it comes from or where it's going. What matters isn't the route but the journey."

Dimas understood almost nothing, but he began exercising his rusty mind. And we continued to walk. Fifteen minutes later, the dreamseller stopped in front of a gathering and headed toward it. We slowed our pace, and let him go on about twenty feet ahead of us. Dimas looked at me and said, apprehensively, "This is a funeral home. I'm not going in there."

"I'm with you. I don't think the dreamseller knows what he's getting into," I said.

It was a family wake, the only place where strangers are both unwelcome and have no desire to enter. But the irreverent Honeymouth, trying to maintain his poise, prodded me, saying, "Come on, Superego. Get over yourself. Let's go to the wake."

Just then I felt like slapping him. I don't know whether he was humoring the dreamseller or truly following his heart. But since we were close to the wake, a place of respect, I contained my anger. The atmosphere was riddled with pain. There was a crowd mourning a man who had died of a rapidly growing cancer, leaving an only son, twelve years old.

The area where the dead were mourned was grand and ostentatious, decorated with several rounded, marble-covered arches and lit by chandeliers. It was a physically beautiful place to house so much sadness. Fear of causing a scene in a place where silence should reign made us slow our pace even more. We distanced ourselves from the dreamseller, remaining about fifty feet behind him. Looking back, he saw our apprehension and approached his timid disciples.

"What is the most clear-thinking place in the great madhouse of our society?" he asked. "The courts? Editorial rooms of large newspapers? The politician's pulpit? The universities?"

"The bars," Honeymouth tried to joke, then quickly apologized. "Just kidding, chief."

The dreamseller answered:

"It's here, at wakes. They are the most lucid places in society. Here we disarm ourselves, strip away our vanities, remove our makeup. Here we are who we are. If we can't be ourselves here, then we are sicker than we can possibly imagine. For those closest to the deceased, a wake is a source of despair. For those a bit more removed, it's a place to reflect. But for both, the truth is stark: We fall into the silence of our crypts not as doctors, intellectuals, politicians or celebrities, but as mere mortals."

These words made me see that it was at wakes where we ceased to be gods and truly came in contact with our humanity, realizing our frailty and accepting our mortality. At wakes, we, the normal, engaged in an intuitive group therapy.

Some said, "Poor man, he died so young." These were the ones who could empathize with the deceased and started to wonder whether they, themselves, could live a kinder life. Others said, "Life is full of risks. In the end, death comes to us all." These saw the urgency of relaxing, slowing down their lives. Still others commented, "He worked so hard, and just as he was about to enjoy the fruits of his labors, he died." These discovered that life passes like a shadow, that, in their search for riches, they neglected their own health. And they realized that they needed to change their unhealthy lifestyles.

People at wakes were trying desperately to buy dreams, to remember the reasons for being alive, but the system steam-rolls them in a matter of hours or days. Everything returns to "normal." They didn't understand that dreams will last only if they're woven with fine thread in the secret places of the mind. I had always tried to make myself immune to these feelings. To me, the misery of others was like a movie, nothing more than fiction trying to take root in my mind, but never finding fertile ground.

"Don't expect to see flowers growing in a place where seeds haven't died first," the dreamseller said. "Don't be worried. Let's go." And he smiled.

To him, these words were enough. To us, they merely took the edge off our hesitation. Death is worrisome, but so is life. The former extinguishes courage, but the latter can choke it out. What could the dreamseller offer in a setting where words fail? What could he say in a venue where all arguments fade away? What could he possibly say at a moment when people are disinclined to listen and taste only the bitterness of suffering in the face of their loss? What words would offer them relief—especially coming from a stranger?

We knew the dreamseller would not behave like just another mourner; that was a problem. We also knew he would not stay quiet and stand idly by. And that was a greater problem still.

CHAPTER 14

A Solemn Homage

WENT THROUGH THE SAME ORDEAL WHEN I LOST MY MOTHER. The expressions of sympathy, the prefabricated advice, nothing helped ease the pain. All the comforting words didn't make a dent in the bars that imprisoned me. I would have preferred the silence of embraces or just a few tears shed at my side.

The dreamseller asked to be let through the crowd, and we followed. The closer we came to the coffin, the more the people seemed to be suffering. Then we saw a young man, near forty, with thinning black hair, a drawn and anguished face, lying motionless in the coffin.

His wife was inconsolable. Relatives and close friends were all drying their tears. The son was lost in despair. I saw myself in him and felt his pain more than my companions could. He had barely begun his life and had already begun losing a great deal. I had only just started to understand life when my father ended his, and then I lost my mother, too. I dined with loneliness and slept in my own sealed-off world, plagued by unanswered questions. God ignored me, I thought. I felt bitter toward him in my adolescence. Finally, in adult life, he became a mirage and I an atheist, a specialist in pessimism. Realizing the emptiness in this young boy, I couldn't hold back the tears.

The dreamseller, seeing the boy's despair, hugged him and asked his name and his father's. Then, to our amazement, he turned to those present and in his deep voice offered words that shook them, words that could provoke an uproar: "Why are all of you grieving so hopelessly? Marco Aurelio isn't dead."

Immediately, Bartholomew, Dimas and I tried to distance ourselves. We did not want to be recognized as his disciples. The people had different reactions to his claim. Some went from tears to mockery, albeit well contained. They secretly laughed at the crazy man. Others were extremely curious. They thought he was some eccentric spiritual leader invited to officiate the funeral. Still others wanted him thrown out, outraged at the invasion of privacy and disrespect for other people's feelings. Some of these grabbed him by the arms in an effort to usher him out.

But the dreamseller wasn't upset. He said in a strong, firm voice:

"I'm not asking you to silence your pain, only your despair. I don't expect you to stanch your tears, only the depth of your anguish. The emptiness never goes away, but despair can be alleviated, for it does no honor to the departed."

Those grasping him released their grip and began to understand that the strangely dressed man with a heavy beard might be eccentric, but he was intelligent. The deceased's widow, Sofia, and his son, Antonio, stared at him.

Then, with an air of serenity difficult to describe, he added:

"Marco Aurelio experienced incredible moments. He cried, he loved, he fell in love, he won, he lost. The reason all of you are sad—thrust into an existential vacuum because of his absence—is because you're letting him die in the only place where he must remain alive: inside you."

Seeing the people more introspective, he resumed his penetrating Socratic method: "What scars did Marco Aurelio leave on your emotions? Where did he influence your paths? How did his actions and words color your way of looking at life?"

After offering these words, the dreamseller said something that shocked everyone, including us. Once again we were ashamed of our lack of wisdom and sensitivity. He repeated the question that had shaken his audience: "Is this man alive or dead inside of you?"

The mourners answered that he was alive. Immediately, he made a comment that lifted them out of their despair and soothed their spirits:

"Shortly before Jesus was killed, a woman named Mary, who loved him, poured the most expensive of perfumes over his feet. It was all she had. By anointing him with her perfume, she was praising him for all he had done and experienced, and he was so moved that he praised her magnanimous gesture, while the disciples scolded her because she had wasted an extremely valuable perfume that could have been used for other purposes. Scolding his disciples, Jesus told them that he was preparing them for his death, and that wherever his message was spread her gesture would be recounted as a timeless homage."

The mourners pondered his words. The ones who couldn't hear clearly squeezed closer to him. Then he concluded:

"Jesus wanted to demonstrate that a wake may be a place of tears, but it should, above all else, be an atmosphere flooded with praise and solemn remembrance. Mourning should be a perfume, an homage to the departed. A setting for recounting his life and his words. A word of praise can be said about any person. Please, tell me of this man's deeds. Tell me how he impacted your lives. His silence should give wing to our voices."

At first the mourners just looked at one another. Then what happened was incredible. Many of them began relating unique stories that they had experienced with him. They spoke of the legacy he had left. His kindness. His loyalty. His capacity to deal with failure. His unyielding affection. His friendship.

Others, now more at ease, joked about his mannerisms. There were those who said he loved nature. One friend said, "I never met anyone as stubborn and obstinate." And in a setting where usually no one smiles, people laughed at the memory, including Antonio and the widow, because they knew how stubborn he could be. A friend added, "But he taught me that we must never give up on what we love."

There were twenty incredible minutes of heartfelt memories. People didn't know how to describe the fascinating emotional experience they had had. Marco Aurelio was alive. At that moment, the dreamseller looked at us, his disciples, and said, whether joking or serious I don't know, "When I die, don't despair. Instead, speak of my dreams and my wild desires."

Some people laughed at the strange and amusing man who had lifted them from the valley of despair to the peak of serenity. As incredible as it seems, even young Antonio smiled. There, in that room where so many lavished praised on the deceased, the dreamseller sold a dream to the young boy who had lost his father.

"Antonio, look what a brilliant human being your father was, despite his shortcomings. Don't hold back your tears. Weep as many times as you desire, but don't let his loss make you lose hope. Just the opposite. Honor your father by living maturely. Honor him by confronting your fears. Praise him by being generous, creative, affectionate, sincere. Live wisely. I believe that if your father could use my voice at this moment to say something to you, he would implore you: 'Son, go forward! Don't be afraid of the journey. Be afraid of missing out on life.'"

Antonio felt his spirits lift. That was all he needed to hear. He would still cry. Longing would beat mercilessly in his chest. But he would know how to put commas instead of periods in his life when he encountered loneliness, when he came upon sorrow. His life would take on new dimensions.

The dreamseller prepared to leave, but first he left the mourners with his final thoughts, the same questions that had shaken me atop the San Pablo Building.

"Are we living atoms that disintegrate and never again become what they were? What is existence or nonexistence? What mortal can know? Who has dissected death to expose its true essence? Is death the end or the beginning?"

Enraptured, people approached me and asked, "Who is that man? Where does he come from?" What could I answer? I didn't know either. They asked the same of Bartholomew and, unfortunately, he found himself answering the questions. Honeymouth enjoyed weaving theories about things he didn't know. Puffing out his chest, he replied:

"Who's the chief? He's from another world. And if you need anything, I'm his adviser on international affairs."

Dimas, the newest member of our group, stunned by everything he'd heard, replied honestly. "I don't know who he is. All I know is he dresses like a pauper but he seems to be very rich, indeed."

Sofia, Antonio's mother, was deeply grateful and bursting with curiosity. When she saw him about to leave without saying anything more, she asked, "Who are you? What religion do you preach? Where do you learn these teachings?"

He looked at her and calmly answered:

"I'm not a priest, a theologian or a philosopher. I'm just a wanderer trying to understand who I am. A traveler who once doubted God, but, after crossing a great desert, has discovered that he is the architect of all existence."

Upon hearing him, I again fell deep in thought. I didn't know that the dreamseller had been an atheist like me. But something had changed in him. His relationship with God troubled me; it wasn't based on religion, tradition or self-pity, but was rooted in an incomprehensible friendship. Who is he, then? What desert had he crossed? Could he have cried more than the people at the wake? Where had he lived, where was he born? Before more questions could bubble up in my mind, he started to leave. Sofia extended both hands to him and wordlessly declared her gratitude. Antonio couldn't contain himself. He gave the dreamseller a long embrace that moved everyone and asked, "Where can I find you again? Where do you live?"

"My home is the world," the dreamseller replied. "You can find me in some avenue of existence."

And he left, leaving everyone astonished. We, his disciples, were speechless. For the moment, at least, he quieted our uncertainties. We were beginning to believe it was worthwhile to follow him, little knowing the storms that awaited us.

We made our way slowly through the gathering. The people wanted to meet him, speak with him, open up some chapters of their lives, but he humbly passed them by. He wasn't fond of praise. We, on the other hand, were starting to feel important. Dimas and Bartholomew, who had always lived at the edge of society, felt their egos swell, attacked by a virus I knew all too well.

CHAPTER 15

The Eager Miracle Worker

THE DAY WOULD HAVE BEEN PERFECT IF NOT FOR THE surprise awaiting us just around the corner. The funeral home was large, and there were several enormous rooms, each separate from the others so several families could mourn their loved ones at once. When we left the hall where Marco Aurelio was being mourned, we passed through another wake, that of a seventy-five-year-old woman.

But a man who walked by caught the dreamseller's attention. He was a young man of about thirty, curly hair, short, navy blue suit and a white shirt. He was good-looking, with a well-modulated voice, imposing. The dreamseller quietly followed him.

The man approached the old woman's coffin confidently. Apparently he was some sort of priest. To me, he seemed harmless, but the dreamseller didn't see it that way. The man positioned himself at the foot of the coffin and made a gesture of reverence. Little by little he revealed his face, and we soon saw his true intentions.

His name was Edson, but people called him the Miracle Worker. Edson had a penchant for "performing" miracles. Oh, he wanted to help others. But there was always a motive behind his aid: He loved attention. Edson wasn't the spiritual leader charged with offering words of consolation at the funeral. He was there out of self-interest.

Incredible as it seems, the Miracle Worker desired to resurrect the old woman. He wanted to put on a dazzling show capable of making the spectators bow at his feet; he actually hoped to awaken the elderly woman from death and be recognized as the bearer of a supernatural gift. Just as Caligula used his power to be hailed as a god on earth, Edson hoped to use his knowledge of the Bible to invoke the supernatural and be treated like a demigod himself—although he never would have admitted it.

As a sociologist I had learned that there is no power as complete as religion. Dictators, politicians, intellectuals, psychiatrists and psychologists fail to penetrate the minds of others like certain religious figures. Because they represent a deity, these men can achieve a status the likes of which Napoleon or Hitler never could.

In our wanderings, the dreamseller would tell us that spiritual leaders who represented an altruistic, generous God contributed to the good of humanity. But those who represented a controlling, vengeful God—in effect, a God created in their own image—caused disasters, destroyed freedom and controlled people. The dreamseller always warned us that it's easy to construct a manipulative God in our mind. He seemed to want to keep us in touch with our humanity.

But this charlatan we saw at the wake had mixed intentions. At certain times he wanted to contribute to the good of his fellow man and was sincere and caring. At other times he seemed swollen with pridefulness.

But this Miracle Worker, though ambitious, was no fool. He wanted to create a spectacle but not a scene. He wanted to resurrect the old woman but tried to guard against insulting anyone. Many thoughts swirled in his brain. "What if she doesn't come to life? What if I tell her to rise and she just lies there? My reputation will be lost."

The dreamseller watched him closely, like a leopard scrutinizing the landscape. We knew the dreamseller took pleasure in dealing with extremely complicated people, but we didn't understand his true intention that day. Little by little we began to see the kind of show the Miracle Worker was hoping to put on.

After a moment of reverence, the Miracle Worker approached the dead woman and whispered in an almost inaudible voice, "Rise." He hoped not to be heard in case his faith failed him.

The old woman showed no sign of life. Immediately, he repeated in that low voice, "Rise."

If she were to have moved in the slightest, Edson would have shouted to the heavens and proclaimed himself a true miracle worker. It would be his most glorious moment. Countless people hungering for supernatural acts would follow him.

But nothing happened. The deceased remained motionless. Bartholomew, Dimas and I, who were far from saints, were indignant with the Miracle Worker's trickery. What an arrogant jerk, we thought.

But he didn't give up. He filled his lungs and in a louder voice, but speaking between his teeth so no one could understand clearly what he was saying, he declared, "Rise, woman. I command you!"

The unimaginable happened. The woman moved. But not because of the Miracle Worker. An older man, reeking of alcohol the way Bartholomew did the day I met him, bumped the coffin. But the Miracle Worker, wrapped up in himself and in looking for any signs of life from the old woman, didn't notice when the deceased's nephew came staggering in and smacked the coffin, causing the old woman's hands, gently resting on her chest, to change position.

The Miracle Worker's heart leaped with emotion. He thought his moment of glory had arrived, that his supernatural abilities had finally revealed themselves. Overcome with joy, and desperate to take credit for his "miracle," he yelled out and proclaimed to the mourners:

"Rise, woman! I command you!"

This time, everyone heard and was startled by his command. He expected the woman to sit up in her coffin and the crowd to acknowledge his tremendous power. But the old woman showed no further signs of life.

He figured all he needed was just a little more faith to make the coffin move again. And this time, he gave the order to the body again, glancing at the crowd: "Rise, woman!" he begged the corpse, which would not respond to his appeal.

The longer the woman remained motionless, the weaker his knees became. He broke into a cold sweat, his mouth dried out and his heart raced. Half dazed, he finally saw the drunk trying to regain his balance by steadying himself on the coffin. The Miracle Worker knew he had made a fool of himself. He felt like a wounded deer amid a pride of lions. But this Miracle Worker still had a few tricks up his sleeve. He raised his voice again and said firmly:

"Woman! If you won't rise to live in this evil world, then rest in peace!"

Several "normals" answered in chorus, "Amen!"

The Miracle Worker ended his performance by taking out a handkerchief to dry invisible tears and said solemnly, "Poor, *poor* woman. She was *such* a good person."

CHAPTER 16

A Very Complicated Disciple

ALL SIGNS POINTED TO THIS BEING JUST ANOTHER CON FOR the Miracle Worker: He used his supposed spirituality to take advantage of others' naïveté. "Normals" have a strong tendency to listen to leaders without questioning them. After watching the Miracle Worker's scheme, I looked at Dimas and thought, "Not even Angel Hand would do something that low." In turn, Angel Hand, knowing something of my nature through Bartholomew thought, "Not even this arrogant intellectual would manipulate other people like that." Bartholomew, more honest than either of us, said out loud, "Only after two bottles of vodka could I hallucinate like that guy."

As soon as my friends and I criticized the Miracle Worker, our legs trembled. We looked at one another and had the same thought: "Why is the dreamseller so interested in this character? Could he be interested in calling him to join the group?" The thought rattled us so much that we said, simultaneously, "I'll leave!"

This worried us. We watched the dreamseller's actions carefully, hoping he would turn and leave, but he went up to the man who had captured his attention. Our hearts pounded. The Miracle Worker met the dreamseller's gaze and, to our relief, our leader said nothing, merely shaking his head in disapproval.

The dreamseller may have had his faults, but he never set

out to manipulate another person. To him, a person's conscience was sacred. Freedom of choice should always prevail. His strongest criticism of society was that it surreptitiously sold a nonexistent freedom, a freedom found in the pages of democracy but not in the pages of history. Too many had been enslaved by their troubled minds.

After disapproving silently, but without exposing the Miracle Worker publicly, the dreamseller made two statements and two conclusions:

"Miracles don't convince people. If they did, Judas would never have betrayed Jesus. Miracles can change the body, but not the mind. If they could, Peter never would have denied knowing Jesus."

Edson remained silent. He didn't know how to reply because he had never considered that. Then came the bombshell that rocked me as a professor.

"The man you claim to follow never used his power in order to control people," the dreamseller said. "Jesus never used his power to seduce audiences and win over followers. That's why he, unlike politicians, told his followers, 'Don't tell anyone!' Unless they followed him out of the spontaneous emotion of an unfathomable love, he didn't want followers. He wanted friends, not servants."

These words got me to thinking about our own history. I remembered that in centuries past, atrocities were committed in the name of Christ: People killed, tortured, waged war, conquered, wounded, excluded in his name. They ignored the gentleness of Jesus, who never manipulated anyone, who would not hear of servants. Centuries of opposition and hatred toward Muslims followed, an animosity whose roots are perpetuated even today. In traveling with the dreamseller, I had begun to suspect I wasn't the confirmed atheist I thought I was. Deep down, my disgust was with organized religion.

The Miracle Worker was dumbstruck: Never had anyone corrected him without scolding him. The dreamseller, having said all he needed to say, turned and left, leaving several who witnessed the confrontation confused. We were immensely relieved. For how long? We didn't know.

The next day, a newspaper report on the recent events appeared in *The Times,* under the headline, "A Stranger Turns a Wake into a Garden." A photo taken secretly as we left the wake was on the front page of one section. The reporting wasn't an attack; instead, it contained many interesting facts. It said that a bold stranger wanted to change the dynamic of wakes, to transform them from settings of despair into platforms for paying homage to the dead.

The journalist had interviewed people who had heard the dreamseller speak. Some said they planned to write their families to say that, when they died, they didn't want a funeral marked by despair, loss and self-pity, but one highlighting their best moments. Mourners should instead be revelers, recalling the deceased's acts of love and kindness, their words, their dreams, their friendships—even their foolish moments. They wanted those saying good-bye to remember that day joyfully, despite the pain.

The article said that the stranger was the same one who had caused a flurry near the San Pablo Building. And it ended with two questions: Are we witnessing one of the greatest atheists ever, or a man with incomprehensible spirituality? Are we witness to a modern-day prophet, or a lunatic?

When we awoke the next morning, we found the dreamseller off by himself, deep in conversation. It was the second time we'd seen him carrying on this monologue. He gestured as if he were having hallucinations or questioning his own reasoning. Ten minutes later, he came to us relaxed. He seemed to have cleansed his mind of the day-to-day noise.

The sky was darkening, threatening a heavy rain. Lightning ripped across the sky. Dimas didn't fear the police or jail time, but he was terrified of lightning storms. We were walking along a wide street when the thunder made our usually unflappable friend cower.

I tried to calm him by telling him that by the time we heard the thunder, the lightning—and the danger—had already passed. But the mind is riddled with traps; he understood my words but they could not calm his irrational fears. I couldn't criticize him, though. I was no different. I had always valued logic over emotion, but it was no consolation from the esoteric pain of my past. It haunted me.

The rain soon began to fall. We quickly sought shelter in a large shopping mall. At the entrance was a vast department store. As we went inside, we heard the earsplitting crack of lightning strike. Dimas dove beneath the first table he found. He was like a child who had seen a ghost. I thought to myself, "The dreamseller is right. There are no heroes. Eventually, every giant encounters obstacles that transform him into a child. All you have to do is wait."

The last lightning bolt overloaded the mall's grounding system and the electricity pulsed down the walls of the building. Two painters, cousins, were repainting the store. One of them, who had a stammer worse than Dimas, was working on the walls. When he was nervous, his voice shut down and he couldn't say a word. The other was on top of a six-foot ladder, happily retouching the steel window frames.

When the lightning bolt hit, it coursed through the walls and bounced into the window, striking one painter. The noise was deafening. The painter fell off the ladder, writhing in pain. His cousin, terrified, rushed to his aid. We started forward, but before we could get there, someone rushed past us, looking to be a hero. I don't know where the man came from, but he seemed familiar. When I looked closer, I realized it was the Miracle Worker from the wake.

Edson saw the painter lying on the floor, moaning in pain and holding his right ankle. He saw that the man's foot was deformed. He concluded immediately that it was because of the lightning. Wasting no time, he told the other painter, who was attending the injured man, "It's OK, I've got him. I'm an expert in this kind of thing."

He rushed over to the man and tried to straighten out his foot but couldn't. He sat down on the man's leg and began yelling an order at the ankle, trying to call on his supernatural powers.

"Heal! Repair! Align your bones!"

But the ankle didn't repair itself. The painter, now in agony, moaned again. The Miracle Worker applied still more force. In his mind, he couldn't leave such a simple case unresolved. It wasn't possible, he must have thought, for his moral standing with God to be so low. The painter howled in pain. The crowd gathered and buzzed, which only made the "Good Samaritan" Miracle Worker try harder to show his supernatural powers.

Many of those watching the Miracle Worker thought he was a doctor doing some kind of procedure to alleviate the painter's suffering. The stammering cousin seemed to want to say something to Edson, who instead was distracted by the man's pestering. Losing his patience, he told the painter standing over him, "Calm down! I am *going* to fix this man's leg."

And he did. Two agonizing minutes later, the Miracle Worker completed his task. Wiping sweat from his brow, he told the audience, "There, the ankle is as good as new." But the man's pain was worse than ever.

The painter looked at his ankle and appeared more desperate. We thought he was still in shock.

Just as the crowd was beginning to applaud the Miracle

Worker, the painter's cousin finally managed to untie his tongue. He came swinging at Edson, shouting, "Get away from him, you butcher! You worthless liar!"

No one understood what was happening, not even the dreamseller. We all thought the stuttering painter was being ungrateful. Then, stammering, he explained:

"My cousin's crippled. He's had a limp for thirty years, but he's never had surgery to correct it. Now this bastard comes along and fixes it—without anesthesia."

A crowd, that only seconds earlier was ready to applaud the Miracle Worker, was now growing into a mob ready to pummel him. But the dreamseller stopped them. With one question he tamed an angry mob and rescued the man who loved power:

"Wait! Why do you want to hurt this man? What matters most, his actions or his intent?"

Tempers cooled and people began to disperse. Bartholomew, still confused, said, "Chief, you need to explain to me what you just said."

Calmly, with the Miracle Worker still shrinking from the crowd, the dreamseller explained:

"A man's actions may warrant our outrage. His methods can be criticized. But what we should focus on are a person's intentions."

For the first time in his life, Edson had performed a real miracle—and had almost been lynched for it. We had criticized his attitude, looking only at his actions. Unlike the dreamseller, we hadn't seen the altruistic reasons for what he had done; we simply wanted him as far away as possible from us and our little sociological experiment. But before we could say a word, the dreamseller did what we feared most. He looked at the Miracle Worker and casually told him:

"Come, follow me and I will show you miracles unlike any you've ever known, miracles that can cure our ailing society."

When we heard the dreamseller's call, my two friends and I embraced one another. Some might have thought we were moved, but actually we were disappointed in ourselves. In that moment, we realized how easy it is to fall under the spell of prejudice. We had accepted scoundrels, drunks and stupidly prideful people into our group, but we had discriminated against the religious types, especially so-called miracle workers. We had to adjust our thinking to the dreamseller's will with a heavy dose of patience and tolerance.

Edson was euphoric about being called. He didn't understand it, but knew that this dreamseller, however strange, possessed great powers of persuasion. He thought that if he learned the dreamseller's techniques, he could use them to go far. He couldn't imagine the depths of the journey he was about to begin. He couldn't imagine the bitter pain he would suffer curing himself of his obsession with power. Deep down, he was as addicted to power as Honeymouth was to alcohol, as I was to my ego, as Angel Hand was to the art of the con. We were addicts, all of us.

CHAPTER 17

An Obsessive Dream

WE WERE NO SECT, NO POLITICAL PARTY. WE WERE NOT part of a foundation or any official organization. We didn't rely on public welfare, didn't even know where we'd sleep or what we'd eat. We depended on spontaneous donations from people, and sometimes we bathed in public shelters. We were a band of dreamers who wanted to change the world, or at least our world. Still, we had no guarantee whether we would change anything or cause more confusion. But I was beginning to love this lifestyle, a pleasant sociological experiment, albeit one full of unknowns.

Some were starting to recognize the dreamseller from the news. They would interrupt his walk, feeling the need to tell him their problems. He enjoyed listening to them. After minutes or hours of hearing them vent, he would encourage them to make choices and understand that every choice comes with frustrations and not merely gains.

Gradually, the dreamseller acquired more disciples, each more interesting than the last. The swallows were learning to fly within a system that threatened to clip their wings. But we also learned not to make grand plans for the future. The future didn't belong to us. Life was a celebration, even though the wine always eventually ran out.

We learned to kiss old people and feel the markings of time. We learned to pay attention to children and delight in their innocence. We learned to talk to beggars and journey through their incredible worlds. Priests, nuns, pastors, Muslims, Buddhists, would-be suicides, depressives, neurotics . . . there were so many beautiful and interesting people around us who were ignored by society.

I was starting to develop a new sensitivity to others, an empathy. Even though my pridefulness was dormant, it wasn't yet dead. I recalled action films I had seen. How many countless extras were killed in movies, faceless people who, in the real world, had entire life stories, complete with fear and love, bravery and cowardice. To the dreamseller, there were no extras in society. He praised the poor, calling them to be his closest friends. He cared deeply for those who lived at society's margins.

Just when I thought my sensitivity was at its height, one of those supporting actors came into my life and made me see that I was still only just a beginner. We were on Kennedy Avenue when we saw a young man of about twenty, close to six feet tall, curly hair, dark skin. His name was Solomon Salles. He had these wild gestures that made even children flinch. He would wink uncontrollably and move his neck restlessly, flexing his trapezius muscles. Before going through a door he would jump three times, believing that if he skipped the routine even once, someone in his family would die. He had severe obsessive-compulsive disorder.

Besides all these bizarre compulsive rituals, the oddest thing of all was that Solomon couldn't see a hole, whether in walls, the ground or furniture, without feeling the urge to stick his right index finger into it. As we were watching him, he was crouching, sticking his finger in various small openings in the sidewalk.

Passersby made fun of him. To tell the truth, we couldn't hold back either, though we tried to disguise our laughter. We thought we'd finally found someone more messed up than any of us. But the dreamseller was upset at our reactions.

"Is this young man more fragile than we are, or stronger?" he asked us pointedly. "What price does he pay for having to live with his tics in public? Is he weak or gifted with unusual courage? I don't know about you, but beyond a doubt he's a stronger man than me."

We fell silent, but he went on:

"How often do you think this young man has felt he was in the center ring of a circus, as he is now? How many sleepless nights has he spent thinking about the laughter of others? How many times has he felt the white-hot sting of prejudice?" And so we would truly feel the burn of our discrimination, he concluded, "Criticism injures a person, but prejudice annihilates him."

Whenever the dreamseller analyzed one of us, he stripped us, leaving us "naked." I discovered that people like me, who always defended human rights, are grossly prejudiced in some areas, even if this barbarity is subtly manifested in a hypocritical smile or in indifferent silence. We're worse than vampires. We kill without extracting blood. He continued:

"If you want to sell the dream of unity, you have to perceive the suffering of others. You have to learn to dry the tears never shed, the anguish never verbalized, the fears hidden below an impassive face. The ones who don't develop such characteristics will have traces of psychopathy even if they live in unsuspecting settings, like the temples of universities or the temples of business, politics or religion. They'll pressure, wound, coerce, without feeling the pain of others. Is that you?" he asked us.

I tried taking a deep breath to see if I could get oxygen to my brain. Could I have traces of psychopathy? Classic psychopaths are easily discerned, but those with subtle traces of psychopathy can disguise their insensitivity behind their academic titles, their ethics or their spirituality. I wore a disguise.

I never sought out my son to ask him about his fears, his frustrations. I imposed rules on John Marcus, pointed out his mistakes, but I never sold him the most important dream: That I wanted to know him, to love him and to be loved by him. I never sought out a student who looked sad, irritable or indifferent. I never lent my shoulder for another professor to cry on. To me, professors were technicians and not people. My arrogance turned against me like a boomerang.

When I was ready to give up on life, my colleagues and students had no idea of my emotional state. An intellectual like me couldn't declare his pain. To them, depression was something that happened to weak people. No one noticed the suffering secretly drawn on my face. Were they blind or was I incapable of showing my feelings? I still don't know.

As the dreamseller always advised us, no one is a hundred percent villain or a hundred percent victim. I was insensitive but also surrounded by people with low levels of sensitivity. I didn't need applause or praise. What I needed was just a shoulder to cry on, to feel the support of people saying, "I'm here. You can count on me."

When the dreamseller made us see the courage and greatness of the young man with OCD, he offered us a challenge: "Are you going to sell dreams to him?" He said nothing more, awaiting our reaction.

We remained silent. After endless seconds with a lump in our throats, we felt lost. It was an odd reaction for a group of supposedly experienced people. We didn't know what to say. We didn't know what he would think of us. Just a few minutes earlier we had branded him a lunatic, and now we were afraid of being branded lunatics by him. Isn't that what insanity is? We went from one extreme to the other.

The dreamseller remained silent and made us uncomfortable. We knew how to ridicule the misfortune of others but not how to alleviate it. We were creative when it came to exclusion but helpless in matters of inclusion. If someone asked the Miracle Worker to deliver a long, bombastic speech to the young man, it would be an easy task, but asking him to sell dreams paralyzed him. If Bartholomew were under the influence and was asked to make friends with the stranger, it would be no problem. But sober, it was much more complicated. If someone asked Angel Hand to steal his wallet then give it back to win his admiration, it would be easy. But charming someone with words was an almost impossible task for him.

If they asked me to teach a class to demonstrate my sophistication, I'd have no problem. But for me to win over a stranger, my fellow man, without using the power of information, was a hellish task. I knew how to address large audiences but not how to engage a man alone. I had been trained to speak about Kant, Hegel, Auguste Comte, Marx, but not about myself. The system had made a mockery of our humanity. And I had nurtured it.

Since there was no instruction manual for selling dreams to an obsessive, and since the dreamseller refused to offer guidance, I shyly tried my hand. I, the most urbane of the group, was also the most unbending. Honeymouth, worn down by life, crouched down and tried to stick his hands in the holes in an effort to initiate contact. But the young man just laughed at him. Bartholomew felt like a fool, and the young man went on with his compulsion.

Edson couldn't stand watching it. He turned his back and covered his mouth, trying helplessly to stifle his laughter. Suddenly, the obsessive young man stood up and saw the opening in the Miracle Worker's Dumbo-like right ear. He rushed over and stuck his finger in Edson's ear, making the Miracle Worker leap to the heavens and shout, "Away with you, demon, this body doesn't belong to you!"

Solomon was startled at the Miracle Worker's rudeness. Edson put his hands on his head, realizing that once again he had displayed his weakness for the supernatural. This time, however, he'd gone too far. He had wanted to cast out the mental illness lodged in the man's brain. But Solomon looked wounded.

"I've been called crazy, psychotic, mad, demented, insane, bonkers, off my rocker, but possessed by demons is a first," he said.

Edson saw how deeply he had hurt the young man. He realized that deep down, he had trouble accepting people who were different, and, in effect, was selling nightmares instead of dreams.

"Forgive me. Please, forgive me," Edson said solemnly. "I was stupid and unjust and superficial. I actually think you're much stronger than me. You put up with mockery while I look for applause."

Edson's honest and courageous words fascinated us. He had begun to achieve one of the most difficult miracles, that of humility. Like him, I had never asked for anyone's forgiveness. We were small gods, I in the temple of knowledge, Edson in the temple of spirituality. We were beginning to understand that we only became strong when we allow ourselves to be fragile.

That moment of honesty broke the ice. We introduced ourselves to the young man and began to become part of his life. He had attempted to study psychology but had to give it up because his professors said an obsessive couldn't treat the mentally ill. He tried law school but had to give it up because his professors said an obsessive with such wild obsessions wouldn't be taken seriously by his clients, much less when presenting arguments in court.

He hadn't lasted three months at any job. No one wanted to hire a person seemingly unable to control his behavior. He didn't have a girlfriend because no one wanted to be with someone who was constantly being insulted. His whole existence was based on exclusion. Nevertheless, he was a very strong human being, as the dreamseller had imagined. Despite those mounting difficulties he hadn't become depressed or thought about taking his own life, as I had. He had serious issues, to be sure. But despite those moments when he felt rejected, he had learned to enjoy life. He lived better than the disciples. We were the ones who needed to buy dreams from him, and he knew it.

Entering that young man's world was a marvelous journey. We discovered a fantastic human being hidden behind society's ridicule. And we were proud to have him along when the dreamseller called him to be a seller of dreams.

The dreamseller led us to an open green space and began to tell us the story of another Solomon, the great king of Israel. The dreamseller explained that King Solomon had had an excellent start in life. He didn't want gold, silver or political power; he wanted that most coveted of treasures, wisdom. Every day, he breathed and drank wisdom. His kingdom progressed prodigiously, becoming one of the first ancient empires, and its relationship with neighboring nations was marked by peace.

But time passed, and power corrupted him. He abandoned wisdom and sought out the pleasures of the physical world. Soon, nothing satisfied him. He became profoundly depressed and was honest enough to admit that he was bored with his life. That vain existence robbed him of life's joys.

"The great king had hundreds of wives, chariots, palaces, servants, armies, golden garments, honors and victories like few kings before him," the dreamseller said, "but he neglected to love a woman and to regard the delicate lilies of the field, which represent friendship and so many other fundamental things."

As he was about to elaborate on the last lesson, my unpredictable companion chimed in and once more made everyone burst with laughter.

"Chief, may I say something?" asked Honeymouth.

"Of course, Bartholomew," he said patiently.

"Maybe Solomon got depressed because he had hundreds of mothers-in-law?"

The dreamseller laughed and offered, "I don't know, but I do know there are some mothers-in-law more lovable than many mothers." And he concluded with this lesson: "Success is more difficult to deal with than failure. As Solomon learned, the danger in being successful is that the person can turn into a workaholic, forgetting to savor the small things in life and missing out on that which only dreams can achieve. The sight of an idyllic country landscape, of a flower garden, of a painting, can evoke more emotion in the man who seeks to behold it than in the man who seeks to own it. God gave us all equal access to life's greatest pleasures. Rich are those who seek out that treasure, poor are those who seek to possess them."

Placing his hands on Solomon, the newest disciple, the dreamseller said, "Great human beings are at the margins of society. Here is someone who has very little and yet has everything. Thank you for selling us your dreams."

CHAPTER 18

Looking for Life Among the Dead

THE NEXT DAY, THE SUN'S FIRST RAYS BROKE OVER THE horizon and shone down on our makeshift beds, inviting us to a new day of discovery. As always, Bartholomew was the last to get up. I imagine that if he were in a comfortable bed he'd sleep the entire day.

Before we headed out, the dreamseller extended an unusual invitation, one that would become an integral part of our story. He invited us to one of the most important tasks of the mind: to do nothing, merely experience the art of observation.

He led us to a busy tree-lined avenue. There he handed each of us a crumpled sheet of white paper and pens and asked us to write down all the sounds and images that excited us. Anything man-made didn't count. The traffic noise was deafening, the air polluted, the commotion intense. What could excite us if not the colorful stores, the stylish cars, the shape of a stranger? And what does that have to do with changing human thinking? What does the art of observation have to do with selling dreams? To me, it was a boring exercise with no intellectual appeal.

It wasn't long before the dreamseller prodded us.

"Anyone who doesn't develop the art of observation is missing the fullness of life. He may be a warehouse of information, but he will never construct great ideas."

I remembered that the day before I hadn't seen the complex human being hidden behind Solomon's rituals. I was a terrible observer. I saw what every "normal" person acknowledged. Edson and Dimas also didn't know what to write. Bartholomew hummed to summon up inspiration, but none came. He looked up, then to the sides, and remained inert. Minutes passed without our observing anything interesting. Solomon was the only exception. He calmed his compulsions and began writing ceaselessly. He was excited, saying frequently, "Hmm . . . Wow, amazing . . . Fantastic . . ."

He was writing, and I was stumped. The dreamseller gave me a nudge.

"You will develop the art of observation only if you learn the most difficult art of the human intellect." And he didn't provide the answer.

"What is it?" I thought.

"The art of calming the mind," he said eventually. "Minds that once were brilliant have lived a mediocre life because they didn't calm their thoughts. Great writers, notable scientists, magnificent artists have shattered their inspiration because they had a cluttered mind. The thoughts, mental images and fantasies that can make our creativity take flight can also clip its wings, if excessive, robbing us of our intuition and ingenuity."

"That's my problem," I thought. My mind was a dark cavern of disturbance. Thinking foolish thoughts was my specialty. Silence was always my enemy. But for the dreamseller, I tried to silence the voices within. It wasn't easy; I was inundated with images racing through my mind faster than the cars on this street. My thoughts were choked by intellectual pollution.

My friends were also lost. But little by little we entered the infinite world of silence. Starting at that moment, our perception was heightened. I began to make out the sharp songs of a bird. It strummed a beautiful melody with unbelievable fervor.

I jotted it down. Then another bird sang a mournful song. Moments later, a dove performed a courtship ritual with a female.

I observed more than ten extraordinary birdsongs. They had little reason to rejoice in that concrete jungle, I thought, but unlike me they were celebrating life. I observed and noted the resilience of the weathered tree trunks, which, despite the impermeability of the soil and a shortage of water, survived in an inhospitable setting—bravery that I never had shown. More than ten million people had passed by those trees since they were planted, and maybe ten, at the most, had actually stopped to observe them in detail. I was beginning to feel like a privileged person in a societal desert.

Bartholomew, who wouldn't normally notice an elephant in front of his nose, also began to have more luck. He contemplated five multicolored butterflies dancing across the sky. Unlike them, he noted, he only danced when drunk. Edson noted various types of sounds produced by leaves rustling in the wind, humbly applauding passersby, unlike him, who sought applause. Dimas analyzed insects that worked tirelessly preparing for winter, something he had never done. He stole and, like all thieves, was a terrible manager, believing that life was an eternal springtime.

After this gratifying exercise, we spoke one of our favorite phrases: "How I love this life!" Never had doing so little meant so much. I had never imagined that nature was present in such a meaningful way, right here, in the middle of the city. How could a specialist in society never have done this exercise? For the first time, I truly loved silence, and in that silence I discovered that I had not had a childhood.

I don't remember any pleasant experiences as a child. Maybe I've become a rigid adult because I didn't know how to relax as a child. Maybe I've grown into a paranoid man because I'd never experienced the innocence of childhood. Maybe I was a chronically depressive and ill-tempered grown-up because I hadn't lived my first years of life joyfully. The losses in my life made me into an adult very early, a young man who thought a lot, but felt nothing.

As I was recalling my childhood, the dreamseller seemed to be studying me. Taking a deep breath, he commented on the death of childhood in our time, one of the things that bothered him the most.

"The Internet, video games, computers—they're all useful, but they've destroyed something invaluable: childhood. Where is the pleasure of silence? Where is the fun of playing outside? Where is innocence? It pains me so deeply that the system is creating unhappy, restless children—better suited for psychiatric care than happy, carefree lives."

All of a sudden, the dreamseller acted in a way I'd never seen before. He turned to watch as several parents passed us, taking their seven- and eight-year-old children shopping. The children were dressed at the height of fashion, every accessory matching their outfits, and they were each carrying cell phones. But they were clearly disillusioned with life. Some whined and complained and caused a scene for a new dress or a gadget. To simply keep them quiet, the parents gave in.

The dreamseller looked furious and he confronted those parents.

"What are you doing to your children? Take them to know the forests. Have them remove their shoes and let them walk barefoot on the ground. Let them climb trees, and encourage them to invent their own games. The human species has shut itself inside a bell jar of selfishness and materialism. Instead, teach them about animals and let them learn a new way to behave." And he paraphrased Jesus' words: "Children do not live by shopping centers alone, but by all the adventures of childhood."

I was impressed by his boldness in the face of strangers. Some of the parents considered his words. Others reacted brashly. One said, "Isn't that the crazy guy we saw in the papers?"

Another, an intellectual and probably, like me, seething with pridefulness, was more arrogant: "I'm a professor with a doctorate in psychology and I won't stand for this invasion of privacy. Let me worry about my children." Looking us up and down he told his friends, loud enough for us to hear, "What a boorish bunch."

Honeymouth heard the insult and couldn't stifle his compulsive urge to talk. He seconded the dreamseller:

"Listen, pal, I'm not a 'doctorate' of anything," he told the professor. "But let your children be immersed in nature. Let them play and get dirty. That way, none of them will turn out to be a crazy, no-good drunk like me." He made a gesture, asking for patience and added, "But I'm getting better, chief."

He turned to the children and said, "Anybody who wants to fly like a butterfly, raise your hand."

Three children raised their hands, two remained indifferent and three hid behind their parents and answered, "I'm afraid of butterflies."

Offended by the forwardness of the strangers, several parents called the security guards at the entrance to the large Megasoft department store they were about to enter. The guards quickly ushered us out.

"Get out of here, you bums."

But, before leaving, the dreamseller turned to the parents who had argued with him and said, "I ask your forgiveness for my actions and hope that one day you won't have to ask your children's forgiveness for yours."

For some of the parents, the dreamseller's ideas didn't fall on barren ground. Some, even while angry, began to realize they needed to work on their relationship with their children. Their children had received the best possible educations under the existing system; they had become experts in consuming products and using computers, but they were perpetually dissatisfied. They didn't know how to observe, feel and draw conclusions. These parents realized that nature may not be as important to the mental survival of the human race as it was to its emotional survival. They began to frequent forests, zoos and urban gardens.

Nature is a more invaluable teacher than all the other educational theories for expanding the mind's horizons.

I was moved at seeing the dreamseller's and Bartholomew's tenderness with children. I had never thought too much about them. I was too busy criticizing society in the classroom. I didn't understand that the true educational material was the student and not the information. I was only concerned that they keep quiet and pay attention in class.

That same afternoon, we passed through a residential district. We came upon a large, gloomy building. The garden was overgrown with tall grass. Enormous trees cast looming shadows, preventing the low plants from flourishing. The old building with its arches was beautiful, but its paint had faded. The wooden window frames were rotting and seemed painted in the green moss. Plaster was peeling from the filthy white walls. It was a nursing home, but definitely not a pleasant place to live out the last years of one's life.

Many elderly people went there not because their families had abandoned them, but simply because they had no close relatives. The majority of those residents had only one child or at most two. When an only child died or moved to a different city or couldn't physically or financially care for his aging parents, the elderly were sent to these institutions for their medical and daily care. They fled from the suffocating trap of loneliness to these nursing homes.

Looking at the building, the dreamseller told us, "Behold a good setting for dreams. Go and bring joy to the people who live there."

In our "holy" prejudice we thought, "Dreams? In a nursing

home? Those people are bored and depressed. What could possibly excite them anymore?" We had been in the world of children, and now we were entering the world of the elderly. Worlds so far apart yet so alike. The problem was that the dreamseller took a step back. We were waiting for him to at least guide us with some instruction, but he simply said he was going for a walk. Before the dreamseller left, Dimas, who began stuttering and blinking uncontrollably, expressed his uncertainty:

"Make . . . the . . . the old folks hap . . . happy? How, dreamseller? They ha . . . have one foot in the grave." He knew how to pick old people's pockets, how to worry them half to death, but he had never cheered up or had a deep conversation with one of them.

"Dimas, prejudice will age you more than the passing of time. Inside, you're older than many of them," the dreamseller said.

"If it were up to me, I could solve their problems in about two minutes," Bartholomew added. "I'd give 'em a couple quarts of booze and get the party started."

He immediately apologized. Edson and Solomon also didn't know how to achieve the miracle of happiness. We were all at a loss.

Before we realized it, the dreamseller had already set off for some unknown destination. The group gathered, each one explained his ideas, we formulated a strategy and went in search of materials, returning two hours later.

Honeymouth was wearing a long wig and dark glasses and was chewing gum. Excited, he told us, "Guys, I've got it! We'll pretend we're normal." We all burst out laughing.

We headed for the nursing home. Before I could say anything, Bartholomew again took the lead. He made up what sounded like a pretty good story to get us in.

"OK, here's the deal. We're a professional band of musicians and we want to put on a show for the people here. For free. We don't need money but any donations are welcome."

When he mentioned donations, I poked him. That wasn't in the script. Dimas was wearing a red hat and dark Ray-Ban–type glasses. I had on a long pigtail wig. Solomon sported thick sideburns like Elvis Presley's. Edson had a red ribbon on his head and a long collarless T-shirt. We borrowed the outfits saying we were putting on a fund-raiser and had promised to return them afterward.

The nursing home staff looked suspiciously at our costumes, but since young people rarely came to visit the elderly, the staff wanted to see what we had in store. I said to myself, "What are you doing here? This isn't going to work." An impromptu audience was arranged. More than a hundred retirees sat down quietly in front of our so-called band.

We had two battered guitars. The Miracle Worker, who claimed to have learned to play in his church band, played way out of tune. And Solomon, who had the other, wasn't much better. I blew into a sax, trying to recall the handful of notes I had learned in a few classes with my grandfather. Dimas had a double bass and didn't know what to do with it. Honeymouth was—what else?—on lead vocals. But he assured us that he could carry a tune and said he used to sing in nightclubs when he was more or less sober.

We played our first piece of music, a rock ballad. But we were nervous and stiff. Honeymouth's voice was a disaster; he couldn't keep up with the music and it probably would have been better if he had just danced along—not that he realized how awful he was. Our audience just watched us. We thought maybe things should be livelier. We stopped halfway through the first song and broke into a heavy metal jam. Oh, what a ruckus we made. We were really worked up, shaking our hips, jumping around the stage, but from the old folks? Nothing. Not even Honeymouth's verbal gymnastics with that off-key voice drew a laugh.

I thought: "We're toast. We've just made these people's depression worse." Bartholomew broke into his anthem, a samba, and we just tried to keep up: *"I drink, yes I do, I'm livin', there's folks who don't drink and are dyin', I drink, yes I do."*

And he repeated the refrain, looking at the old people, believing a little alcohol in some form would get them moving.

But no one sang. Or clapped. Or smiled. Or so much as moved. Instead of selling dreams, we were selling embarrassment. We looked at the nursing staff and saw that they were motionless, too. Like us, they thought the elderly had one foot in the grave and were just waiting for death. Just when the afternoon was looking like one of the worst since we started following the dreamseller, he returned. When they saw him, several of the old men and women rushed to hug him passionately. That was when we realized that he was a frequent visitor here.

The dreamseller handed out our instruments to the audience, though they could barely hold them. We thought they wouldn't even realize what a guitar, saxophone or double bass were, much less be able to play them. To our surprise, three of the men, Mr. Lauro, Mr. Michel and Mr. Lucio, took the two guitars and the double bass, positioned them correctly, and began to play in tune. The sound that emerged made us tingle. We couldn't believe what we were hearing.

A woman picked up the saxophone and put on a show. I was speechless. "Wait," I thought, "isn't this supposed to be a warehouse for old people awaiting death?" We were shocked— and humbled—to realize this place was a prison for full, rich, gifted people with incredible repressed potential.

The dreamseller delighted in hearing them. Then he took Bartholomew's microphone, and gave it to a much older gentleman, who could barely walk. But when he breathed into the microphone, his voice was unrivaled even by Frank Sinatra.

Then the dreamseller called the elderly who could still

move about to the floor and began to dance with them. Even I started to dance. It was a riot. These old folks turned that nursing home upside down. Smiles sprang onto their faces and they felt like people once again. Of course they had looked at us like we were idiots. We had underestimated them and given them our worst, thinking that just because they were old—that their muscles were weak, their memory failing—they would swallow whatever pathetic show we put on.

Many of them had enjoyed a wonderful childhood, much better than mine. And now, the child within awakened from its slumber. Later, the dreamseller would tell us he had sent us to the nursing home not with the intention of our selling them dreams but so we could buy dreams from them. He showed us there is no such thing as a person without worth, only someone who is grossly undervalued.

Upon hearing these words, I realized another mistake I had made. My grandfather, Paulo, was fun and sociable. He died almost fifteen years after my mother, but I never let myself into his world. I had felt rejected by my uncles and cousins, and so I ended up rejecting my grandfather. Every victim bears the scars of a hostage. I had admired my grandfather's ability to play instruments, but had never asked about his tears and his fears. I never valued his great sense of humor and his lifetime of experiences. I missed out on enjoying such a surprising human being.

That day, the dreamseller wove together thoughts that still echo in my mind:

"The time between youth and old age is shorter than you can imagine. Whoever doesn't delight in reaching old age isn't worthy of his youth. Don't fool yourselves: A person doesn't die when his heart stops beating. He dies when the world tells him he's no longer of any value."

The Temple of Electronics

THE EVENT THAT OCCURRED IN THE NURSING HOME CAME to light not because a journalist was present but because a nurse photographed it and gave the information to a newspaper. Ever since our visit to the nursing home, our days were filled with commotion. As the days went by, our group became ever stronger. We formed close ties despite our bickering. We held lively outdoor round tables to discuss our own stories and what we'd seen in society.

At least once a week the dreamseller invited new people—bricklayers, painters, sculptors, gas station attendants, mechanics, garbage collectors—into our expansive "home" to sit on fruit crates and tell us about their lives. They were delighted at the invitation. And we had never had as good a time communing with our fellow man, listening to stories of their real difficulties and expectations, dreams and nightmares, passions and disillusionments. It was a unique sociological experience, a magical apprenticeship.

Meanwhile, the dreamseller's fame was growing. He had become a mythic figure in the city. People in cars would point at him and tell one another, "Isn't that the guy who stopped traffic near the San Pablo Building?" "Isn't that the same one who shook up an old folks' home and a wake?" Judging by how "normals" like a spectacle, they'd soon be saying he raised the dead.

One day, a man of about sixty with a serious and tormented expression recognized the dreamseller on the street. He called to the dreamseller and hurried to catch up to us.

"Master," he said. "For thirty years I worked for the same company. I truly started to come into my own as a manager and distinguished myself among my peers. But my boss didn't like it and started finding all sorts of ways of making my life hell for years until he finally fired me. I gave that company my all, but I was tossed aside like trash. I became depressed. I felt betrayed and didn't have the courage to start all over again with a new company. Besides, they prefer young employees who'll take less pay. I hate my old boss with all my heart. What can I do?"

The man's lips trembled. He appeared to be looking for some kind of relief amid the agony. The dreamseller looked first at us, then at him, and stated:

"Envy and revenge are phenomena exclusive to the human race. No other species has them. He envied you because you had something he didn't. But there's a way to exact revenge on him."

I was confused. "What kind of man am I following?" I thought. "Isn't he the master of forgiveness?"

Bartholomew liked the dreamseller's attitude. Echoing his words, he said, "That's right. An eye for an eye, a tooth for a tooth. Give the guy a good punch in the mouth."

Dimas puffed out his chest. "If you need somebody to get your back, you found him," he said and began making karate gestures.

Honeymouth was emboldened. He began to shout and make disjointed karate chops like he was some kind of sensei. The two started play-fighting and Dimas, without meaning to, popped Honeymouth upside the head and dropped him like a bad habit. He went out cold and was slow to get up. When we rushed to his side, he rubbed his head and told Dimas, "Are you mad at me?"

Bartholomew realized this eye-for-an-eye was a dangerous business. The fired manager, watching this, didn't know whether to laugh or cry.

"How should I get even?" he asked the dreamseller.

"By killing him," the dreamseller replied flatly.

My legs buckled. I never thought I'd hear those words come out of the dreamseller's mouth. My heart was pounding and I even thought about leaving the group that very moment. Then, dripping hatred, the man bared his true intent.

"You're right. That's what I'm going to do. That son of bitch doesn't deserve to live." But before the man could leave, the dreamseller searched for the root of his hate.

"The greatest revenge you can take against any enemy is to forgive him. Kill him inside yourself."

"How do I do that?" the man asked, surprised.

"The weak kill their enemies' body; the strong kill how they regard their enemies. Those who kill the body are murderers. Those who kill what they represent are wise."

The man started to feel light-headed. We had to grab him and lean him against the closest wall. The dreamseller went up to him again, looked him straight in the eyes and said:

"Take your revenge by reclaiming your peace of mind and by shining even more in your next job. Otherwise, he will haunt you for the rest of your life."

The man stood paralyzed for several seconds. Then he regained his composure and realized that he couldn't behave like a victim, like a poor fool who only fuels his anger. He should take action, but a different kind. He gave the dreamseller a long embrace, the way a son hugs his father. And when he left, he was clearly headed down a different path.

That's when I noticed the revolver bulging under his shirt. I was flabbergasted. The man really was ready to commit murder. Only then did I understand the dreamseller's shocking attitude. No gentle words would have dissuaded this man, just like when I tried to commit suicide. The dreamseller hadn't wiped out his desire for vengeance; he had just redirected it.

"What kind of therapy is this?" I wondered.

Days later, the Consumer Electronics Show, the greatest consumer electronics fair in the world, was taking place in the wealthiest part of the city. More than 2,500 companies were participating and some 140,000 visitors from more than 130 countries were expected. Even in a down economy, end-users and retailers eagerly flocked to the event, which proved the industry had experienced uninterrupted growth.

The dreamseller turned his attention toward the big event; he wanted to stand in the temple of electronics. We couldn't understand why he was so interested in the event since it looked like he had never even used a computer. But he simply said, "Let's go to the fair."

Skittish, we followed him. The event was way too upscale for people like us. After all, we were unkempt in torn shirts and frayed and patched jeans. We weren't part of any corporation, and of course, didn't have an invitation. We looked as if we had teleported from some rural area of the 1900s into the peak of the twenty-first century.

Bartholomew, trying to put us at ease, repeated his famous phrase: "Guys! Let's pretend we're 'normals.'" Immediately, our posture improved, we tried to smooth our hair and walked upright and confident.

As we approached the doors, Dimas put his arm around Solomon's shoulder and tried to keep his nervous tics under wraps. Pulling away from him, Solomon joked, "Watch it, Nimble Fingers. I'm all man, here!"

"Hey, it's Angel Hand or Saint's Hand, to you," Dimas said.

"More like Devil's Hand," Bartholomew joked.

Dimas didn't like the joke and his eyes grew wide and angry.

"In the old days, Dimas. In the old days—many hours ago," he joked again, and ran away, afraid of retaliation.

Our group was impossible; I swear we were like children, sometimes. But our sense of humor faded as soon as we set foot in the fair. Seeing the apprehension on our faces, the dreamseller told us:

"Does rejection still frighten you? Do these tense settings still threaten you? Haven't you learned that someone can injure your body but not your mind, unless you let him?"

His words just fueled our anxiety. The entrance hall alone intimated us: a beautiful patio with a multicolored water fountain. Dozens of vases with roses, hibiscuses, daisies and tulips decorated the place.

Endless panels of illuminated ads for the major corporations glowed at the entrance. A red carpet led visitors inside. But to get in, besides showing an invitation and ID, guests had to submit to a full-body scan and a metal detector. It's a dangerous world and a man's word apparently was worth little.

In that moment, I realized that I, the intellectual of the group, was the most insecure of all. I drifted behind the others. The dreamseller didn't actually want to go into the fair, he wanted to stand in the entrance hall and watch people. But Bartholomew, demonstrating uncommon boldness, tried to get in. But two security officers quickly intercepted him. One of them asked him to spread his arms and ran a security wand over every part of his body. When the guard began to touch his private parts, Bartholomew jumped: "Easy, there, buddy!"

We went to his aid. The dreamseller tried to calm him and asked the rest of us to hang back. When several other security officers approached, they took one look at our band of misfits and asked to see invitations. Since we had none, they started scanning us with their machines and frisking us as they'd done to Bartholomew. The guards got angry when Solomon said he was ticklish and wouldn't let himself be searched. They tried to throw us out of a public area.

Then, one of the guards recognized Angel Hand from his past life. He gave him a hard shove and said, "Get outta here, you crook."

As he fell, he stole the guard's wallet in a moment of weakness. But he regretted it before he even hit the floor and returned the wallet. The dreamseller was pleased, but it only made the guards more suspicious.

Edson was fuming. I felt if he actually had supernatural powers, he would have rained down fire on those guards. But the dreamseller displayed a disquieting calm, like he had fully expected that situation.

While pushing us toward the door, the guards began mocking us.

"Maybe these guys are the clowns the fair hired as entertainment," one of the guards said as they followed us to the door. And they all laughed. In fact, we did look like something out of a comedy—or a horror film. Another guard shoved the dreamseller, who almost fell.

"Why do you attack me when I didn't attack you? What have I done to incur your wrath?" the dreamseller said, regaining his balance.

One of them said what the other guards were thinking. "Get lost, you lousy bunch of con artists."

Suddenly, I said something I never imagined I'd ever say: "How I'd love to be a millionaire so I could give those guys a swift kick in the ass."

I spoke before I realized what I'd said. For the first time, I had expressed a love of money. The power of money had subtly seduced me, but I had never admitted it, not even to myself. I loved luxurious cars, cruises and summer homes. It was a secret love. I criticized the petty bourgeoisie who traveled first class in planes, but deep down I envied them. I detested flying coach class, where we were packed in like sardines.

Since we couldn't go inside the fair, we stayed outside in the reception hall. Undaunted, the dreamseller told us, "Let's approach people as they enter and leave the event. After all, our stage is the world."

"Approach people? But I thought we were here to see computers," I said to myself. Angel Hand wondered aloud whether any kind of dream could be sold in a place like this.

But then I noticed something odd. What looked like a businessman, dressed impeccably in a suit and tie, examined us from head to toe as he walked by and into the event. His badge read Megasoft Group, one of the world's largest computer companies. I looked out of the corner of my eye and saw him stop to talk to other men in suits, who we later learned were undercover antiterrorism agents. He pointed at us as he spoke.

The agents quickly approached, and one of them again asked the dreamseller to identity himself. They ignored the rest of us. When he couldn't produce any kind of identification, they acted fast: One of them punched him unexpectedly in the face, dropping him to the floor with an awful thud. They pounced on him, shouting "terrorist!" and quickly overpowered him. It all happened so fast that for a few seconds we stood paralyzed. When we tried to protect the dreamseller, we were also attacked.

Honeymouth again feigned his karate pose but was knocked out by a single blow. I'd never seen such violence. In the confusion, one of the agents drew his gun, ready to shoot the dreamseller. He might have been shot dead on the spot if not for two local police officers who had been driving by in their patrol car and ran toward the commotion. Staring at the supposed criminal, one of the police officers drew his gun and shouted at the agents.

"Drop your weapons! I'm the police chief of this district," he said. The agents lowered their guns. "I know this man. He's no terrorist."

"Yeah? Well, where's his ID? Who is he?" the head agent asked.

The cop searched for a plausible answer. "He's, uh . . . a salesman. A traveling salesman. And if you don't leave him alone, I'm going to arrest you for using excessive force," the chief threatened.

The police chief was the same one from the top of the San Pablo Building. Since that day, he had not been able to get the dreamseller out of his mind. He had spent several sleepless nights after the dreamseller's comments about his relationship with his son, and had since followed the dreamseller's "ministry" in the papers.

I was overjoyed and felt my faith in the police restored.

Though he was bleeding, the dreamseller tried to play down the situation and told the chief, "These are good men. There was just a misunderstanding."

It was only then that Bartholomew started to regain consciousness and asked, "Where am I?"

Remembering he'd been knocked out but realizing the situation was under control, he jumped back up in a karate pose:

"Oh, now these guys are in trouble! I'm a black belt in judo, karate, kung fu and lots of other stuff. Hold me back or things are gonna get ugly."

Instead of holding him back, we let him go. Honeymouth leaped up in a bound and seeing that the agents were eyeing him again, told them, "Yeah, well, I'm calm now . . ."

The agents moved on, and so did the police officer, but not before the chief thanked the dreamseller for the few words on that rooftop.

"My son would like to meet you," the chief said.

"Someday. Tell him to have many dreams and to fight for them," the dreamseller answered.

The dreamseller's right eye was swollen, and blood was dripping from the left side of his lip, but he didn't complain. We knew that following him meant running the risk of mockery and scorn, but now we realized we were also risking our lives.

I was shocked to see how quickly people could snap from tranquillity to brutality. What shook me most was that the specter of aggression was also inside me. I knew about my pridefulness, but not about the latent violence.

I was beginning to believe in the concept of harmony and solidarity, but I felt like attacking anyone who hurt the gentle dreamseller. I never imagined that love and aggression could live so close to each other. I never thought that peace and war could inhabit the same person. Mild-mannered people, as it turned out, also harbor monsters in the recesses of their minds.

CHAPTER 20

Living Longer in a Shorter Time

Things had been too intense at the electronics fair. We thought the dreamseller should see a doctor right away and then rest. We lifted him up under his arms and started to carry him outside. But instead he climbed onto a low wall surrounding a multicolored fountain and courageously started inviting people to hear about the latest innovations at the fair.

We couldn't believe our eyes. Some began to approach us because they recognized the rabble-rouser described in the newspapers. Controversial as ever, he continued provoking the participants and exhibitors of the Consumer Electronics Show.

"The most vulnerable child has a more complex mind than all the computers in the world strung together. But where is more money and research invested, in helping children or in building machines?"

Paying attention only to the first part of the question, a scientist addressed the dreamseller:

"You don't know anything about artificial intelligence. In a few years we'll have machines superior to the human brain. They'll have the programming of the human mind, but with superior memory. It'll be the greatest invention. Just wait and see!"

The dreamseller accepted the challenge:

"Well, I disagree. Computers will forever be condemned to the sleep of unawareness. They will never know conflicts. Never be disturbed by the search for their origins and their purpose. Never produce philosophy or religion. They will always be slaves to their programming."

I thought: "Where did the dreamseller learn that information? How does he manage to confidently discuss controversial matters?" On the other side, the computer engineers and programmers listening to him seemed at a loss.

"Can it be that computers will never know they exist?" the scientists asked.

"Our conflicts speak to our complexity. If we're not capable of being happy because we have computers, at least we should admire them as the fruits of our ingenuity," the dreamseller said.

I looked at some of the members of our group and realized that they understood nothing. Bartholomew, in particular, was lost. But I bit my tongue, and later he surprised me by reading my mind and whispering, "Hey, Superego, I've always been a deeply complex person, but I just can't stand hearing all your back talk."

Bartholomew was always giving me a hard time when he knew I couldn't answer back. I wanted to crush him with my intellect, but I needed to work on something I'd never had: patience. I, who was never religious, asked, "God, grant me the patience to not lose my temper with this *deeply complicated* character."

Meanwhile, the dreamseller, after criticizing blind faith in machines, turned his guns on the Internet.

"The system produced the Internet and cell phones, sparking a revolution in communications the likes of which history had never seen. People lost their inhibitions to technology, and felt more comfortable dealing with machines than with other people. Not to engage others is a tolerable act, but to not engage oneself is indefensible."

Now I understood why the dreamseller often isolated himself. When I first saw him talking to himself, I found it extremely odd. To me, such behavior had always been a sign of madness. But he turned the concept upside down, considering it a clear sign of sanity.

More and more people gathered, forcing him to speak louder. They had come to the magnificent fair to see the newest innovations in computers and instead discovered the latest news about their own mental "computers." The dreamseller made an argument bolstered by numbers unknown to me to shine a light into the audience's mind:

"Millions of people have never had an encounter with their own being. Their tombs will hold foreigners who never found their true home," he said.

The people meditated on these words as if they were a prayer. At that moment, Honeymouth raised his hand. He should have kept his mouth shut to not spoil the mood. But he was even more addicted to the sound of his own voice than he was to alcohol. He said, "Chief, I think we're in worse shape than everyone else here."

"Why, Bartholomew?" he asked patiently.

"Because we don't even have an address. We live under a bridge."

The crowd roared with laughter and Bartholomew realized what a blunder he'd made. But the dreamseller just smiled at his disciple's spontaneity. Honeymouth was a hyperactive, mischievous child. And to the dreamseller, freedom grew in that spontaneous terrain. Most people killed their spontaneity in school, church, at work, even here, at this electronics fair; they're robots admiring other machines. They don't say what they think. At that moment, I looked within myself and realized that I was no exception. In the name of discretion, I was formal, deliberate, guarded. I didn't know myself or let others know me. I was an expert in pretending everything was fine. It wasn't easy to admit that Honeymouth had an advantage over me.

Calmly, the dreamseller said, "Yes, Bartholomew. We have no home, but we seek the best home of all. Remember our song."

And once again he startled a crowd with his eccentricity. He interrupted his speech to sing his song, even making the gestures of a conductor. We joined in. During the first verse I was stiff. Honeymouth and Dimas went all out. We left the hilltops of reflection to revel in a relaxing waterfall of fun.

I'm just a wanderer
Who lost the fear of getting lost
I'm certain of my own imperfection
You may say I'm crazy
You may mock my ideas
It doesn't matter!
What matters is I'm a wanderer
Who sells dreams to passersby
I've no compass or appointment book
I have nothing, yet I have everything
I'm just a wanderer
In search of myself.

Hearing that song, some of the listeners were completely stunned. They asked, "What kind of group is this? Where did they come from? Who's this conductor? Could he be a speaker from some corporation in disguise as some sort of publicity stunt?" Others loosened up, followed the beat and began to sing with us. They lost their fear of getting lost, lost the fear of letting go, discovering for a few moments that they were not researchers, engineers or businessmen, just wanderers themselves. And still others moved away from the audience muttering, "That guy's stark raving mad!" Whatever their reactions, it was impossible to remain indifferent to the dreamseller's words. He penetrated the most intimate reaches of loneliness.

We looked around us and saw that several people were moved, especially two well-dressed female executives. Despite being surrounded by people, they felt crushingly alone. They were successful professionally, but they were unhappy with their lives.

Seeing the crowd become reflective, the dreamseller touched on another matter. He asked something apparently obvious: "Do people live longer today or in the past?"

One person, taking the initiative, answered, "Today, beyond the shadow of a doubt!"

But the dreamseller, looking at his disciples, particularly at me, turned to challenge the crowd: "No! We die younger today than in the past!"

Many jeered the dreamseller. I thought this time he had it all wrong. One scientist couldn't resist. Laughing, he said confrontationally, "This is nonsense! Even the poorest student knows that average life expectancy has expanded because of new sanitation methods and vaccines."

The dreamseller was no fool and knew what he was saying. Addressing the scientist, he replied:

"In Roman times the average life expectancy was barely forty years. In the Middle Ages, forty-five. Today we're nearing eighty. But I'm referring to the average life of the mind. In our minds, we die earlier. Doesn't it seem you went to sleep and woke up at your present age, ladies and gentlemen?"

And, raising his voice, he declared:

"Technology and science have their upsides. They have produced vaccines, antibiotics, water treatment plants and sewers, agricultural techniques, preservation of food, all of which have led to a longer average physical life. But the same system that has made us free has imprisoned our minds with its excesses. Do you understand me?"

We didn't understand, at least not fully. He was often sparing with his words, speaking almost in code. We didn't know what he meant by "excesses" of the system. To clarify, he once again did what he loved to do: He told a story.

"In 1928, the Scottish bacteriologist Alexander Fleming was analyzing a fearsome bacteria in his lab," the dreamseller said. "Distracted, like any good scientist beset by an overload of activities, he left the door open when he went home. A fungus found its way into the Petri dish, producing a mold. What seemed to be a disaster generated a notable discovery: The mold killed the bacteria. From that discovery came the first antibiotic, penicillin. Millions of lives were saved. But penicillin came to be used excessively and indiscriminately. The result? A disaster. The excessive use of antibiotics has produced resistant bacteria which are now much more dangerous. Penicillin, one of medicine's greatest gifts to humanity, stands accused today of creating so-called superbugs. By the same token, the system that expanded average physical life, through its excesses, is burying us mentally earlier than in the days of smallpox."

Pausing to take a breath, he concluded his story:

"We live longer physically than in the past, but time seems to pass so much faster. The months rush by, the years fly by. Many are in the infancy of their mental development but look at themselves and discover their bodies are seventy or eighty. Nowadays, eighty-year-olds have the mentality of history's twenty-year-olds. And what about all of you? What are the excesses that have damaged you?" he asked his listeners. They shouted out answers:

"Excess of commitments."

"Excess of information."

"Excess of social pressures . . . excess competition . . . goals . . . demands . . . the need to keep up."

We were the society of excesses, even an excess of insanity.

Bartholomew wasn't about to be left out. Fortunately, he was on target.

"Excess of drinking," he said. And because he never let anyone have the upper hand, he looked at each of us and added, "Excess of ego, of crookedness, of religiousness."

We pinched him playfully.

People were beginning to see how excess had invaded our lives. They needed to buy dreams. And the dreamseller wanted to sell them.

"How do we turn back this eccentric, stress-filled life?" asked a worried man of about sixty.

The dreamseller was direct and to the point:

"Cut out the excesses, even if it means losing money and status. If you don't want to be old people complaining about your lost youth, you have to find the courage to make cuts. There are no cuts without pain."

I started thinking, "Had the dreamseller found the courage to make such cuts in his own life, or was he one of those theorists who talk about something they haven't experienced? Can a person without experience open up the mind of others?" He made me see that my own life was passing me by. I was mired in the quagmire of excess. Excess of classes, worries, thoughts, depression, complaints, debts. I had created "superbugs" that were infecting my mind.

Besides talking about cuts in lifestyle, he sold the art of observation that we did weekly. And he concluded his ideas by saying:

"Life passes quickly in this small interval of time. To live it slowly and meaningfully is the great challenge of mortal men."

These words made me remember that in the past, the days

sped by so rapidly that I didn't notice. Now, with this uncommon family, my days stretched long and lavishly. We lived intensely.

Just as he was speaking, the dreamseller began to feel dizzy. The stress of the beating and the strain of the speech had drained him. We helped him down from the wall, and Solomon and Dimas took him by the arm and led him outside.

He left to warm applause and went to rest under the Europa Avenue Bridge across the street.

One man caught up to him just to say, "I've never heard so much craziness in one day. You're a fraud!"

We turned purple with rage. But the dreamseller calmed us and responded: "I hope my ideas are those of a crazy man and yours are those of a sage." And he walked away.

People were watching the dreamseller as he left.

"Maybe he wants to found a new society," one said.

"How will I find the strength to make the necessary cuts in my excesses?" another told a friend.

Some wanted to go live in the countryside, grow orchids and raise animals. Others wanted to make a fresh start in society, change jobs or work as volunteers for children's hospitals or cancer centers. They went home haunted but fueled by the dreamseller's words. None of them slept well, understanding that each needed to lose the fear of getting lost. As it turned out, our teacher wasn't only a seller of dreams but also of insomnia.

As we were leaving the temple to electronics, a well-dressed woman, seeing the dreamseller's weakened condition, approached him. We told her it wasn't the right time, but the dreamseller ignored his dizziness and gave her his attention.

"My wonderful daughter Joana, six years old, has cancer," she said, on the verge of tears. "When the doctors said she probably had only three months to live, my world collapsed. I wanted to die in her place. Worse, I can't even stay at home. I'm here because when I look at her I drown in despair, and she's so special that in those moments she tries to console me."

We were stirred and, once again, ashamed of our insensitivity.

"My dear, I have no supernatural power to help little Joana. But I can say this: Three months lived badly pass like seconds, while three months lived fully are an eternity. Don't bury your daughter in the tomb of your fear. Go home, discover her and let her discover you. Live intensely with her during the time she has left."

The woman left encouraged, eager to make each minute a unique moment with her daughter. We didn't know if it would help Joana live any longer. But we were certain that in those three months, they would live a richer life than most parents do with their children in a span of thirty years.

I thought about the job I had done as a father. And I felt like running to John Marcus and begging his forgiveness.

CHAPTER 21

The White-Hot Spotlight

A S WE WERE HELPING THE DREAMSELLER TO A PLACE WHERE he could rest, Bartholomew separated from the group. A reporter wanted to write a story about us, in particular about our mysterious dreamseller and his intentions. Seeing that during his speech Bartholomew had asked a question, the reporter called him aside and asked for an interview. Bartholomew was excited, unaware he was entering dangerous territory.

The journalist wasted no time.

"Is it true that this man called you all to follow him, without promising money or offering the least bit of security?"

"Yes," he replied simply.

"Is it true that you actually live under a bridge?"

"Not just one," he answered. "We live under lots of bridges."

"Why? Who are you all? Who do you follow?"

Not being able to give any precise answers, Bartholomew, without thinking much about it, said, "Us? We're a group of artists."

"Artists? Are you painters, sculptors, a theater group?" asked the journalist, thinking he was dealing with a bizarre group of performers.

Smiling, Honeymouth replied, "No, no, nothing like that.

We practice the art of complicating life." And he laughed that distinct laugh that could be heard fifty yards away.

The journalist thought he was being spoken down to. But my friend had been sincere and spontaneous. Then, trying to better explain his thought, he added:

"Throughout history, we've complicated life, but now we're going through a complicated process of *uncomplicating* our lives. It isn't easy, but we'll get there."

Honeymouth was enthusiastic because it was the first interview he'd ever given. He felt drawn—at least a little—to the white-hot glow of the spotlight.

"But who is this leader of your group? What does he do?" asked the curious reporter.

"I don't know who he is. But I do know that he sells dreams," Bartholomew said innocently.

"He sells dreams? How does that work? Isn't the guy dangerous? Isn't he crazy?"

The disciple looked all around and said:

"I don't know if he's crazy, but I know he says we're all in a world of madness. And the chief wants to change the world," he said, making the dreamseller's goals seem fanciful. In reality, the dreamseller wanted to stimulate people to thirst and hunger for change, for only they could be responsible for their transformations.

Puzzled, the interviewer inquired:

"Wait, what? That raggedy character said that *we* live in a world of madness? And *he* wants to change the world? And you people *believe* him?"

"I don't know if he's gonna change the world," Bartholomew said. "But he's changing my world."

"Are you anarchists?" the reporter said, changing directions.

Bartholomew knew nothing about the anarchist movement. He didn't know that Pierre-Joseph Proudon, who inspired that movement in the nineteenth century, defended the idea of building a new society, one capable of expanding individual freedom and liberating the worker from the exploitation of big business. In that social order, constituted by organizing the workers, people would treat their fellow men fairly and develop their potential. Anarchists didn't recognize the governments power, its laws or its institutions. They lived under their own governance. Without the intervention of the state, they thought, humans could live freely.

But the dreamseller disagreed with the central idea of anarchism. To him, without constitution and institutions, human beings could commit atrocities, trounce the rights of others, assassinate, extort, live only for themselves and display unrivaled savagery. Nor did he want to replay the hippie movement, which had emerged in the wake of America's war in Vietnam. Young people's frustration with the war generated disillusionment with institutions, and that had become the seed of a movement of peace and love, but one without social commitments.

The dreamseller's plan to sell dreams, on the other hand, was replete with commitments to society, especially to human rights, freedom and mental health. That's why he recommended to those who would follow him that they not abandon their activities in society. Only a few, maybe the weirdest, were called to his training.

Bartholomew didn't know what to answer. He just scratched his head and replied with philosophical simplicity: "Look here, my friend, I don't know if we're anarchists or not. What I do know is that until a short time ago I didn't know who I was."

"And now you do?" the interviewer asked. But our friend tied his mind in more complex knots.

"Now? I know even less. I don't know who I am or what I am, because what I used to think I was isn't what I am at all. I

still don't understand who I am, but I'm searching to find myself. You understand?"

"No!" answered the reporter, completely confused.

"Thank goodness! I thought I was the only one who didn't,"
Bartholomew said. "Look, my friend, I only know that I used
to live falling down drunk every day, but now I'm lifting others up." And, staring at the journalist, he extended a friendly
invitation: "Wouldn't you like to be part of the group?"

"Not me! That's crazy stuff," the other man scoffed.

At that, Bartholomew countered, "Now, wait a minute.
What do you know about being crazy? Being crazy is a beautiful thing!"

He playfully hopped up, spread his arms and began to
dance and sing his favorite song in that unsteady voice: "I'm
going to go crazy, too crazy . . ." The reporter left without saying good-bye, as Bartholomew sang on: "Oh, how I love this
life!" He shook his hips and sang, "I'm going to go crazy, too,
too crazy . . ." He was lost in the moment.

The journalist, before interviewing Bartholomew, had already mapped out his article. He merely needed to confirm
some facts with Bartholomew. He had let prejudice guide him.

But Bartholomew was so euphoric with his first interview
that he lost his way. He decided to celebrate the only way he
knew how. He went to a bar and got wasted. It was his third
relapse since he was called, except that the first two had been
mild. This time he ended up passed out on the sidewalk.

We started to worry when he went missing. The dreamseller set us out to look for him. My friends and I said impatiently to each other, "Again? The guy's hopeless." After an
hour, we found him, almost unconscious. We tried to lift him
to his feet, but he could barely stand, and he just let his body
dangle like deadweight. We each took an arm and lifted, while
Dimas pushed from behind.

Bartholomew, his voice slurred, complained to Dimas, "Not so hard, bud. My bumper's a little temperamental . . ."

And he passed gas—often and loudly and noxiously, joking, "Sorry about the broken tailpipe, guys."

We all felt like smacking him. I said to myself: "I left the world of ideas in the academy to listen to the ideas of a drunk. Unbelievable!" I had never loved my fellow man unless there was something in it for me. Now I was taking care of someone who, besides offering me nothing in return, drew me away from serious reflection and made fun of me. We had to carry him the last hundred feet to the bridge. The hardest part was putting up with his declaration of love for us:

"I love you, guys, I love you so, so, so, so much . . ."

"Shut up, Bartholomew!" sweating and exhausted, we said in chorus. But it was no use. Asking him to keep quiet just made him louder. Twice more on the way to the bridge he loved us. Maybe he was being sincere, maybe his affection was greater than ours. As soon as we got to the bridge, he tried to give us all kisses of gratitude. We dropped him on the ground like a sack of potatoes.

"*Mis amigos,* it's a privilege for you to take me in your arms," he said.

Impatiently, we complained to the dreamseller. "What this guy needs is Alcoholics Anonymous." But without Bartholomew, there was no laughter in our group.

"Send him to a mental institution," Dimas said.

"Master, how long do we have to put up with this?" the Miracle Worker asked.

We weren't happy with his response.

"It's a privilege to carry him," the dreamseller said.

Bartholomew, even intoxicated, felt validated. "You heard the chief. I'm not worthless!" he said almost incomprehensively but clear enough to raise our tempers.

"It's better to carry than to be carried," the dreamseller said. And he added something that once again flew in the face of my atheism:

"The god constructed by man, the religious god, is merciless, intolerant, elitist and prejudiced. But the god who hides behind the scenes of existence is generous. His capacity to forgive has no limits. It inspires us to carry those who frustrate us as often as necessary."

While the dreamseller was speaking, I started to doubt him. I remembered my sociological analysis of texts from the Old Testament, which portrayed a rigid, aggressive, intolerant god. "Where is the generous god, if he accepted only the people of Israel?" I asked myself. As if reading my thoughts, the dreamseller said:

"God's generosity and forgiveness was shown by Jesus when he called Judas his friend, amid the act of betrayal, and when Jesus called out from the cross, 'Father, forgive them, for they know not what they do.' He protected those who hated him, he loved his enemies and that love made him intercede on behalf of his torturers."

His words exposed my own lack of generosity. I had never known how to forgive. I had never forgiven my son for using drugs. To me, he had taken his excellent upbringing for granted. I had never forgiven my wife for leaving me. To me, she had left one of the best men in the world. I had never forgiven my father for killing himself. To me, he had committed the greatest of crimes in having abandoned me while I was still a child. I had never forgiven my faculty colleagues who betrayed me after they had promised their support.

Now, with the dreamseller's guidance, I had the chance to forgive by carrying a childish, confused, irresponsible alcoholic. How could I do that without complaining? It was incredibly difficult for me. But I was actually coming to love that clown. Bartholomew had what I'd always wanted: authenticity and self-esteem. Sociologically speaking, irresponsible people are happier than responsible people. The problem is that the irresponsible depend on the responsible to carry them.

The next day, we saw the consequence of Bartholomew's interview. Plastered across the front page of the major newspaper was a photo of the dreamseller under the headline: "Psychotic Calls Society a 'World of Madness.'"

The journalist wrote that there was a lunatic who claimed that mankind was on its way to becoming a gigantic worldwide insane asylum. But this time—according to the lunatic—that asylum wasn't some gloomy, ugly, stinking, dark place like the psychiatric hospitals of the past, but a pleasant, colorful setting full of sophisticated machines, a perfect place to indulge our madness without being inconvenienced by it.

He gave speeches in public places, with the intention of changing the mind-set of people. No one knew his origins, but to deceive people he called himself by an attractive name, "the Dreamseller."

The article included photos of onlookers hypnotized by him and went on to say the guy was stark raving mad but charismatic and provocative. His power of seduction was unrivaled. Even intelligent businessmen fell into his trap, the article said. A gang of misfits followed him. The story said that the dreamseller didn't work miracles or consider himself a messiah, but not since the time of Jesus had the world seen a lunatic so boldly trying to reproduce his steps.

The reporter made no mention of the dreamseller's provocative ideas. He said nothing about the need to dialogue with one's self, the sleep of unawareness to which computers are eternally condemned, the excesses of society that cause us to die prematurely in our minds. He concluded the piece by saying that the dreamseller's followers were a band of anarchists who put democracy at risk and who might commit terrorist acts.

The article burned our real story to the ground, devastating our project and our true intent. We were profoundly depressed and discouraged. We couldn't go on, I thought. Once again, the dreamseller tried to ease our minds:

"Remember the swallows," he said, calming us. "It's not our calling to be myths.

"Never forget that it's impossible to serve two masters: Either we sell dreams or we concern ourselves with our image in society; either we remain loyal to our conscience or we fall prey to what others think and say about us," he said.

And once again he gave us the option to leave:

"Don't worry about me. You have already brought great joy to me and to many others. I've learned to love you and admire you the way you are. I don't want to put your lives in danger. It's better that you go."

But where would we go? We wouldn't any longer succeed as "normals," servants to a system wracked with tedious social routine, slaves complaining about life as we waited for death. The selfishness of the past still lived inside us, but was slowly losing ground to the pleasure of serving others.

We decided to stay. After all, if the person most defamed by the story felt free, why should we chain ourselves?

That very day, we saw the article had backfired. The story, instead of killing the movement, added fuel to it. People couldn't take more news about murders, accidents, rapes, robberies. In a city marked by sadness, the dreamseller became a social phenomenon.

People were hungry for something new, even if it were clothed in madness. The dreamseller became that novelty, made into a local celebrity, which was precisely what we most feared. From then on, he began to be followed by paparazzi.

Upon realizing his growing fame, he warned us:

"To create a god, all that's needed is a bit of charisma and leadership in a climate of social stress. Be careful, the system gives but also takes away, especially our humanity."

I understood the dreamseller's warning. The most cultured people on earth, a people who had won Nobel Prizes in the early twentieth century, enthroned Hitler in a period of social crisis. Times of crisis are times of change, for better or for worse. Recalling the risks of power, the dreamseller said:

"The majority of people are unprepared to assume power. Power awakens phantoms—blackmail, vanity and a hunger for power—which are hidden beneath a cloak of humility.

"Power in the hands of a wise man makes him into an apprentice," he continued, "but in the hands of a fool turns him into a tyrant. If you acquire great power one day, what demons will you face?"

His question shook me. When I took over as chair of the department, I became hard, inflexible, demanding. I came to understand that we cannot judge a person by the mildness of his voice, the kindness of his acts or the simplicity of his attire, but only after he has been given power and money.

The dreamseller spoke in a way that intrigued me. He gave the impression of someone who had tasted real power. But what power could someone so poor, with no home and no identity, have had?

Some religious people began to hold his ideas in great esteem, but others were concerned about the attention he was gaining; God was their personal property. They were the erudite theologians, experts in divinity. A penniless man who lived under bridges wasn't qualified to talk about God, they said. Some religious radicals wondered, "Couldn't he be a prophet of evil? The Antichrist foretold centuries ago?" He had become an emblematic figure. He wanted to move about unnoticed, but it was impossible for him to hide.

People began asking for his autograph everywhere we went. But, looking them in the eye, he said to their surprise:

"How can I give an autograph to someone as important or more important than I am? It would take decades to get to know you a bit, to understand some of the pillars of your intelligence and unveil some of the phenomena that make up the construction of your thoughts. I'm the one who feels honored to meet you. Please, give me your autograph."

They would leave his presence speechless and reflective. And some even bought the dream that there are no celebrities or "ordinary" people, only complex human beings with different places in society.

CHAPTER 22

The Superiority of Women

I N THE DAYS THAT FOLLOWED, IT WAS ALL BLUE SKIES FOR US. No social trouble. No rejection. We were enjoying prestige, attention and recognition. Not bad for someone who challenged the powerful system and resided in inhospitable places. But we had no idea what lay ahead.

Just as everything was progressing in perfect harmony, the dreamseller challenged us once again. He invited us to the most charming of all temples, the temple of fashion. In the southern part of the city an exquisite fashion show of famous designers was taking place. The powerful Megasoft Group was again represented by their worldwide chain of feminine apparel called La Femme, which encompassed over ten international designer labels and had two thousand stores in twenty countries.

We found the dreamseller's invitation bizarre. It seemed like a strange place to sell dreams. After all, we believed that at least in that environment self-esteem had found its most fertile ground.

"What's the dreamseller looking for in a place like that?" we wondered. "How would he respond to it? Who could he possibly approach?" We were hoping he'd be discreet and not cause a scene, but, at this point, we knew better.

Just getting into the event would be a problem. After all, if we hadn't succeeded in getting into the computer show, how would we get into the fashion show—especially looking the way we did?

That day, the dreamseller was wearing a faded, patched black blazer that he'd gotten in a secondhand store and was a size too large. His faded black pants were hemmed oddly and the back pockets were patched with blue cloth. He was wearing a wrinkled moss-green shirt with a few pen stains.

I was wearing a polo shirt and beige pants that I had been given by a traveler who had found his dreams. We were all disheveled, but Bartholomew's clothes were the funniest and the most ridiculous. A widow who lived near the Europa bridge had given him clothes that belonged to her husband. His yellow pants ended well short of his ankles. His left sock was navy blue and his right sock baby blue. His white T-shirt boasted an eloquent slogan that faithfully reflected his personality: "Don't follow me. I'm lost, too." There was no way this ragtag bunch would ever be allowed into the show, I thought.

As we approached the immense hall of the fashion show and carefully watched the exquisitely dressed people, the dreamseller once again scrambled our thinking. He neither gave a speech nor criticized the world of fashion. He said with assurance:

"I'm thinking of calling a few women to sell dreams. How do you feel about that?"

Our roving bachelor pad was rocked. We were an eccentric, admittedly weird group, but we had adapted. We had our differences, but we were adjusting. Our arguments away from the dreamseller were heated but capable of being overcome. Calling women to join our brotherhood seemed like too much. How could it work?

I immediately posed the question: "A woman? I think it's a bad idea."

"Why?" he asked.

Luckily, before I could reply, Honeymouth came to my defense. "They won't be able to bear this lifestyle. How will they stand to sleep under bridges?"

"What bathroom will they use? What mirror will they use to comb their hair?" asked Solomon. But the dreamseller replied:

"Who said they have to leave their own homes to follow us? After all, everyone should sell dreams, whether to himself or to others, wherever he—or she—is."

For the first time, his words brought us no relief. We didn't believe a woman could participate in the group. We considered ourselves revolutionaries, protagonists of a fantastic sociological experiment. We didn't want to share our macho glory. Infected by discrimination, we thought that women would diminish our boldness.

"Following you, Dreamseller, is for . . . real men, and good ones. Besides, women talk too much and act too little," Angel Hand said with conviction. Then he realized his arrogance and tried to backpedal. We had taken over the dreamseller's project and given it a masculine feel.

The Miracle Worker also was against the dreamseller's proposal. He used his knowledge of theology in an effort to dissuade him.

"Dreamseller, Buddha, Confucius and Jesus all had men as disciples. Why would you want to call women to follow you? Look at history. It'll never work."

For the first time, the group was unanimous in showering praise on the Miracle Worker. We began to think he could make interesting contributions. Nevertheless, the dreamseller had an answer for our theologian.

"When Jesus called his disciples, where did he put them, at the periphery or at the center of his plans?" he asked.

"The center, of course," the Miracle Worker replied without hesitation.

"And women?" he asked, testing him.

Edson thought, reflected and rubbed his forehead. After a prolonged moment of analysis, he answered shrewdly:

"I can't say at the periphery, because they provided material support, but they weren't at the center of his work, because they weren't active participants in his project."

Wow," I thought to myself. I had always thought Edson wasn't much of a logical thinker, but he was proving me wrong.

Then, the dreamseller looked at him and then at all of us.

"Wrong," he said, then fell silent.

Because I had studied these sacred texts, I thought Edson was right. I waited for the dreamseller's arguments, but suspected this time he wouldn't convince us.

"They were always at the center of the project. First, according to Scripture, God didn't choose a caste of Pharisees, Greek philosophers or priests to raise the young Jesus, but a woman, an adolescent uncontaminated by the ruling class, someone outside the system."

"Second, the first person who talked about Jesus was a female, the Samaritan woman. She had lived a promiscuous life, been with many men, but his words were enough to satiate her hunger. She gathered her people and spoke of the man who had moved her." After uttering these words, he stopped to take a breath and took ours away by adding, "A prostitute was more noble than the religious leaders of his time."

Bartholomew came out with a phrase that broke the tension hanging over us. I don't know how he came up with such imagination.

"Chief, I've always thought women were smarter than men. The problem is, the credit card was invented . . ." And he started laughing. Ironically, he'd given the impression that he was the one who had supported the women in his life. In reality, they had supported him.

The dreamseller, unhappy with our prejudiced masculinity, attacked even further. He asked our acting theologian:

"Tell me, Edson. In the most important moment in Jesus' life, when his body was withering on the cross and his heart was weak, where were the men, at the center or at the periphery of his plan?"

Edson, paling, was slow to answer. And our faces were flushed. In the silence, the dreamseller said:

"His disciples were heroes when he was shaking the world, but they were cowards when the world came crashing down on him; they kept quiet, fled, denied they knew him, betrayed him. But even then, he loved. Men, I say again, are more timid than women."

"But don't men make war? Bear arms? Don't they start revolutions?" the sociologist in me blurted out.

"The weak use weapons; the strong, their words," he answered and asked the question we feared most:

"Where were the women when he was dying?"

Humbly, because we were familiar with the Bible, we muttered, "Near the cross."

"More than anything, they were at the epicenter of his project. And do you know why? Because women are stronger, more intelligent, more humane, generous, altruistic, supportive, tolerant, faithful and sensible than men. Suffice it to say that ninety percent of violent crimes are committed by men."

We were stunned by so many favorable adjectives about women. The dreamseller didn't seem like a feminist, nor did he appear to be trying to cast words into the air in an effort to compensate for millennia of discrimination against women. He seemed totally convinced of what he was saying.

To him, the system that controlled humanity was conceived in the hearts of men, although its creators could never imagine that one day they would become the victims of their own creation. It was time for women to come into the picture and sell dreams. Lots and lots of dreams.

CHAPTER 23

The Temple of Fashion

THE DREAMSELLER GAVE US FAIR WARNING. HE REMINDED us that the most cultured of Jesus's disciples, Judas, betrayed him. The strongest, Peter, denied knowing him. And the rest, except John, ran in fear. After demonstrating masculine fragility and feminine greatness, the dreamseller revealed why he was in the temple of fashion.

He told us that in the past, the male-dominated system had subjugated women, burning them, stoning them, silencing them. In time, they freed themselves and partially reclaimed their rights. He paused and, out loud, said the number "one." This numerical citation in the middle of a speech made me uneasy. I'd seen how that movie ended.

The dreamseller noted that women had begun to vote, to excel in the academic world, to increase their numbers in the corporate sphere, to occupy the most varied social areas. Women had become more and more daring. They began to change vital sectors of society, to introduce tolerance, solidarity, affection and romanticism. But the system was unforgiving about their audacity.

It set for them the most cowardly and underhanded trap. Instead of extolling their intelligence and obvious sensitivity, it began to exalt the female body as never before in history. It was used tirelessly to sell products and services. They started to feel special. It seemed as if modern societies were trying to make up for millennia of rejection and intolerance. The dreamseller paused to take a breath.

Staring at the immense, colorful temple of fashion, he became outraged and in a loud voice began inviting people to talk about what was so great about the latest fashions. Nothing could be odder for someone dressed like him. But, since the fashion world makes room for the eccentric, they all thought he represented some designer rebelling against conventions. We felt out of place seeing such finely dressed people around us. Some of them recognized him.

He quickly began a discourse about his controversial ideas: "When women came to feel they occupied the throne of the male-dominated system, the fashion world locked in on the most subtle stereotype." And he recited the number "two," deeply saddened.

I didn't know where the dreamseller was heading with this. I knew that stereotypes are a sociological problem. The stereotype of the crazy person, the addict, the corrupt politician, the socialist, the bourgeois, the Jew, the terrorist, the homosexual. We use stereotypes as a vile standard to brand people with certain behaviors. We don't evaluate the content of their character; if they show certain characteristics, we immediately imprison them behind the bars of a stereotype, classifying them as junkies, corrupt, unstable.

But what does the beautiful world of fashion have to do with stereotypes? The women were free to wear whatever they wanted, to buy any clothes they fancied, and have the body they desired. I didn't understand why the dreamseller was so concerned. Nevertheless, the more he spoke, the more I was impressed.

"What a crime that what the fashion world has stereotyped as 'beautiful' is nothing more than a genetic accident."

Bartholomew wasn't sure what the dreamseller was talking about.

"Chief, is that stereotype expensive?" he asked, thinking it was some kind of clothing. The dreamseller told him:

"Its implications are extremely expensive," he explained. "To maximize sales and create an ideal image for women, the fashion world began using the bodies of uncommonly thin young women as the epitome of beauty. One young woman out of ten thousand with a very thin body and exceedingly well-formed face, hips, nose, bust and neck became the stereotype of beauty. What consequences that had for the collective consciousness . . ."

More and more people were gathering around. After a brief pause, he continued:

"The genetic exception became the rule. Children looked to their Barbie dolls for direction, and adolescent girls turned runway models into an unattainable standard of beauty. That process engendered a compulsive quest for the stereotype, as if it were a drug, in hundreds of millions of women. Women, who were always more generous and supportive than men, turned on each other without realizing it. Even Chinese and Japanese women are mutilating their anatomy to come closer to the beauty of Western models. Did you know that?"

I didn't know that, but how could he? How could someone completely outside of fashion be so well informed about it? Suddenly, he interrupted my thoughts by uttering the number "three," and a moment of sorrow washed over his face.

He continued by saying that such a distorted model of beauty had sunk into the collective unconscious, imploding women's self-image and committing an act of terrorism against self-esteem. In the past, stereotypes didn't have serious collective consequences because we weren't yet a global village. And just when women thought they liberated themselves, the system clipped their wings with the "Barbie syndrome."

A male designer challenged him tensely, "I don't believe any of that. That's ridiculous."

"I wish it were. I would love for my ideas to be foolish." And he spoke the number "four."

At that moment, a young woman, confused, asked, "Why do you count while you speak?"

The dreamseller turned and stared at me silently. It seemed like some great force was dragging him into the hearts of families who were losing their sons and daughters. His eyes swimming with tears at the thought, he turned to the crowd and said:

"Lucia, a shy but lively young woman—creative and an excellent student—weighs just seventy-five pounds, despite being five feet, five inches tall. Her bones stick out under her skin, forming a repulsive image, but she refuses to eat for fear of putting on weight. Marcia, a smiling, extroverted young woman, an enchanting girl, weighs seventy-seven pounds and is five-foot-three. Her cadaverous face drives her parents and friends to despair, but even so she refuses to feed herself. Bernadette weighs less than ninety-five pounds and is five-seven. She used to like to talk to everyone but has isolated herself from her boyfriend, her friends and lives in chat rooms on the Internet. Rafaela weighs one hundred and five pounds and stands six feet tall. She played volleyball and liked going to the beach and running on the sand, but now she's starving to death."

He paused again, looked attentively at his audience, and said:

"In the time you've been listening to me talk, *four* young women will have developed anorexia. Some will survive their troubles, others will not. And if you ask these young women why they don't eat, they'll answer, 'Because we're obese.' Billions of cells beg them to be fed, but these woman have no compassion for their bodies, which lack the strength to exercise or even walk. This desperation to reach this ideal body type, this stereotype of what is beautiful, has managed to suppress a vital instinct living things have never managed to block out naturally: our instinct to eat."

And he stated that if those individuals lived in tribes where the stereotype wasn't so powerful, they wouldn't be sick. But they live in modern society, which not only propagates an unhealthy thinness but places excessive value on a certain type of eyes, neck, bust, hips, the shape of a nose—in short, a world that excludes and discriminates against anyone who doesn't measure up to the standard. And the worst part is that all this is done subtly. He emphasized:

"I don't deny that there can be metabolic causes for eating problems, but the social causes are undeniable and unforgivable. There are fifty million anorexics in the world—as many as the number of deaths in World War Two."

Suddenly the dreamseller put aside his somberness, changed to a more pleasant tone and climbed on top of an armchair beside him and called out:

"The social system is clever: It shouts when it should keep quiet and keeps quiet when it should shout. Nothing against the models and the intelligent and creative designers, but the system forgot to shout that beauty can't be standardized."

Various people, international models and famous designers who were passing by, were attracted to the eccentric man showcasing his ideas. There were already people across the world fighting those stereotypes in society, but their voices were but a whisper compared to the monstrous system. Drunk with indignation, the dreamseller once more turned to his incisive Socratic method:

"Where are the heavier women in these shows? Where are the young women with less shapely hips? Where are the women with prominent noses? Why, in this temple of so-called beauty, are there no young women with saddlebags or stretch marks? Aren't they human beings? Aren't they beautiful, too? Why is the world of fashion, which came about to promote well-being, destroying women's self-esteem? Isn't that a socially acceptable rape of self-esteem?"

Listening to this indictment, I began to feel disgusted with the system. However, just when the dreamseller had taken us to the heights of reflection, along came Bartholomew to once again wreck the mood. He raised his hand and clumsily attempted to second the dreamseller:

"I'm with you, chief. I don't discriminate when it comes to women. I've dated every type."

The audience burst into laughter. But we were so nervous already that we hushed Bartholomew.

"Pretend you're normal, Bartholomew!"

The people were split by the dreamseller's ideas. Some were enthralled, their mouths agape; others hated the ideas down to their last thread. Paparazzi began taking photos, eager to record the scandal of the year.

As the buzz from the crowd died down, the dreamseller lowered his voice to make an emotional request:

"I implore you, the brilliant designers, to love women, all of them, to invest in their mental health by using not just these unattainable body types to express your art. You may not make as much money as you otherwise might, but you'll realize immeasurable gains. Sell the dream that every woman has a unique beauty."

Some people applauded, including three international models to my right. Later we learned that models were exposed to a host of mental conditions. They were ten times more likely to be anorexic than the population as a whole. The system both enthroned and incarcerated them, and after a short career, it discarded them.

Three people booed the dreamseller. One of them threw a plastic water bottle at him, opening a cut over his left eyebrow, which bled profusely. We took him by the arm and asked him to stop talking, but he wasn't intimidated. Wiping away the blood with an old handkerchief, he called for silence and continued. I thought: "There are many who hide their thinking for the sake of their public image; here's a man who's faithful to his ideas." Then he offered a proposal that made our skin tingle:

"Most women in modern society don't see themselves as beautiful. So in every clothing store and on every label there should be a warning, like on packs of cigarettes, that reads: 'Every woman is beautiful. Beauty can't be standardized.'"

These words got quite a reaction from the press. At the very moment he said them, a paparazzo photographed him from an angle that caught the upper half of his body and, in the background, the logo of the international clothing chain of the Megasoft Group.

His ideas about discrimination in fashion reminded me of when he told us: "Discrimination can be constructed in a matter of hours, but can take centuries to dismantle. A full century after Abraham Lincoln freed African-Americans from slavery, Martin Luther King Jr. was on the streets of major American cities, still fighting discrimination." I kept asking myself, "Who is this man who makes these revolutionary proposals? Where does his knowledge come from?"

The dreamseller told the crowd that our existence can never be standardized. All of us experience life differently, from sex and the taste of food to our appetites, art, even beauty.

"What's the normal frequency for having sexual relations? Every day? Every week? Any classification would generate serious distortions. What's normal if not that which satisfies each person? Isn't being satisfied enough?"

A stunningly beautiful international model named Monica, deeply moved by his speech, interrupted him and had the courage to say publicly:

"My whole life, all I knew how to do was strut, strut, strut down a runway. My world was the runways. I've been photographed by the best international photographers. My body has been on major magazine covers. I was raised to the top by the fashion world, but the same world that praised me cast me aside when I gained ten pounds. Today I have bulimia. I eat compulsively, then feel so guilty about it that I have to make myself throw up. My life is a living hell. I can't even bear the taste of food. I don't know who I am or what I love anymore. I've tried to kill myself three times."

There were no tears in her eyes, none left to cry. The dreamseller, seeing the model's suffering, took two deep breaths. He thought it better to remain silent, realizing that Monica's experience spoke more eloquently than his words. But first he wanted to see her smile. He switched from reflection to humor.

"When women are in front of the mirror, they say a famous phrase, even unconsciously. What is it?" The women present answered in unison, "Mirror, mirror on the wall: Who's the fairest of them all?"

"No," the dreamseller said. "They all say, 'Mirror, mirror on the wall. Who's got the most defects of them all?'"

The crowd smiled. Monica laughed a beautiful laugh; it had been five years since she laughed like that. That was what he wanted: to sell her the dream of happiness. It was an admirable sociological experiment. It was the first time I'd ever seen humor grow out of such despair.

Bartholomew told the dreamseller, "Chief, I don't see any defects when I look in the mirror. Have I got a problem?"

"No, Bartholomew. You're simply beautiful. Look at your friends. Aren't they marvelous?"

Honeymouth took a long look at the group of disciples.

"Don't push it, chief. The family's kinda shabby."

We broke into laughter and headed for the door. We'd never felt so beautiful.

CHAPTER 24

Calling a Model and a Revolutionary

WHEN WE LEFT, MONICA CAME OUTSIDE TO EXPRESS HER profound gratitude. She hugged the dreamseller affectionately and gave him a kiss on the cheek. The rest of us were green with envy.

The dreamseller looked at her and suddenly took the most extraordinary attitude:

"Monica, you shone on the fashion runways, but I want to invite you to parade down a different runway, one harder to cross, one tougher to keep your balance on, but definitely more interesting to experience. Come sell dreams with us."

Monica didn't know how to answer. She had read several stories about the dreamseller but had no idea where this would lead. When we heard the call to the enchanting model, we, who had rejected letting women into the team, changed our position immediately. We agreed with the dreamseller that women were not only more intelligent than men, they were also much better to look at.

Noting our enthusiasm, the dreamseller moved on to talk to another person. He left it up to us to explain to the newcomer the fascinating world of selling dreams. We'll surely convince her, we thought. We tried to explain, then explain our explanations. But we stumbled over one another and over our words. We were like a pack of stray dogs in mating season.

Seeing that Monica looked far from convinced, the Miracle Worker withdrew to pray. He didn't want to fall into temptation. Angel Hand was euphoric, unable to articulate his words, but nevertheless he tried to invent a poem to attract the model:

"A life without . . . dreams, is . . . is . . . like a winter without . . . snow, an ocean without . . . waves . . ."

Monica had never seen such a band of lunatics—dirty, poorly dressed, weird—trying to win her over at all costs. She grew more doubtful. After all, we were like a swarm of bees around the queen. While we were speaking, Monica glanced to the side and several times saw the dreamseller listening attentively to the person with whom he was talking. After half an hour, the model looked like she wanted to get out of there. Unfortunately, that was when Honeymouth went into action.

"Monica, hon, selling dreams is the craziest experience I've ever had. Not even when I was soaked in vodka was I so delirious," he said, scaring the girl.

"Pretend you're normal, Bartholomew!" we all said again.

But he didn't know how to pretend; he was what he was. Then something unexpected happened. When Bartholomew spoke of the craziness of the project, she took heart. She wanted something more exciting than the world of fashion runways. But she was still undecided about this sociological experiment.

When the dreamseller returned, Monica asked him, "Sir, I know the man you were talking to."

"Really? He's a fascinating person," he said effusively.

"He's a deaf-mute and doesn't know sign language," the model replied, suspicious of the dreamseller's motives. If the deaf man didn't know sign language, it wasn't possible for them to communicate. We fell silent. It was clear she wouldn't follow him.

"I know," replied the dreamseller. "That's why it's rare that anyone pays attention to him to free him from his loneliness. I heard the words he didn't say. Have you spent any time trying to understand him?" She fell as silent as the deaf man.

Monica agreed to join the journey, but at the dreamseller's request she would sleep at her own home. She didn't know about the sleepless nights that awaited her.

The next day, the dreamseller was in every major daily newspaper in the city and on all the television morning newscasts. His ideas were spreading. Some papers were already calling him by the name he liked: "Dreamseller." They said he had turned the fashion world upside down.

Some journalists, extremely concerned with the eroding self-image of today's youth, wrote about the Barbie syndrome and came to conclusions that expanded on what the dreamseller had said. They said he had shouted that because of the unrealistic standards of the fashion industry many adolescent girls lose a grip on reality and are perpetually dissatisfied with their bodies, finding defects in their faces and constantly complaining that their clothes didn't fit.

Young people who didn't like to read newspapers clamored for the articles. Some took it to school, where it spread from hand to hand. Many boys and girls breathed a sigh of relief when they read the articles because they so often had agonized about the "anatomical defects" they saw in themselves. Soon they began laughing at their "paranoia." They felt the story covered conflicts almost never discussed at school. From that point on, a rebellious streak started forming within some of the students. They began criticizing the social system and wanted to learn firsthand the ideas of that mysterious dreamseller.

Monica met us that afternoon and told us about the waves the article had created in the fashion world. She said that some of her designer friends as well as some stores had bought into the dreamseller's ideas and were beginning to spread the view that beauty couldn't be standardized.

Seeing the model more enthused, we decided to tell her about the countless adventures we'd had in the last several months. A week later, the dreamseller told us he wanted to invite another woman to the group.

The way Monica looked, we felt he could invite not one or two or three, but ten women. "How we've changed our stance," I thought. I, who had always criticized politicians who were enemies one day and the best of friends the next, began to understand that such fluctuation was a sickness inherent to the human mind. It all depended on what was at stake.

Convinced of the wisdom of his new plan, the dreamseller looked upward and then to the sides, placed his hands on his chin and began moving away from us. He was lost in thought again. I heard him ask himself in a low voice, "Which woman should I call? What characteristics should she have?"

The dreamseller was about fifty feet away, walking in circles in the lobby of the shopping mall where we met. Just as we were celebrating the proposal of bringing more women into the group, an elderly woman appeared and gave Honeymouth a light tap on the head with her cane. It was Jurema.

"How are you, boys?" she said.

"Just fine, Jurema. How nice to see you again," we said politely.

Suddenly we looked over at the pensive dreamseller, then back at the little old lady and had a terrible thought: "She might be the next to be called! We better get her out of here fast."

The dreamseller, his gaze turned toward the sidewalk opposite where we stood, raised his voice and said to himself, "Whom to call?" We felt a shiver run down our spines. We tried to hide Jurema. We had to get rid of her.

"The sun is . . . scalding. You could get dehydrated, you're sweating so much. You should . . . go home," Dimas, the great manipulator of hearts, told the old woman, trying not to stutter. But she insisted on staying.

"The weather's fine, my boy," she said assuredly.

Edson took her arm politely.

"You look tired. At your age one needs lots of rest," he told her.

"I feel just great, son. But thanks for your concern," Jurema said.

I also gave it a shot, trying to remind her of something she might have forgotten—an appointment, a doctor's visit, a bill to pay. But she told me everything was taken care of.

Monica didn't understand our concern over Jurema. She thought we were being a little too nice. Bartholomew, who had always been the most honest of any of us, slipped up again. Seeing that she had no intention of heading home, he appealed. He raised one eyebrow and said:

"My dear, beautiful Jurema," he said, and she seemed to melt, batting her eyelashes. Just when he'd gotten her attention, he blurted out, "I'm sorry to tell you that you're as red as a beet. I think you might be having a heart attack. You need to get to a hospital right away."

Solomon tried to cover Bartholomew's big mouth, but it was too late. Jurema did the job. She hooked his neck with the crook of her cane, yanked him close and said flatly:

"Bartholomew, with your mouth shut you're absolutely perfect."

We roared with laughter. But Jurema was bothered, realizing we were hiding something from her. To show us she was still strong and full of life, despite being more than eighty years old and having a touch of Alzheimer's, she crouched down and did a few push-ups. She asked us to try and match her, but we couldn't keep up. Then she leaped into a pair of ballet pirouettes and dared us to try. But we all clumsily almost fell on our faces.

"You guys are a bunch of old geezers," she said. "I feel younger than any of you and I'm as healthy as a horse. Now, where's that guru of yours?"

Guru? I thought. The dreamseller didn't like even being called master, much less guru. We said he was having some problems . . . had an appointment . . . couldn't talk to her now. We tried to block her view of the dreamseller, but she poked her head between us. By then, Monica had already figured out our little game and I think wondered whether there was any hope of redemption for any of us.

Jurema shouted even louder, "Where's the guru?"

We cringed when we heard the dreamseller's deep, powerful voice.

"How wonderful to see you again!" he told her, and then said the words we had all dreaded: "Come with us. Come and help us sell dreams!"

Monica couldn't help laughing and laughing, but we were worried. We wandered off to one side and began to whisper questions to one another. "What will society think of us, a band of eccentrics followed by an old lady? We'll be a laughingstock. Oh, the newspapers are going to love this. What'll it be like living with her? We'll probably waste all our time waiting for her to catch up. And that old-lady smell? Does she wear dentures?"

We worried that our journey would suffer with the addition of Jurema. The dreamseller patiently watched our boys-only conference as Monica tried to explain the calling to Jurema. But she was a beginner herself and had trouble making it clear.

Jurema, an honest woman, called us aside and said, "I've never sold anything in my life. What type of product is it?"

The dreamseller went off to speak with Monica and left us alone to explain the project to Jurema. This gave us a golden opportunity to dissuade the old woman. In the privacy of my thoughts, I wondered whether the dreamseller hadn't seen Jurema first and was testing us again, in an attempt to unveil the subtle prejudices in our minds.

We had had a fantastic experience at the nursing home, where we had discovered the greatness of the elderly, but we insisted on harboring a prejudice against them. We were convinced the old lady wouldn't be able to keep up with the pace of the group. We thought that, with her, the dreamseller would have to be less aggressive with some of his plans.

We spoke honestly with Jurema about the adventure of dreams. After all, even when our interests were thwarted, we were learning to be transparent. But, to dissuade her, we emphasized the dangers we faced, the public shame, the insults, the beating the dreamseller had suffered.

She listened attentively, nodding her head. She arranged her white hair, as if wanting to massage her restless brain. We were sure we were leaving her more uncertain than before. Solomon looked to the heavens and made the sign of the cross. "I'm getting scared just thinking about the dangers that lie ahead," he said.

He signaled to Bartholomew to keep quiet for once because we seemed to be making progress. But, not thinking twice, the bungler said in a trembling, horror-movie voice: "It's very risky to follow this man, Jurema. We could be arrested. We could be kidnapped, beaten, tortured. We could even be killed!"

We thought, for once, he'd managed to say just the right thing. Little did we know his words would be a kind of prophecy. Jurema's right eye widened, her left eye closed. Just when we were sure we had convinced her, it was our turn to be startled.

"Fantastic!" she said. We exchanged dumbstruck glances.

"Fantastic? What do you mean, 'fantastic,' Jurema?" I

asked, thinking that her senile mind had somehow misunderstood everything we had said.

"Everything you've told me is fantastic," she said. "I'm absolutely ready to be a wanderer and I accept the invitation to join the group! I was always a rebel in my student days, and later as a university professor. But I was punished, subjugated by the educational system. I had to follow an agenda I disagreed with, a curriculum that did nothing to form thinkers."

Our little brotherhood was shaken. We couldn't breathe. As if the mysterious identity of the dreamseller weren't enough, now we had a mysterious old lady to contend with. Some of us snorted, disturbed by her. I tried to dab the beads of sweat off my face.

"I've always wanted to sell dreams, to stimulate minds, but I was silenced," she said. "I get disgusted every day when I think about modern society steamrolling young people's intellect, mashing them all together, crushing their critical thinking and turning them into tape recorders of information. What has society done to our children?"

I asked what her full name was.

"Jurema Alcantara de Mello," she said flatly.

When I heard the name, I took a step backward, even more shocked than before. That's when I discovered that Jurema was a renowned anthropologist who had been a university professor at the highest level. She had even done postdoctoral work at Harvard. She was internationally known and had written five books in her field of study and they had been published in various languages.

I leaned against a nearby post to steady myself. I remembered having read several journal articles of hers, as well as all her books. She had played an important role in helping me formulate my ideas. I had admired her organized power of reasoning and her boldness. And here, just minutes earlier, I had wanted to kick her out of our group. I thought to myself: "Damned prejudice! Who will free me from this intellectual cancer? I dream of being a free and open person, but I'm hopelessly stubborn."

Her ideas were right in line with the dreamseller's. Jurema went on to say that societies, with some exceptions, had become quagmires for conformist minds that were untroubled by the complexity of existence, devoid of great ideas, and they never questioned who they are.

"We need to stimulate people's intelligence," she said.

The dreamseller smiled in delight. He must have thought: "I hit the bull's-eye." Jurema was more of a rebel than all of us. As she aged, she became more determined. She began to challenge us the second she joined us. Since age brings an incurable courage and honesty, she was very outspoken. She started pointing out things that Monica hadn't yet had the courage to say. She confronted the dreamseller and criticized the group's look.

"Being a band of eccentrics that sells dreams is fine, but being a band of filthy ragamuffins is absurd," she said.

Oh, did we get angry at that. But even after seeing us pout, Jurema didn't back down.

"Calling a group eccentric in order to create a spirit of solidarity is laudable," she said, "but not caring whether that group looks shabby and unkempt, that's just wrong-headed."

The dreamseller remained silent. But Dimas couldn't take it.

"Jurema, sweetie . . . li . . . lighten up," he stuttered, attempting a familiarity that only Bartholomew could get away with.

She didn't let it slide. She came close to him, took several whiffs of his body and scowled, "Lighten up? You smell like rotten eggs."

Bartholomew roared with laughter.

"Didn't I tell you? I'm a saint for putting up with that guy's smell!" Bartholomew said. And he laughed so hard he couldn't hold back and ripped a sonorous thunderclap of his own.

"You should be ashamed of yourself," she told him. "If you can't hold it, you should at least do it so no one can hear you."

We were starting to get worried. We looked at the dreamseller and began to realize that this new member of the family wanted to pour cold water on us—literally. For the first time we saw him scratch his head, without taking action. Jurema was a revolutionary, but she was unbalanced. She turned to the dreamseller and did what we never thought anyone would be bold enough to do: She confronted him.

"And don't give me that story about how Jesus called those who cleansed the outside of their body but forgot to cleanse the inside hypocrites. Yes, we must emphasize the inside, but without ignoring the outside. His disciples bathed in the Jordan and in the houses where they were guests. But look at you. Look at your followers! How long has it been since they've had a real bath?"

We had bathed in public bathrooms, but not as often or as well as we probably should have. The master didn't argue. He simply nodded his head in agreement. He had taught us many lessons, and the greatest one was to have the humility to learn from others.

And if that weren't enough, Jurema turned to Edson and boldly asked him to open his mouth. He did so cautiously. We felt that the dreamseller had to have regretted his choice at this point. But maybe not. "Wasn't a female disciple with just these characteristics what he was looking for?" I thought.

"Good lord, what a stench! You need to brush your teeth," she told the Miracle Worker, pinched her nose and told him to close his mouth.

I laughed—but between clenched lips. She noticed it and said, "What are you laughing at?"

She didn't spare anyone, except Monica, who hadn't had this much fun in years. She felt that we were a traveling circus.

The dreamseller said Jurema wouldn't sleep under the bridge with us, because of her age. She and Monica would return home and reunite with us the following day.

At the end of the day, Jurema invited us to bathe and eat supper together at her house. The prejudice virus, which was dormant, reawakened. We looked at one another and thought that, given her age, a professor's meager pension and what she had to pay for medicines and doctors, her financial situation couldn't be much better than ours. We probably couldn't even all stand in her house, much less have dinner there. And with the old woman plodding away at the stove, it would be midnight before the meal was ready.

Jurema turned her head up the street and whistled.

When we asked what she was doing, she said she was calling her driver. We thought she must have been suffering some kind of dementia and Dimas said under his breath, "It must be the bus driver."

There was no sign of any driver. She whistled again, this time more loudly. Nothing.

"I think 'Driver' is the name of her dog," Bartholomew said. Jurema shot him a dirty look and wagged her cane, but instead of smacking him, she seemed amused by the joke.

"Just imagine everybody cramming into some old Ford straight out of a museum," Edson said.

Our group always had some kind of retort. In the few months we had been together, I had enjoyed myself more than I had in my entire life, even when we were making fun of each other. The dreamseller fostered that environment. Monica felt as if she were always at a street fair. In her former life, she had been wealthy, but what she hadn't blown on luxury items, she lost in the stock market. But traveling with the group, she was getting something the free market couldn't sell.

While we were joking, a beautiful white limousine pulled up in front of us, almost running over Bartholomew's foot. An impeccably dressed chauffeur said, "Sorry, ma'am. It took me a long time because there was traffic."

Our jaws dropped. And I'm sure we all, conveniently, had the same thought: "What a great new disciple!"

CHAPTER 25

The Butterflies and the Cocoon

JUREMA WAS THE WIDOW OF A MILLIONAIRE. BUT SHE never felt a need to flaunt her wealth. Sometimes she bypassed cars, chauffeurs, designer clothes and other benefits that her fortune might have afforded her. She lived modestly. We had never been in such a luxurious vehicle. We were smitten, but the dreamseller, someone who seemed never to have driven a car, remained indifferent. He asked Jurema for the address and said he would walk. He needed to think.

He met us at her house two hours later. The millionaire widow had made a quick stop at a store and bought clothes for all of us. We looked civilized again. We had already taken a bath and were nibbling on delicious cheese and cold cuts. It was all so delicious that it made us remember there are some wonderful things about the system. Honeymouth was so hungry that he used his hands to grab the snacks instead of the metal toothpicks. Solomon didn't talk, making time only to eat. Funny, but I noticed that his tics and quirks had diminished considerably with a filling belly. I didn't know whether it was hunger or a lasting improvement.

Dimas stuffed his mouth with cheese, like a rat, and stared at all the expensive objects on top of a china cabinet and the beautiful paintings hanging on the walls. I think that if he hadn't been called by the dreamseller, he might have returned to clean the place out. Monica ate discreetly. She was so happy about being part of the group that nothing distracted her. I never imagined that such a good-looking person could live such a nightmare.

The dreamseller was led into the main area of the house, which comprised over 5,000 square feet of space, divided into five rooms. Jurema's luxurious mansion barely fazed him and that seemed to make her happy. She was tired of people who fawned over her house but had nothing to say to her. He then went to bathe and was given new clothes.

As all of us were beginning to enjoy a delightful dinner, the dreamseller had a request for her: "Tell us about your husband."

She was surprised, for people seldom asked about the dead, not wanting to cause any awkwardness. But she loved to talk about him and had always admired him. She told us about the time when they were young, their courtship, the marriage. Then she spoke of his tenderness, boldness and intellect. Twice, the dreamseller said, "What a great man. He was also a dreamseller."

She mentioned that her husband had been CEO of one of the most important companies of the Megasoft Group, which was made up of more than thirty firms. We thought the business world would be of no interest to the dreamseller, but he unexpectedly asked, "How did he become wealthy?"

To tell the story of her husband's rise, she first had to give us some background on the Megasoft Group's president. She said that the owner of an important firm had died and left a fortune to his twenty-five-year-old son. The young man had an exceptional mind and was endowed with unusual enterprise and leadership ability. He far surpassed his father. He took the company public and, with the money from his booming shares, expanded the business and invested in the most diverse activities in the corporate world. He invested in oil, clothing store chains, communications, computers, electronics and hotels. Within fifteen years he had put together the Megasoft Group, which became one of the ten largest corporations in the world.

She told us that when the company went public, the young president gave all the employees the chance to buy stock, and her husband became a minority stockholder in the company. With the phenomenal growth of the group, he made a lot of money. When I heard Jurema's story, I interjected:

"When you mentioned that young millionaire's enterprising spirit, I remembered that the largest shareholder at my university was precisely the Megasoft Group. After it became the university's biggest booster, there was no shortage of money to underwrite research and theses."

The dreamseller then asked Jurema a few questions:

"Did you know the young man who expanded that group so explosively? Was he free or a prisoner of the system? Was his philosophy to love money more than life or life more than money? What were his priorities? What values motivated him? Was he conscious of the brevity of life or did he position himself as a god?"

Jurema, caught by surprise, didn't know how to answer, as she had rarely seen the young man personally. He was extremely busy, courted by kings and presidents, while she was simply a professor. But she said that her husband liked him a lot.

"Judging by the comments he made," she said, "I believe he was a very good and well-bred person. But after my husband passed seven years ago, I heard little about him, except that some misfortune had struck his family. It appears he had mental problems. They said he passed away, but the press covered up the story. They say that if he were alive today he would have displaced the old magnates and be the richest man on earth."

The dreamseller looked at us and said:

"My dear Jurema, you were very generous to that millionaire. I, too, have heard of his boldness, his story and his death. But we have the tendency to make the deceased into saints, to exalt their good qualities and conceal their defects. Someone who knew him intimately told me he was ambitious and had no time for anything except increasing his wealth. He forgot what mattered most in his life."

Sadly, displaying the heavy air of one who disagreed with the path taken by that leader, he added some memorable observations:

"I don't ask you to hate money or material goods. Today we sleep under bridges with the sky as our blanket; tomorrow, who can know? I ask you to understand that money itself doesn't bring happiness, though lack of it can diminish it drastically. Money can't make us crazy, but the love of it can destroy our serenity. The absence of money makes us poor, but its misuse makes us miserable."

We all fell silent.

"Chief, being broke and happy is fine by me, but with money life's a lot better," said Bartholomew, drinking coconut water while the rest of us had French and Chilean wine.

The dreamseller smiled. It was difficult for him to have a deep conversation with those street "philosophers."

As we moved from town to town and people recognized the dreamseller, people wanted to hug him immediately. Their eyes shone when they saw him. Some kissed him. Little by little, he was becoming more famous than society's politicians, and that was stirring envy.

Seeing people gather around him in front of an imposing shopping mall, the dreamseller climbed a few steps leading to the main entrance and began one of his fascinating speeches. He gave a philosophical interpretation of Jesus' most famous homily, the Sermon on the Mount.

He had told us he loved that text and agreed with Mahatma
Gandhi that if all the sacred books of the world were banned
and only the Sermon on the Mount survived, humanity would
not be without light

"Happy are the humble of spirit, for theirs is the kingdom
of wisdom," the dreamseller shouted. "But where are the truly
humble, those who have emptied themselves of themselves?
Where are those who recognize their mistakes? Where are
those who courageously admit their smallness and fragility to
be found? Where are those who struggle daily against pride?"

After speaking these words, he stared attentively at the apprehensive, anxious faces of the crowd. He took a breath and
continued:

"Happy are the patient, for they shall inherit the earth.
Which earth am I referring to? The earth of tranquillity, the
soil of enchantment with life, the terrain of simple love. But
where are these gentle souls? Where are the open-minded?
Where can we find those who are intimate friends of tolerance? Where are those who temper their irritability and anxiety? Where are those who act calmly in the face of setbacks
and frustration? Most people are not gentle even to themselves. They live a pressured life of unending demands and
self-inflicted punishment."

The crowd flowed more and more around him. He raised his
eyes to the sky, slowly lowered them and finished his interpretation of the second beatitude, inverting the classical motivational thoughts:

"Stop the neurotic need to change others. No one can change
anyone else. Whoever demands more of others than of himself
is qualified to work in finance, but not with human beings."

And he continued:

"Happy are those who mourn, for they shall be comforted.
But why do we live in a world where people hide their tears?

Where are those who shed tears over the selfishness that blinds our eyes and keeps us from learning what goes on in the minds of those we love? How many hidden fears have never been revealed? How many secret conflicts have never been given voice? How many emotional wounds have we caused and never admitted to?"

As he spoke, the people reflected. Many were lamenting the pitfalls in their personal relationships.

"Happy are the peacemakers, for they shall be called the children of God. But where are those who calm the waters of emotion? Where are the masters at solving interpersonal conflicts? Aren't we all experts at judging others? Where are those who protect, challenge, surrender themselves, reconcile and believe in others? Every society divides its people, and every division implies a subtraction. Peacemaking is not, therefore, teaching the mathematics of addition but understanding the mathematics of subtraction. Whoever fails to understand that is qualified to live with animals and machines, but not with human beings."

I was speechless. I was schooled in how to be an academic, but was very poorly equipped to live among people. I had owned dogs, and I had no problems with them—or at least they never complained. But dealing with human beings was a constant struggle. I was very demanding. I was qualified to work, but didn't understand the human toll of the mathematics of subtraction. People were free to think, as long as they thought like me. Only then did I begin to comprehend that living well means learning how to lose before learning how to win.

More were congregating to hear the dreamseller speak. Traffic stopped, creating mass confusion. The chaos grew and he quickly had to bring his explanation to an end. That day, the dreamseller chose more disciples, all with particular characteristics. None of them was a saint. None had a calling to be perfect.

Many began to accompany the dreamseller wherever he went. Word had spread on the Internet, and people kept track of where he was and where he was headed. Despite being followed by many now, he was privately training only a few of us. Not because we were the most qualified, but maybe because we were his toughest cases.

CHAPTER 26

The Journey

THREE DAYS LATER, HE CALLED A SPECIAL MEETING. Apparently, he was going to tell us about his greatest dream. I could see it burning inside him. He took us to a calm grassy clearing where there was barely any noise or people. He had us sit in a semicircle. It was seven AM and dew had settled on the lawn. The first rays of sunlight were glittering on the horizon and lighting the petals of the hibiscuses, forming a kind of arch of gold. Birds were chirping, celebrating the dawning of a new day.

More people were joining the group. Unlike us, the closest group, they had their lives like any other member of society. They had jobs, families, friends, hobbies. That day, there were thirty of us. Among them were manual laborers, managers, doctors, psychologists, social workers. There were Christians, Buddhists, Muslims and people of several other religions.

To our surprise, he started the meeting by telling us something tangible about his mysterious past.

"In the past, I had unimaginable power at my fingertips, a level of control that spanned more than a hundred countries. But there came a period in my life when time stopped. I lost all peace in my life. I cried endlessly and inconsolably. Finally I isolated myself on an island country in the Atlantic Ocean and stayed there for more than three years. The food was good, but I wasn't hungry. I only hungered for knowledge. I devoured books. I had access to one of the most spectacular libraries. I read day and night, like an asthmatic gasping for breath. I read more than a dozen books a month, almost a hundred and fifty a year. Books on philosophy, neuroscience, theology, history, sociology, psychology. I read while eating, sitting down, standing, walking. My mind was like a machine that photographed page after page of knowledge. All that knowledge helped me understand my past and deal with all I had been through. That's how I became the human being you see, a small and imperfect seller of dreams."

He offered no further explanation. His words gave me the wings to fly far off into the heavens of my mind. I saw that while he told his story, some of my friends looked lost. But I can't say my mind was any better at fitting the puzzle together. "How can he say that his power was so great? What power is he referring to: financial, political, intellectual, spiritual? He seems so fragile, so docile, so poor. He eats with paupers. There are times when he's tense, but he knows how to control his tension. He demands nothing. He sleeps anywhere. Puts up with aggression. Protects those who oppose him. How can someone who once had so much live so meagerly? Could that power be a figment of his imagination?" Interrupting my thoughts, he elaborated some important recommendations:

"The project to sell dreams doesn't conflict with your religion, culture or beliefs. In fact, respect your beliefs, value your culture, appreciate your nation's past and the traditions of your people. I only ask that you change one thing . . ."

He paused for a long time, as if slowly moving toward his fundamental goal.

"I ask you to expand your horizons. To value and, above all else, respect your condition as human beings. My greatest dream is that we can form a network of people without borders, in every nation, among all peoples, all religions, all scientific environments. A network of people to rescue human nature, the instincts our species has lost. Humanity lives in a pressure cooker of stress because of the ruthless way in which we compete, because of our lack of respect for the international rules of commerce, because of social conflicts, because of the devastation to the environment. The French Revolution took place over two centuries ago, but we speak of it as if it had occurred yesterday. Yet, when we look to the future we have no guarantee that our species will survive one or two more centuries."

Then he spoke of his model. He said that Jesus repeated more than seventy times in the New Testament that he was the son of man. "Throughout history, few have understood what he meant. He revealed that he was for all mankind. By insisting he was the son of man he wanted it known that he was the son of humanity—the first human being completely without borders. His culture, his race, his nationality were important, but his humanity was much more so. His passion for his fellow man was at a level that theology doesn't understand and psychology can't reach. Only a human without borders could say that prostitutes should enter heaven before illustrious Pharisee theologians. His limitless love was a scandal during his time, and still is in our own." And the dreamseller added solemnly:

"I have thousands of shortcomings. I've made more mistakes than any of you can imagine, but Jesus' philosophy and psychology is my model." And he proposed founding a society of human beings without borders, based on just four principles:

To go beyond race, culture and nationality and position ourselves as humans without borders, with a vital commitment to protect man and the environment;

To fight discrimination in all its forms and support all
    forms of inclusion;
To respect the differences that make us unique;
And to promote interaction among people of different
    cultures and beliefs.

The dreamseller knew that his proposals shared the principles
of the French Revolution, the United Nations Declaration of
Human Rights and the Magna Carta of many nations. But the
difference was that he dreamed of taking pages from those
charters and printing that text within the hearts and minds of
humans without borders.

"It's too utopian," I muttered to myself. But the dreamseller
read my lips.

"You're right. Nothing could be more utopian, imaginary,
romantic. But take away the dream of utopia and we are left
as machines. Take away hope and we are left as slaves. Take
away dreams and we are left as robots. If business and political
leaders thought in terms of humanity, two-thirds of the world's
problems would be solved in a month. And that's no dream."

I nodded my head, recognizing that he was right. I remembered all the times I had felt like a teaching machine whirring
steadily for students who became learning machines.

The dreamseller seemed more fixated than ever. He measured his tone more than he normally did. Anyone could see
this was a special day for him. And he seemed to have something important left to say. Then he told us the parable of the
cocoon.

"Two caterpillars each spun a cocoon. In that protected
atmosphere they were transformed into beautiful butterflies.
Just when they were ready to fly free, their fears gripped them.
One butterfly, being so fragile, thought to herself: 'Life outside
has so many dangers. I can be torn to bits and eaten by a bird.

If a predator doesn't kill me, I might be torn apart in a storm. A lightning bolt could strike me dead. The rain could weigh on my wings and send me crashing to the ground. Besides, spring is ending. What if the nectar runs out? Who will help me?' The risks were in fact many, and the little butterfly had reason to be scared. Frightened, she decided not to leave. She remained in her protected cocoon, but, having no means to survive, she died a sad death, starved, dehydrated and, worst of all, walled in by the world she had spun.

"The other butterfly," he continued, "was also apprehensive. She was afraid of the world outside, knowing that many butterflies didn't last a day outside the cocoon. But she loved freedom more than she feared the dangers that could befall her. And so she set off, flying in the direction of all the dangers. She chose to be a wanderer in search of the only thing that defined her essence."

When he finished telling the parable, the dreamseller unveiled his intentions. He paused briefly to listen to the exquisitely beautiful birdsongs that seemed to be sung in his honor and made a series of simple yet profound requests. There were so many that I found it hard to take notes:

"I called you here so early because for two days I'd like you to go out and live the principles of being 'a human being without borders.' I'm sending you out in pairs into the social landscape. Take with you neither purses, money, checks, credit cards, nor food—nothing that provides survival support, only medicines and personal hygiene products. Eat whatever you're offered. Sleep in the beds prepared for you. Discriminate against no one. If someone rejects you, don't resist, treat him with gentleness. Act like social therapists. Give and receive. Don't feel the need to win people over. Don't defend your beliefs, don't impose your ideas. Instead, emanate humanity. Ask those you meet on the road how you can be of help to them.

Talk to people, get to know their hidden stories, uncover dazzling human beings among the anonymous. Don't look at them through your eyes but through theirs. Don't invade their privacy, don't try to control them, go only as far as they allow. Listen to them humbly, even those who are thinking of ending their lives, and encourage them to listen to themselves. If they manage only to listen to themselves instead of you, you have succeeded. Remember that the kingdom of the wise belongs to the humble."

He paused and seemed concerned when he warned us:

"We're living in the third millennium. Selling the dream of being a human without borders in a society that has reached the pinnacle of selfishness seems like the absurdity of all absurdities. Being true, generous and considerate when others ask it of us already seems like going beyond extraordinary; just imagine how difficult it will be to teach others to be this way when no one asks it of them. You'll be called fanatics, lunatics, proselytizers. But if they accepted me, they'll also accept you."

Other than that, he offered no rules about how to approach people or whom to look for: rich or poor, educated or illiterate, city dwellers or those in rural towns. He gave us no map, only the inspiration to continue the journey. His hair blew in the wind, and we were dripping sweat. We were all scared of what awaited us. I thought to myself, "This isn't going to work. We'll be misunderstood, maybe even reviled. And what if I run into one of my colleagues from the university? What will they say about me?" The dreamseller added:

"There are many ways to contribute to the good of humanity, but none of them is easy, and none of them come with applause. People will be suspicious of your motives. You may be famous in the morning, and infamous by nightfall. You may be heralded one moment and treated like the dregs of society the next. The consequences are unpredictable. But I guarantee you that if you overcome these obstacles, you'll emerge much more human, much stronger, and able to understand what books can never teach you. You'll understand, to some small degree, what millions of Jews experienced at the hands of the Nazis, Christians in the Coliseum, Muslims in Palestine . . . You'll begin to understand the kind of oppression that homosexuals, blacks, prostitutes, the deeply religious and women have suffered throughout history."

I thought to myself, "Letting Bartholomew and Dimas loose to represent the dreamseller without monitoring could be a disaster. It's not that different from letting a medical student perform surgery without a supervisor."

What the dreamseller was asking of us was to create a social laboratory unlike any I had studied in sociology. He didn't want us to do charity work in Africa with financial backing, or give philanthropically to some institution, or to support a religion or a political party. He wanted us to return to our roots. We could take nothing with us, not even our prestige in society. We would have to be merely human beings connecting with other human beings.

He insisted that we had a right to choose.

"I encourage you to leave the cocoon at least this one time, but no one is obligated to do so. There are many risks, and the consequences are unforeseeable. The choice is yours, yours alone."

The room shook with tension, but no one backed down from the dreamseller's challenge, not even a pair of eighteen-year-olds near the front. Youth yearns for adventure, and they were ready to experience the journey.

CHAPTER 27

Sending Forth the Disciples

W HEN THE MEETING WAS OVER, HE SENT US OFF FOR OUR two-day journey. Each took the person who'd been sitting on his right as his partner. He gave the women the option to sleep at home, but they all declined.

"We want the full experience. We choose to leave our cocoons for those two days," Jurema said, speaking for the women. Four other people asked to be excused, though they promised to return on the appointed day.

Our results couldn't have been more mixed. We were taken for thieves and kidnappers. We were rejected, ridiculed, threatened. Several pairs had to explain themselves at the police station. But in spite of everything, we had spectacular experiences. We enjoyed ourselves and learned so much. It seemed as if we were traveling in another society, that we had entered a completely different world, the world of "the other person." Everyone said they felt totally insecure without money or credit cards. Sometimes we felt like a wandering people with no home, no country and no protection, wondering how we would survive from day to day. We were just humans and nothing more. The dreamseller's sociological experiment proved that we were concealing our true humanity behind concepts like ethics, morality, titles, status and power.

Honeymouth, with Dimas as his partner, set off to sell dreams in the places he knew best, bars and nightclubs. He was met with countless hassles. Some threw vodka in his face, others humiliated him, some cursed him, and still others simply threw him out. "Get outta here, you drunk!" He lost his patience five times and threatened to punch two alcoholics. He began to realize just how difficult a calling this would be.

Despite the setbacks, he helped alcoholics to their feet, listened to rambling conversations and consoled them. Many told him they drank to drown out the pain of losses, betrayals, financial crises and deaths in the family. He had no magic solution, but he lent his ear. At the end of the first day, he went up to a middle-aged man sitting by himself at a table and said, "Sir, I don't mean to bother you. I'd just like to know how I can be of service."

The answer was swift: "Get me another shot of whiskey."

He said he had no money. The alcoholic shoved him rudely.

"Then get out of here or I'm calling the police."

Bartholomew was a husky man. He grabbed the alcoholic by the collar and was about to shake him when he remembered the dreamseller's counsel.

"Oh, if this had happened a couple of months ago . . ." he said angrily. Dimas was also indignant.

The drunk put his hand on his head, quickly regaining his composure. Even with his judgment impaired, he saw he had been rude. He apologized and asked them to sit with him. Then, without explanation, he sobbed for twenty solid seconds.

When he regained his composure, he introduced himself. He said his name was Lucas and he was a failed surgeon. He had made a mistake that didn't threaten his patient's life, but the patient's lawyer used that mistake to take him to the cleaners. He was sued and lost everything he had built up in twenty years of practicing medicine. Deep in debt, he couldn't make his mortgage payment and was about to be evicted. He couldn't meet the monthly payment on his car, and that was about to be repossessed soon, too.

"Don't cry, my friend. You can live under bridges," said Bartholomew, which only depressed the man even more.

Dimas jumped in. In an effort to console the doctor, he told part of his story, a story Bartholomew didn't know. He said his father had served twenty-five years for armed robbery. His mother soon took up with another man and abandoned the boy, just five years old at the time, and his two-year-old sister. They were sent to separate orphanages. She was adopted and they never saw each other again. Dimas wasn't adopted and grew up without a father, without a mother, without a sister, without schooling, without friends and without love, until he aged out of the system.

Bartholomew tried to console his friend:

"*Mi amigo*, I always thought you were just a crook and a cheat. I didn't really know you," he said, putting his arm on Dimas's shoulder. "You're the most normal one in the whole crazy group."

Dr. Lucas was moved by his story. The effects of the alcohol had started to wear off. They became friends, chatting for more than three hours. They left arm in arm and singing, "For Lucas is a jolly good fellow, for Lucas is a jolly good fellow . . ." They felt the pleasure of a true friendship. They understood that living outside the cocoon has its undeniable risks but also irrefutable charm.

Bartholomew and Dimas slept in a guest room at the doctor's house. His wife had heard of the social movement of "dreams," and she made them a delicious spaghetti dinner. The next day, she thanked them. It had been six months since she'd seen her husband motivated to face his life.

Dimas and Bartholomew continued their journey. At the

end of the afternoon of the second day, they found another alcoholic in a pitiful situation, slumped over the counter of the bar. Bartholomew appeared to know him. When he turned his head, he recognized him immediately. It was Barnabas, his best friend from bars and nightlife. He was well under six feet tall and weighed 242 pounds. He was always boozing and eating. Alcohol hadn't succeeded in taking away his appetite. They called him the "Mayor," as he loved to give speeches, argue about politics and come up with fanciful solutions to society's problems. He and Bartholomew were two peas in a pod.

"Honeymouth?" Barnabas yelled, almost in code because of how badly he slurred his words.

"Mayor, how good to see you!" And they embraced.

Dimas and Bartholomew took him to a park near the bar. They stayed together for hours until the alcohol had worn off. After Barnabas became a bit more lucid, he told Bartholomew:

"I've seen you in the papers. You're famous now. You're tending bar. No, no, sorry, you're playing Santa Claus, distributing free gifts, right? Cool," he said, his voice slurring, "You're one of the good guys, now. Not one of us sloppy bohemians."

"I am still the same. I just slightly changed my way of looking at things," Bartholomew said. And he took advantage of being among friends to tell a story of his own. Like Dimas, he had been in an orphanage in childhood, but for different reasons.

"My father died when I was seven, and cancer claimed my mother two years later. I was taken to an orphanage on the outskirts of the city. I stayed there till I was eighteen, then I ran away," he said.

Dimas looked at Bartholomew in surprise and said:

"Wait, don't tell me you're 'Goldfoot.'" That was Bartholomew's nickname at the orphanage because he was such a great soccer player. Bartholomew hadn't heard that name in a long time. He really looked at Dimas and recognized him, too. They both had felt they knew the other from someplace but could never quite place the face. As children, they had known each other for a year, and now, twenty years later, they had found each other again.

"That's great. A family reunion. I guess I'm the only one who doesn't have anybody," said Barnabas, feeling suddenly dizzy and holding his head in his hands, his elbows on the table.

Bartholomew felt sorry for his friend. He looked at the clock and saw they were late for the meeting with the dreamseller. He asked Dimas to go on ahead. He wanted to chat a bit with Barnabas about the new family.

Jurema and I went to speak to students in a university across town from mine. I tried to challenge their thinking. I urged them to develop the Socratic method, to develop their own social experiment and to expand the world of ideas. Everyone was impressed by Jurema's eloquence. She had more vigor and drive than they did. The students were weary, apathetic, discouraged.

Suddenly I saw two professors I recognized coming toward me, and my face immediately flushed. They were colleagues from my university who were teaching a course in that same building. They approached us, laughing. I could read their lips, saying to each other that the authoritative head of the sociology department had lost his mind.

Jurema told me, "It's time to face them. It's time to leave the cocoon."

That was the price I had to pay for being such a tyrant. One of the professors who hadn't kept up to date, a guy I thought had been a terrible teacher and thought I was too hard on him, didn't hesitate to open with, "So, how goes the life of a crazy person?"

I wanted to turn and run. But Jurema took me by the arms and tried to ease my mind.

I got myself under control, looked him in the eye, and replied:

"I'm trying to understand my madness. When I used to hide behind intellect, I thought I was completely healthy, but since now I'm a wanderer in search of myself, I know I'm sicker than I ever imagined."

They were astonished. They saw that I still had my rapid power of reasoning, but they had never seen me acknowledge an error, never seen me with any semblance of humility. They began to sheathe their swords.

I tried to explain myself, not really expecting anyone would understand.

"Do you know the essence of who you are? How many moments of real pleasure have you had today? Have you had time to relax? Have you invested in your personal projects or have you buried them? Have you behaved like intellectual giants isolated in your brilliance, or have you been men without borders who know how to share your pain? Have you been teaching machines or have you been agents who mold thinkers?"

They felt the crazy man who had wanted to commit suicide had become a better debater than the professor they had once known. One of them, Marco Antonio, a professor of sociology who was the most erudite in the department, but whose teaching methods I had always criticized, praised me:

"Julio, I've been following your work through the press and through our students. I am truly impressed by the courage it must have taken to break from your life and to reorganize it. Sooner or later everyone should take such a break to try to find himself, to rethink his story."

I told them about the dreams project. I said that it wasn't

a motivational, self-help project, but one of forming humane thinkers. It was a project to mold "a man without borders."

Professor Marco Antonio thought for a long time and confessed that he was bored with social conformity and weary of the pernicious paradox of "personal isolation versus mass interaction." I asked him to explain the paradox, as I didn't understand the full extent of his idea.

"Human beings choose to live on islands when they should be on continents. And other times, they are on continents, when they should be on islands. In other words, they should be sharing ideas and experiences to help everyone overcome frustrations. But we should be islands—individuals—when it comes to taste, lifestyle, art and culture. Television, fast food, the fashion industry all have served to homogenize our tastes and styles. We've lost our sense of individuality."

I thought to myself, "This professor's thoughts are very close to the dreamseller's." Then, he asked us how he could get acquainted with the sociological experiment of being a person without borders. And I was happy to tell him.

All the pairs returned flushed with enthusiasm. They had encountered unforeseeable tribulations but had experienced notable deeds. Deeds that did nothing to increase our bank account or our social standing but brought us back to our origins.

Some of the pairs brought with them friends whom they'd met along the way. Monica brought five model friends of hers. They were excited about parading on unfamiliar runways. Jurema and I brought two professors and two students. Dimas brought Dr. Lucas and his wife. Solomon brought his old psychiatrist, who specialized in anxiety disorders but was constantly depressed. He had been infected by his patient's happiness and wanted a dose of this social antidepressant.

Everyone spoke to each other about their simple but meaningful experiences. They spoke euphorically about the joy it had brought them to really know people who might otherwise have been just anonymous extras in the movie of life. They discovered the indescribable pleasure of contributing to someone else's story and the anonymous solidarity that came with it.

All told, thirty-eight new "strangers" were added to the group. Among them, two Orthodox Jews and two Muslims. Suddenly we noticed the absence of the most vibrant person in our group, Bartholomew. Dimas told us he was with his friend and would be along shortly.

We were so excited that we improvised the first of the project's many festivities to come. There, rich and poor, intellectuals and illiterates, Christians, Muslims, Jews and Buddhists ate, danced and spoke free of the world's prejudice. Our only goal was to share a bit of each other.

Not even Robespierre in his philosophical delirium could have imagined that the three pillars of the French Revolution— Liberty, Equality, Brotherhood—would be lived so richly by people who were so different from one another. The dreamseller, seeing our joy, told us:

"We are all different at our core: in the intrinsic fabric of our personalities, in the way we think, act, see and interpret existence. The dream of equality grows only when we respect each other's differences."

But not all the pairs had been successful. My friend Edson returned with two black eyes. He appeared to have fallen down or been punched a couple of times. We were curious to hear the story.

He told us that, after succeeding in winning over people with his selflessness and kindness, someone had offended him. He said:

"A fifty-year-old man asked me if I was familiar with the Sermon on the Mount. I said I was." Edson's voice caught in his throat. He was a little ashamed. Trying to encourage him, I asked, "But isn't that a good thing?"

"Yes, but the problem is that he asked me to recite some of the words from the sermon, which I did enthusiastically because I knew the text by heart." Edson paused again. He started to turn red. His silence provoked Dimas's question: "But isn't that wonderful?"

"Yes, but when I got to the part where we're supposed to turn the other cheek, he asked me if I believed in that. Without batting an eye, I said I did." He fell silent and blushed as the dreamseller listened closely.

"But that's wonderful, Edson," Monica told him. Edson lowered his voice.

"Yes. I mean, no. At that moment, he slapped me on the left cheek. I've never felt so much pain, or so much anger. My lips trembled, and I wanted to strangle him. But I held back."

"Congratulations," said Professor Jurema. "That was truly a miracle." But our friend's clothes were torn, his cheek was bruised and the dreamseller was suspicious.

"Why's your right eye black, too?" asked Solomon.

"After he hit me on the left, he asked me to turn and offer my right cheek. I didn't want to, but before I realized it he slapped me again. I wanted to grab the guy by the throat, but I remembered everything we've been through together. I remembered the gentle Jesus of Nazareth and the dreamseller's project. I held back. I don't know how, but I held back. He had heard of our project and he called me a 'nonsense seller.'"

People started clapping, but he asked them to let him finish his story. Because he had failed. Finally, he finished explaining what had happened:

"Then he asked me for my right cheek again. I was dripping with rage. I knew that Jesus had said to turn the other cheek, but not to turn the same cheek twice. I looked toward heaven, asked for forgiveness and started pounding the guy. But he was stronger, and he beat the hell out of me."

It was no time to laugh, but we couldn't hold back. Even the dreamseller, who didn't approve of violence, was fighting back a smile. Then he gave us an unforgettable lesson.

"Being a human being without borders doesn't mean risking your life unnecessarily. Remember that I didn't call you to be heroes. Don't provoke, much less confront, those who offend you. Turning the other cheek isn't a sign of weakness, but of strength. It's not a sign of stupidity, but of great vision."

He paused to allow us to assimilate his ideas, then continued:

"Turning the other cheek is a symbol of maturity and internal strength. It doesn't refer to the physical cheek but to the mental one. Turning the other cheek means trying to do good to someone who disappoints us, it means having the grace to praise someone who defames us, the altruism to be kind to someone who hates us. It means walking away from those looking for a fight. Turning the other cheek prevents murders, injuries and lifelong scars. The weak seek vengeance; the strong protect themselves."

Edson soaked in these words like rain to dry earth. That episode helped him take a major emotional leap forward, polished his wisdom and expanded the frontiers of his mind. He contributed greatly to our movement.

The dreamseller's words penetrated all of us like a bolt of lightning. They had such an impact that the Orthodox Jews and Muslims who were present turned and hugged each other. I looked at my friend, Professor Marco Antonio. I remembered that I had come down hard on my enemies at the university. I never learned that those who turn the other cheek are much happier, much calmer and sleep soundly at night.

Jurema whispered in my ear, "I taught for more than thirty years. But I have to admit that I produced many aggressive, vengeful, heartless students."

And I thought to myself, "So did I. Without realizing it, in the structured confines of universities, we produced dictators in the making."

A commotion broke out as I was deep in thought. Bartholomew and Barnabas had finally appeared—completely drunk. Bartholomew had been so happy at finding his old friend that he let down his guard. He knocked back a few drinks to celebrate and got drunk on vodka again.

They had their arms around each other. Their legs got tangled up as they walked, and to keep from falling down, each clung to the other. They showed up singing a Nelson Gonçalves song:

Bohemia, I'm back again, begging to rejoin you.
Crying for joy, I've come to see the friends I left behind.

As if his bingeing weren't enough, Bartholomew looked at the group and yelled out his favorite phrase: "Oh, how I love this life!"

"Shut up, Bartholomew!" we called out in chorus, laughing.

But he didn't shut up. Instead, almost falling over, he called out the dreamseller and questioned his project. His face flushed, and emboldened by everyone watching him, he said:

"Listen, chief, this whole deal about being 'humans without border,' that's old news. Real old, you know?" He tried, and failed, to snap his fingers to emphasize his point. He continued, "Alcoholics have known about that for years and years and years . . . No alcoholic is better than any other. They all kiss each other, they all hug, they all sing together. We don't have a country or a flag. You get what I'm saying?"

I watched the dreamseller. He had invested so much of his time in training us. He had had the patience of Job, and now, as his dream was becoming a reality, he had to deal with this mess. But the dreamseller just walked up to them and hugged them. And jokingly, he said, "Some people can live outside the cocoon forever. Others need to come home now and then."

And instead of being disappointed, he seconded Honey-mouth's idea.

"It's true, alcoholics are human beings without borders, especially when they're not aggressive. Why? Because in certain cases the effect of alcohol blocks the memories that hold our prejudices and our cultural, national and social barriers. But it's better and safer to achieve that goal while sober, through the difficult art of thinking and choosing."

And he began to dance among us, filled with energy. He understood that one person could not change another; it has to come from within. He knew, better than any of us, that the dangers of living outside the cocoon were many and unforesee-able.

Watching the dreamseller lovingly coach his "students" who had strayed completely, I was convinced that the greatness of a teacher lies not in how he teaches his perfect students, but in how he teaches the most difficult ones. How many crimes against teaching had I committed? I had never encouraged a rebellious student or helped one who was struggling.

I took Jurema aside and told her, "I've buried students in the basement of the educational system."

Jurema, examining her own history, had the courage to confess:

"Unfortunately, so have I. Instead of encouraging creative rebellion, intuition and thoughtful reasoning, I demanded only the 'right' answers. We molded paranoid young predators, desperate to be number one, and not peacemakers, tolerant individuals who feel worthy of being number nine or ten."

It felt like we were leaving behind our sociological infancy and entering into childhood. The celebration lasted till the early hours. We were drunk with joy. Barnabas was invited to join our team of dreamsellers, and he and Bartholomew became the most eccentric pair in the bunch. We didn't know whether they had been reformed or whether they would make us even crazier than we already were. But it doesn't matter. We, too, were learning to love this life.

CHAPTER 28

The Living Dead

THE DREAMSELLER'S FAME WAS GROWING EACH DAY AND was starting to seep into the world of finance. Businessmen and executives had heard about this unusual stranger, and because they were always eager to learn new inspiring leadership styles, they asked me to invite the dreamseller to give a lecture. They wanted to meet this man who was setting society on fire.

In my experience, the elite were only interested in three things: money, money, money. I almost told him immediately that the dreamseller wouldn't accept the invitation, but not wanting to be presumptuous, I passed along the news.

However, I was in for a surprise. After thinking about the invitation for a while, the dreamseller said he would talk to them, but in a setting of his choosing. And he gave me the address. It was a location I had never heard of. I didn't know the size of the amphitheater, whether it had air-conditioning and comfortable chairs. I only knew that his audience was used to luxurious accommodations and to getting their way.

I was told the audience would consist of close to a hundred businessmen and executives, of whom only five were women. There were entrepreneurs, bankers, owners of large construction companies, of supermarket networks, of retail chain stores and other sectors. They represented the richest and most powerful people in the state.

They were delighted that the dreamseller had accepted the invitation. But since I had always been suspicious of these people, I wanted to scare them, to tell them they had no idea what awaited them. I said that the dreamseller was so radical, he would make Lenin the communist seem ordinary. My jibe made them squirm, but I only doubled the threat. I told them that the dreamseller might call them capitalist vipers who lived to exploit the poor. They were not amused. They seemed to be rethinking the invitation, but even so, they wanted to hear this man's fascinating ideas.

The leaders received their invitations, and some found it strange that they didn't recognize the address, since they were used to attending events at the city finest venues. The night of the meeting, the dreamseller set off ahead of us. He seemed to want to meditate before the event. "Could he be preparing for battle?" I thought. "Was he asking God for the wisdom to be able to rattle these elite individuals? This is his golden opportunity to break the backs of the financial elite," I thought. But I was wrong. I had no idea that what was about to happen would leave me at a loss for words.

We didn't know the address either, so we asked around as we walked. We were nearing the address, but couldn't find the location on the dimly lit street. Eventually, we came across another group of people who seemed lost, the businessmen and executives. They thought I'd given them the wrong address. But I assured them that it was the address the dreamseller had given me. Still, I thought they might be right. Maybe he had mistakenly given us the wrong address, since he didn't run in these high-society circles and didn't know exactly where the city's amphitheaters were.

The business leaders thought they'd been fooled. But we decided to go a bit further up the street together in search of the site. Suddenly, we found ourselves at the entrance to a huge, gloomy cemetery. It was the famous Recoleta Cemetery. We checked the street number the dreamseller had given us and the numbers matched. I thought to myself, "If people thought the dreamseller was crazy before, they're sure of it now."

"I don't mind confronting my mental demons, but this is too much," Solomon said. "I hate cemeteries, especially at night. Let's get out of here."

I took his arm and asked him to stay calm. The elite participants were beginning to arrive in their luxury cars and to gather around the gates. Everyone was confused. For the first time, I humbled myself in the presence of that group, apologizing for the mistaken address.

Suddenly, just as we were about to leave, the gates of the cemetery swung open, their hinges creaking. Honeymouth clung to Angel Hand.

"I'd need a couple of bottles of vodka in me before I went in there," he said trembling.

No sooner had Bartholomew said this than a strange, terrifying figure appeared. We couldn't see its face in the inky night. But it clearly was gesturing for us to step through the gates. Inside, under gas lamps throughout the cemetery, we saw the face of tonight's speaker, the dreamseller. The address was no mistake.

All of us, disciples and businessmen alike, moved slowly and apprehensively toward a wide open area where everyone could stand. We looked at one another for answers, all thinking the same thing: "What am I doing here?" This would be the first time in history a leadership conference had been held in a cemetery. And it was appropriate. Because it would be the first time that the hurried world of the living would be discussed among the dead.

As we gathered around, the dreamseller used his deep, vibrant voice to greet the participants in an unusual manner:

"Welcome, all of you, the future rich residents of the cemetery. Please, make yourselves at home."

The businessmen's legs weakened. They were used to great competitive battles, to taking phenomenal risks, but they had never faced a challenge like this. They had been knocked out in the first round by a stranger. I didn't know what to say or how to react, and those around me were frozen. Recoleta Cemetery is imposing. It's a cemetery for the wealthy. Its mausoleums are truly works of art.

Seeing us deep in thought, the dreamseller continued to let his ideas flow.

"The notable men and women of society lie here. Dreams, nightmares, secret feelings, visible emotions, anxiety attacks, moments of rare pleasure made up the lives of each human being who rests here. Their stories sleep here, forever. And other than their loved ones, no one ever thinks about them."

We didn't know what the dreamseller was getting at, whether the conference had begun or even if there would be a conference. We only knew that his words were taking us on a journey through our own stories. That in the past of those buried here we might see our own future. His talk, which seemed intended to cause fear, began to take on an unexplainable tenderness. Then he made a request of all of us:

"Take ten minutes to read the gracious epitaphs on the front of the mausoleums."

I had never taken the time to do anything like that. Despite the failing light, we began moving through the cemetery's passageways, reading the engraved messages that celebrated the existence of people now departed. So much longing! So many inscriptions! So many words laden with noble sentiments! Some messages said, "To my kind and gentle husband, who will be greatly missed by his loving wife. May God grant him peace"; "To our beloved father: Time stole you from us, but it can never steal the love we feel for you"; "Dad, you are unforgettable. I will love you forever"; "To my irreplaceable friend: Thank you for having lived and having been part of our lives."

I don't know what happened to me when I read those messages, but I became lost in emotion. I began to remember the ones I had lost. I never wrote a plaque for my father. Nor even thanked him for giving me life. His suicide blocked out my feelings. Not even for my brave mother had I written a message, other than the one I carry silently in my mind: "I love you. Thank you for having put up with my rebelliousness."

I looked to the side and saw that my friends and the businessmen were moved. They had traveled through time, opened the doors of their subconscious and encountered their excruciating frailty. They were men who ran companies with thousands of employees, but now they were simply mortals.

At that moment, I saw that the dreamseller had stripped them of their pridefulness, shut off their defense mechanisms, removed the security they took in their financial status. When he opened his mouth, he said something every businessman hates to hear, "Where are the proletarians of today, and who are they?"

I thought to myself, "These businesspeople won't stand for this." No one answered. The question, though seemingly obvious, was not. Then he stood the theory of utopia on its head.

"You're today's proletarians," he said.

I thought: "What's he saying? Doesn't he know the audience he's talking to?" I thought the dreamseller had no idea what he was saying. But he quickly threw my thinking into a tailspin.

He said that Karl Marx (1818–1883) had left his native land and gone to Paris, where he met Friedrich Engels (1820–1895).

The two refined their ideas, joined socialist groups and initiated a lifelong collaboration. To them, the manner in which goods are produced and wealth distributed are the forces that shape all aspects of our lives: politics, law, morality and philosophy. Marx believed human history was governed by the laws of science and rejected all religious interpretations of nature and history. He thought these laws would help people, especially the working class, make their own history.

But this dream never materialized, he said. When a group of socialists seized power, they became ruthless, crushed their opponents, silenced dissenting voices, infringed on human rights and crushed the freedom they had preached. The working class did not construct its own history, rather, the ones in power wrote the history books. Religion was replaced by the cult of personality of those leaders.

"Their revolution was extreme," he said. "Unlike them, my dream isn't to destroy the ruling political system in order to rebuild it. I don't believe in change from the outside. I believe in change that begins from within, a peaceful change in our ability to reason, to see, to critique, to interpret social phenomena and, especially, to reclaim pleasure. My dream lies within people."

After he showed that he knew what he was talking about, he said that when Marx launched his ideas, the project failed not because the ruling class didn't distribute income, but because they used political and financial power to oppress the working class. A small minority lived like princes while the majority lived like paupers.

Today, he said, this separation of the classes remained. Social inequalities hadn't been eradicated. In fact, with the advent of globalization, the system had created a new class of exploited people: "You!" he emphasized again.

Again I thought, "But aren't they the privileged ones? Don't they live in the lap of luxury? How can they be called an exploited class—the proletarians of this millennium?"

But to ground his ideas, the dreamseller crushed a popular saying of ours:

"In past centuries, before the system developed, it took three generations for a family's fortune to disappear. So the old saying held true: rich grandfather, lordly son, poor grandson. But these days that saying doesn't hold up. A solid business can vanish in five years. A successful industry can be out of the market in a short time. Several fortunes over can be lost in a single generation."

After that initial shock, the businessmen began to agree with this mysterious thinker.

"For your companies to survive, you can never stop competing. To stay ahead of the competition, you are forced to find ways to reinvent yourselves each year, each month each week."

And he asked a basic question that everyone got wrong:

"Does the system crush companies that show weakness?"

Unanimously, they answered yes. But he said no.

"The system doesn't crush the *companies*. It crushes their *leaders*."

He saw that doctors, lawyers, engineers, journalists—people of all professions—were being crushed in the same way. These masters of finance began to realize they weren't as rich as they thought. These proprietors of power began to understand they weren't as strong as they imagined. Some in the audience were still skeptical. But the dreamseller loved skeptics. He could pin them down with the sharpness of his ideas. So he left no doubts:

"Ladies and gentlemen, the time of slavery has not been expunged from the pages of history but merely changed its form. I'm going to ask you some questions, and I want you to be completely honest. Anyone who isn't will have to answer to his own conscience. Tell me: Who has migraines?"

People were a bit embarrassed, but one after the other they raised their hands.

"Who has muscle aches?" Again, the vast majority raised their hands, this time more quickly.

Then he began asking countless other questions:

"Who wakes up fatigued? Whose hair is falling out? Who feels his mind is always racing? Who worries about problems that have yet to happen? Who feels like he's always hanging by a thread? Who loses his temper over the tiniest of problems? Who has wildly fluctuating emotions—calm one minute and explosive the next? Who's afraid of what the future will hold?"

Most never lowered their hands. They had all the symptoms. I couldn't believe what I was seeing. I rubbed my eyes and asked myself, "Aren't these society's elite? How can their quality of life be this terrible? Aren't they the ones who drink the best wines and champagnes? Don't they dine at the best restaurants? Why are they so gravely stressed?" I was shaken.

My mind wouldn't reconcile the two images. The rich traveled in luxury cars, but they were paralyzed by their stress. They would go to their beach houses, but their emotions didn't surf the waves of pleasure. They slept on soft mattresses but lacked the mental comfort to sleep at night. They wore the finest suits but stood naked against the worries in their lives.

"What insanity!" I thought. "Where is the happiness the system promised these people who've reached the top of their professions? Where is the peace for those who've accumulated riches? Where is the reward for competence? They take out insurance on their homes, their lives, their businesses, even against kidnapping. So how can they be so insecure?" The system, it turned out, crushed its leaders.

CHAPTER 29

Midnight in the Garden of Broken Dreams

THE DREAMSELLER'S QUESTIONS IN RECOLETA CEMETERY
sent our heads spinning. I had attacked the business elite
for years on end in my classroom, but I realized I needed to
reexamine a few concepts. I began to understand that the
system betrayed everyone, especially those who nurtured it
most. It even affected celebrities, not just because they lost
their private lives but because their success was fleeting. In this
society, it was easy to become insignificant overnight.

In the name of competition, the system sucked out their
last drop of mental energy. They expended more energy than
many manual laborers, and were constantly fatigued from an
overload of thinking. They were victors, but they didn't carry
away the ultimate prize.

The stress was even greater for companies who specialized
in production. There was an international price war, distorted
by government subsidies that contaminated the value of products, and could crush companies on the other side of the globe.
Now, add in the taxes on products coming in and out of the
country, the disparity of wages paid to workers in different
countries and the fact that some firms lowered their prices
below the cost of production to corner the market. Survival
was a hellish art.

It took its toll on everyone involved. Thirty-five percent of them had heart problems or were hypertensive. Fifteen percent had cancer, and some of those wouldn't live to see the New Year. Thirty percent suffered depression. Ten percent had panic attacks. Sixty percent had marital problems. Ninety-five percent exhibited three or more mental problems and most of those had as many as ten different mental issues.

Yes, the proletariat were still being exploited across the globe. But in developed and emerging societies, where labor laws were just and human rights were respected, the ones who were exploited were the those engaged in intense intellectual work, like managers, directors, business magnates, professionals, professors, journalists.

The oppression was so devastating that many executives took their problems home with them, even on vacation. Workers who had a decent salary but weren't in a position of leadership or management had time for friends, food, relaxation on weekends. They could go to bed and wake up without being suffocated by worry. But for the business leaders those simple pleasures were luxuries. In the best sense of the word, "the serfs lived better than the feudal lord."

It was then that I understood why the dreamseller said that success is harder to deal with than failure: The danger of success is that one can become a perpetual-motion machine. Marx and Engels would spin in their graves if they knew that the final stage of capitalism would attain the socialist dream: It would tax the elite more than the workers—physically, anyway.

Although there were exceptions. The problem for the working class was consumption: the compulsion to buy, to use credit cards, to live beyond their means. Capitalism, it turned out, made workers king and exploited the minds of those in power.

The interesting thing is that there were no statistics to tell us about this new group of exploited workers. They were apparently strong, self-sufficient demigods who needed no help, much less dreams. But they were not beings without borders; they were enslaved to this way of thinking. Aside from an annual medical checkup, nothing was done for them.

It was clear the dreamseller knew what he was talking about and to whom he was speaking, after all. But we didn't understand how he could know that. How could this ragged nomad possess that information? What kind of person is this who moves with equal ease among paupers and millionaires? Where does he come from?

Bartholomew couldn't keep quiet any longer after seeing these giants of industry admit their frailties. He raised his hand and told the dreamseller:

"Chief, these guys are in bad shape! But I think we can help them."

It was the first time in modern history that someone so poor had called members of the financial elite paupers. It was the first time that a proletarian felt richer than society's millionaires. His utterance was so spontaneous that what had been tragic turned suddenly comical. The participants looked at one another and broke out in broad smiles. They needed to buy lots of dreams if they wanted to regain their mental health.

As if the night didn't hold enough surprises, another one arose in that darkened cemetery. Suddenly, from inside a tomb about fifty feet away, a terrifying figure with an old white coat over its head emerged with a horrifying cry: "I am death! And I have come for you!"

Even the dreamseller was startled. And for the first time in my life, I truly believed in ghosts. Our hearts jumped up in our throats, and reason completely leaped out of our bodies. Some started to run for the gates, but the ghost laughed and laughed.

"Take it easy, folks. Calm down! Why so nervous? Sooner or later we'll all be sleeping in a place like this," it said.

The figure removed the coat from his head. It was that Bartholomew's worst half, Barnabas. Those two managed to make a joke wherever they were, even in a cemetery.

Every time we reached the heights of seriousness, they plunged us into wild laughter. They spoiled everything. If in the past, had they been students of mine, I'd surely have expelled them. But fortunately for them, they had found a patient teacher in the dreamseller. I didn't understand how he managed to love those two degenerates.

Seeing that the audience was still tense, Barnabas took a chocolate bar from his pocket, bit into it, and started in on a story of his own.

"I used to come to this cemetery drunk and depressed for a little self-therapy. Since the living seldom spoke to me because they thought I was drunk or crazy, and the ones who did speak to me insulted me or offered me fortune cookie advice, I'd come here to talk to the dead. Here, I could cry about my mistakes. Here, I could allow myself to be frustrated, a man who wanted to start all over, but I always failed. Here, I confessed that I felt like human refuse. Here, I asked God's forgiveness for everything: For my many drunken binges. For the 'one for the road' that left me sleeping in the park. For abandoning my family. I never had a dead person complain about my foolishness."

The businessmen were moved by Barnabas's sincerity and his willingness to share his feelings, characteristics rarely seen in their circles. They desperately needed to open up but wouldn't dare show weakness. They couldn't be human.

Hearing Barnabas confess his woes, Bartholomew took the stage again. He embraced the other man and tried to console him as only Bartholomew could.

"Don't cry, Mayor. My problems are bigger than yours. I'm immoral."

"No, mine are worse. I'm a pervert," Barnabas stated in a louder voice.

"No, my mistakes are too many to count. I'm a scoundrel," Bartholomew said in a still louder tone.

"No, no, you don't really know me. I'm completely depraved . . ."

Amazingly, they started arguing about which one was worse. The businessmen had never seen anything like it. They only ever saw people bragging about who was better. We wanted to break it up, but we were afraid of making a bigger scene. And to show he really was the worst of them, Bartholomew lost his patience and said:

"I'm corrupt, dishonest, a liar, I don't keep my word, I don't pay my bills, I covet my neighbor's wife. I've even stolen your wallet when you were drunk . . ."

"OK, stop, stop, stop!" Barnabas said. "You're right. You are the biggest good-for-nothing on the face of the earth."

"OK, wait. Now, you're exaggerating, Barnabas!" Bartholomew said, now trying to defend himself.

Watching this madness, I looked up at the stars and said softly, "God, take pity on these idiots. Please, shut them up." But the businessmen loved watching them. If anything, they wished they could express themselves so honestly and openly as those two. They had worked beside their colleagues for years—or decades—but their spirits were sealed as tightly as the tombs that surrounded them in that cemetery. In the professional world they lived outside the cocoon; in their private lives, they hid inside. They didn't know how to be a shoulder to cry on. Instead, they disguised their feelings.

"Thank you, you two," the dreamseller said to my surprise. "You've made me recall my own imperfections."

"You can count on me, chief," said Honeymouth, shooting me a look. "See that, Superego? You could learn a thing or two from me."

Then the dreamseller began another story. Many species, he stated, had physical and instinctual advantages over humans. They saw farther, ran faster, leaped further, heard better, could smell aromas a mile away and bite down with incredible force. But we had something they didn't: a sophisticated brain with more than a hundred billion cells with which to think. Such a sophisticated brain should grant independence, he offered. Nevertheless, he asked his listeners:

"So why do our brains make us dependent on others, especially as infants? Rarely can a four-year-old child survive on his own, while other mammals and lizards the same age no longer have any contact with their parents. Some creatures are already in their full reproductive phase, and others are already elderly at the age of four. Why are we more dependent than the other species, despite loving independence?" he asked.

No one spoke up. They didn't know the dreamseller was leading them into his marketplace of ideas, the warehouse where he kept his dreams.

An elderly businessman, at least seventy and apparently one of the richest in the audience, took me aside and said in a low voice, "I know that man. Where does he live?"

"You wouldn't believe me if I told you," I said, adding, "I think you must be mistaken."

"No, I know that extraordinary mind from somewhere," he insisted.

Meanwhile, another businessman of about fifty, who had gone bankrupt three times but always made socially responsible investments, answered the dreamseller's question with a single word: "Education."

"Magnificent. Education is the key!" the dreamseller said. "Our brain made us totally dependent on gathering the experience accumulated over generations of humans, from our parents to grandparents. The only way to get these experiences is through education. They're not genetically transmissible. Education is irreplaceable."

Then he shook the participants by showing them how deeply their minds were being exploited—and how they could be passing on that mental exploitation to their children.

He explained that parents too often pressured their children to compete, to study incessantly, to take courses, to prepare themselves to survive in the future, without realizing that excessive pressure annihilates the creativity of childhood. It weakens existential values, closes them to new experiences, destroys their humanity.

"Do your children know about the failures in your lives?" he asked. "Do they know how you overcame them? Do they know your fears and your worries? Do they know how courageous you've been? Have they explored your most important ideals? Do they know your philosophy on life, about your ability to reason, to analyze, to reflect? And have they seen your tears? Forgive me, but if they don't know any of this, then you're simply building machines to be used by the system. If they don't know these things, they're missing out on their humanity. And you're ignoring the very reason our brains made us dependent."

Then he said something that really unsettled the crowd.

"For just thirty seconds," he said, "put yourself in your children's place and think about the epitaphs they would write for the entrance to your tomb."

The suggestion alone sent many people into a nervous breakdown.

I would hate to know what my son would write about me. He doesn't know me. I always hid from him. "How can someone living at the edge of society carry around this knowledge? What motivates him? What secrets is he hiding?" I thought.

Finally, the dreamseller took aim at his real target.

"The capitalist system brought about, and continues to bring about, unimaginable gains for society. But it runs a serious risk of imploding in less than a century. Maybe in just a few decades. But it won't happen the way socialists imagine, through class warfare. There is a problem that lies at its core: It produces freedom of expression and possession, but not freedom of simply being. Capitalism depends on our wants, not on our needs. It depends on chronic dissatisfaction as its engine for consumption. If at some point in time humanity were composed only of poets, philosophers, artists, educators and spiritual leaders, the world's gross domestic product would collapse, because, in general, these people are more satisfied with just what is necessary. The GDP might suddenly drop thirty or forty percent. Worldwide, hundreds of millions would be unemployed. It would be the greatest depression in history. There would be wars and endless conflicts."

These arguments left some in the audience with jaws agape. The businessmen hadn't thought of that. But then, he started to sell the dream of relaxation.

"Getting back to the symptoms I asked you about, I'm going to ask one more question, and if you answer collectively I'll invite you to open a psychiatric hospital."

The audience actually laughed.

"Who among you is forgetful? Who has memory lapses?"

Almost everyone raised his hand. They would forget commitments, everyday information, telephone numbers, where they had put items, people's names.

"Some people are so forgetful that they put their car keys in the refrigerator and look for them all over the house," he said casually. People laughed. And he went on: "Even funnier are the ones who look for their glasses without realizing they're wearing them. Others forget the names of colleagues they've worked with for years. The cleverest would ask, 'Say, what's your *full* given name?' when in reality they didn't even remember their first name."

Some of the businessmen chuckled because they had used that tactic. I suspect that even the dreamseller had used it.

"Ladies and gentlemen, for those everyday memory lapses, don't go to a doctor. Why not, you ask?" he asked.

"Because he's forgetful himself!" yelled out an older man wearing a blue suit and striped gray tie.

They shook their heads at their own stressful lives. They were beginning to understand that the memory lapses, in most cases, were a desperate attempt by the brain to reduce the avalanche of worries.

Bartholomew had raised both hands, indicating that he was super forgetful.

"Chief, how come I always used to forget the names of my mothers-in-law?"

Sometimes we couldn't stand him. Barnabas, who had known him for years, jabbed back:

"Bartholomew's been married three times and lived with seven other women. He hasn't had enough time to learn their names to begin with."

Honeymouth looked at the audience and opened his hands, as if to say, "I never said I was a saint." As hard as he tried, for better or worse, he just couldn't be normal

"I didn't choose you because of your failures or your successes," the dreamseller told him, "but because of who you are, because of your heart."

"I'm forgetful myself, Bartholomew," the dreamseller continued. "Some people tell me, 'Teacher, my memory's lousy.' And I tell them, 'Don't worry, mine's even worse.'"

I was forgetful, too, but I never would allow my students the same courtesy. I was a tyrant when it came to correcting exams. I recalled Jonathan, a brilliant debater, who nevertheless couldn't put the information down on paper. The other professors and I consistently gave him failing grades. Eventually, he failed out. We had called him irresponsible, but he might have been a misunderstood genius. We were the voice of the system. We tossed potential thinkers in the trash bin of education without a trace of remorse. Only now, after I learned to buy dreams of a free mind, did I realize I should have been evaluating my students' minds. And that might have meant giving the highest grades to someone who gets all the answers wrong.

I felt helpless and heartbroken at seeing all my shortcomings laid bare. I had been unforgiving even with my son. John Marcus suffered from mild dyslexia and couldn't keep up with his classmates. But I kept the pressure on, asking for more than he could give. If I'm being honest with myself, I wanted him to be an outstanding student in order to enhance my image as father and professor. Any message my son or my students would leave at my tomb wouldn't be one of praises and longing.

Jurema seemed to understand what I was thinking. She touched my shoulder and said quietly:

"Alexander Graham Bell said that if we tread the path that others have taken, at best we'll arrive at the places they've already been. If we don't sell new ideas so that students take new paths, they may end up right where these businessmen and -women are today, with ravaged health and broken dreams."

One by one, the businessmen left, carefully observing the mausoleums they passed. Some of them remembered that from the sixteenth to the nineteenth century an inhuman system had bought and sold black-skinned human beings as if they were animals, locked them in the holds of boats and shipped them off to a terrifying future. Left behind were their friends, their children, their spouses, their freedom.

Today, the system had created a new, erudite slave. It paid them high salaries and gave them health benefits. Their future promised an endless crush of stress, anxiety, dog-eat-dog competition and forced mental labor. Left behind were their children, their spouses, their friends, their dreams. As the dreamseller said, history loves to repeat itself.

CHAPTER 30

A House Divided

THE DREAMSELLER'S LATEST CONFERENCES, ESPECIALLY THE one at Recoleta Cemetery, were all over the media. People noted that even the giants of industry had been seduced by this enigmatic wanderer. The same questions that kept me up nights flooded their minds.

Some said he was the greatest imposter of our time. Others said he was a thinker far ahead of his time. Some argued that he was destroying peace in our society, while others said he was its most ardent defender. Some called him an atheist. Others, a vessel of unfathomable spirituality. Some believed he came from another planet, while others said he was the most human of us all. Maybe it was a mix of all of those things—or none of them at all. Discussing the dreamseller's identity was the topic du jour in bars, restaurants, coffee shops and even in schools. And the discussions were heated.

The more his fame grew, the more difficult his mission became. He neither gave interviews nor announced the following day's schedule. Even so he was in the news every time he spoke. When we got angry at the coverage that distorted his ideas, he would calm us down by saying, "There is no free society without a free press. The press makes mistakes, but silence the press and society will plunge into an endless night without light. It will have a mind without voice."

He couldn't go anywhere without being photographed. The dreamseller didn't appreciate being a celebrity and he was considering moving to another city or country. He thought of selling dreams in the Middle East, Asia, anyplace where people would see him as a mere mortal.

It was no longer possible to hold discussions in small venues. He was a magnet for crowds. Often hundreds would gather spontaneously to hear him speak. He would have to raise his voice, and even so, those farthest away in the crowd couldn't make out his words. His teaching was passed by word of mouth. He didn't like holding discussions in closed amphitheaters or using multimedia, preferring to speak outdoors. He liked that anyone who didn't agree with his ideas could freely and easily leave.

Companies wanted to sponsor him just to associate their image with his. They wanted their marketing to show they, too, were bold, innovative, unpredictable. The very idea of it sent shivers down the dreamseller's spine. After his refusing countless gifts and offers of money for the use of his image, something unusual happened. Several well-dressed representatives of the powerful Megasoft Group approached us individually, without the dreamseller present, to make what they thought was a lucrative offer.

They first contacted Solomon and Dimas and me. They started out praising the dreamseller's social work effusively. Society had become more unified, kinder and more human since he had come onto the scene, they told us.

"We know that humility guides his life, that he hates fame, but we want to surprise him with an homage to all that he's done for society," they said. "This tribute won't be about giving him any kind of prize or money—we know he would never accept material goods. But we'd like to show our appreciation by offering to let him use the city's largest covered stadium, which our group owns, so he could address more than fifty thousand people all at once. His sermon would be televised, and later rebroadcast as a special prime-time event, to the entire country. Millions would get to hear his message."

We were excited but suspicious about the offer. Still, the leaders of the business group seemed to have the purest of intentions. To seduce us further, they told us:

"Please don't deny us or society this privilege. Everyone wants and needs to hear the dreamseller's wisdom. His words could help save countless anguished people thinking of suicide, using drugs, wracked by their own demons. We insist on honoring him and giving the people of this country this gift. The only thing we ask is that it be a surprise."

The entire group decided we should talk over this delicate matter. After reflecting on the proposal and analyzing the benefit to society, we felt it could be a good thing. After all, millions could be reached. Honeymouth and Barnabas were quite excited about that. Jurema was the only one who wasn't sold on the idea, she of all people, who still owned Megasoft shares. But she finally gave in.

We had to set up a secret plan to get the dreamseller to the stadium at the appointed date and time. That day, as we walked closer to the stadium, we could see traffic snarled in all directions and hundreds of people pouring through the main gates. When we came to a private entrance to the stadium, the dreamseller found it all strange and asked, "Why do we have to come to this place?" And he seemed nervous.

Since we couldn't say anything about the tribute, we asked him to trust us and go along with our request. We told him we were going to a show, but when he continued asking questions, we backed him into a corner.

"Throughout all our time together, you've asked countless

things of us and we've always obliged. Just this once, can't you go along with what we're asking?"

We knew it was a kind of blackmail, especially since the dreamseller had always listened to us and supported us. Still, he followed us without saying another word.

When we were about to enter the VIP room, he asked apprehensively, "Who set up the event?"

"Some people who really care about you. Wait and see," we said, without offering anything further.

The Megasoft executives were in a separate room, preparing the event. We found ourselves in a green room with a lavish buffet of fruits, cold cuts and juices. But the dreamseller didn't eat anything. He seemed to turn inward to reflect. The rest of ate ravenously.

Barnabas stuffed a handful of seedless grapes in his mouth and muttered almost incomprehensibly, "These guys are the best!"

Bartholomew, with three slices of salami and two of ham in his mouth, babbled, "I'm starting to like those businessmen," then immediately started humming to cover up what he'd said. We tried in vain to shush them.

The dreamseller sensed something in the air. He fidgeted and looked to the sides, uneasy, as if wishing he could go off alone and meditate. A long twenty minutes passed. When the time for the conference finally arrived, three glamorously dressed young women led us to the stage. The dreamseller trudged unusually slowly down the corridors. He seemed out of sorts.

Before directing us to our seats, the organizers of the event, wearing perfectly tailored suits, came to greet us. They greeted the dreamseller last.

They were five executives and the last one appeared to be the leader, maybe the CEO of one of the firms in the group. He shook the dreamseller's hand and, in a joking tone, said, "Welcome to the stadium. And thank you for your delirious ideas. Great men have great dreams."

The dreamseller, who was always in a good mood, usually never cared if someone called his dreams a delirium. But he just aimed a penetrating stare deep into the executive's eyes. The man was immediately flustered.

Until that moment, the dreamseller might have believed we would be attending a show.

The organizers took their seats to the right of the stage, and we sat on the left.

High on the stage was a huge screen, twenty-six feet tall and fifty-five feet wide. Other screens were scattered around the stadium. The master of ceremonies for the event appeared onstage, wearing a dark suit. He didn't mention the names of the executives or the sponsor. He did everything simply, as he should. In a resonant voice, he began to introduce the dreamseller. The immense crowd fell silent.

"Ladies and gentlemen, it is our great pleasure to present to you the most complex and innovative person to appear in our society in recent decades. A man with no marketing team, money or credit cards, and without revealing his origin or academic background, has spread his sensitivity and altruism throughout society. He has achieved a prestige that many have not. He has achieved a fame that is the envy of celebrities. He is truly a social phenomenon!"

At that moment, echoing his words, the crowd interrupted the presentation to applaud the dreamseller. We looked at the dreamseller and could see he wasn't happy. He, who always felt at ease wherever he was, who had a superb ability to adapt to the most diverse settings, seemed uncomfortable with the praise. But there was no denying that he was a social phenomenon. We followed him because he was an exceptional person. The master of ceremonies continued:

"Children and adults alike follow him. Icons of society and the common man listen to him. This man leaves political liberals speechless and conservatives amazed. For months we've been intrigued. The media, the authorities and even the man on the street asks: Where did he come from? What were the most important chapters in his story? Why does he seek to rock the pillars of society? What is his objective? We don't know. He calls himself only a seller of dreams, a merchant of ideas in a society that has ceased to dream."

After defining the indefinable man that we followed, he called the dreamseller to the stage with a wink and a smile, and a joke that put the audience at ease. "And now, I give you the seller of *nightmares*!"

It was then that the dreamseller realized this event had been staged in his honor. He rose awkwardly from his chair and headed for center stage. It was an emotional sight to see the crowd applauding him at length. We, his disciples, fell into step with them, and clapped wildly, emotionally. In turn, as he walked, I could see his lips moving, and he seemed to be telling himself, "I don't deserve this . . . I don't deserve this . . ." A microphone was quickly attached to his lapel while the applause continued.

It was a sight to behold. And a little unbelievable to know that a man in an old black coat with patched elbows and a wrinkled yellow shirt, an unshaven man with long unkempt hair who spoke in public yet craved anonymity, could be so loved. The applause died down and the audience awaited his words.

Onstage, he looked over at the event's organizers, but said nothing to them. Instead, he took a couple of unsteady steps and, staring out at the crowd, began with these words:

"Many kneel before kings because of their power. Or before millionaires because of their money. Or before celebrities because of their fame. But I humbly bow down to you, because I'm not worthy of your praise."

The stadium crowd went crazy. People rose to their feet again and applauded. They had never seen an honoree solemnly honor the audience in attendance. He waited silently for the applause to die down before he continued. But as he was about to resume, the emcee interrupted.

"Ladies and gentlemen, before this mysterious and intelligent man graces us with his magnificent words, we would like to pay tribute to everything he has done for society," he said.

We were confused. We thought the introduction had ended. The emcee looked at the dreamseller and asked him to kindly remain on center stage to watch an unusual film that had begun playing on the enormous stadium screen. At the same time, they cut off his microphone.

When the film began, we were expecting scenes of the countryside, flowers, valleys and mountains as tribute to the dreamseller. But the film didn't show springtime, rather the rigors of winter. And not a physical winter, but rather a harsh winter of the mind.

The film opened with the camera lens stepping through the main entrance of a large and rundown hospital. We could read that it was a mental institution, one of the few left in the region. The outer brown walls were peeling and cracks throughout the ancient structure formed odd horizontal fissures. The building was three stories high, a rectangular prison unlike the human mind, which revels in free forms and defies predictability. Instead, the building forebode claustrophobia and sadness.

The camera dove into the hospital and panned to different mental patients, some talking to themselves, others with trembling hands, some staring vacantly from the effects of drugs. The camera continued down hallways and revealed other patients sitting on uncomfortable benches with their gazes fixed on infinity or with their heads between their legs.

That the movie had no audio track and was deathly silent

only added to the cold feel. We found it all extremely strange. The camera seemed to be handheld, and we figured whoever took this film must have been some kind of amateur. From time to time, the film cut to a live shot of the dreamseller's face. He looked worried, disconcerted. We couldn't imagine what was running through his mind, whether he was more confused than we were or whether he understood something about this tribute that we failed to grasp. Maybe he was feeling the pain of the patients in that hospital. And maybe the film would later show him showering that dreary place with his dreams.

Suddenly sound burst from the film as if someone had released the mute button. The entire stadium jumped, as if watching a horror movie, and they were startled to hear someone screaming from inside a room, "No! No! Get away from me!"

A desperate mental patient was moaning on the other side of a closed door. The camera moved in as the door opened slowly. A patient rocked back and forth on a bed, covering his face with his hands and tearfully calling out, "Leave me alone! Get out of my life!"

The patient was wracked with uncontrollable anxiety, trying to flee from the monsters haunting his mind. He continued covering his face with his hands and rocking back and forth, like an autistic child. He was wearing a rumpled white shirt with its buttons in the wrong holes and his hair was disheveled.

The person filming him asked, "What's making you depressed?"

The sound was muffled, but possible to make out:

"I'm scared! I'm scared! Help me! My children are going to die! Help me get them out of this place!" he moaned, panting, overwhelmed by unfathomable panic.

The one filming him repeated the question. "I'm here to help you. Calm down. Why are you so worried?"

Shaken, he replied, "I'm inside a house that's collapsing, a house that's fighting against itself." Then the hallucinating patient spoke to the entities only he could see and hear. "No, no don't destroy yourself! I'll be buried alive! You're suffocating me!"

The people in the stadium fell into a suffocating silence. We, too, felt our throats tighten. The patient said that the house itself was beginning to fight ferociously against itself. We were confused by the film. No one understood anything. We had never heard of a house battling itself. It was the height of insanity. We couldn't understand why the filmmaker would record this patient's mental breakdown. Maybe the dreamseller would come along and rescue him later in the film?

"Tell me what you see," the cameraman asked.

Still covering his face, the patient's voice trembled:

"The roof is screaming, '*I'm* the most important part of this house! *I* protect it. I and *I alone* can withstand the sun and the storms . . .'"

The filmmaker wanted to know more about the hallucinations.

"Tell me more. The more you let out, the better you'll feel," the cameraman said.

The patient began to shake and writhe in fear.

"The paintings! The paintings on the wall are shouting back!" he roared. "They complain and complain and won't stop!"

"What do they say?"

"*We're* the most important things in this house! *We're* the most expensive, the most precious thing you have! Everyone who comes through the door admires *us*!" the patient said. He broke out in a cold sweat and begged for the voices to stop yelling.

"Get out of my head! Leave me alone!"

At that moment, I remembered myself on top of the San Pablo Building. As much as I might have been suffering, I hadn't lost my mind; I hadn't been seized by hallucinations; I hadn't felt like a man trapped inside a dungeon his mind had created. I, who had been ready to kill myself, couldn't imagine the pain and suffering of this young man, who had fallen into the darkness of madness. His suffering sent shivers through the audience.

Monica, who had experienced the valleys of emotional misery in her own life, said, in a frightened, almost inaudible voice, "What could make the human mind collapse like this, to make it reach the depths of despair?"

The suffering shown on the screen was so great and so captured our attention that some of us forgot why we were there. The dreamseller remained on center stage, his back to us, his gaze fixed on the screen. I couldn't imagine what he was feeling. He must have been sharing the same sadness we all were.

The patient turned his face into the corner and said, "No one understands me! All they do is give me drugs!" He continued talking about his hallucinations. The furniture, he said, wanted to cannibalize other parts of the house. He shouted: "The furniture wants to swallow the paintings. It's yelling at them! It's saying, '*We're* the most important parts of this house! We give comfort and add beauty!'"

I looked over at the executives of the Megasoft Group and saw them smiling. I thought to myself: "How can they smile in the face of such pain? Maybe they know the movie has a happy ending. I mean, otherwise, they're psychopaths . . ."

The macabre film continued as the young patient wrestled with other parts of the house fighting all around him. Now, an imposing, domineering voice was shaking the patient's crumbling home. The cameraman, interested in capturing the smallest details of his mental break, asked again, "Who is it that's upsetting you?"

The patient turned his back to the camera, removed his hands from his face, and placed them against the wall. His lungs fought desperately for air. The rise and fall of his shirt

betrayed his panting. The cameraman persisted, without soft-
ening his tone: "Talk to the monsters inside you! I'm offering
you the chance to exorcize your demons."

The patient fell back into his initial terror.

"I'm afraid! I'm afraid!" he screamed. "Now it's the safe!
The safe is threatening to destroy everything. It's threatening
to devour the entire structure. It roars like thunder. '*I'm* the
one who pays for everything. I'm the one that bought all of you.
I brought you into existence. Bow down before me! *I* am the
god of this house!'"

The patient panted like an asthmatic. I thought at any moment he would have a heart attack. I had never seen anyone so
weakened, someone so much in need.

At that moment, trying desperately to escape his prison, the
patient turned his face to the camera and screamed hopelessly,
"We're going to be buried alive! I'm scared! So scared! Help,
please! Everything's tumbling down!"

The camera zoomed in on the young patient's uncovered
face for the first time. His panicked expression filled the gigantic stadium screen. And when we saw his face, it wasn't
his house that we saw come tumbling down; it was our whole
world. The floor seemed to shake beneath us, our bodies trembled. Our voices caught in our throats. We were paralyzed in
our seats. The scene was unbelievable, surreal. The patient in
the film was . . . the dreamseller.

Outside, I was frozen. But inside, my mind was a storm. My
inner voice screamed, "This isn't possible! We've been following a mental patient, a maniac? This can't be!" The sociological experiment shattered into a million little pieces. We'd been
fooled. Our revolutionary leader showed his damaged, fragile
form. I couldn't tell whether I felt rage for letting myself follow
this man, or compassion for the misery he had suffered. I didn't
know whether to feel sad or ashamed.

The audience was astounded. Like me, they couldn't bring themselves to believe that the person on stage was the same one in the movie. But the resemblance was unmistakable, despite our dreamseller's longer beard. My friends grabbed each other's arms, trying to shake themselves awake from a dream they wished they had never dreamed.

The event's emcee, so as to leave no lingering doubts, had them turn the dreamseller's microphone back on and asked him, as if he were facing an Inquisition, "Sir, can you confirm that the man in the film is you?"

The audience of tens of thousands fell into a deafening silence. We were hoping against all hope that he would say no. That there was some mistake, that it was a lookalike or maybe a twin brother. But, true to his conscience, he turned to the crowd, fixed his gaze on his group of friends with tears in his eyes and said unequivocally, "Yes, it's me. That man from that movie is me."

Immediately, his microphone was cut off again. But the dreamseller didn't try to defend himself.

"A *mental* patient," the announcer scoffed, shaking his head.

"Ladies and gentlemen," he said, turning to the television cameras and now speaking in a high and mighty tone. "We have finally discovered the true identity of the man who plunged this great city into disarray. This is the man who captured the imaginations of millions. Indeed, he is truly a great social phenomenon."

Sweeping his hand toward the lonely dreamseller at the center of the stage, he said, sarcastically, "Behold: The greatest imposter of all time. Society's greatest con man. The greatest swindler, the greatest illusionist and the greatest heretic of the century. And to show our gratitude, we confer on him the title of the greatest seller of lunacy, of nightmares, of trash and falsehood and stupidity that this society has ever produced."

A lightning storm of flashes erupted. A stunningly beautiful model walked up to him and handed him a diploma. The organizers had planned everything down to the tiniest, insulting detail.

Incredible as it seems, the dreamseller didn't refuse it. Instead, he graciously accepted the scroll. We, his disciples, were perplexed. The audience was frozen. No one in the stadium dared say a word.

The muscles of my face as well as my ability to reason were paralyzed. My mind was roiling with questions: Had all the ideas we'd heard, ideas that had so swept us away, come from the mind of a psychotic? How is that possible? What had I done to my life? Had I dived into a sea of dreams or of nightmares? Had I been saved from a physical suicide only to suffer an intellectual one?

CHAPTER 31

Psychotic or Sage?

A FTER REVEALING THAT THE DREAMSELLER WAS, IN FACT, the young, tormented psychiatric patient from the film, the event organizers turned to us smugly, as if to say that we had been the biggest fools of all. They seemed to want revenge. "But for what?" I wondered. What was behind this ambush? Why destroy a man's image so publicly? Why so much hate for a seemingly harmless human being?

Only later did we find out that one of the dreamseller's speeches was to "blame" for the plummeting stock price of the La Femme fashion giant, part of the Megasoft conglomerate. Prices fell immediately after the dreamseller recommended emphatically, in the "temple of fashion," that designer labels should carry a warning that beauty cannot be standardized, that every woman has her own particular beauty, and that women should never identify with models who represented a genetic exception in the human race.

The real problem started when the CEO of the fashion giant— one of the organizers of the event—wrote an op-ed saying these were nothing more than the ramblings of a lunatic. And if attacking a humble man weren't enough, he finished his thought with a quote that showed the depth of the Barbie syndrome: "With apologies to all the ugly girls, beauty is important." The statement had circled the globe, not only in newspapers but also on the Internet, generating heated debates in the media and producing a chain reaction of repudiation on the firm. Thousands had sent messages to the countless La Femme stores around the world opposing its philosophy. The company's stock fell by thirty percent in two months, a loss of more than a billion and a half dollars. It was catastrophic for the company.

Revenge, which exists only in the human species, reared its ugly head. Unmasking the man who had caused all the damage became a question of honor for the leaders of the company, a matter of survival. They wanted to publicly unmask the dreamseller to discredit his ideas and regain their credibility.

We didn't know where to hide in the stadium. We'd lost our courage, our adulation and our enthusiasm. I who had learned to love the dreamseller now couldn't find the energy to defend him. Now I understood the pain in John Lennon's famous phrase after the Beatles broke up: *The dream is over.*

"Our movement is dead," I thought, and figured the rest of the group felt the same way. But I was surprised by Monica and Jurema's defiant attitude.

"It doesn't matter if the dreamseller was or is psychotic," they said. "We were with him through the applauses and we'll be with him through the jeers."

"Were women stronger than the men?" I wondered. I don't know, but I do know that they displayed an irrational idealism. Then, two of the men stood up in solidarity,

"If the chief's crazy, then I'm crazy, too!" Bartholomew yelled out.

Not to be outdone, Barnabas stood up emphatically.

"I don't know if he's crazy, but I do know he made me feel like a person again. And I won't abandon him now. You know what? *I'm* crazier than the dreamseller," he said, then added, "But not as crazy as you, Honeymouth."

"Thank you, my friend," Bartholomew replied, feeling flattered.

The dreamseller turned to leave and headed for the exit when the crowd started buzzing. We thought they might rush the stage to lynch him, and then, suddenly, they broke out in a chant that soon filled the stadium.

"Speak . . . ! Speak . . . ! Speak . . . !"

The chant reverberated throughout the stadium until the entire building shook with nervous energy. The executives looked worried. The last thing they wanted was to start a riot that would give them more bad front-page press. So they turned his microphone back on and gestured for him to return to the stage and speak. Doubtless, they figured the dreamseller would crush what was left of his image by trying to worm his way out with superficial explanations and accusations. But clearly, they didn't know the depth of this man they were so eager to discredit.

He looked out at the audience, and then at us, his disciples. He gently raised his voice and, without fear of repercussions, he dissected his own history the way a microsurgeon does with the tiniest of blood vessels.

Softly, he told us his story, the most dramatic one I'd ever heard. Except that this time it was no parable; it was his true story, raw and uncensored. For the first time, the man I had followed exposed the very depths of his being. And I realized that I hadn't known him fully, either.

"Yes, I was mentally ill, or maybe I still am. I'll leave that for the psychiatrists and psychologists, and all of you, to judge. I was committed to an institution because I was suffering from a deep and severe depression accompanied by mental confusion and hallucinations. My depression was fed by a crippling feeling of guilt. Guilt over the indescribable mistakes I'd made with people I loved the most."

He paused for breath. He seemed to be trying to rebuild his dismembered being, to organize his thoughts in order to tell his shattered story. "What mistakes did the dreamseller make that unbalanced him?" I wondered. "Wasn't he strong and generous? Didn't he demonstrate the height of camaraderie and tolerance?" To our surprise, he declared:

"I was a rich man, very rich, and powerful, too. I was more successful than anyone else of my generation. Young and old alike came to seek my advice. Every venture I touched turned to gold. They called me Midas. I was creative, bold, intuitive— a visionary, unafraid of uncharted territory. My ability to absorb a failure and come back stronger astounded everyone around me. But gradually the success I always thought I controlled came to control me, to poison me, to invade the intimate reaches of my mind. Without realizing it, I lost my humility and became a god—a false god."

We were stunned by his words. I wondered, "Could he really have been rich? What kind of power did he have? Or is he hallucinating again? Didn't he walk around in tattered clothes? Didn't we depend on the kindness of others just to survive?"

At hearing the dreamseller's admission, Bartholomew became emboldened.

"Aha, *that's* my chief! I knew it! I knew he was a millionaire," Bartholomew said. Then, scratching his head, asked, "Wait, then why were we always so broke?"

There was no good explanation. "Maybe, like so many businessmen, he went bankrupt," I thought. "But could financial ruin trigger such a serious mental illness? Could it break someone's sanity and plunge him into the realm of madness?" My thoughts were interrupted when he continued his account.

"My only goal was to stand out, to compete, to be number one, as long as it meant playing by the rules," the dreamseller confessed. "I didn't want to be just another face in the crowd.

I wanted to be unique. And so, I became a machine, tirelessly dedicated to success and making money. The problem doesn't start when we possess money, however much we have. It starts when the money possesses us. When I realized this had happened to me, I saw that money could, in fact, impoverish a man. And I became the poorest of men."

I was flabbergasted at seeing this man, who had supposedly been so rich and powerful, remove his mask and become an unflinching critic of himself. I tried and failed to think of any leader in history who had ever spoken so courageously. I looked at myself and realized that I, too, lacked such bravery. His bold words began to invigorate me. My admiration for this man was being rekindled. Then, he told the story of how he, his wife and their two children were scheduled to go on an ecotourism vacation with friends to see one of the planet's few remaining great rain forests.

But, for him, time was a scarce commodity, he said. So he planned the trip months in advance. Everything was set, but at the last minute, he was asked to participate in a video conference with some of the company's investors. Vast sums of money were involved. His family and friends postponed the trip by a day to wait for him. The next day, he had to quickly resolve a business matter that had been dragging for months: He had to sign off on the purchase of another large company or lose it to his competitors. Hundreds of millions of dollars were at stake. The trip was postponed again. On the day they were finally set to travel, the board of directors of his petroleum firm presented him with a new problem. More make-or-break decisions had to be made.

"So as not to put off the trip again, I apologized to my wife, my children and our friends and told them to go on without me. I would charter a flight later and meet them there," he said, his voice beginning to crack. "My wife didn't like the idea.

My seven-year-old daughter, Julieta, was sad, but she kissed me and said, 'You're the best daddy in the world.' Fernando, my loving nine-year-old son, also kissed me and said, 'You're the best father in the world—but the busiest, too.' I answered, 'Thank you, children, but someday Daddy will have more time for the greatest kids in the world.'"

The dreamseller heaved a deep and heavy sigh. "But that time would never come . . ." He paused and started to cry. In a choked voice, overcome with emotion, he told the audience:

"While I was in the middle of a meeting, hours after they had taken off, my secretary rushed in to say there had been a plane crash. My heart started to pound. I turned on the news and heard that an airliner had crashed into a dense tropical rain forest . . . and there did not appear to be any survivors. It was the flight they were on. I collapsed to the ground and cried inconsolably. I had lost everything. There was no air to breathe, no ground to walk on, no reason to live. Between tears and pain, I put together a rescue mission, but we never found my wife and children's bodies; the plane had burned to a cinder. I couldn't even say good-bye to the most important people in my life, to look into their eyes or touch their skin. It was as if they'd never existed."

Overnight, the man so many had envied became the object of pity, the indestructible man became the most fragile of beings. And to add to his indescribable pain, he was tortured by guilt.

"The psychologists who treated me wanted to ease my guilt. They tried to tell me I wasn't responsible for the loss. But I knew, indirectly, I was. They tried to protect me instead of making me face the monster of my guilt. But they couldn't ease my desire to punish myself. They were good doctors, good men, but I resisted and closed myself up in my own world."

Still reading out from the chapters of his past life for the audience, he began asking himself aloud:

"What did I build? Why didn't I prioritize what I loved the most? Why did I never have the courage to cut back on my schedule? When is it time to slow down? What is so important that it is more important than life itself? If you lose that, what does it matter if you have all the money in the world?"

What an unbearable burden. What colossal pain. As I listened to him, I began to understand that all of us, however successful, we all miss out on something. The warm sun sets on us all, no one sails forever on tranquil seas. Some lose more, others less; some suffer avoidable losses, others unavoidable. Some lose in the social arena, others in the theater of the mind. And if someone manages to get through life untouched, there is still something he loses: youth. I was a man of losses and I continued to be an expert in losses. But suddenly, recalling the last few months we had been together, I was startled. This man has lost everything in front of the entire world. How did he manage to dance? Why was he the happiest of wanderers? Why did he manage to always put us in a good mood? How did he manage to be so tolerant when life had been so unfair to him? How could he lead such a gentle life after having been the victim of such a brutal tragedy?

As I was pondering these questions, I glanced at the organizers of the event and saw they were visibly shaken; it seems they didn't know the true identity of the man they had mocked. I looked out at the crowd and saw people crying. They might have felt compassion for the dreamseller or, perhaps, some were recalling losses in their own lives. At that point Jurema squeezed my hands and told me something that surprised me even more.

"I know that story. It's *him*!" she said.

"Him, who? What are you saying, professor?" I asked, even more confused.

"It's him! The sergeants have laid an ambush for their own

general. How is it possible?" Jurema was so worked up that she wasn't making any sense.

"I don't understand. Who is the dreamseller?" I asked again.

She stared at the leaders who had organized the event and said something that floored me.

"Incredible. He's standing on the very stage that belongs to him," she said and could say nothing more.

My mind went into a tailspin, like a kite cut free of its string. Repeating her last sentence—"He's standing on the very stage that belongs to him"—I began to understand what Jurema meant.

"I don't believe it! *He*'s the owner of the powerful Megasoft Group? The sergeants laid a trap for their own general, thinking he was just a soldier. Could it be? But isn't he dead? Or had he just gone into hiding? Then again, the dreamseller had severely criticized the leader of the Megasoft Group at dinner at Jurema's home. We must be dreaming!" I thought.

A film began to unreel in my mind. It struck me that the dreamseller had involved himself in many events linked to that corporation. He had rescued me at the San Pablo, a building belonging to the Megasoft Group. And mysteriously, they almost shot him at that same building. He had been beaten at the temple of computing, apparently at the behest of an executive of that same group, and had kept silent. A reporter from a newspaper owned by that group had slandered him, and he had said nothing. Now he was humiliated by leaders of the same corporation and hadn't rebelled. What was going on? What did it all mean?

I took a deep breath, trying to bring order to my whirlwind of ideas. I brought my hands to my face and told myself, "This can't be true! Or is it? No, it can't be! We're experts at making up facts when we're under stress." I took Jurema's arm and asked:

"How can one of the most powerful men on the planet sleep under bridges? How can a billionaire eat other people's leftovers? It makes no sense!" The professor shook her head; she was as upset and confused as I was.

Just then, the dreamseller seemed to be answering the questions on all our minds. He said his losses had been so great, his suffering so deep, that he began to lose all rational thought. He said he couldn't organize his ideas. He refused to eat and finally had to be committed to a psychiatric hospital. At the hospital, he began hallucinating just as we saw on the video. His brain seemed ready to implode.

In a firmer tone, he revisited the story that the organizers had used to destroy him publicly. He spoke of the second part, surely unknown to them.

"After the roof, the safe and other structures in that house fought against each other to claim supremacy, I heard another area of the house making itself known. But this time it was a soft, gentle, humble voice. It was a voice whispering beneath the ground, and it didn't terrify me."

Looking out at the audience, the dreamseller stated:

"It was the voice of the foundation. Unlike all the other parts of that mansion, the foundation didn't want to be the greatest, the best, or the most important. It wanted merely to be recognized as part of the whole."

I strained to understand what the mysterious man was trying to reveal, but it was difficult. But then it started to be come clear.

"When I heard the voice of the foundation, all the other parts of the house condemned it vehemently. The safe was first. Bursting with pride, it said, 'You're an embarrassment to us. You're the dirtiest part of this house.' The conceited roof said, 'No one who has ever entered this house has even ever asked about you. You're completely unnoticed.' The beautiful paintings declared arrogantly, 'You're ridiculous to suggest you have any worth, at all. Just accept your lowly role.' The furniture was adamant: 'You're insignificant. Just look where you're located.' And so the foundation was rejected by all the other structures of the home. Humiliated, shunned and without any way to go on being part of that building, it decided to leave. And what do you think the result was?" he asked the crowd.

They all answered as one, even the children in the stadium: "The house collapsed!"

"Yes, the house caved in. My house, which represents my personality, caved in because I dismissed my foundation. When it collapsed, I shouted at God: 'Who are you, and where were you when my world collapsed? Do you not intervene because you don't exist? Or do you exist and you simply just don't care about humanity?' I fought with the psychiatrists and psychologists. Fought with their theories and medications. I fought with life. I thought it so unjust to me, nothing more than a bottomless well of uncertainties. I fought with time. In short, I fought with everything and everyone. But when the foundation made itself heard, I was heartened, enlightened. And I understood that I had been profoundly wrong. More than anything else, I had fought with my own foundation. I had cast aside my values, my priorities."

Hearing that explanation, we finally began to comprehend some of the secrets of this fascinating dreamseller.

He started to understand himself when he was able to interpret his hallucinations. The safe, he said, represented his financial power, which he had always valued. The roof was a metaphor for his intellectual capacity, which he had prized greatly for helping him overcome so many difficult tasks. The works of art represented his prestige and fame, and the furniture, all the luxuries and comforts in life.

"But I betrayed and neglected my foundation," he said. "I

swept my love for my wife and children under the rug of my
activities and mounting concerns. I gave them everything, but
I forgot to give them the one fundamental thing that I had re-
garded only as trivial: myself. My friends were barely a con-
sideration and my dreams were forgotten completely. How can
one be a good father, a good husband and a good friend if the
people we love are excluded from our agenda? Only a hypocrite
could believe it, a noted hypocrite who so many held up as an
example."

He said bravely that he hid his mistakes, his shortcomings,
his stupid attitudes, which represented the dirty part of his
foundation, but which were also fundamental to the structure
of his personality. Now I understand what he meant when he
said that whoever fails to recognize his shortcomings has an
outstanding debt to himself and to his humanity.

I began to further understand why this man had had such
an affect on me. To get through to me, he had to be more than
an ordinary man. He had to be more than a thinker, more than
a brilliant mind, more than a teacher of uncommon sophistication. A man with those qualities might have attracted my admiration, but he wouldn't have captivated me as he did, wouldn't
have broken down my prideful ego. The dreamseller had to be
someone who had known the darkest valleys of fear, who had
been mired in the morass of psychological and social conflict,
who had been torn apart by predators of the mind and been
lost in the mazes of madness. And, after surviving all of that,
he remade himself with uncommon strength and written a new
story based on his own experiences.

This, *this,* is the man I would follow.

His ideas were as incisive as a philosopher's, and his humor
as vibrant as a clown's. His actions were a paradox, fluctuating between the extremes. He was sought out by icons of society, but he made no distinction between a prostitute and a

puritan, an intellectual and a mental patient. His sensitivity overwhelmed us.

Whenever I saw someone on television being arrested by the police, he would hide his face in an effort to protect his image. The man standing on the stage in front of me wasn't hiding. I remember what he had said to the psychiatrist at the building where we met—that there were two kinds of insanity, and he had dared to say that his was the visible kind. Now, when his opponents had tried to ambush him inhumanely, he displayed his wounds in front of more than fifty thousand people, unashamed of his past. His honesty was crystal clear.

When I heard him confess that he had betrayed his foundation, my mind was wracked by sociological concepts. Who isn't a traitor at some point? What puritan is not at some moment immoral to himself? What believer doesn't at some point betray God with his pride and his underlying desires? What idealist doesn't betray his beliefs in the name of hidden interests? What person doesn't betray his health in order to work a few extra hours? Who doesn't betray sleep by turning his bed into a place of tension? Who doesn't betray his children for his ambitions, arguing that he's working for them? Who doesn't betray his love for his spouse by failing to communicate in his marriage?

We betray science with our absolute truths, betray our students with our inability to listen to them, betray nature with development. As the dreamseller warned us, we betray humanity when we pick up a banner to call ourselves Jews, Palestinians, Americans, Europeans, Chinese, whites, blacks, Christians, Muslims. We are all traitors who desperately need to buy dreams. We all harbor a "Judas" in our mind, a specialist in hiding our true feelings under the carpet of activism, ethics, morality, social justice.

It was as if he were reading my thoughts. He fixed his gaze on mine and then raised his eyes to the audience.

"My interpretation of that vision—regardless of whether some might call it a hallucination—made me realize that my mental illness started long before I'd lost my family." He smiled and joked with the crowd. "I warn you, ladies and gentlemen, you're dealing with someone who's been crazy for a while, now . . ."

The audience settled into smiles. The emotion of that scene is hard to describe.

"When I realized I'd betrayed my foundations, I had to find out who I really was. That's when I left the hospital and went off to find myself. It was a long road and I got lost many times on the way. But when I discovered myself, I left my nest and transformed into a delicate swallow, gliding down the streets and avenues, helping others who were also searching for themselves." And he again demonstrated his sense of humor by saying, "Careful, friends, this craziness is contagious."

People smiled again and burst into applause, as if breathing in that contagion just as Bartholomew, Barnabas, Jurema and I—and so many others—had. I can still remember the day I was ready to give up on life and the dreamseller recited a poem that resonated with my own foundation. Even now, it echoes in my mind:

Let the day this man was born be struck from the record
   of time!
Let the dew from the grass of that morning evaporate!
Let the clear blue sky that brought joy to strollers that
   afternoon be withheld!
Let the night when this man was conceived be stolen by
   suffering!
Reclaim from that night the glowing stars that dotted the
   heavens!

Erase from his infancy all his smiles and his fears!
Strike from his childhood his frolicking and his
*   adventures!*
Steal from him his dreams and his nightmares, his sanity
*   and his madness!*

This dreamseller's contagious ideas taught us not to deny who we really are. His ideas were an antidote; before meeting him, we had all been "normal," and we had all been sick. We wanted in some form or another to be gods, not knowing that being a god means having to be perfect, to worry about our image in society, to give too much importance to the opinions of others, to demand too much of oneself, to punish oneself, to make constant demands of ourselves. We had lost the joy, the simplicity of being. We were brought up to work, to grow, to progress, and unfortunately also to betray our very essence in our short time in existence.

What kind of a madhouse are we living in?

CHAPTER 32

If I Could Turn Back Time

NSPIRED AFTER REVEALING AND INTERPRETING THE STORY of the house, the dreamseller offered his final ideas. Once again he recited poetry in the desert, when his lips still thirsted. He looked out into emptiness, as if on another plane, and displayed an intimate relationship with a god I didn't know. Forgetting that he stood before the large stadium crowed, he called out:

"God, who are you? Why do you hide your face behind the curtain of time and why won't you help cure my foolishness? I lack wisdom, as you well know. With my feet I walk on the surface of the ground, but with my mind I walk on the surface of knowledge. I am too prideful if I think I know anything about this world. And even when I admit I know nothing, it's my pride that allows me to admit I know nothing."

He lowered his eyes, glanced at the leaders who hated him, then at the audience, and delivered a philosophical speech that stealthily penetrated the depths of our being.

"Life is very, very long for making mistakes, but frighteningly short for living. And being aware of that brevity erases my mind's vanity and makes me see that I'm simply a wanderer who is nothing more than a flicker in this existence, a flash that dissipates with the first rays of light. In that brief time between flickering and dissipating, I seek to find who I am. I've looked

for myself in many places, but I found myself in a place without
a name, in the place where jeers and applause are all the same,
the place where no one can enter without our permission, not
even ourselves.

"Oh, if I could only go back in time! I would achieve less
power and have more power to achieve. I would drink a few
doses of irresponsibility, position myself less as a problem-
solving machine and give myself permission to relax, to think
about the abstract, to reflect on the mysteries that surround me.

"If I could go back in time, I would find the friends of my
youth. Where are they? Which of them are still alive? I would
seek them and relive the uncomplicated experiences plucked
from the garden of simplicity, where there were no weeds of
status or the seduction of financial power.

"If I could go back, I would call the woman in my life, the
love of my life, during breaks in meetings. I would try to be a
more distracted professional and a more attentive lover. I would
be more good-natured and less pragmatic, less logical and more
romantic. I would write silly love poems. I would say 'I love
you' more often. I would acknowledge freely, 'Forgive me for
trading you for business meetings! Don't give up on me.'

"Oh, if only I could fly on the wings of time! I would kiss
my children more, play with them more, enjoy their childhood
the way dry soil absorbs water. I would go out into the rain
with them, walk barefoot on the grass, climb trees. I would
be less afraid that they would hurt themselves or catch cold
and more afraid that they'd be contaminated by this society. I
would try less to give them the world, and harder to give them
my world."

Beholding the magnificent stadium, its intricate columns,
its expansive roof, its plush seating, he continued, intensely
touched:

"If I could go back in time, I would give every penny I had

for one more day with them, and I would make that day an eternal moment. But they went away, and the only voices I hear are those that remain hidden in the ruins of my memory: 'Daddy, you're the best father in the world—but the busiest, too.'"

Tears streamed down his face, proving that great men cry, too. And he concluded with these words:

"The past is a tyrant and it won't allow my family to come back to me. But the present generously lifts my downcast face and makes me see that, although I can't change what I was, I can construct what I will be. They can call me crazy, psychotic, a lunatic, it doesn't matter. What matters is that, like all mortals, one day I will end the theater of existence on the tiny stage of a tomb, in front of an audience in tears."

This last thought reached the roots of my mind. Breathing heavily, he ended his speech:

"On that day, I don't want people to say, 'In that tomb rests a rich, famous and powerful man whose deeds are recorded in the annals of history.' Or, 'There lies an ethical and just man.' Because those words will merely sound like an obligation. But I hope they say, 'In that tomb rests a simple wanderer who understood a little of what it means to be human, who learned to love humanity and who succeeded in selling dreams to others travelers . . .'"

At that moment, he turned his back to the audience and left the stage without a good-bye. The crowd in the stadium broke their silence, rising to their feet and applauding him uninterruptedly. His disciples couldn't hold back and burst into tears. We, too, were learning to lose the fear of showing our emotions. His supposed enemies also rose. Two of them applauded. The CEO sat still, not knowing where to look.

Suddenly, a boy broke through security, climbed onto the stage, ran after the dreamseller and gave him a long, heartfelt embrace. It was Antonio, the twelve-year-old boy who had been in such despair at his father's wake, the wake the dreamseller had transformed into a solemn act of homage.

"I lost my father, but you taught me not to lose faith in life," the boy told him. "I'll always be grateful . . ."

Touched, the dreamseller looked at the young boy and surprised him by saying, "I lost my children, but you also taught me not to lose faith in life. And for that, *I* will always be grateful to *you*."

"Let me follow you," the boy said.

"How long has school been in you?" the dreamseller asked.

"I'm in the sixth grade."

"You didn't understand my question. I didn't ask what grade you're in, but how long school has been *in you*."

I had made teaching my life, my world, and even I had never heard anyone phrase a question that way, much less to a young boy. The boy looked confused.

"I don't understand the question," the boy said.

The dreamseller looked at him and sighed. "Well, the day you understand it, you'll become a seller of dreams like me, and in your free time you can follow me."

The boy walked away confused, but then suddenly, something dawned on him. The stadium camera caught him just as his expression changed. He radiated pure joy. Instead of returning to his seat, he came over to us. We all wanted to understand what had happened, but none of us understood at the time.

The dreamseller headed toward the door, without a destination or an agenda or a map, living each day unhurriedly, blowing like a feather in wind. This time he left without inviting us to follow him. And we felt a deep sadness.

Would we ever see each other again? Had the dream of selling dreams ended? What would we do? Where would we go? Would I write other stories? We didn't know. We only knew we were children playing in the theater of time, children who understood very little about the mysteries of existence.

Who is the dreamseller really? Where does he come from? Is he one of the most powerful men in the world or a pauper with an uncommon imagination? To this day, we still don't know. But it doesn't matter. What matters is that we broke out of the prison of routine, and we left the cocoon to become wanderers.

Bartholomew and Barnabas touched me on the shoulder. I don't know whether they had understood everything that happened in the stadium or nothing at all.

"Don't follow us. We're lost, too," they joked.

We hugged each other warmly. I had learned to love my fellow man in a way not found in textbooks. Despite our uncertain futures, we looked at one another and said, "Oh, how I love this life!"

The other members of the group joined in the embrace. We might have been saying good-bye forever.

Before taking his last step off the stage, the dreamseller turned and saw us. Our eyes met, slowly and intensely. The image filled our hearts with joy. Immediately, our dream was reborn.

We ran across the stage and followed him, knowing that unpredictable adventures lay ahead of us—as well as unexpected storms. We left the stadium, joyfully singing our anthem.

I'm just a wanderer
Who lost the fear of getting lost
I'm certain of my own imperfection
You may say I'm crazy
You may mock my ideas
It doesn't matter!
What matters is I'm a wanderer
Who sells dreams to passersby

I've no compass or appointment book
I have nothing, yet I have everything
I'm just a wanderer
In search of myself.

THE END
(of the first volume)

The
Dreamseller
THE REVOLUTION

A Novel

To all the anonymous people in society who understand that existence is a great contract with risk. And to those who read the clauses of that contract that drama and comedy, loss and gain, desert and oasis, calm and stress are privileges that belong to the living.

Preface

THE DREAMSELLER IS A SAGA TOLD IN SEVERAL VOLUMES with the same characters. In this saga, drama and comedy, pain and laughter, sanity and madness permeate the texts and roil the story. Though there is a sequence, each book can be read separately. I was not expecting the first book, *The Dreamseller: The Calling,* to have such explosive success overseas, especially because it is intensely critical of the social system and denounces modern societies as having become huge mental institutions in which being sick is normal.

The Calling introduces a mysterious character—the dreamseller, whose origin and history are unknown and who "calls" the wanderers to follow him on a risky journey to reflect upon and denounce the madness of the social system. The disciples are wild, eccentric, complex and confused. The dreamseller prods his listeners to search the most important place of all, a place that even kings have rarely found: the inner reaches of the human soul.

In the second book, *The Revolution,* the dreamseller continues to turn society upside down. His "crazy" disciples, among whom Bartholomew and Barnabas stand out, spread their wings, revealing a surprising creativity and causing endless and unexpected adventures. They provoke everything and everyone, including the dreamseller himself. This novel demonstrates that societies are made up of anonymous heroes.

Among the anonymous are the depressed, who confront their emotions with dignity; the anxious, who dream of calmer days; cancer patients, who fight for life and make each day an eternal moment; parents, who exhaust body and mind to support and educate their children; teachers, who, for meager salaries and without praise from society, move the world by teaching critical thinking to their students; students, who quixotically believe they can change history, unaware that they live in an unbending social system hardly sympathetic to new ideas; workers in offices and firms, who go unnoticed unless they cause a scene but who have uplifting stories. All of them are in some way dreamsellers—although they also sell nightmares.

Every human being is a vault of secrets. Exploring them, spending time with them is a privilege. As a psychiatrist, psychotherapist and author of a theory that studies the intriguing world of complex thinking, I have learned a great deal from each of those anonymous individuals. I've discovered a treasure buried in their minds. I feel small next to many of them.

The Dreamseller: The Revolution, by emphasizing these anonymous figures, reflects the amazing complexity of our history, which is written with tears and joy, calm and anxiety, sanity and madness.

CHAPTER 1

A Controversial and Surprising Man

WE WERE LIVING IN A TIME WHEN PEOPLE, DEVOID OF creativity and caught in a web of sameness, were overly predictable. Actors and actresses, show business personalities, politicians, religious leaders, executives of large corporations— all were tiring, boring and often insufferable. They were repetitious in their worn-out jargon. They neither appealed to emotion nor inspired the intellect. They needed a marketing strategy and a media makeover to repackage them and render them interesting. Even young people no longer had any enthusiasm for their idols.

Suddenly, as we rode the waves of tedium, a man appeared, breaking the imprisonment of routine. He turned our minds upside down, or at least my mind and the minds of those closest to him. He became the greatest sociological phenomenon of our time. Though he shunned the attention of the media, it was all but impossible to remain indifferent to his thoughts.

Without revealing his identity, he declared himself a seller of dreams and, inviting others to join him, soon blew like a hurricane into the heart of the great city. He was an enigmatic stranger followed by strangers. And he made demands:

"Whoever would follow me must first recognize his madness and face his stupidity." And he proclaimed to passersby,

"Happy are those who are transparent, for theirs is the king-dom of mental health and wisdom. Unhappy are those who hide their sickness behind their schooling, money or social standing, for theirs is the kingdom of insanity. But let's be hon-est. We are all experts at hiding. We squeeze into the tiniest of holes to hide, even under the banner of sincerity."

The man rocked society, astounding those who heard him. Wherever he went, he caused a ruckus. He lived beneath bridges and overpasses or in homeless shelters. Never in our time had someone so unassuming had such impact. A pauper without health insurance, welfare or money for his meals, he had the courage to say:

"I ask not that you be wanderers like me. My dream is that you will be wanderers in your own right, that you make your way through territories few intellectuals dare to explore. Fol-low no map or compass. Search for yourselves, lose yourselves. Make each day a new chapter, every twist in the road a new story."

He criticized modern man, who lived like a machine, never pondering what it meant to be a thinking being or reflecting on the mysteries of existence. Mankind walked in the shallows of existence and intellect. Some protested, "Who is this audacious invader of our private lives? What insane asylum did he escape from?" Others discovered that they had no time for what was essential, especially for themselves.

Only a small group of friends slept where he slept and lived where he lived. I was one of them. Those who crossed his path didn't know if what they were seeing was real or imagined.

His origins were unknown even to his disciples. When asked about his identity, he would repeat, "I'm a wanderer moving on the path of time, looking for himself."

He was destitute but had what millionaires lacked. His

home was expansive: sometimes park benches, sometimes the steps of a building or the shade of a tree. His gardens extended throughout the city. He contemplated them as if they were the Hanging Gardens of Babylon, cultivated only to enchant his eyes. Of every flower, he made a poem, of every leaf a dart to plunge into the wellsprings of sensibility, of every weathered tree trunk a moment to soar on the wings of imagination.

"Dawns do not go unappreciated. Sunsets do not go unnoticed but invite me to repose and to think about my folly," the dreamseller would say. He behaved unlike anyone we'd ever met. While others loved to glorify themselves, he enjoyed reflecting on his smallness.

One morning, after barely sleeping under a highway overpass, he stretched, took several deep breaths, and drank in the morning sunlight. After reflection, he went to the center of a nearby university campus and shouted to the students:

"We are free to come and go but not to think. Our thoughts and choices are restricted to the confines of our brains. How can we be free if we cover our bodies with clothing but our minds are stark naked? How can we be free if we contaminate the present with the future, if we steal from the present our inalienable right to drink from the fountain of tranquillity?"

On one occasion, three psychiatrists passing by heard one of his speeches. One of them was taken with the ragged stranger, but the other two said, "That man is a danger to society. He should be locked up."

Reading their lips, he replied, "Don't worry, my friends, I'm already locked up. Just look around at this grand and beautiful mental hospital."

In modern societies, child labor was outlawed, but the dreamseller said that those same nations committed a crime against children by encumbering their minds with mass consumption, allowing them to grow up too fast, and overloading them with activities.

"Our children are spared the horrors of war; they don't see houses destroyed or mutilated bodies, but their imagination is obliterated, their capacity for play inhibited, their imagination kidnapped by unnecessary trinkets. Isn't that its own form of horror?" he said. "There's a reason that depression and other emotional disturbances among children and adolescents have increased so much." He said this with tears in his eyes. His own children had perished in a tragic accident, but at the time, we knew nothing about the details of his mysterious past.

Once, at the end of classes, he "invaded" a private elementary school whose pupils were the children of upper-middle- and upper-class parents. Granite floors, marble columns, stained-glass windows, air-conditioned classrooms. Every pupil had a personal computer. The only problem was that the children were restless, found no delight in learning and were not developing critical thinking. To them, school and the educational environment were almost unbearable. As soon as they heard the bell, they would dash out as if released from prison.

Their parents, when they came for them, didn't have a minute to spare. They would scold their children if they were late. The dreamseller slipped past security, put on a clown nose and began running, jumping, dancing in the patio. When they saw this crazy man, many of the nine- and ten-year-olds forgot they were on their way out and went over to watch him.

Opening his arms like an airplane, he pretended to fly to a small garden. There, he imitated a toad, a cricket and a rattlesnake. Then he performed magic tricks. He produced a flower from his sleeve and a bunny from his jacket. And after a few minutes of amusement he told the attentive children:

"Behold the greatest magic of all." And he took a seed from

253

his pocket. "If you were a seed, what kind of tree would you like to grow into?" He asked them to close their eyes and imagine the tree they would be. Each child imagined a different tree, from the diameter of the trunk, the shape of the crown and the size of the branches, to the most diverse types of leaves and flowers.

Several parents were desperately looking for their children. They had never been ten minutes late leaving class. Some feared they had been kidnapped. The teachers also went looking for them. When they found the dreamseller in the garden, they were impressed by how quiet the children were, especially at that time of day. They saw the ragged man and realized that the person stirring up the school was the same stranger who was inciting the city.

Then he told the children, "A life without dreams is a seed without soil, a plant without nourishment. Dreams don't determine the kind of tree you'll be, but they give you strength to understand there's no growth without storms, times of difficulty and misunderstanding. Play more, smile more, imagine more. Cover yourselves in the dirt of your dreams. Without dirt, a seed can't germinate." And he scooped up some of the clay beside him and smeared it on his face.

Amazed, several of the children also stuck their hands in the clay and dirtied their faces. Some stained their clothes. They would never forget that day, even when they were old. However, when their parents arrived and saw their children dirty and being taught by a ratty-looking stranger, they were horrified. "Get that maniac away from our children!" some said.

"We pay a fortune in tuition and the school doesn't offer the least bit of security. It's an outrage!" others shouted.

They called security, who roughly tossed the dreamseller out of the school in front of the children. Juliana, a nine-year-old with the most dirt on her face, ran to him and shouted, "Stop, stop!"

Surprised, the guards stopped. Juliana handed the dreamseller a flower and said, "I'd like to be a grapevine."

"Why, my child?"

"It's not pretty or strong like you. But anyone can reach its fruit."

"You will be a great seller of dreams," the dreamseller said.

Some of the teachers asked the security guards to go easy on the man. As he left, some applauded. Turning to them, he said:

"A society that encourages those who punish over those who educate will always be sick. I would not bow to the famous or the great leaders of our society, but I bow down to the educators."

And he bowed before the open-mouthed teachers.

It was not easy to accompany that mysterious man. He spoke in places where you were supposed to keep quiet, danced in places where you were supposed to sit still. He was unpredictable. Sometimes he would distance himself from his disciples to avoid involving them in the tumult he caused.

One of the things that most disheartened him was how unhappy people seemed to be in the digital age, something unforeseen by Freud. He would often say:

"We are morbid, weary and perpetually discontent. Yet the entertainment industry is at its peak, and the sale of depression medication has gone through the roof. Doesn't that bother you, ladies and gentlemen?"

People did seem troubled. Some by his words, others by the man himself.

"We watch sitcoms every night, but where are our smiles the next morning? We have pleasures the Greeks never dreamed of, but where is the enduring joy? And the patience?"

The dreamseller didn't worry about whether he was lauded or ridiculed. He was concerned only with being faithful to what he believed. To him, life was far too short to be lived in a false, futile, mediocre way. One of the manifestations of mediocrity that he fought against most fiercely was the cult of celebrity.

"Those who live outside the media spotlight, the anonymous toilers who struggle to survive, the health professionals who save lives, the assembly line workers, the trash collectors, those are the true stars in society. But just as it trivializes these heroes, the system handpicks its celebrities. A society that promotes celebrities is emotionally stunted and sick."

To some, the dreamseller was the craziest of crazies. To others, a thinker of unprecedented daring. And some saw him as a man who had been great and fallen from his throne. To me, he was stimulating, extraordinary, controversial. His speeches cut like razors, his ideas were enthralling. He was both loved and hated like no other.

I had been a prideful intellectual and egotistical professor of sociology who always felt the need to be praised and to control my students. For six months, I had been following this man with the long, unruly hair and untrimmed beard, this man who wore clothes so wrinkled and torn, you'd never even find them at a secondhand store.

But this man was so captivating that groups of teenagers would wake up at sunrise on Saturdays and Sundays to seek him out. They wanted to find out what kind of uproar he and his disciples would get into. Some of his disciples seemed so crazy that their illnesses couldn't even be found in psychology textbooks. And, to be honest, there were times when I felt like running away and abandoning our group. But something about his mission fascinated me.

The dreamseller wasn't balanced like a Christian monk, serene like a Buddhist monk, and he was much less deliberate than a philosopher from Greece's Golden Age. Sometimes he led us to calm waters, other times into the eye of the storm. When people praised him, he might say, "Careful, I'm not normal. Some think I'm mentally ill. Following me is risky."

He could spend hours talking to a blind man and say that of the two, the blind man could see more than he. Young people wanted to discuss their crises and passions. He might interrupt a brilliant speech and abruptly leave a crowd if he spotted an elderly man having trouble walking. He would accompany his halting steps for blocks on end and listen with delight to the conversation.

I asked myself what kind of man was this who expended energy on things we considered irrelevant. He was capable of creating poetry from a glass of water and drinking it in a way we never did. Raising the glass, he said:

"O, water that quenches my thirst, one day I will disintegrate in a tomb, and you, in a thousand particles, will return to the bed of the sea. But you will weep with longing for humanity. Released, you will evaporate, travel to distant places and, like tears, once again fall to refresh other people."

Free of the neurotic need for power, he did not worry about his image. He lived without glamour, ostentation or self-promotion. When we walked with him, the hundred billion neurons that make up our brains were in a constant state of alert. Living with this man meant laying bare our foolishness, revealing our madness.

This man rescued me when I was on the verge of suicide. Afterward, he might have gone on his way and I mine, perhaps never to meet again. But what he said to keep me from killing myself floored me. For the very first time, I bowed before another man's wisdom. I was ready to end my life, to punctuate my existence with a period when he made me a disturbing offer:

"I want to sell you a comma."

"A comma?" I asked.

"Yes, a comma, so you can pause, then go on writing your life, for a man without a comma is a man without a history."

That was the moment I realized I had used periods instead of commas throughout my life. If someone frustrated me, I would eliminate him, putting a period to our relationship. Someone injured me? I would erase him. If I encountered an obstacle? I would change directions. If my plan had problems? I would replace it. If I suffered a loss? I would turn my back.

As a professor, I learned from the books of others but didn't know how to write the book of my existence. I considered myself an angel and those who frustrated me, demons, without ever acknowledging that I had been the one who alienated my wife, my only child, my friends and my students.

Whoever eliminates everyone around him will one day decide to eliminate himself. And that day had arrived. But luckily, I had found the dreamseller and come to understand that frustrations, disappointments, betrayals, abuse and conflict are all part of life. And commas are essential.

I lived comfortably in my small apartment on a professor's meager salary. Then I, a socialist who had always criticized the bourgeoisie and sang the praises of society's poor, came to experience the pain of poverty in my own life.

I became a follower of a seller of ideas who had nothing. Marx, a theoretical thinker who never knew what it meant to be a proletarian, would have been perplexed by this man. When I began following the dreamseller, I realized Marx was a hypocrite who defended something he didn't know. Therefore I left behind the frontiers of theory to become a wanderer, a small seller of commas to help people free their minds, rewrite their history and develop critical thinking.

Being mocked, jeered, branded a lunatic, an impostor—

these were the smallest risks in joining the group. The worst? Being beaten, arrested, labeled a rioter, kidnapper and a terrorist. Selling dreams in a society that has stopped dreaming came at a very high cost.

But nothing was more exciting. Those who joined our group knew nothing of boredom, anguish or depression. We did, however, run unforeseeable risks.

CHAPTER 2

Deliver Me from These Disciples!

FOLLOWING THE DREAMSELLER DOESN'T SEEM SUITED FOR someone who had been applauded in universities and respected by his fellow professors.

Some of my old colleagues from the university thought I'd lost my mind. I discovered that just as cattle are marked with a hot branding iron, in some sectors of the university, colleagues are branded with the flames of prejudice. I was among the worst offenders, but this time, I was the one being prejudged.

Was it insane to follow this man? Probably. But it seemed a more lucid insanity than living the life of "normals" who spend hours a day in front of their televisions, waiting for death, without ever venturing forth and fighting for a dream. An insanity saner than spending your days clutching a cell phone, in touch with the world but out of touch with yourself. An insanity more fertile than those who defend their theses in order to avoid controversy, not knowing that great ideas are born of the soil of risk and humiliation. As thesis adviser, I avoided controversy—and suffocated thinkers.

What I have been doing since is the most fantastic sociological experiment in recent times. Naturally, there are side effects to this journey, and they have nothing to do with prejudice or the hardship of following a fearless, bold and critical man.

They're due mainly to the team of disciples he has invited to follow him. They drive me crazy, especially Bartholomew and Barnabas.

Bartholomew is a recovering alcoholic. Still, his greatest problem isn't alcoholism but compulsive speech syndrome—CSS. He's hooked on always offering his two cents. He likes to philosophize but trips over his words. His nickname says it all: "Honeymouth." His mouth is bigger than his brain. Unlike the dreamseller, he's brash, but I have to admit that he has a contagious happiness, an enviable sense of humor.

Barnabas is also a recovering alcoholic and was a longtime boozing companion of Bartholomew's. Both are experts at putting their foot in their mouth. Barnabas is addicted both to alcohol and to giving political speeches, thus his nickname, "The Mayor." Whenever he sees a gathering of people, his brain goes into a trance, he swells his chest, modulates his voice, and tries to persuade people to vote for him—for what office, no one knows. Unlike the dreamseller, he loves applause and recognition. Honeymouth is thin, lanky. The Mayor is an obese, good-natured slob and always has something hidden in his jacket to chew on. Honeymouth is a street philosopher; the Mayor, a street politician.

To them, intellectuals like me are imbeciles. They love to provoke me. Despite being irreligious, I sometimes pray, "God, deliver me from these disciples!" To make things worse, Bartholomew and Barnabas compete with each other like children. Besides trying my patience, they diminish the dreamseller's philosophical depth. Whenever they're around, drama turns to comedy.

Even when they have no problems, they find a way to create some. And the worst part is they drag in everyone around them, including the dreamseller. Frankly, to this day I can't understand why he chose them. I thought he should have chosen cultured, experienced, well-behaved individuals such as executives, psychologists, teachers or doctors. But he preferred those rabble-rousers.

Once, in the middle of a discussion, the dreamseller stated poetically a truth about human existence that applies directly to every mortal, rich or poor: "Existence is cyclical. No applause lasts forever and no jeers are eternal."

That thought led me to reflect on the great men in history. Jesus Christ was loved by many but was betrayed by his closest friends. Julius Caesar's closest friends, Brutus and Cassius, betrayed and assassinated him. Napoleon rose and fell like few others. Lincoln, Kennedy, Martin Luther King—all had short lives.

Bartholomew couldn't keep quiet, and looking to stand out from the crowd, he disagreed with the dreamseller.

"Boss, I'm afraid your theory doesn't apply to me," he said. "My life isn't cyclical. I've been down for years. I'm made fun of, cursed, called a bum, a shameless good-for-nothing. I go from one mess to another."

Barnabas, the Mayor, upon hearing Bartholomew hold the crowd's attention, couldn't resist jumping in like a stumping politician.

"Distinguished dreamseller, ladies and gentlemen, if Honeymouth has been living years of misery, I must declare that I have lived a miserable life as long as I can remember. I'm lost in the woods without a compass, a cell phone, a credit card or money." He raised his voice and added, "But, I trust the dreamseller's words that life is cyclical and the day will come when I will be called upon by the people. For in this city there are only two types of voters: those who vote for me and those who haven't met me." This pair was so shameless that they competed not only to be the best but also to be the worst. I could only conclude the dreamseller had called them to follow him because he pitied them.

Once, he commented to his circle of friends:

"I leaped among the mountaintops like a ram, never imagining I could fall. But the day came when I stumbled through the hostile valleys of anguish, in a place where few mental health specialists have gone. That's when I discovered that I knew nothing about myself. I learned I was a stranger in my own home, unknown even to myself."

Astonished by that discovery and shaken by his unfathomable losses, he isolated himself on an island for more than three years. Time stopped. Everything and nothing became one and the same. Profoundly depressed although his table overflowed with food, he had an appetite only for knowledge.

"I would consume books day and night, sitting or standing, walking or running. I devoured books on philosophy, neuroscience, history, sociology, psychology, theology. Books became my passport to travel the world of the mind."

After this process, he pulled himself together and returned to society. But, no longer the same man, he didn't look upon life as he had before. He did not become a hero or a messiah, but a human being conscious of his imperfections, aware of his own madness and the madness of the world around him. He did not want to change the world but to shout about other paths. Selling dreams became his reason for being.

Many questions still torment me when I think about his story. What does he want from us? Why is he bent on challenging others' minds? Is he running away from something? Had he really been such an important figure? How can someone who was once highly respected let himself be labeled an impostor, a psychotic, a rebel? Who was he?

After telling us a little bit about his past, he fell silent. He spoke no more about it. We didn't know whether he was being figurative or if everything he said was true. But what worried us most is that he started risking his life.

We couldn't imagine who would want to hurt—much less assassinate—a man who radiated such gentleness and generosity. Concerned about the safety of his friends, he tried to distance himself from us. But we insisted on staying.

"Boss, if you need a man to protect you, here I am!" Bartholomew said. "Nobody close to me has ever died. Well, I mean, they've been beaten, battered, pummeled, but not killed."

In a serious tone, the Mayor declared his loyalty to the dreamseller: "With me at your side, you'll be safe from all dangers, including the ones Honeymouth causes."

I couldn't take it. He was talking his head off and not paying attention to the dreamseller's words.

I felt like slapping him. But we were dealing with protecting the dreamseller.

Dimas, the con man in our group, decided to show his loyalty, even though no purse or wallet was ever safe around him.

"Dreamseller, safety is my middle name. You can count on me."

Dimas was in recovery, but he was still a kleptomaniac; when certain objects came into sight, they would trigger a compulsive attempt to possess them.

At that moment, Edson, the group's religious voice, saw his favorite pen in Dimas's pocket. "Hey, that's my pen," he said.

Without missing a beat, the cunning Dimas told him, "I know. I was taking care of it for you." And he returned it.

Edson thought he had supernatural gifts and was always trying to perform miracles. After getting his pen back, he told the dreamseller:

"My prayers will protect you."

After weighing the band of misfits around the dreamseller,

I wondered whether he wouldn't be safer surrounded by his enemies. We were the most unconventional family ever. The dreamseller trained us to be patient and calm, but those virtues were luxuries to us. We broke all the sociological rules.

How long would we follow him? We didn't know. What surprises and setbacks awaited us? We couldn't guess. Would we sell dreams or worsen an already tottering society? Everything was tinged with doubt. The future was the mother of uncertainty.

CHAPTER 3

A Market of Crazies

THE DREAMSELLER NEVER SERVED UP HIS IDEAS ON A platter. He made us enter the "kitchen" of our intellects and fend for ourselves. To him, whoever can't fend for himself doesn't know how to think.

Once, we were in the beautiful but busy courtyard of the federal courthouse. There was a huge monument to independence, with a cast-iron horse nine feet high, atop an enormous thirty-foot concrete pillar. Mounted on the animal was a soldier, also iron, holding a sword. He seemed to be shouting, rallying his troops to battle. As he passed the monument, the dreamseller pointed to the soldier and said:

"Behold a reflection of how mankind has always believed more in arms than in ideas. But who are the strong ones—those who use weapons or those who use ideas?"

Honeymouth had no doubts. "Those who use cannons, machine guns, rockets."

"But isn't it ideas that build the weapons, Bartholomew?" the dreamseller replied, hoping to correct him.

"Yes."

Then the dreamseller said, "If ideas are strong enough to build weapons, they should be strong enough to find solutions to avoid our having to use them. But, once built, weapons turn us against ideas. The creature destroys the creator."

We went on walking. The country's legal eagles passed through the courtyard. Lawyers, judges, prosecutors, public defenders, justice officials—all wearing impeccable suits that contrasted with our rags, especially the dreamseller's. He was wearing a threadbare and wrinkled coat with a large tear on its left side, ventilating his back.

Watching the others rush by, he began inviting them to a forum on the human mind. He bombarded them with questions as they passed.

"Doesn't the ability to formulate thoughts enchant you, ladies and gentlemen? How we penetrate the immense area of the cerebral cortex, millions of times more complex than the districts of this great city, and succeed in finding the pieces that comprise even the poorest of thoughts? Doesn't that astound you? Isn't the most despicable of human beings, by possessing this capability, a genius, even if he fails in school or has a below-average IQ? How do we penetrate the unfathomable labyrinths of the mind and, amid billions of options, pull verbs from our mental files and conjugate them without knowing beforehand where they're found and what tense we'll use? Doesn't this feat dazzle you? We may act different from one another, but the phenomena that make us *Homo sapiens* are exactly the same, whether we're judges or prisoners, prosecutors or criminals."

This bombardment of queries perplexed me. I wondered: Where did he get his ability to ask questions and draw these conclusions? His questions were so complex that they knotted the minds of his disciples.

The jurists passing through the courtyard were disturbed by the avalanche of questions. They used their brains all the time, but they never thought about thinking. One said, "Who is that madman?" Another, more thoughtful, asked, "What university does this thinker come from?" And still others wondered, "Is this some kind of street theater?" The dreamseller's questioning penetrated the cerebral circuits of those men, hard workers who never had time to reflect on the mental phenomena behind thought, or on human anguish and conflicts. Only a few stopped.

The Mayor, whispering in our ears, came out with this piece of nonsense: "Once I've had a few, I know the answers to all those questions," the Mayor joked.

Although others ignored him, the dreamseller went on: "I have something extremely dear to sell you, ladies and gentlemen. Come closer! Lend me your ears."

Some of them stopped to look at the stranger, wondering what he was selling. His most befuddled disciple broke the silence.

"I'll take one, dreamseller! I'll pay for it! It's mine!" Bartholomew said, without actually knowing what the dreamseller was selling.

But his big mouth actually started a bidding war. And seeing Honeymouth gaining attention, the Mayor shouted louder, "No, it's mine. I'll pay more! Two thousand."

Passersby were annoyed with the noisy pair. People asked, "Buy what?" "How much does it cost?"

Drawn in by an eccentric selling an invisible product and two lunatics willing to spend everything they had to buy it, people finally stopped to watch the show.

"I'll pay a million!" Honeymouth said.

Barnabas bid louder. "I'll pay a billion!"

Watching these two clowns, I, the first to be called by the dreamseller as a disciple, wanted to find a hole to crawl into. Once again they were diminishing the dreamseller's ideas. The somber courtyard became like Babylon: No one understood anyone else.

And then, I had a disturbing thought: "Could it be that the dreamseller chose Bartholomew and Barnabas to serve as mirrors so people like me could see their own insanity?"

As I struggled with these thoughts, my reasoning expanded. I began to think these loons were authentic, and I was the one pretending. They said whatever came to mind, while I hid my real intentions. They smiled without fear and cried without regret. No one ever learned about my emotional troubles until they exploded.

I began to realize that society, and later the university, had taught me to gloss over my emotions. Actors work in theaters, intellectuals in the arenas of knowledge, but down deep we're all masters of disguise.

The Mayor, still trying to win this mythical auction, upped the bid. But Bartholomew, who never conceded defeat, especially to the Mayor, shouted, "I'll give a trillion!"

The Mayor filled his lungs to make an even higher bid, but since he didn't know the word "quadrillion," he appealed to the dreamseller. "Noble Master, Honeymouth is the biggest deadbeat in the world. He buys, but he doesn't pay."

"That's a lie, ladies and gentlemen," said Honeymouth. Turning to the lawyers witnessing the scene in astonishment, he asked, "Who wants the privilege of being my lawyer to sue this man for slander?" No one raised his hand. However, more than a few burst into laughter. It had been a long time since they felt relaxed.

I was shaking with rage. We had lost the philosophical atmosphere the dreamseller had created. Peter denied Christ three times. Silently, I have been denying the dreamseller daily. It's hard for me to acknowledge that I'm part of this group of troublemakers.

Just when I thought the dreamseller was disappointed with his disciples, I saw his calm, smiling expression. The breeze spread his hair softly onto the right side of his face. The wind stirred the leaves on the trees.

It was a circus and a classroom, all at once. He didn't care at all about the humiliation. For him, jeers and applause were one and the same. He didn't let either get to him. I dreamed of such freedom, but I was a prisoner of my mental dungeon.

CHAPTER 4

What Is Truly Dear

INSPIRED, THE DREAMSELLER GAZED ACROSS THE ALMOST
fifty people gathered in the courtyard, then turned to his
two bungling disciples and gave them a great lesson. I was
fascinated.

"Barnabas, Bartholomew and friends. Everything that can
be sold is cheap; even if it costs a billion dollars, there's someone with the money to buy it. Only that which can't be sold is
expensive," he stated. "Money buys tranquilizers, but not the
ability to relax. It buys hangers-on, but not the shoulder of a
friend. It buys jewels, but not a woman's love. It buys a painting, but not the ability to contemplate one. It buys insurance,
but not the capacity for protecting our emotions."

He breathed deeply before continuing: "Money buys information, but not self-awareness. It buys glasses, but not the ability to see unexpressed feelings. It buys a manual with rules for
raising our children, but not a manual for life."

Hearing the dreamseller's simple yet cutting words, I remembered my son John Marcus. And how I had gone so wrong with
my boy. Only now did I understand that I had never given him
what can't be sold. I criticized, confronted, punished and put limits on him. I was nothing but a soulless manual of rules and ethics.
I abused him emotionally. I corrected him in front of his peers.

I never once gave him a shoulder to cry on. Never said that his father also had fears, had made mistakes and countless times was inconsistent. The dreamseller's first rule: to recognize your madness and your stupidity. I didn't recognize them. I was more machine than teacher, trying to shape thinkers. I considered myself a god educating a human being.

From a sociological point of view, I knew that men who have committed history's greatest atrocities were those who acted like gods. They killed, injured and conquered, never knowing their own frailties, as if they were immortal. We reproduce the attitudes of such atrocious men in the least expected places—in our living rooms, classrooms, offices, courts.

I looked around and saw illustrious judges and attorneys, their eyes swimming with tears. They were like me, cultured but vulnerable; gigantic but small; eloquent when speaking of the outside world but reluctant to speak about themselves with their loved ones.

Some of the attorneys around us were extremely rich, but had only bought what was cheap in life. They were never really millionaires. While the dreamseller had the attorneys' heads in the clouds, Bartholomew appeared to bring them back to earth. He yelled to Barnabas:

"I'm richer than people loaded with dough. I don't buy jewels, but women love me. I don't buy paintings, but I contemplate the sky. I don't have groupies, but I have an interesting set of friends." And to jerk our chain, he added, "Hey, Julio Cesar, Edson and Dimas snore like goats but I still don't need pills to sleep."

The Mayor wasn't about to be outdone. Seeing the captive audience, he tried to win it over by using a big word he didn't understand.

"I am richer than you, Mr. Bigmouth. I'm a very *turpitudinous* person." He didn't know that "turpitudinous" meant shameful, wicked, depraved. Actually, he didn't realize how right he was. And he continued, "Ah, cherished society! If you but knew who I am you would love me."

The lawyers bursted out laughing. When the laughter died down, the dreamseller elaborated a thought I'd never had. "When we leave the womb of our mother and enter the womb of society, we cry. When we leave the womb of society and enter the womb of our eternal graves, others cry for us. Coming into life and leaving it, tears punctuate our story. Why, ladies and gentlemen?"

I wondered how he managed to think straight in this commotion. His disciples were disruptive, traffic on the streets was snarled, but as if removed from all of it, he displayed a startling ability to construct unusual ideas.

The dreamseller asked questions we had forgotten how to ask. I didn't know the answer to his question. Seeing our silence, he prodded us:

"Whoever isn't amazed by the phenomenon of existence is like a child who lives without having the slightest awareness of life."

Living has become a banal phenomenon, no longer amazing. Many spent a dozen or more years in school without being even minimally conscious of their role as human beings. The dreamseller resumed his questioning and redirected it to the lawyers:

"Why, ladies and gentlemen of the legal profession, do we cry when we leave the maternal womb and others shed tears when we leave the social womb for the cold womb of a grave?"

I was hoping Bartholomew and Barnabas wouldn't open their mouths this time and spoil the intellectual journey. But this time it was young Solomon who spoke up.

Solomon is a sensitive, intelligent disciple who is also obsessive and a hypochondriac. He improved alongside the dreamseller but frequently suffered relapses. If the day was sunny, he feared he'd suffer heatstroke; if it rained, he feared he'd catch a cold. And his most irresistible obsession was sticking his finger into any hole he saw.

"Tears in this life are due to cancer, encephalitis, pancreatitis, duodenitis, heart attacks, aneurisms, cerebrovascular accidents . . ." And he went on to list more than a dozen other diseases we had never heard of.

The audience looked at each other as he rambled on. I furrowed my brow, Bartholomew and Barnabas scratched their heads. The dreamseller thanked the young man for his participation. To him, debate was as important as finding an answer.

"Well, done, Solomon. But I'm going to take a different approach. The tears at the beginning and the end of life reveal that existence is the greatest of all spectacles, marked by countless emotions. Drama and comedy. Gentle breezes and heavy storms. Health and sickness. All are privileges of the living. From young children to the elderly, from Westerners to Asians, all of us experience success and defeat, fidelity and betrayal, relief and pain to some degree."

I pondered his words. I had never considered pain and failure a privilege, but indeed only the living can experience them. I had bombarded my students with information but never prepared them for the miracle of existence. I educated the young with college degrees but I left them unprepared to deal with loss, adversity, scorn, betrayal, frustration.

The dreamseller didn't want us to be masochists and seek out suffering. Just the opposite. But neither did he want us to be naïve. He believed that whoever denies or flees from pain only increases it. Facing one's losses fearfully merely adds fuel to his anguish, turning our spectacle of an existence into a limited script. I had the impression that he had learned this lesson from his own past. He seemed to suggest that when he had succumbed to his emotional demons, he had tried to ignore them and only succeeded in making them stronger. At the same time, I had the feeling, right or wrong, that he wanted not only to sell dreams to the lawyers but also to prepare his disciples for the tumult we would face at his side. I felt afraid and forgot for a few moments what he had just taught us. It's so hard to learn the language of emotion.

While I was meditating on his words, Bartholomew intervened again, and this time he touched everyone, including me. He fearlessly told his story, speaking in a voice filled with emotion:

"Master, when I was expelled from my mother's womb and entered the womb of society, I shed lots of tears. My father was an alcoholic and often beat me. He died when I was seven. My mother left me at an orphanage. She told me she had cancer and couldn't take care of me. Three or four years earlier, she had taken my only brother to an orphanage, or to a foster family, I'm not sure. They told me my mother died, but they never told me about her funeral. I never had a chance to grieve. I shed tears and more tears crying for her and for my brother, but no one heard me. I was adopted for a short time, but my adoptive parents couldn't stand me and left me at another orphanage. I grew up without a family. I grew up alone, deeply alone. I was battered in the womb of society," he said, with a sensitivity he had never before expressed. He didn't seem like the Bartholomew I knew. But, in fact, this helped explain the Honeymouth who always sought a place in society where he could finally be seen and heard. "The only affection I received was from my dog. I named him Terrorist. Terrorist had fleas for company, and Terrorist was company for me."

I was very moved. The Mayor listened to Bartholomew's tale and, wiping tears from his eyes, recounted a part of his own existential desert.

"I understand you, my friend," he said, sadly. "I was the prettiest little plump child in the world, but my parents abandoned me on the doorstep of a skinny couple who—on top of everything else—were vegetarians. They tried to nourish this body with spinach, carrot juice and vegetables. I went to bed hungry every night. They saw eye to eye on food but not on life. They would fight every day. I was their punching bag. Whenever I cried, they would stick a carrot in my mouth. To this day I shudder when I see a carrot. As if that weren't enough, they spanked me. Finally, they put me in an orphanage at the age of six—an orphanage run by vegetarians. I was so hungry I wanted to eat an entire cow out of spite!" He paused and grew solemn. "Who would ever adopt a little boy that age—no matter how cute he was? I grew up without love or affection."

Hugging his friend, he said, "And just like you, Honeymouth, the only kisses I ever got in the orphanage were from my dog, Spook. I would fall asleep every night with Spook at my feet."

The Mayor didn't care who was starting at him or judging him. Now I understand why he always has food stashed away. He had gone hungry. I felt guilty for having criticized them. The closest onlookers teared up. A couple placed a hand on his shoulder. The dreamseller was moved. But, just as everyone was touched by their stories, the incorrigible pair inevitably reverted to their usual selves.

"Mayor, this show's way too depressing," Honeymouth said. "The only way to drown our sorrows is with a pint—or ten."

"I hear you, Honeymouth. This womb of society is too sad to endure. I think we need to go get hammered."

Professor Jurema, another of the dreamseller's disciples, an elderly former educator, was a patient and intelligent woman, just like Monica, the ex-model who was also part of the group. When the two heard the nonsense Bartholomew and Barnabas were spouting, they both started to cough, trying to drown out their words. I joined in. The three of us were the most level-headed of the disciples.

But the crowd was enjoying itself. The attorneys, judges, and prosecutors came down from the heights of existential reflection to the level of barroom humor.

Jurema grabbed her cane and hooked it around Bartholomew's neck, uttering the famous phrase, "Bartholomew, with your mouth shut you're irreplaceable."

"Settle down, folks. I didn't mean get loaded on booze—but on philosophy, wisdom, ideas."

Inspired by Bartholomew's cleverness, Barnabas, as if on the campaign trail, forgot his painful past, looked at the audience, and like an all-knowing politician, said:

"Yes, most noble friends of this portentous courthouse! Faced with the tears that fall during this all-too-brief show called life, it behooves us to intoxicate ourselves with the wisdom of Jesus Christ, Confucius, Augustine, Rousseau, Auguste Comte." And, looking in my direction as if to needle me, added, "And of the great emperor Julius Caesar."

The audience of learned men applauded them vigorously. I pulled Professor Jurema aside and muttered, "Professor, I doubt they've ever read a book. They're just trying to win over the crowd."

Jurema nodded, "The world belongs to the shrewd. They grew up alone."

Barnabas had the audacity to tell the lawyers, "Esteemed Mayor and distinguished attorneys, we mustn't forget Montesquieu and his great book *The Spirit of the Laws*."

Several of them knew who Montesquieu was. When they heard that reference, they applauded the two shabby men more enthusiastically. I felt the dreamseller should have been jealous of those scene-stealers; after all, he carries the piano, tunes the piano, plays the piano, and it's these buffoons who get the applause. But my cheeks burned when I saw the dreamseller was also clapping.

I was always an austere, stubborn professor who rarely laughed, very different from the dreamseller. He gives his disciples the freedom to do silly things, while I was a believer in absolute silence in the classroom. Respect above all. He wanted to disappear and allow the anonymous to stand out; I, on the other hand, never let any student win a debate. Obedience above all. I overvalued drama and disdained comedy in the small world of the classroom. The dreamseller valued both. I fear I prepared servants of the system rather than human beings to correct it. The dreamseller did the opposite.

That's when I noticed three men whispering next to me. They didn't realize I was part of the group. They were talking about the dreamseller. One of them took out a handheld computer and reviewed a series of images. I thought I saw the dreamseller on the screen. I tried to get closer, but they quickly removed the image. However, I was able to see a very strange message on the screen:

"The eagle lives. It must be destroyed." And they quietly left.

I remembered the dreamseller's revelations in the city's stadium: that he had been a giant in the financial and social world. But since he lived in tatters and was highly critical of the system in which we found ourselves, I took his revelations as symbolic, not literal. After watching him shiver from the lack of warm clothing, or get sick and not have medicine to treat his illness, or go hungry, I was convinced it was impossible he was once a multimillionaire. I figured he was a poor man who was rich in wisdom—but one who had no place to lay his head.

Then some teenagers in the audience bumped into me, trying to get closer to the dreamseller. They were students from a nearby school who had been passing by and were captivated by our two clowns.

Bartholomew and Barnabas, encouraged by the applause, took a bow. Then, Barnabas went into a trance, his politician's spirit once again taking over. He liked to use difficult words but often mispronounced them. As if in full campaign mode, he declared, "Hear me, people, the hoi polloi, the great unwashed masses of this noble city . . ."

"Yea! Very good!" bellowed Bartholomew, urging the crowd to break out in another round of applause. Extremely encouraged, the Mayor thanked them and continued his speech:

"I ask for your votes! I promise to clean up political skulldugging." Barnabas gave a wan smile, unable to pronounce "skullduggery." He tried again and still got it wrong: "Skullduggeny! Skulldugness!" And the more he spoke, the more he spat on those nearby. A judge came to his aid.

"Political *skullduggery*."

"Thank you, my future attorney-general," Barnabas said.

Edson, "the Miracle Worker," wasted no time. He took a cap from his jacket and brazenly added, "Well, good people, man does not live by talk alone. The Mayor, with that delicate little body of his, needs to eat. Who would like to contribute?" And he passed the cap among the onlookers, collecting enough money for a bountiful supper for the group.

The dreamseller left quietly. He was an artisan of ideas, while his two subordinates were artisans of eccentricity. But the lawyers remained thirsty for his knowledge. Some were already familiar with his reputation; now they knew his reasoning. They couldn't define him. Neither could we.

They understood, at least for the moment, that some write the laws, while others apply them. Some wear coats and ties, while others go around dressed in rags. Some write books, others read them. But fundamentally we are all children at play, not comprehending the most important phenomena of existence.

CHAPTER 5

A Master Who Disturbed the Brain

As the months passed, the dreamseller defended the idea that the scientific discoveries that should free us were instead imprisoning us. Our minds were paralyzed by technology and excess information. We were like children living in the shadow of the "fathers of knowledge."

Pythagoras faced prejudice. Socrates submitted to the wrath of the Athenian elite. The world, symbolized by an apple, fell on Newton's head. Einstein had to disarm the bomb of truth while working in a patent office. Freud had to break the chains of a medicine that exalted the body at the expense of the mind.

The dreamseller argued that thinkers journeyed through pitfalls of injustice, disorder and lack of control on the road to true knowledge. We have forgotten this in our universities. We applauded courageous pioneers of knowledge but we were timid. We had a primal fear of confronting chaos and thinking freely.

"Don't blindly follow me. Don't swallow my ideas without letting them pass through the stomach of your criticism. Every great social and political disaster comes from the unquestioning worship of truth, the passive acceptance of ideas." Then what the dreamseller said shocked us: "The passive acceptance of ideas is worse than minor criticism aimed at them. I'm not looking for servants but followers who think. If they're not able to criticize me, they're not worthy of following me," he said emphatically.

Indignant, he said that the majority of students spent their twenty years from kindergarten to graduate school without ever formulating an original thought, without having opinions of their own and without the courage to think differently from their peers. We criticized the German youth who were seduced by Hitler to commit atrocities against Jews, Gypsies and homosexuals but were unaware that the social system was silencing the world's young people in our own century.

So one day, the dreamseller came onto the campus of one of the city's largest universities and shouted to the students:

"Venice is dying at the rate of half an inch a year. Doesn't that bother you? But who cares that the most charming of all cities is being drowned in the waters of the Adriatic? Where are the student protests against climatic disasters? Hunger kills between two hundred and three hundred poor, starving children daily. But who has time to listen to their cries? A small fraction of the funds world leaders spend to shore up the financial system could have wiped out world hunger. Doesn't such apathy bother you?"

Incensed, he would go from campus to campus, roaring:

"Fortunate are those who feed their brain with doubt, for theirs is the kingdom of new knowledge. Happy are those dissatisfied with our pitiful answers and false beliefs, for they arrive at places never before reached. Oh, how perverse a system that stones those who dare to think differently! Who will find solutions for the great problems of humanity?"

Some of the university students said, "What's that lunatic saying? Feeding the brain with doubt? We live in the time of scientific certainty and logic. How can anyone praise disorder?"

Seeing that none of the students raised their hands, Bartholomew stood up and said, "I'll try to solve the problems of humanity! I've been beaten down by society. I never fit into the normal way of doing things. I'm a wasted talent."

I couldn't believe his audacity. At the same time, the Mayor saw an eight-year-old boy drop his sandwich. The boy was the son of a professor standing a few yards away, concentrating on the bizarre characters who had invaded their campus.

The Mayor grabbed the sandwich, spat on it to clean it, rubbed it on his dirty clothes and then, with a subtle glance, offered it back to the little boy. The boy was disgusted and refused the sandwich. The Mayor began eating it like a starving dog. Between bites, he heard Honeymouth holding court and spoke up with his mouth full:

"Men like me, who personally know human suffering, should run the country." Lifting the remains of the sandwich he was eating, he added, "Don't be fooled by appearances. I'm an excellent product in a bad wrapper. Of the people and for the people, I sanctify myself."

I could keep quiet no longer. "'Sacrifice myself,'" I corrected him, "not 'sanctify myself.'"

Then the shameless reprobate looked at me and either praised or knocked me, I don't know which. "Saintly man! Thank you for your early vote. This man can see the pearl hidden in this handsome skull."

I raised my hands to my head and snorted to keep from lunging at him.

Days later, we were strolling casually down a wide street when we saw men and women in white clothing coming from and going into the convention center. A sign read "International Convention of Cardiology."

Without hesitating, the Master entered the lobby. We couldn't get into the private areas of the event because we didn't have badges, and given the clothes we were wearing any attempt to do so would lead to expulsion. I felt the setting was too sophisticated for us and tried to distance myself from the group.

The pharmaceutical industry, with luxurious booths, was displaying its latest heart medicines and inventions: antihypertensives, anticoagulants, antiarrhythmics and a whole series of other drugs and devices. Cardiology professors from countless medical schools from around the world were here. The dreamseller, with his trained eye, carefully observed their movement, their gestures, the muscles in their faces, their way of speaking. He noticed something strange.

A few minutes later, he decided to make his presence felt, raising his voice, regardless of whether he was making a scene or not.

"Distinguished cardiologists, you treat heart attacks and other coronary diseases. But who among you is healthy in his mental heart?"

Seeing that intriguing man with his booming voice and his crazy clothes talking to thin air, a small group of the curious soon gathered. Some thought he must be an actor hired to announce the launching of some new drug. But then came a bombshell:

"How many of you have mental arrhythmia or maybe even mental infarction? How many of you have an agitated mind, overactive, racing like a runaway heart? How many have emotions whose 'arteries' are as blocked as the coronaries that kill the tissues of the heart? Who among you relaxes and oxygenates his mind with pleasure?"

The audience of cardiologists had never heard such questions. Could the mind alter their intellectual pulse rate by generating an unhealthy overload of thoughts and mental images? The dreamseller believed it could. Could emotion block the flow of pleasure? He believed it could.

CHAPTER 6

Scream Therapy

THE DREAMSELLER'S KNOWLEDGE IMPRESSED ME. I DIDN'T know if he had an undergraduate degree or had done postgraduate studies, but I knew he read newspapers, magazines, scientific journals and books wherever he had a chance—even under bridges and overpasses, by candlelight. In fact, he kept small private libraries under two of the overpasses where we slept. A piece of bread satisfied him, but nothing nourished him like a good book. No one at the cardiology conference answered the dreamseller's questions. Though they remained silent, he knew that in many of the listeners' minds was a cry, an unheard cry indicating that something was amiss in their mental heart. They were overly agitated, excessively busy, thought too much and worked too hard. Like the businessmen, ninety percent of them had three or more psychosomatic symptoms such as headaches, accelerated heart rates, gastritis, hair loss attributable to stress, fatigue and memory loss.

"Can a person with mental heart disease take good care of someone with physical heart disease?" he asked. "Yes, he can. But not for long and not well."

Suddenly, a man appeared amid the small audience, bellowing so much that he almost gave them heart attacks. Yes, it was

Honeymouth, disturber of minds and hearts. He began screaming as if he were dying.

"Aaaahhh! Uuhhh! Aaaahhh! Uuhhh!" And then he fainted.

I went over to him, not knowing what was happening. For
a moment I thought, "This time Bartholomew's had a heart attack. Incredible, right in front of a group of cardiologists!" Solomon began to rub his hand on the left side of Bartholomew's
chest. I had to hold him up so he wouldn't pass out. Edson,
the Miracle Worker, kneeled and started praying for his dying
friend. Dimas panicked and said, "Honeymouth is going to die!
Honeymouth is going to die!" Monica and Jurema were in despair. They begged the doctors, "Help him, please! Don't let
him die!"

Bartholomew was immediately tended to by several doctors. They laid him on the floor and listened to his heart. A
doctor quickly brought a defibrillator to administer a shock.
The dreamseller was worried.

Suddenly, the Mayor rushed in. With total self-confidence,
as if he were the most experienced doctor on the planet, he said:

"Stay calm, my dear doctors. I'm familiar with the case.
He's my patient." Hearing this, they made way for him. He
abruptly grabbed Jurema by the hand and said, "This lovely
lady of some eighty-plus years will perform mouth-to-mouth
resuscitation on my patient."

"Me?" said the professor, startled.

Realizing that he was about to be kissed by Jurema, Bartholomew immediately sat up. Now, if it had been Monica, he
would have remained as still as a stone. Bartholomew opened
and closed his arms three times, breathing deeply, and gave
three small cries: "Aaahhh! Aaahhh!" Then he explained:

"My dear doctors, I have just done primal scream therapy.
A therapy that my friend Dr. Mayor and I created to de-stress
the heart!"

When they saw they'd been fooled, some of the cardiologists raised their hands to their heads. They felt like idiots, and so did I. Some of them reprimanded the pair; others wanted to punch them. The dreamseller had to intervene once again.

"Friends, have you noticed how our emotions can go from one extreme to the other in a fraction of a second? We're calm one instant, explosive the next. Peaceful one moment, aggressive the next. Isn't that a sign of mental collapse? Have you ever noticed how our mind suffers over foolish details, fluctuates because of small frustrations, taking on problems that aren't its own? Isn't that mental arrhythmia? Why get mad at these two young men? At least they tried to lower the stress level. They didn't hurt anyone."

In the field of sociology, we joked about surgeons, especially heart surgeons. Some of them had enormous egos. When they went into the operating room they thought they were gods, and when they left they were sure of it. Deep down, however, as the dreamseller tried to demonstrate, they were people who treated others with affection but were unaffectionate with themselves.

The doctors were speechless. They had never imagined that a beggar would tell them they had seriously fluctuating mental arrhythmia. And the dreamseller added, "The health care system has led you to partly betray the ethics of Hippocrates, the father of medicine: you took care of your patients but ignored yourselves . . ."

In fact, many doctors worked seventy-hour weeks. The excess of work conspired against their enjoyment of life. An elderly and experienced French professor of cardiology, already aware of the dreamseller's fame, took the liberty of speaking up:

"The incidence of cancer, heart disease, anxiety, panic attacks and depression among doctors is startling. We don't even have time to cry or lament."

A dismayed Brazilian heart surgeon added:

"It's true, the health care system has turned into a vampire that sucks the blood out of the most idealistic of professions. We spend our lives taking care of others and, before we know it, there's little time left for us to live. And the worst part is that we have to use our crumbs of time to reclaim the health we've lost along the way."

"If doctors themselves are sick," I thought, "then how bad off is the rest of the world?" I did a rundown of my past and remembered rarely meeting healthy, calm, sedate students and professors. And even the calm professors I knew had their fits of fury when contradicted. I, particularly, was tense, impatient, nervous, frenetic, angry. My emotions would go to extremes, from calm to irritable in a matter of seconds. I needed prescription tranquilizers to keep from erupting in the classroom, and just to sleep four or five hours a night—if I could sleep at all.

Just when the conversation was heading toward a higher plane, the Mayor asked a question to which I knew the answer: "Dreamseller, what do you think? Am I normal?"

This time, I laughed so hard that it startled the others. I couldn't hold back and told the dreamseller, "You're exceedingly normal, Mayor," if it was normal to be sick, I thought.

A smile plastered on his face, the Mayor said gratefully:

"Thank you, Julio Cesar, emperor of weary hearts. Someday, when I come to power, you will be my adviser for 'irrelevant' affairs."

I didn't know if I should be flattered or offended. All I know is that he managed to confuse me. While these thoughts were running through my mind, Bartholomew said to the Mayor:

"Wake up, Mayor! 'Superego' here called you a nutjob, batty, off your rocker. Get it?" Bartholomew had given me a nickname I hated: Superego. To that insulting alcoholic, "superego" meant superproud, superhaughty—not the way Freud conceived of it.

"Lay off, Honeymouth," the Mayor said. "You're the one who's unhinged." Infuriated, Honeymouth told the dreamseller, "You know I was a karate champion. Hold me back or that guy's going to get what's coming to him."

"Bring it on, you wimp."

Some of the doctors tried to separate these idiots. The Mayor took a boxer's stance, accidentally hitting the elderly French professor. Already stressed, fatigued and having gone several nights without sleep, the doctor fainted.

"Oh, no! I've sent the doctor to meet his maker," he said.

I raised my hands to my head, feeling partially responsible. Society was already smothering doctors, and we were making it worse. The world was one gigantic mental hospital, and the dreamseller's disciples were setting fire to it. The doctor quickly regained consciousness, stood up and began screaming:

"Aaaahhh! Uuhhh! Aaaahhh! Uuhhh!"

Everyone tried to help him, but suddenly, after the primitive grunts, he spread his arms, breathed deeply and said, "Take it easy, people. It's scream therapy! It *does* feel great to de-stress!"

Two other doctors also began screaming. Immediately, other formal, extremely well-behaved physicians started to shout. Security called the paramedics.

For a crazy moment, I had the urge to let out some screams of my own to relieve my stress. Craziness, I discovered, is contagious.

CHAPTER 7

A Psychotic with Quite an Imagination

WE SLEPT THAT NIGHT BENEATH THE AMERICA BRIDGE, which connected to the city's major arteries. It wasn't the place where we usually slept, since the nightly traffic of buses and trucks was nearly unbearable. But we had a reserved spot in that enormous "hotel" for the homeless, where we kept a few thin mattresses in a corner. No one touched our meager belongings, for among the homeless there's a code of mutual protection: each one respects the crumbs of the other.

Geronimo, an elderly and likable beggar who had been sleeping at the America for twenty years, liked it when we spent the night there. He would perk up when we arrived, serving us stale crackers and cookies. Incredible as it seems, he made delicious coffee over a small campfire. He was schizophrenic and, from time to time, he hallucinated. During those attacks, he would talk about the monsters that pursued him. His imagination would be the envy of horror story writers. While we drank coffee, he told us that the night before he had faced the most terrifying monster:

"The beast had seven heads with seven horns. He had a sword in his hands and another that stuck out of his belly. I could see his heart beating in his chest. And he sucked the blood out of anything that came near him. The monster howled like a dinosaur. He wanted to eat me alive. He was as hungry as the Mayor and as ugly as the Miracle Worker," he said, pointing at Edson. We nearly died laughing.

Geronimo's mind was sometimes a scattered mess. He interrupted the story of the monster and started telling us about an airplane that had flown under the bridge. Bartholomew said anxiously, "Wait, what did you do about the beast?"

Like Don Quixote recalling windmills, Geronimo remembered the story. He puffed out his chest and finished his epic tale:

"I fought the demon for two hours. That beast with his two large swords and me with just this little knife." He showed us the blade as if it were his trophy. "The monster was angry. He jumped around like a monkey and talked like Honeymouth: 'I'll kill you, old man! This overpass belongs to me!' It was a battle of giants. He almost cut open my chest, almost gashed my neck, almost fractured my skull. Almost, but I was more agile than the beast. As quick as a cat, I stabbed him in the back. And seeing that he couldn't defeat me, the monster ran away."

Bartholomew said enthusiastically, "Next time you come and get me, Geronimo, and I'll get rid of it. I used to be a monster hunter under these bridges."

"Right," I thought to myself, "you hunted the monsters you created when you were having alcohol withdrawal symptoms." I had witnessed one of those attacks.

"You can count on me, too," said the Mayor. "I've killed ten tyrannosaurs in my time."

The Mayor went on to demonstrate to Geronimo just how he had dispatched those fierce animals. Awkward as always, he tripped and landed on top of the poor old man, knocking him off his feet. We helped Barnabas up and he pulled Geronimo from the rubble. Regaining his composure, the old man said:

"Rest assured I'll call you the next time the monster shows up . . ." He paused, then concluded, "Actually, maybe I'll just wait and watch that fight on television."

I chuckled. Even Geronimo wanted to get away from the pair. I don't know whether they believed his story, whether they had psychotic attacks of their own, or if they were just up for anything that promised a bit of amusement. All I do know is that one lunatic understands another.

The next morning, I got up early with an aching back. My monster was the mattress pad. We said good-bye to Geronimo and resumed our journey. Three blocks later, we saw an apparently nervous man coming toward us. He was about forty and had slightly graying hair, a light complexion and was wearing a white shirt and black blazer. He could have been another of the dreamseller's admirers—or one of his critics.

The dreamseller, the Mayor, Bartholomew and I were just ahead of the group, and Professor Jurema and Monica had just caught up with us. We were telling them about Geronimo's feats and when the stranger came up to him and said:

"Dreamseller, I've got a present for you." He immediately put his hand inside his blazer and pulled out a revolver. Just as he was about to fire point-blank, the dreamseller, with impressive reflexes, knocked the gun from his hand, tossed it into the air and caught it. We were amazed. The astonished criminal ran off.

"Please bury this," the dreamseller told Bartholomew, handing him the gun.

"How did you do that?" Edson asked.

Smiling, he replied, "Experience. I'm an expert in certain kinds of hand-to-hand combat."

"Are you joking?" Solomon asked in surprise.

"Life is one big joke," he said, and went on walking.

Meanwhile, the Mayor was busy hurting another innocent

bystander. As he told the story of the dreamseller grabbing the gun, he thrust his right fist forward and brought his left elbow back quickly, yelling "Yah!" and unwittingly hit Jurema in the stomach. She fell backward.

"Oh, God, I've killed Jurema!"

But Jurema didn't die. She had practiced ballet for more than thirty years and had sharp reflexes. When she saw the Mayor's elbow, she managed to pull back and cushion the blow. We rushed to her side.

"The Mayor's going to kill one of us yet," she said, as we helped her up.

I started to think about the danger the dreamseller had exposed himself to. I was especially worried about the way the guy had approached him. He didn't look like a mugger, more like an assassin. It looked like a hit job. But who would want to kill him, and why? I had little time to think about the matter, however, because the dreamseller soon offered us some more beautiful lessons.

He saw an olive tree that was over three hundred years old. Its gnarled trunk was twisted and mutilated by the effects of weather over the centuries. Contemplating it joyfully, he said:

"Olive tree, you are stronger than the strongest of men. How many generals have passed by you, proud, arrogant, as if they were immortal, but succumbed to the perils of time? And you, humbly, have endured. How many kings have passed by you with majestic processions, only to face certain ruin? And you, simple and nameless, endure to this day, continuing to tell your story."

He turned to us and said, "The best stories are written in anonymity. It's time for the anonymous revolution."

Along our journey, I suspected that the dreamseller wished to bring about a revolution in the fabric of society. A revolution of ideas, one without weapons. A simple, implosive, penetrating revolution, but one without pressure, coercion, manipulation or aggression. However, considering the team he had chosen to carry out that revolution, I felt he had already failed. Could it be he didn't realize that the complicated group of disciples wasn't up to the task? Who would listen to them? Do politicians listen to a band of troublemakers? Would Congress treat them like clowns or wise men?

But I didn't realize that the sparks of revolution had already been lit. Not only were his disciples more outspoken in debating ideas, countless people who would follow us were braver, no longer lowering their heads when confronted, exercising their rights, feeling like citizens.

The ideas he offered went viral. I was not the only one writing them down, so were journalists and students. They were beginning to think critically, to construct ideas of their own and to have the audacity to express them.

CHAPTER 8

The Great Mission

TWO WEEKS LATER, WE WENT BACK TO THE ENORMOUS courtyard outside the federal courthouse. This time the dreamseller did not address an audience. He sat down on the grass in silence, near an old concrete bench with peeling paint. He gazed calmly at the horizon as if both close to and distant from us. We sat down around him and I was glad to not have a crowd around us.

The dreamseller brushed his hair away from his brow and said softly:

"Rousseau said that man is born good and society corrupts him. But that idea needs some refining: to me, *man is born neutral and society educates or accentuates his instincts, frees his mind or imprisons it. And it usually imprisons it.*"

The dreamseller was always warning us that we must seek the true breath of freedom. We were suffocated by the shrinking of pleasure, creativity and spontaneity.

"Every baby," he continued, "is born with an instinct for aggressiveness and selfishness. It's a parent's job to polish that mind by filling it with thousands of life experiences to mitigate those primal instincts and breed altruism, compassion, friendliness and the ability to think before acting."

Hearing his words, I sifted through my own memory. I had

met many social scientists and authors but never anyone like this. I wondered if I was seeing history in the making. I asked myself how far this revolutionary dreamseller would go with his plan and whether the texts I'd write about him would reach the people.

At that moment, Edson, the Miracle Worker, suddenly ran up, panting, almost out of breath. He had gone to use the bathroom, and as he walked back, he happened upon a scene that shook him. Nervously, he told us about a young man climbing the thirty-foot high monument to independence, most likely to take his own life. People were gathering anxiously around the site.

A chill ran down my spine. I remembered when I was at the top of the San Pablo Building, depressed, hopeless, with no reason to go on living. Images flashed through my mind, images I wanted to erase but couldn't. The past can't be erased. It only assumes other guises.

The news shook our group. We all looked at the dreamseller. We expected he would immediately rise to his feet and rescue the young man, as he had done with me. But he didn't move. We expected he would use his incisive intelligence to break through the resistance of a youth who had lost the enchantment of life. But he didn't react. We tried to lead him by the arm, but he insisted on staying where he was.

To our amazement, he told us, "Go there and sell dreams to the man."

"What? Us? It's too big a risk, Master!" Monica said, and we all agreed.

The simple thought of someone killing themselves right before our eyes, and our being unable to do anything about it unnerved us. We were imprisoned by fear.

Tears are shed at the beginning and the end of life, but it's hard to witness a young person cutting off his own breath. Who is he? Who are his friends? What torments him? We were un-prepared to confront that volatile situation. What if we failed?

The dreamseller remained seated. Seeing us rooted along-side him, he recited the poetry of dreams:

"Dreams inspire emotion, free the imagination, nurture the intelligence. Whoever dreams rewrites his story and reinvents his history. Will you reinvent yourselves?"

Suddenly, his emotions flashed, he stood up and finished his thought:

"Without dreams, we're the servants of selfishness, vassals of individualism, slaves to our instincts. The greatest dream to be sold in this society is the dream of a free mind!"

"Do you dream of a free mind?" he yelled, startling pass-ersby. "If you dream, why don't you take risks to rescue that young man? The risk of failing, of looking ridiculous, of being embarrassed, of crying, being labeled stupid, psychotic, a fraud are all part of being a dreamseller. And that's why I have called you!"

And he urged us:

"That man doesn't want to kill himself. He has a thirst to live but doesn't know it. Use his self-destructive energy to explore his thirst. How? I don't know! Free his mind! Do the dance of life. Approach him with a flexible, loose, imaginative mind."

I tried to gulp down the knot in my throat. This is one thing a university never taught me to do.

"Dancing's something I understand!" Honeymouth said. And that's just what I was afraid of.

"And so do I!" said the Mayor, suddenly grabbing Monica to dance.

A man was dying, and these two found time to play.

CHAPTER 9

Good Samaritans or Funeral Home Partners?

W E WEREN'T PRIESTS OR DOCTORS, AND CERTAINLY NOT psychologists. We weren't perfect or self-confident, and we had no experience in rescuing depressed people. We were just people, fascinated by a stranger who used every means to free us from the place where we were imprisoned.

The dreamseller's words played in my mind. I couldn't remain indifferent, especially since I had come close to killing myself under similar circumstances. But I was paralyzed. "But why am I paralyzed?" I wondered. "From fear that the man will kill himself or from fear that I won't be able to help him?"

It bothered me to realize that my fear of failure mattered more to me than this man's life. I had spent years speaking about freedom while being imprisoned by this society. I was a critical intellectual and, as such, thought that critics were free, but critics rarely stick their necks out. They hide their shortcomings. I needed to try, needed to go beyond the frontiers of my ego, but my legs wouldn't obey. Stress shook the balance between my brain and my body.

What now, I thought: Do I react or retreat? Hold out my hands or pull them back? Face the shame or hide? I needed to make a choice and accept the consequences. I had made a thousand excuses for not reaching out to help others in the past. But now I was out of excuses.

Solomon was hyperventilating at the thought, rubbing his hands on his chest. He asked the Mayor to sit down, and thankfully, he came to his senses. Noting our hesitancy, the dreamseller asked once more, "Who will go?"

Professor Jurema rubbed her forehead. I lowered my eyes. Edson mediated. Dimas snorted. "Send me, Boss. I accept the challenge," Bartholomew said.

Barnabas rose and said, "Dreamseller, count me in. I'm a freethinker, so how can I refuse to free other minds?"

I thought I was going to have a panic attack. A closeted atheist, I found myself calling on the divine. "Oh my God, not those two!"

But the pair was emboldened. Resolute, they rose to their feet. And foreseeing the worst, I tried to warn the dreamseller as politely as I could.

"Bartholomew and Barnabas are good, well-meaning guys who like to help their fellow man. But don't you think it's better for them to stay here?"

They wrinkled their noses.

"Why are you worried, Superego?" they responded unflinchingly.

I couldn't take it. I forgot about the guy on the verge of killing himself:

"Why am I worried? For a million of reasons," I replied, irritated. "You can't control your tongue! You're impertinent, insubordinate, rebellious. With the two of you, what's already a difficult task will become mission impossible!"

"I know that movie!" the Mayor yelled.

Although Jurema had been more patient than I, she couldn't stand it anymore, either. She feared these two recovering alcoholics would ruin the dreamseller's plan: The revolution of the anonymous would never strike a blow.

"Master, I really like Bartholomew and Barnabas, but you're the only one with enough experience to keep this man from committing suicide."

But all of this only made the two more determined.

"My dear and lovely Jurema, esteemed Superego, please remain calm. Barnabas and I are experts at dealing with suicides."

"We are?" Barnabas asked. But then he coughed and corrected himself: "I mean, yes, of course we are. We've already sent ten to their graves."

"Ten?" I asked, thinking it must be a joke.

"Yes, ten!" confirmed the inveterate talker, spreading his hands.

We almost fainted when we heard this statistic, but no one doubted they had sent ten people to meet their maker. Just imagine if they had tried to save me when I wanted to give up on life. I'd be gone. I ran a hand over my head and neck to reassure myself I was alive. The lump was still in my throat.

Monica, ever patient and amused, had a soft spot for the two of them, but she knew they had no place in a situation that called for calm, clear thinking.

"Dreamseller, I hoped that with time your disciples would become calmer, restrained, balanced. But some of them seem . . . not quite ready."

I don't know whether Bartholomew understood her criticism, but he was grateful. "Thank you, dear Monica."

The Master replied patiently:

"Monica, no one can change anyone else. My plan isn't to change them but to encourage them to rewrite their story. Wisdom doesn't lie in changing others but in respecting our differences."

Edson, the Miracle Worker, was anxious, thinking about the young man who had scaled the monument. After a few silent prayers, he tried flattery:

"Honeymouth, Mayor, you're the most gifted of the group. I suggest you stay with the dreamseller while we try to do something for this poor man . . ."

Even Dimas, aka Angel Hand, a skilled pickpocket and recovering rogue, tried to stop them. Dimas, who was stuttering less and less, began stammering again. "I'll st-stay wi—with you, dear fr—friends."

But nothing deterred the determined duo. The Mayor, sticking out his chest like a politician, proclaimed, "Voices of the opposition wish to silence me!"

"You're only hearing the voices in your head," I said, unable to restrain myself.

"Trust in God and in us, too," Honeymouth said.

The dreamseller shook his head. We were wasting time squabbling. "Arguments are excuses for inaction! Let them go. You're a family.

"Be social activists. Act."

For the first time, I realized how demagogues are created; we had fallen victim to something I had dedicated so much time railing against in my writings. It was time to act.

Bartholomew tried to put us at ease. "Rest assured, my friends. Ours are complex minds in search of the uncomplicated. We'll only come to the rescue if the rest of you fail."

"How can we stop them?" I asked Monica and Jurema. "Those two are nothing but trouble."

And they would cause much more trouble than we ever imagined.

CHAPTER 10

Paralyzed by Fear

L IVING IN OUR DYSFUNCTIONAL FAMILY MEANT CONSTANT surprises, sometimes spectacular, sometimes pathetic. Young Solomon and Edson took me by the arm and hurried me along. We wondered whether we might be too late.

On the way to the other end of the square, we passed dozens of towering trees—pine trees, palms, and acacias—blocking our view of the cast-iron horse the man had scaled. On the way, Bartholomew decided, "Superego, you'll be our leader!"

"Leader? Me? Fat chance!" I said. But they all wanted me to lead the mission. After all, I was the one with the most personal experience with this. But my mind was racing, my fragile courage stripped from me, my spirits stolen away. I thought, "What can I say? And how to say it? How should I act? This was going to be a catastrophe."

Barnabas was so overweight and out of shape he was out of breath and lagged behind. "It takes one to save one," he said between bites of a sandwich.

I wanted to pummel him, but I tried to regain control. For years on end I prepared tirelessly for every class I taught, but now I was in uncharted water. And I wished I had a compass. Just then, Bartholomew looked at the group and said, "People. Let's pretend we're normal."

Monica replied tensely, "Then hide your face and shut your mouth, Bartholomew."

Despite how nervous they made me, Don Quixote and Sancho Panza—Honeymouth and his faithful squire, the Mayor—were invariably festive. "There are advantages to being that crazy," I told myself.

As we neared the monument, we saw people clustered around the base. I looked up and saw a man younger than thirty years old near the top. Knowing the dreamseller was nowhere near to help me, my anxiety clouded my thoughts.

Monica and Jurema trailed behind me, breathlessly, followed by Bartholomew and Barnabas, who were chatting about trivial matters.

Honeymouth asked for a bite of the Mayor's sandwich. And the Mayor, realizing it was almost gone, guarded it like a lion with its prey. I couldn't understand how they could eat at a time like this. More than a hundred people had formed a semicircle in front of the monument. The fireman hadn't arrived yet. A few policemen were patrolling the courtyard of the federal courthouse, but they had no idea what to do. The jumper had already made his way up the sixty-foot pedestal and was now climbing up the gigantic cast-iron horse. All he had was a grapple and a rope for support. He slipped frequently, making the onlookers gasp. He didn't appear to be an amateur rock climber or thrill-seeker, just a human being in the terminal stages of pain.

Bartholomew and Barnabas looked at me and said, "Well, leader, what now?"

I didn't know where to begin. I saw myself in him, sensed myself in him but was at a loss for what to do or how to get him to come down. It only managed to awaken the demons slumbering in my unconscious. They no longer haunted me, but it was uncomfortable to revive them.

I knew the young man wanted to find a place that existed only in his limited imagination, a place without pain, tears, memories—nothing. He must have tried to overcome his problems and perhaps had taken medication or alcohol in search of relief. He must have heard advice and sought alternatives to ease his troubled mind. But nothing had comforted him, apparently. Language is a crude instrument when it comes to describing a crisis. When I passed through the arduous valley of clinical depression, I was a stranger even to myself.

Monica grabbed my arm. She had once been a slave to bulimia; she would binge eat and then purge. Her self-image was distorted. As a model, she was applauded for her beauty, but her self-esteem was nonexistent. On this day, she urged me to take action:

"Quick, you have to do something. He's going to jump at any moment."

I didn't want the burden of being the leader. After all, I wasn't even the leader of myself. I'm a genius, and like many geniuses, I have faith only in science and in numbers, not in life. Though I have an IQ of 140, far above average, that IQ hadn't humanized me. I still couldn't manage to take a risk for the young man. What good is a high IQ if I can't think straight when the world is crumbling around me? What good does it do to have an extraordinary cerebral cortex if I react like a child in tense situations?

When I turned and found Edson praying, I snapped at him. "Stop praying," I said, "and show us your miraculous powers!"

Since I wasn't taking any action, others more human than I risked themselves. Bartholomew was actually behaving himself, realizing there was very little he could do. Trying to unblock my mind, he asked, "How did the dreamseller rescue you?"

I remembered how he had broken through the police tape

and gone to the top of the building, sneaking past the psychiatrist and the police chief. When he approached me, I screamed that I would kill myself. But he unnerved me when he sat down on the ledge and began eating a sandwich. I shouted again that I would end my life, but he astonished me by saying, "Could you not interrupt my dinner?" I remember thinking, "I've met somebody crazier than I am."

When I told Bartholomew that the Dreamseller had begun his rescue with nothing but a sandwich in his hand, the Mayor jumped in. He took his sandwich from his old black coat and presented it to me, saying "It's up to you, my friend!"

It was like a 10,000 volt shock. I swallowed hard. I didn't know what to do with that sandwich or how to start my intervention. I only knew that I could very well hasten this man's suicide. I had lived that story and I knew banal words are useless.

I had to use something unexpected to break into his conflicted mind, as the dreamseller had done with me. But it didn't come to me. My anxiety paralyzed my body and mind. I began to exhibit nervous tics, blinking my eyes, and rubbing my face compulsively. I was stripped of my pride in public.

CHAPTER 11

A Devilish Confusion

WHILE I FLOUNDERED, OTHERS TRIED TO DO WHAT I COULD not—save the young man. Professor Jurema, the most daring, shouted up at him, "Life is hard, son, but don't give up on it. Fight back!"

Nothing. The man didn't even react. Another woman, who appeared to be about seventy-five, called up to him: "Think about the people who love you."

But he remained unmoved. This was a man who was tired of thinking, of caring and he saw none of the beauty in life. His sole desire was to end his emotional suffering.

A psychologist stepped forward from the crowd, went up to the monument, and tried to draw his attention. "Please, give me the chance to listen to you! You have a friend in me. Let's talk!"

It was an interesting, respectful, intelligent approach. But the man didn't want friends or to talk about his problems. Resolute in his decision, he wasn't seeking opportunities to find relief. When he had almost reached the horse's back, he stumbled and nearly fell. Panicked people covered their eyes.

Two psychiatrists who specialized in prescribing antidepressants were passing by and stopped to try to help. They conferred with each other but didn't know how to proceed. They were successful in medicating cooperative patients but were at a loss in a situation like this.

One of the doctors, a gray-haired man, ventured the obvious: "Don't take your life. There's no suffering that can't be overcome."

But the young man seemed deaf, hearing only the voice in his nightmares. Others tried: a policeman, a cardiologist, a social worker. All failed. The young man looked down and finally spoke, shouting angrily at the spectators, "Get out of here if you don't want to see a man's final moments."

He had climbed atop the horse and was trying to reach the shoulders of the soldier. Suddenly, he lost his grip and started to fall off the side, clutching onto the soldier's sword with one hand. The crowd gasped. He continued scaling the monument, unaware that unconsciously he wanted to scale the heights of his anguish and transcend it. He wanted to jump from the highest point. I saw this as a breath of life, a spark of hope. And I tried to use it to save his life.

I pushed aside my fears and attempted to win him over by putting myself in his place. I took a deep breath and said, "Listen, my friend! I've been where you are. I understand, at least a little, the pain you must be going through. Tell me your stories, your troubles. Life is worth the trouble."

The young man stopped climbing. I thought I had reached him. But I was quickly disillusioned.

"Your words make me want to throw up."

I was shaken. I saw that I'd done worse than the others. Nothing seemed to move him. He finally made it to the top of the monument and stood on the shoulders of the iron soldier. It was hard for him to keep his balance.

That was when the two "gravediggers" of the group showed

up at the worst possible moment. Both came dangerously close to the monument and, instead of speaking to the jumper, started trying to calm the crowd.

"Take it easy, folks! Don't lose hope!" said Honeymouth.

"We're going to get this guy down in a hurry," the Mayor said.

The crowd fell silent. The young man was flabbergasted. He looked down, blinked, and couldn't believe what he heard. "Do those guys want to see blood?" he must have thought. I looked at him and immediately put my hands over my eyes.

Suddenly, Honeymouth began to shout like a lunatic. "Come down from there so I can kick your ass," he said.

Everyone, from the crowd to the young man, was shocked— speechless. There was no doubt these two were out of their minds.

"Right! Just because you climbed that monument you think you're hot stuff? Come on down from there so I can slap you around," the Mayor added, and started making karate moves.

The scene was so absurd that the suicide thought he must be delirious. He shook his head to see if he was hearing right.

Without missing a beat, Honeymouth yelled, "Suffering is a privilege of the living, you jerk. Face your life, you pile of Jell-O. Come down here and I'll smack you around a little to wake you up."

We almost fainted. I saw the color drain from the faces of the rest of the group. All of us were astonished. Once again I asked myself what I was doing in that group.

I was convinced those two were born to be partners in a funeral home. They weren't selling dreams; they were selling coffins. I imagined the guy jumping from the monument and landing at our feet. I felt the urge to pounce on Bartholomew and Barnabas and gag them.

The Mayor went even further. He began to scoff at the reasons that people kill themselves.

"What are you afraid of, huh? That you're in a financial hole? I'm in a deeper one. There's over a hundred bill collectors on my tail, son."

The man atop the monument writhed with rage. Then, seemingly indifferent to the young man, Honeymouth started chatting with the Mayor. The would-be suicide paid attention to their conversation, spoken loudly enough for him to understand what was being said.

"Mayor, every time I pass a bank, I make the sign of the cross and feel like sending flowers."

"Why, Honeymouth?"

"Because that's where I'm buried."

Both broke into laughter. Those nearby laughed at these clowns, momentarily forgetting they were at a horror show.

"I'd need to send an entire florist shop, man," the Mayor added.

Seeing them first humiliate each other and then collapse in laughter, the suicide trembled with anger. He didn't know whether to kill himself or them. They were stealing the scene. As if this weren't enough, Honeymouth began speaking of other reasons people kill themselves.

"Wake up, kid! What, did you make a fool of yourself? Did somebody insult you? Do wrong by you? I've been there. I've been kicked out, handcuffed, tied up, imprisoned. They say I'm a hopeless bum, an incorrigible nut, a characterless drunk."

"But you *are* all that, Honeymouth."

"Am I? Yeah, I guess you're right." Then he resumed his verbal assault on the young man. "You're running away from your little depression! I've been through one of the biggest. Even my shrink couldn't put up with me. Did your wife cheat on you? I've been cheated on five times!"

The young man's face was starting to twitch with rage. He scratched his head, snorted, wished he had wings so he could fly down and pummel these two.

"Five women cheated on you, Honeymouth?"

"Five, Mayor. The women don't know what they missed out on. *C'est la vie,* my friend," he said, mixing French and English.

Then it was the Mayor's turn to attack. "Are you running away from your mother-in-law? I've taken crap from three of them. One of them tried to shove my head into a microwave!"

The crowd again forgot the young man and laughed. Some began to believe it was all a show by some local theater group.

"But you *are* a scoundrel, Mayor. You deserve to be cooked alive," said Bartholomew, turning his back on the young man.

The Mayor claimed he was innocent, and to leave no room for doubt, related some of his run-ins with his former mothers-in-law. "I'd rather go to war than face a crazy mother-in-law."

Atop the monument, the young man's lips were twisted in rage. He looked like a lion trying to roar.

"You wanna die 'cause you've suffered losses? I've lost more than you have, you wimp! I lost father, mother, brother, wife, uncles, cousins, friends, jobs, respect, home."

"And even your sense of shame," the Mayor added.

"But I never lost faith in life!" Bartholomew said defiantly.

Then the Mayor began bouncing around like a boxer. He leaped and punched the air, saying, "Come on down here and face my fist of fury, you little worm!" And, like the lousy fighter he was, he tripped over his own feet, stuck out his right fist, and unintentionally hit Honeymouth on the chin.

"Where am I?" Honeymouth said, staggering. Dizzy, he blinked, saw Monica, and said, "What a lovely place. I must be in heaven." Then he looked at me, came to his senses, and said, "What's so funny, Superego? You never took one on the chin from a friend?" And he rubbed his jaw.

Solomon began to feel his obsessive-compulsive urge to stick his forefinger into a hole. But he couldn't find any available orifice. Suddenly, he noticed Edson, the Miracle Worker, praying for an angel to rescue the young man. He saw the available opening and stuck his finger deep inside it. Edson leaped forward and bellowed:

"Be gone from this body, evil spirit!" he said, thinking it was a demon trying to possess him.

I shouldn't have laughed at such a tense moment, but I couldn't hold back. I covered my mouth to avoid an explosive guffaw.

Fortunately, the police showed up to put an end to the festivities. They grabbed and handcuffed the two troublemakers and were about to haul them off to the precinct for attempted manslaughter. The young man was ecstatic as he watched; now he could finally kill himself in peace.

But suddenly Professor Jurema stepped forward.

She had white hair, a face marked by the passing of time but was dressed impeccably with beige pants and a crisp white blazer, and gave off the air of someone trustworthy. "Take it easy, officers, take it easy. These two are family."

The cops didn't understand, but they stopped to listen. She explained: "We're one big family."

"What? You, these two, and the guy up there on the monument are all related?" the confused policemen asked.

"Sure," she said, hugging Bartholomew and Barnabas. "Can't you see the resemblance?" Then, addressing the two nutty disciples, she said, "Don't you worry, boys. I'm here."

"You sure the jumper up there is one of you, too?" the taller of the two cops, a muscular dark-complexioned man, asked Honeymouth.

"My younger brother."

Hearing this, the jumper was so angry he thought he was going to have a heart attack.

And that's how the strangest family ever to walk the earth was formed.

CHAPTER 12

A Really Crazy Family

THE POLICEMEN FREED OUR FRIENDS. THEY MIGHT HAVE
doubted the two men, but not the elderly woman. Barnabas
led Bartholomew by the arm and together they whispered to
Jurema, "He's part of the family?"

"Yes."

"But what family?" Bartholomew asked, curious.

"This family of lunatics, for heaven's sake!" Professor Jurema said.

"Hey, you're right!" He looked up and said, "I even feel like
I know that guy."

The jumper was curious about what was going on beneath
his feet. He tried to turn his ear to the wind to hear their whis-
pers as the two troublemakers thanked Jurema:

"Thank you, Granny!"

Sure, Jurema was old enough to be their grandmother, but
she didn't take well to being called that. "Granny? No, Mom's
more like it."

Her words tapped something lost in them. Both had been
abandoned by their parents. Upon being adopted in public by
the professor, they started kissing her. Perhaps with an eye to
an inheritance, they told her:

"Mommy, we love you. You saved us!" Jurema tried desperately to get them off her.

"All right, all right! Enough! I'm Granny, okay? Forget I said anything."

The scene was so bizarre that the young man was no longer the center of attention but just a supporting character. He was now part of the confused audience watching this ragtag team of dreamsellers.

Solomon, Dimas, Monica and Edson all began to hug and kiss Jurema and call her Granny. I was the only one who kept my distance.

At that moment, Barnabas once again caught the spirit. Turning to the crowd, he tried to explain the inexplicable. "Noble members of the public, fear not. We're simply resolving a family matter. The guy up there is our brother."

The jumper was dumbstruck. He was so angry he was almost spitting fire. Being insulted by these two vagrants was one thing, but being adopted into a family of nutjobs was too much to bear. He lost the will to die. All he wanted was to focus his anger on these loons and end their little circus. But he thought he had gone too far to give up. So he decided to watch the events unfold.

To make things worse, Jurema decided to climb on the shoulders of her two stooges. Their alcoholic pasts had left them with the worst sense of balance. She almost fell several times, but thanks to the ballet classes she took in her youth, she kept her balance.

I expected her to be gentle with the young man. Boy, was I wrong. "Get down from there, you miscreant! Come to Granny so I can spank that pale little butt of yours."

I couldn't believe what I was hearing. Professor Jurema, a woman with a doctorate in psychology, a noted writer highly respected in academic circles, had come down to Bartholomew and Barnabas's level? I nearly fainted.

When he heard the old lady challenging him, the man became dizzy, the world began to spin around him. He got so woozy that he fell and landed—hard—straddling the horse's hindquarters.

Solomon cringed. "P-poor guy, now he's st-sterile, too."

The expression on the young man's face was at first inscrutable . . . and then suddenly tortured. He looked down and emitted a war cry: "Aaaargh!"

"Hey, he's using our scream therapy, Honeymouth," the Mayor said.

The man didn't know whether to cry or scream or kill himself. I looked at him and realized that his brain was paralyzed by testicular pain. He was as motionless as the statue.

"Come on down, little brother," Honeymouth said. "If you don't, I'm gonna climb up and grab you by the arm." And, looking at Jurema, he said dramatically, "Hold me back, Granny, or I'm climbing this thing!"

"No, don't do that," she begged him.

"No! It's too dangerous!" Edson added.

The crowd shifted. The only thing worse than witnessing one death was watching two.

"Mayor, I'm gonna end this once and for all," Honeymouth declared.

The Mayor called his bluff. "An excellent idea. Godspeed!"

Honeymouth gulped. "Well, only because Granny insists, I'll stay. I'm staaaaying!" he yelled up to the young man.

He walked close to the Mayor and whispered, "You'll pay for this, you rat!"

While they were arguing, the young man rushed down the monument to settle his debts. He was panting, in a frenzy by the time he reached the ground. Jurema, frightened, ran to hide behind Monica and me.

Bartholomew and Barnabas hadn't realized the young man had come down and was rushing up to them. The crowd applauded when he reached the ground, but the two thought the applause was for their heroism. Their backs to the monument and facing the audience, they bowed their heads in acknowledgment.

Raising his right hand to the heavens and lifting his voice like a politician, Barnabas launched into a short speech:

"Thank you for the most distinguished homage, my generous people. I pledge to issue a decree destroying all the monuments in the city so that no future idiot can try to kill himself."

The Mayor didn't know that the young man was standing right next to him, ready to explode. We all closed our eyes. This, we couldn't watch. Just then, Honeymouth made things even worse.

"No, not idiot! Jackass!" And he turned to put his hands on the shoulder of the guy next to him—unaware that it was the young man.

Trembling with rage, the young man said, "Who *are* you?"

The bungling buffoon tried to imitate the dreamseller's deep quotations. "Who am I? I don't know. I'm simply in search of myself."

"Yeah? Well, now you've found me!"

But before the young man could make a move, the Mayor, looking up at the statue, was startled to see that the jumper wasn't there. "Honeymouth! Our brother's gone to meet his maker!" he yelled.

Little did they know he was inches away from punching their own one-way tickets.

CHAPTER 13

The Great Surprise

THE YOUNG MAN WAS MASSIVE IN STATURE. BLOND, HUSKY, muscular, with powerful arms and a chest chiseled from working out. He was a professional boxer—a heavyweight. He stood almost six feet tall and weighed two hundred and ten pounds. He grabbed Bartholomew and Barnabas each by the collars and told them:

"Get ready to meet your maker, you jackasses!" he said. And then the boxer started pummeling our friends.

No one had any idea what was going on. Most thought it was bad blood between brothers. We jumped on the young boxer and managed to prevent a massacre. Even the cops joined the melee. Once they were separated, Honeymouth, bleeding and confused, groggily asked his buddy, "Mayor, are we in heaven?"

"I suspect we're in hell," Barnabas replied.

When the two realized the brute was the man from the monument, they fell to the ground on their knees. It seemed like they were thanking God for still being alive.

Jurema whispered to Monica. I could read her lips saying "This was their plan, all along." "How ridiculous," I thought. There was no way these two idiots could have consciously used such a tactic to save the young man. *Or could they?*

I began to bombard myself with questions. "Aren't these two total imbeciles? Thoughtless loudmouths? These guys can't account for their own actions, much less some one else's. How could they have outsmarted everyone and used an actual strategy to rescue him?"

I turned to see them still on their knees, mouthing the word "eleventh." I was shocked. And the windows to my mind opened. It's not easy to break through the walls of prejudice, but I began to see their actions from a different angle. I finally understood how they reached him. They had provoked him to the point of rage so that he would focus on punishing them instead himself—something I would never have considered.

They didn't use philosophical words as the dreamseller did to rescue me from the top of the San Pablo Building, but they did use the same passion, the same surprise attack, the same ability for disarming the mind and demolishing false arguments. I was amazed.

Later we would learn that Bartholomew and Barnabas hadn't sent ten men to their deaths—rather, they had saved ten from jumping from the President Kennedy Bridge near the bar where they drank. Only after police, firefighters, paramedics, psychiatrists, psychologists and even spiritual leaders failed would they leap into action.

They were drunk and disorderly, but they understood the finer points of emotional peaks and valleys. They knew that psychological jargon had little effect on someone who had condemned himself to death. My friends taunted the victim to make him project his anger onto them.

It moved me profoundly. Although I had known depression in the past, I was still an empty intellectual, a coward, an insensitive thinker who detested compromising his image by turning to others for help. As the dreamseller said, we're all experts at hiding things.

The young boxer was still drunk with rage. He struggled to break free to continue beating them.

"Why would you hit someone who saved your life?" I told him. "Why would you punch someone who gave of himself and loved you without knowing you?"

My voice was so strident that he stopped in his tracks. The crowd fell silent. I continued:

"Don't you realize they provoked your anger on purpose? Don't you understand that they made you hate them so you wouldn't hate yourself? They wouldn't let you use a period to end your life. They sold you a comma so you could go on writing your story."

The young man's anger cooled as my words washed over him. His name was Felipe, but people called him "Crusher" in the ring. He had always dealt violently with his opponents, until he was knocked out by events in his life. Sooner or later everyone is KO'd in life, but Felipe never accepted his defeat. A man who had always been violent with others could act no differently with himself.

The boxer came to his senses and concluded that the two agitators had served as sparring partners—without using any protective gear.

He looked at the two men. Bartholomew had a dark ring forming around his left eye and was bleeding from a cut just above it. The Mayor's lips were swollen and he was bleeding from the right side of his mouth.

The young man collapsed and started crying unabashedly, with no fear of the audience, no fear of criticism, no fear of his own feelings. The onlookers fell totally silent. Each teardrop spoke to the young man's pain.

It was just as the dreamseller had told us: Each person has his reasons for crumbling. Life is cyclical and there are no heroes who can be on top forever. Every person has his reasons for crying—some tears we see, while others are hidden from sight. Crusher had his own demons, and they were many. But he left behind a world of self-destruction to enter our world of sublime kindness.

He got up from his knees and hugged Honeymouth and the Mayor with uncommon affection. Bartholomew and Barnabas, who hadn't any family until they found us, melted in light of such caring. Crusher brought his chest up against theirs. He thought nothing could keep him from killing himself, but then he had met two lunatics so in love with life that they torpedoed his plans.

All three were crying. Tears and blood mixed like ink to write a new story. It was the first time I'd seen men who were strangers cry and embrace like that, a phenomenon not found in psychology texts but one described in the dreamseller's manual.

Crusher then turned to hug Professor Jurema and kissed her on the cheek. "Thanks for the spanking, Granny."

She, too, had tears in her eyes. On days like this, she felt it was easy to follow the Dreamseller. She had once shined in the classroom. And now, as her days to pass on new lessons out in the world became fewer, she shined at selling dreams.

Bartholomew and Barnabas had taken real beatings when they used this strategy to convince jumpers to get down from the bridge. The price they paid was high. Twice they had to stay in the hospital. They had bones broken three times.

After Crusher had asked their forgiveness, it was my turn to do the same.

"I'm sorry for misjudging you," I said.

This time Honeymouth spared me. "I might have done the same thing in your place." Turning to Crusher, he said, "I'm sorry for pissing you off. I was already buried under the banks, but you almost sent me to the cemetery."

We all laughed. The Mayor interjected, "You rearranged my face, dude. I won't be able to chew for an hour."

The tension had dissipated and Crusher felt comfortable enough to tell us about the problems that had sent him to the top of that monument.

"I'm a professional boxer. I was suspended for six months for using a medication they considered 'performance enhancing.' They killed me in the press. My father, my best friend, died of a heart attack two months later. I was a week from getting married, when I lost my shirt in the stock market. I lost my money and my fiancée."

That's when the dreamseller walked up to us. He had been watching from a distance, allowing his anonymous disciples to act on their own. "My son, we all have forty-six chromosomes in our cells, but we're all very different in how we handle adversity. There's no such thing as a sky without storms." What he said next shook the disciples, especially me. "I once stood on a bridge, at the height of my despair. I didn't want to die, but I had no spirit to go on living. But then, I ran into two young drop-down drunks. They provoked and insulted me. They were relentless. I half expected them to toss their whiskey in my face."

Bartholomew and Barnabas couldn't believe it. They didn't know the dreamseller was one of the people they had rescued. Because they were drunk most of the time, they couldn't remember much at all about who they had rescued. I was stupefied and I wondered, "Could these two have shaped the dreamseller's desire to sell dreams? Can the pupil teach the master? Can the patient cure the doctor?"

"After that shock, I went into hiding and spent a lot of time rethinking my life. That was when I came to understand that frustrations are a privilege of the living and transcending them is a privilege of the wise," said the dreamseller.

A few people in the crowd wrote down that sentiment. And then the dreamseller began to applaud Felipe, Bartholomew, Barnabas and Jurema. Soon, the entire crowd was clapping. However, applause is a dangerous thing for the Mayor. Although he was injured, he leaned on the person nearest him and launched into a short speech

"Thank you very much, my splendid and abyssal public," he said in a slurred voice, as if he were drunk. "Vote for me in the coming election." By this point, three people were holding up his mammoth frame.

"What office are you running for?" asked a crowd member who realized there were no upcoming elections.

Honeymouth answered for him. "Chief lunatic of this global insane asylum," he said, gesturing all around him.

They all broke out laughing, even Crusher. He got the message. He was one more inmate learning to laugh at his own madness. "You've got my vote," he cheered.

The dreamseller seconded his vote.

The people around them all pledged their votes. Inspired, the dreamseller looked Crusher in the eye and invited him to become a follower. Honeymouth looked approvingly at Barnabas and said, "I'll be your secretary of finance, brother."

"Anything but finance, you old pickpocket!"

"How can you say that, Mayor? I'm an upstanding citizen now," Bartholomew said. But, he turned to the dreamseller and asked him for forgiveness for his life before they met: "Master, before I met you, I thought there was a chance I wasn't a saint. Today . . . well, today I'm sure I'm not."

None of us were saints. We all understood that. And although the dreamseller and those two knuckleheads might not change our insane asylum of a world, we knew they could make it a fun place to live.

We left hugging one another, leaving behind a crowd of

more than a hundred people looking for a taste of adventure. As we departed, we sang our song:

I'm just a wanderer
Who lost the fear of getting lost,
Certain of his own imperfection;
You may say I'm crazy
You may mock my ideas
It doesn't matter!
What matters is I'm a wanderer,
Who sells dreams to passersby;
I've no compass or schedule,
I have nothing, yet I have everything.
I'm just a wanderer
In search of myself.

CHAPTER 14

Unusual Leaders

―――――

DAYS LATER, A WINDSWEPT FLYER LANDED AGAINST THE dreamseller's chest. He read that a Leaders of the Future seminar was to be held that night, and he decided to participate. Since the event was sponsored by the Megasoft Foundation and admission was free, we were confident we could get in. However, as always, our ratty clothes made us a target for the security guards.

People of all ages and nationalities entered without a problem, but vagrants were once again kept out. The security guards checked us from head to toe, asking us to spread our arms and scanned us for guns, bombs and dangerous chemical products.

"Very generous of those guys. I enjoyed the free massage," the Mayor said.

We took our seats in the center of the amphitheater, in the thirteenth row. We were about fifty feet from the speakers, who spoke about the molding of political, business and institutional leaders who would change the future of humanity.

The Mayor and Honeymouth sat next to each other. In less than fifteen minutes they were sound asleep. The rest of the crew was barely able to keep their eyes open. Some of the speakers were so technical and monotonous. Obviously, it was too much to ask that the dreamseller's followers develop a taste for this since they had never been taught to develop a taste for the fare of the academic world.

I never understood how the Mayor and Honeymouth, who loved to cause a scene, could always keep such sound minds. They managed to fall asleep effortlessly. I remembered reading an article that said that major business leaders relied on pills to sleep. Without their tranquilizers, their minds were restless.

The Mayor's snoring was as loud as a dissonant orchestra, the noise thundering five rows in all directions. Even the speakers looked to see what all the racket was about. I kept nudging the Mayor to quiet his snoring.

But the Mayor was on cloud nine, dreaming he was swimming in a pot of spaghetti *al sugo*. He mumbled, "delicious . . . tasty . . . delectable." The spectators in front of us started turning around. I stuffed a handkerchief in his mouth. He started chewing on it and soon calmed down.

Honeymouth was so relaxed that he began dreaming he was floating through the clouds, riding a winged horse. Making small hand movements to control the animal, he touched the heads of those in the next row. Monica, Jurema, and I tried to keep his hands to himself.

"If we depend on these two," I thought, "humanity is in for a dark future."

Soon, though, they quieted down and we were able to listen to the lecture series. During the final address, Bartholomew and Barnabas began dreaming simultaneously that they were fighting each other over a beautiful woman. It was a familiar dream, which often caused us problems under the bridges and in the shelters where we slept.

At the exact moment when they imagined they were vying for the princess's hand, the event's final speech began, dealing with great leaders of the past and their fundamental characteristics. The speaker mentioned the self-confidence, determination, concentration, focus and transparency of King Solomon, Napoleon, Henry Ford, Thomas Edison, John F. Kennedy and others.

Just as the lecturer spoke about the leaders, Bartholomew and Barnabas, lost in their dreams, shouted, "Scoundrel! Rogue! I'm gonna rip your heart out!" People thought they were being critical of the lecturer and shouted them down. It was all we could do to keep them quiet.

Suddenly, they started caressing each other's heads, imagining they had finally reached the princess. And that was when the panic ensued. They opened their eyes, stared at each other and screamed.

"Help!" they shouted simultaneously, as if they'd seen a ghost. The lecturer and other participants thought the building was on fire. The lecturer interrupted his speech and I sank down in my seat, trying to make myself invisible.

The room was a veritable summit of political and social heavy hitters from around the world. The organizer of the event, along with three security men, came to investigate the source of the disturbance. When he approached, he saw me with my head down, as if I were responsible. He asked me to look up, which I did reluctantly. Startled, he recognized me.

"Julio Cesar?"

It was Tulio de Campos, a colleague from the university. Tulio was a professor I had frequently criticized when I was chairman of the sociology department. His ego was as big as mine, and equal egos repel. We couldn't stand each other. Having heard that I was wandering the streets with a strange man, he took his revenge. He humiliated me in public, calling me irresponsible, a rabble-rouser, a cut-rate intellectual. He tore me down just as I had done to him a little more than two years earlier.

"Everyone knows you went crazy, Julio Cesar. And now you're trying to undermine my work?"

"It's true. The guy's nuts. But he's a good man," Honey-mouth, said, humiliating me even more.

"So this is your group of bedlamites, eh? Why don't you spare us all the headache and get out of here," Tulio said.

"What's going on, here?" the Mayor asked. "We're nuts, crazies, weirdos, but not bedla—bedla—bedlamites!" Then he gestured to Professor Jurema for help with the meaning of the word.

"Bedlamite," she explained, "means insane, unhinged, a lunatic."

"Oh, gooood! Then he got it right." And he gave Tulio a thumbs-up, irritating him even more.

The dreamseller raised his right hand to speak.

"Sir, these men are not perfect, but each is brilliant in his own way, just as you are clearly a great leader as the organizer of this event. And a great leader, in order not to have a heart attack at an early age, must possess, among other qualities, two in particular: good humor and tolerance. Good humor to avoid stressing at one's own stupidity and tolerance to avoid stressing at the stupidity of others."

Tulio reeled. He realized for a few seconds that he was both punitive and self-loathing, neither tolerant nor good-humored. But, raising a finger, he stated in an authoritative tone, "Any more noise and you'll be immediately removed."

My mouth was filled with the bitter taste of humiliation. I had never allowed anyone to speak to me with such self-importance. I had fired five professors after minor confrontations. Now the shoe was on the other foot, and it hurt. It was tough seeing myself reflected in Tulio.

The lecture resumed, but the speaker had gone off the rails. Like many lecturers, he could only speak brilliantly if everything worked flawlessly. He stumbled on and mercifully brought an end to the event's final presentation.

A Megasoft executive thanked everyone for their participation, adding "except for some," while clearing his throat. He praised the conglomerate to which he belonged, stating that its focus was investment in shaping human beings, and in the rights of citizens and the promotion of society's well being. And he concluded by saying that this seminar would help change the course of history.

After the applause died down, I thought we might leave without further disruption, but the dreamseller rose from his seat and brandished some words that woke up the more than two hundred people present. As he began to speak, the house lights came back up.

"How can we shape future leaders without reforming our educational system? A society that pays its judges many times what it pays its teachers will always face major difficulties in creating great leaders. Our system is sick, turning out sick people for a sick society. What kind of future awaits us?"

The audience was surprised at the audacity of this shabbily dressed man. Who was this man? Was he trying to restart the seminar? In a way, he was. Some wondered who he was. Others recognized him immediately and began spreading the word that he was the wanderer who had been taking the city by storm.

CHAPTER 15

Newspapers: A Source of Nourishment

THE DREAMSELLER FOCUSED ON THE IMPORTANCE OF molding young leaders, something that worried him greatly, since it would one day be their task to take on humanity's problems.

"Our young are not feeding their minds with the intellectual diet capable of providing the nutrients they need: critical awareness and the development of their role as social activists." What he said next went to the heart of my prejudices as a college professor. Their minds should not be built in the classroom, he said, but through newspapers.

"Free and independent newspapers currently represent the major source of intellectual nourishment for the human mind. But young people have neither easy access to them or interest in reading them. Editors, reporters, columnists organize their minds daily to shape a newspaper. To me, newspapers are as important—or more important—than books. But they're dying. The ritual of leafing through a newspaper, the pleasure of informing oneself and diving into the information sweeping across the nation is a delight. But new technologies, spearheaded by the Internet, are strangling that delight. How will we form new leaders if the young spend hours a day watching TV or surfing for entertainment sites and don't spend even a

minute a week informing themselves about the political, social and economic facts that permeate the globalized world? We
won't form leaders but slaves."

I was impressed. I've always talked about critical thinking,
but I never imagined that the dreamseller thought newspapers contributed more to such thinking than outdated school
curriculums. Now I know why the he read them late into the
night and encouraged his disciples to read them, even if they
were two or three days old. Now I understand why my uncultured and noisy partners were enriching their brains. And the
dreamseller commented on another aberration of the system.

"It's a crime against education for students to spend years
studying a tiny atom they'll never see and an immense outer
space they'll never tread and yet not spend time getting to
know the world inside them. They must learn how thought is
formed and how thinkers are formed, how to act upon their
mind and how to act in society."

The audience broke into applause. Suddenly, no one wanted
to leave. They wanted to stay to hear this intriguing and controversial prophet, the street thinker.

"To those who would be leaders, I recommend they spend
time getting to know what is in the mind of the anonymous.
Politicians should bow down to their most humble of voters.
Psychiatrists should learn from the mentally ill. Intellectuals
should be taught through the imagination of the illiterate. And
celebrities? They should cede the spotlight to the unknowns.
Train yourselves to see the world through the eyes of others."

He let his words hang in the air, preferring to let people
think and draw their own conclusions. But the audience went
from applause to scorn in less than a minute. They broke into
laughter, thinking it was a joke to lighten the mood. After all,
since the time of the Greeks and Romans the lesser members
of society were always led, controlled and subjugated by the

more powerful. It would be counterintuitive to bow to their inferiors.

In modern society, our beliefs hadn't changed but had merely taken on new trappings. The blood rushed to my cheeks when I heard the laughter around me. I was hoping the dream-seller wouldn't expand on his thinking, but then his disciples raised their voices to echo his thoughts. Again, I wished I were invisible.

"Dreamseller, I've always thought that celebrities should bow down before us," Bartholomew said, pointing to us. I tried to hide my face. "It's finally our time, the time of the under-privileged, the poor, the nobodies. Let's revolt and show soci-ety our strength in numbers!"

Suddenly, the Mayor sprang into action. "Yes, the revolu-tion of the bedlamites, the crazies, the lunatics, the unhinged," the Mayor said, puffing out his chest. "I've always thought psy-chiatrists should learn from my noteworthy ideas."

I tried to cover his mouth to keep him from uttering more nonsense, but he was standing up. I refused to be a part of that ignoble band of revolutionaries. These eccentrics hadn't under-stood a single word about the dreamseller's revolution. Hadn't understood that he had chosen us, the craziest of society, to shame the sages and make the leaders blush.

"Yes, it's the time of con men and scam artists," Dimas said then quickly caught himself: "I mean *recovering* con men."

"And the time of the obsessive-compulsives and the hypo-chondriacs," Solomon yelled.

"Hallelujah! It's the time for the faithful to display their miracles," Edson added.

If I were the dreamseller, I might have run from their delu-sions, but he listened to them patiently. But in the back of my mind, a voice was telling me that I was as sick as anyone in this

world-wide insane asylum. Suddenly, beautiful Monica, the
first female disciple to follow the dreamseller, spoke up.

"Yes, it's time for women who aren't in the fashion magazines, who have been swept aside by the media because they
don't measure up to the dictatorial standard of beauty," she
said. Monica proclaimed these words as if she were Joan of
Arc trying to liberate women from the tyrannical yoke of
thinness imposed by the leaders of the fashion world. Monica
knew what she was talking about; she had been one of the most
sought-after international models until she was discarded after
gaining a few pounds.

"Yes! And it's time for the elderly to bombard society with
Factor E!" said Professor Jurema. "You young people," she continued, "are shiftless, lazy, fragile, spoiled, timid, and narrow-
minded. You're like gravediggers watching over the dead. You
talk a lot but don't act." And she said nothing more. She didn't
have to.

"Factor E for empty-headed. The old lady's batty," a young
student muttered under his breath.

Suddenly, she thumped him on the head with her cane. "E
for experience," she said. "Knowledge without experience is
useless."

Only Crusher and I didn't speak up. Though very strong, he
remained silent, for fear of being lynched. I felt embarrassed,
spewing an opinion in a place where I hadn't been invited.

Without another word, the dreamseller left, and we quickly
followed him. The audience stayed behind for a few moments
thinking about all that had been said, digesting our ideas. But
some of them were clearly experiencing heartburn.

A few blocks away, the dreamseller called me aside. He was
an expert at correcting in private and praising in public, never
the other way around. "What's bothering you, Julio Cesar?"

"Master, your disciples just don't grasp your philosophy."

"They grasp it within their limits. Why not respect those limits?"

"They bring shame down on you, and they can destroy your image, destroy your plan for selling dreams. It's because of them that people don't know how to define you, as either a wise man or a lunatic."

Like a father correcting his son, he told me, "I've learned to accept being cheered and being booed, being loved and hated, being understood and defamed. What will I take away when the breath of life ceases? No slander can tear away a shred of my being, unless I allow it. Ideas are seeds, and the greatest favor that can ever happen to a seed is for it to be buried. A man without friends is soil without water, a morning without dew, a sky without clouds. Friends are not those who flatter us but those who demystify us and expose our vulnerability. An intellectual without friends is a book without words."

I had to admit that I had had admirers, but I was a man without friends. I neither had anyone to whom I lent a shoulder to cry on, nor had I had ever lent a shoulder. My ego was too big, my pride enormous, but my solidarity was minuscule. I was a man of contradictions.

Over the years, students asked me to act as their mentor for their master's and doctoral theses, but we never plumbed the depths of our personality. Three university students tried to commit suicide the last year I taught. Ten students suffered depression. Several dozen had psychosomatic illnesses. But I never went to visit them. A professor and his students were miles apart.

We couldn't appreciate how to formulate thoughts or thinkers. I was sick and shaping sick people for a sick society. I pretended to teach, and they pretended to learn. And diplomas justified our playacting.

CHAPTER 16

The Intelligent Poor

MANY YOUNG PEOPLE FOLLOWED FADS FOR HOW TO DRESS, talk and behave. To be different from the group caused them anxiety. They lacked a style of their own and were controlled by marketing that permeated every fiber of the fabric of society. Some young people not only followed fads but also rejected anyone who didn't fit into the shortsighted view of the world. They detested the very idea of homosexuals, beggars and other minorities.

Five days after the uproar at the leadership conference, a significant event occurred. The dreamseller had left his disciples on their own as he went looking for a calm setting in which to meditate. To the dreamseller, solitude was an invitation to know himself and embark into the universe of reflection.

A group of about fifteen upper-middle- and upper-class university students began to taunt us when they saw Dimas, Edson, Bartholomew, Barnabas and me in our old patched clothes. The group thought homeless people were a blight on society, a problem worthy of violence.

As they passed by us, one of them stuck out his left foot out and tripped the Mayor, who fell like a ton of bricks. We rushed to help him, but he wasn't injured. We thought it was an accident, but then I noticed they were laughing as one of them said,

"Check out the dregs of society!" We stopped and faced each other. They seemed to be aching for a fight. My nerves were on edge. My instincts as a professor took over and I shouted without thinking, "Get out of my classroom!"

Seeing me act like a crazed professor, they burst out laughing. For the first time in my life, I was humiliated by students.

One of them went further. He walked toward me and yelled, "Get a load of the master of morons!"

Instead of being intimidated, Bartholomew thrust out his chest and said, "Behold the future of society: youngsters who live in their daddy's shadow, who have never fallen but want to lift up the world!" And *he* broke out laughing.

The students hated his cockiness. Some were ready to pounce on him. One of them retorted, "The destiny of great leaders is to rid society of its trash."

The Mayor suddenly injected himself into the scene. "Vote for me in the next election and I'll spare you."

The youths thought they were being ridiculed. They were puzzled by the boldness of this group of ragamuffins. They didn't know anything about the dreamseller who had trained us.

Crusher was enraged. Just as some of the youths were getting ready to confront us physically, I proposed a change in the field of battle:

"Why not fight in the realm of ideas? If you can answer a few questions right, we'll let you kick our butts. If you can't answer, we get to kick yours."

They thought it would be like taking candy from a baby.

"It's a deal. Bring on the questions."

I took a deep breath and began the quiz.

"Who was Immanuel Kant? What was Montaigne's central line of thought? Can you tell us about the accomplishments of Spinoza?"

They took a step back, not knowing how to answer. They whispered among themselves, "Where did these guys get those names?" Seeing their confusion, I started hammering them.

"Do you know the history of the Phoenicians, the Hebrews, the Persians? The Minoan world? The Mycenaean culture, the Homeric period?"

The students were flabbergasted. They looked at each other in a cold sweat. They never expected homeless people to have brains, much less working ones that could leave them speechless.

Outside of their required reading in school, many of them read almost nothing.

They were the Harry Potter generation, the generation of instant gratification who wanted everything as if by magic. Like high-ranking military officers, they demanded that their parents be their servants. They were skilled at complaining but terrible at expressing gratitude. They lacked the will, the ambition, the ability to compete and survive in the world. They used the Internet, but their culture was as shallow as a puddle of water. They had nothing but disdain for history and philosophy, ignorant to the fact that to see the future it was necessary to study the past.

Suddenly, Dimas, the confidence man of the group, jumped in. "Why did the world's stock markets collapse? Do you know what a subprime mortgage is?" We all followed a man who, though very poor, read a lot. Watching the dreamseller devour newspapers and magazines, his uncultured disciples eventually developed a taste for reading. A few days earlier I had seen Dimas buried in the business section of the newspaper.

Edson, the group's theologian, added, "Do any of you have any idea what the Gaza Strip is?"

After some thought, one of the youths ventured, "Is that some kind of pizza?"

Then the Mayor summed it up. "You'll forgive me, my young friends, but it seems you're in the world but from some other world."

"I like that, Mayor," Honeymouth said. "They're aliens making fun of aliens. Well, it's time to pay off the bet, kids. Turn around."

The students began backing away, holding their hands over their butts. But Honeymouth, remembering the dreamseller, said, "Don't worry, we're not gonna kick you. Only the weak use force. The strong use ideas. The future of the world depends on you and not on us vagabonds. It was an honor to meet you."

We waved to the young men and sent them on their way. They were rich, we were poor, but we possessed something that couldn't be bought or sold. The students left wordlessly and quickly dispersed. The students wouldn't sleep that night. Some reconsidered their role in society and began to buy the dream of critical thinking. They began to see beyond the limits of images.

All these experiences led me to discoveries that disconcerted me. I came to understand that it was not only particular groups of young people who were prejudiced and exclusionary but also some groups of intellectuals, especially the radical followers of certain ideologies: like all the "ians," like the Piagetians, or the "ists."

I belonged to the "ists." I was a rabid socialist and saw little benefit of other social theories. Only after I began following the dreamseller and living with that controversial group of friends did I expand my mind and break down barriers. I've been learning that the worst enemies of any theory are those who most radically adhere to it, who don't have the courage to see beyond it.

I was an expert in the ideas of Marx, Engel, Hegel and Lenin but did very little to change the society I lived in—or to change myself. I prepared students to be good test takers but not to debate ideas. I didn't care whether they were creative or slaves to trends. I was a rigid professor criticizing a rigid society.

I didn't stimulate my students to delve into history or philosophy, to go beyond the boundaries of my subject. I was one of the gravediggers who helped to bury their imagination and sensitivity. I did nothing to prevent the formation of psychopaths. After all, some psychopaths have high IQs.

One of the dreamseller's teachings, which cut like a razor, was that any debt can be repaid, or set aside, except the debt of conscience: *whoever is not faithful to his conscience has an unpayable debt to himself.*

I'm learning to pay off debts to my conscience. It's not easy to recognize my immaturity and talk about what I'm ashamed of. But to flee from myself is to perpetuate my misfortunes and to take my problems with me to an early grave.

CHAPTER 17

Flying on a Chicken Wing

WE WERE WALKING THROUGH A POOR DISTRICT IN THE South Zone. The dreamseller loved to go there, where he had several friends who were manual laborers, machine operators, drivers, custodians, and some were unemployed. What they lacked in resources, they made up for in feelings. They gladly shared what little they had.

Sometimes they would invite us to lunch or dinner. The dreamseller was particularly fond of Luiz Lemos, though we didn't know him. Later we learned that he was a man who had suffered, but was happy, balanced and above all uncomplicated. A paraplegic, he had lost the use of his legs in an automobile accident. He was married to Mercedes, a helpful and lively woman though she had only one leg, having lost the other in an accident at work.

The couple had no children of their own but looked after the children of others, despite their limitations. The dreamseller had been in their house before and they loved having him. He and Luiz Lemos appeared to be longtime friends.

Once, the couple invited the entire group to have lunch at their house. Since the house was small, without a yard and with only a tiny living room—between seventy and eighty square feet—this lunch was not for the crowds, but only for the inner circle of disciples.

We took the subway and, after changing lines twice and passing through more than ten stations, we arrived at the Corujas neighborhood where the couple lived. We left the subway and set off on foot to their house. After climbing a steep hill and making several turns, our tongues were hanging out by the time we arrived at their home twenty minutes later.

"Wow, we're really earning our lunch today," the Mayor said, exhausted. His corpulent body wasn't up to physical exertion. He preferred his food to come to him.

Honeymouth, seeing the humble neighborhood where the Lemos family resided, commented good-naturedly, "I can't get over how many poor people there are in the world. Still, I prefer living in our Kennedy mansion." He was referring to our bridge.

Luiz Lemos was a millionaire compared to us. We were paupers, with neither a living room, bedroom or sofa, much less an armoire. To follow the dreamseller meant adhering to a certain lifestyle. Besides learning to recognize our stupidity and inconsistency, we lived with only just enough money to make it through the day. People rightly considered us less fortunate, homeless, hopeless and godforsaken. We slept under the blue star-studded blanket. Luckily, a few doctors carried blankets in the trunks of their cars and on cold nights would distribute them.

The well-off disciples would sleep at home and in the morning try to find us. But because the dreamseller followed no set schedule they weren't always successful. Monica and Jurema were among those who lived like "normals," but they were nevertheless two of the most tireless "abnormals." And they were with us that day.

Our hosts' house was not glamorous. Cracked, peeling walls.

Windows with faded paint and rusted sides. A leaky roof that was rotted through. In the living room was a table with four chairs. The couple barely fit into the cramped space.

As we approached Luiz Lemos's house we saw him eagerly awaiting us in his wheelchair. From ten yards away, the dream-seller was already shouting hello:

"My good friend Luiz Lemos! And how is the man who travels freely where others dare not tread?" They hugged and kissed each other's cheeks.

With uncommon reverence, Lemos replied, "I'm unworthy of having you in my home."

The dreamseller answered, "I'm the one who's unworthy to enter your home." Then he placed his hands on Mercedes's shoulders and asked her, "And how is this enchanting woman?" He hugged her and kissed her delicately on the forehead.

"What an honor to have you in our humble home," they told us as if receiving a king and his princes.

We greeted them warmly. The dreamseller chatted pleasantly with the couple about the latest happenings in his life. Minutes later, the Mayor's CES (compulsive eating syndrome) began to affect his brain. Impatient and starved, and without a spare sandwich in his pocket, his shameless politician persona manifested itself:

"Honorable hosts of this hungry tribe: Are we here to talk or to eat?"

"To talk!" Monica and Jurema said, trying to gloss over his rudeness.

"To eat!" Honeymouth, Dimas, Solomon and Edson said simultaneously and loudly. I wanted to crawl into a hole but, as always, straddled the fence. I was hungry, too, but I preferred to politely disguise my grumbling stomach.

Mercedes, having heard of the dreamseller's imps, said, "Let's eat before the food gets cold."

She had prepared a small roasted chicken, a stew, a green salad and generous servings of white rice. She was an excellent cook.

Given the extremely tight space, at the host's suggestion we moved the table to the bedroom and sat on the living room floor.

"I propose," said Bartholomew, trying to bring order to the chaos, "that we form a line and serve ourselves in the kitchen and sit in this magnificent living room."

And to show his fine manners, he added, "Mercedes and Mr. Luiz Lemos will be the first served."

The host and hostess naturally declined the offer. "Please," Luiz Lemos said, "you first."

That was when I caught on to his scheme. Bartholomew and Barnabas were strategically placed at the kitchen door in order to be the first to serve themselves. I was outraged by their gall, but the dreamseller seemed amused. He was in heaven. To him, everything was a party.

The two wise guys, like soldiers in a war, attacked the chicken, heading straight for the drumsticks and even tearing off a chunk of the breast. To disguise the stratagem, they buried their pieces of chicken under a mountain of rice.

Then Solomon, Edson and Dimas served themselves. They tore into what remained of the breast and ripped it apart. They gave no thought to me, despite knowing I loved roast chicken. Crusher also served himself, though awkwardly. When my turn came, only the mortal remains of the blessed bird were to be seen. Not even the neck had survived. Crusher took one wing and I took the other. The Master had salad and a few pieces of meat. Monica and Jurema did the same.

The two sly foxes waited anxiously for everyone to serve themselves so we could start the meal together, a practice of the dreamseller's. We all sat down, squeezed in like sardines.

Edson was so famished that he didn't even say grace; he merely looked up, down and tore into his food. Solomon and Dimas didn't even blink; they only made time for swallowing. The dreamseller silently gave thanks for the food that nourished him.

Bartholomew and Barnabas ate like barbarians. Suddenly, Honeymouth stopped chewing. With his full mouth, he said, "Hold up, people. Let's thank those who prepared the food." I found his sudden altruism strange.

Everyone stopped eating. We had to quickly swallow the juicy bite that brought joy to our salivary glands. Honeymouth was so euphoric with his piece of chicken that he said:

"Mercedes and Mr. Luiz Lemos, thank you very much for inviting us, I hope not for the last time." Then he had the gall to ask all present to spear the chicken on their forks and raise it to the sky.

I wanted to hide my face in shame, but I followed his lead because I didn't want to look like a spoilsport. He and Barnabas were like two generals carrying their most highly prized spoils of war, firmly and proudly clutching their drumsticks.

I, on the contrary, felt like the conquered, holding up my bony, puny wing. Crusher raised his sad wing, as well. We looked at each other and shook our heads.

I lost my appetite. I felt that even when they expressed their gratitude these two scoundrels were needling me and showing that my intellectuality was worthless. Once again I discovered that intellectuals are no match for street smarts. Subtly, they dominated businesses, universities, politics and even life under bridges, while we spent so much time thinking.

"Lord, forgive me for my covetousness and thank you for this spectacular poultry," he said, trying to excuse himself.

And to sour my appetite even more, the Mayor added,

"Amen! May the chickens of the earth multiply, and peace fill the hearts of the shrewd and the gullible."

Mercedes and her husband were amused by the pair. This time I couldn't ignore the provocation. I turned to the Master and said, "Dreamseller, these two are calling me gullible, an ignoramus."

"Julio Cesar, my hope for all of you is that you may order a taste of tranquillity from the menu of existence. When the intellect is free, food takes on another flavor. A simple meal eaten in peace is better than the finest dishes eaten amid anguish and anger."

I fell silent before the dreamseller's wisdom, but Honeymouth, with his unstoppable capacity for talking, spewed forth like a street philosopher.

"Master, to build on your theory, I'd like to say that Julio Cesar can go further with legs than with his tiny wings . . ."

The Mayor, Dimas and Solomon congratulated him. "Thank you, but I'm merely an emerging genius," he said with false modesty.

And without further delay, they devoured their food. Traveling with Bartholomew and Barnabas, I don't know whether I was training to be humble or training to meet the monsters of rage and indignation buried in my story. I had to learn either to react less to their provocations and make life a party or else I would have a heart attack.

Just as I was promising myself I'd never again eat a chicken wing, I remembered scream therapy and bellowed, "Aaaahhh! Uuuhhh!"

Bartholomew and the Mayor were so startled that they dropped their drumsticks on the floor, only to pick them up again, sheepishly. They'd had a taste of their own medicine.

I burst out laughing. My friends, especially Monica and

Jurema, were impressed with me. I had never acted like that. For the first time, I felt good about playing the clown. I understood that smiling at our idiotic behavior is a miraculous cure for a bad mood. I apologized to our host then went back to eating, happy as a lark.

The dreamseller didn't scold me. In fact, he nodded his head in satisfaction. He realized I was beginning to learn how to savor my meals.

CHAPTER 18

An Assassination Attempt on the Dreamseller

A FTER EATING AND TALKING FOR A WHILE, WE SAID goodbye to the friendly Luiz Lemos and Mercedes. The dreamseller hugged them affectionately. I had never seen people who did so much with so little. Giving of themselves is what nourished their emotional needs. Honeymouth asked for forgiveness, but not for himself. Rather, for the rest of us, me in particular.

"Excuse my friends if they didn't behave well. But in a few decades the dreamseller will change them. Please, every time you prepare a chicken, remember this hungry mouth."

Bartholomew never lost his sense of humor.

Just as the Mayor was about to open his mouth to babble something, I told him, "Save your breath, it's a long way home."

Fortunately, recalling his fatigue, he listened: "Thank you, my chief of staff, for taking care of me."

The way down was truly grueling. We tried a short cut and ended up in a street barely wide enough for a car. Three blocks down, we turned to the left and found ourselves in a dead end. As we tried to retrace our steps, we found our path blocked by five heavy-set, rough-looking men. We hadn't noticed that they were following us. As they came closer, people in the vicinity began closing their windows and doors.

A chill ran down our backs. We knew we were in real danger. When they drew within forty yards of us, they put on hoods. They moved faster. At ten yards away they took revolvers and a pair of machine guns from their long coats. We were dead. I was sure of it.

Three of the criminals were white. The fourth was black, not tall but extremely muscular. The fifth was short, but agile and calculating; he looked as if he had come from the dungeons of the Chinese mafia. He was the leader of the group, and it made me shudder to look at him. From his quick movements, he appeared to be a master in martial arts.

"Freeze!" they ordered, pointing their guns at us. I became dizzy. I had never been in a high-risk situation. Crusher's lips started trembling. Monica and Jurema burst into tears. Edson's voice faltered. Solomon experienced a panic attack.

The Asian man became more violent and merciless as we withered.

"Dead men don't cry. So shut your mouths!" He took a photo from his pocket, looked at the dreamseller and compared the images.

Glancing at his companions, he nodded, confirming that this was the one they were after. They pointed their weapons at the dreamseller and at us. The dreamseller, who seemed to know he would die sooner or later and had no fear of saying farewell to life, told them in a firm voice:

"Even a killer has to have some dignity when he carries a gun. If you want my life, why shed innocent blood? Let the others go," he told his executioners.

Hearing this, the killers were motionless for several seconds. Then, surprisingly, the dreamseller took control and shouted to us, "Leave! Now!"

We all ran, expecting to hear gunshots hot on our trail. The elderly Jurema and Monica ran like rabbits. Dimas leaped like a leopard. Edson appeared to have sprouted wings. Solomon forgot he was having a coronary and darted. Crusher and I had never run so fast in our lives. But the shots didn't come.

We rounded the corner and continued to flee. A couple of hundred yards from the scene, we stopped briefly to catch our breath. Two of the disciples were missing: Bartholomew and Barnabas. We waited for them, but they had stayed behind. Stayed behind to die with the dreamseller. Stayed behind to be at the side of one they loved. Stayed behind because the dreamseller was all they had. I couldn't believe their heroism.

We wanted desperately to get out of that labyrinth and find the police. But the police station seemed a long way off. We asked several people for help, but they were afraid for their lives. We went on as fast as we could, but we knew it was hopeless. The execution would be swift.

Exhausted, I stopped. I began to cry. I couldn't accept the idea of the dreamseller being summarily executed. The man who saved my life and made me love life would be cut down mercilessly. As he said, "We present our story like eternal players in the theater of time and suddenly end the play as if we had never acted." I felt miserable, guilty for having done nothing for the man who had done so much for me.

The disciples who gave him the most problems were also the most loyal. I began to feel sad at the thought of participating in the wake for Bartholomew and Barnabas. I couldn't imagine life without their humor and antics. Yes, they tormented me, but they also brought color to my tedious and suffocating existence. I never imagined they would become a part of me.

While my friends and I cried like children, the assassins were preparing to carry out their mission. They pointed their guns at the three men, who didn't stand a chance. As they were about to pull the trigger, the Mayor spoke.

"One moment, sir. Let me say my last words," he told their

leader, who stood immobile in surprise. "Thank you, kind assassin." Turning his head, he said, "Dreamseller, you embraced
me, believed in me, and invested your attention in me. You
were more than a father. It is an honor to die at your side. Honeymouth, you were a pain for many years, but you were my
brother." Then he dried his tears and made a request to his murderers: "You can kill me, but bury us both in the same coffin."

Hearing this, Honeymouth forgot he was at gunpoint and
found the energy for one last confrontation with Barnabas:

"Easy there, Mayor. Not together! It was hard enough putting up with you in *this* life." And, looking at his killers, he
uttered not a request but an order: "Go ahead and shoot, but I
demand a coffin all my own."

The killers had never encountered victims who behaved
like that. They wanted to concentrate on their job but kept
wondering, "Just who the heck are these guys?"

When they were about to fire, it was the dreamseller's turn
to intervene.

"I don't believe these jerks are going to kill us without
amusing themselves," he said, defiantly. And he began jumping around like a clown, trying to imitate a martial arts expert.
He tripped over his own feet and fell.

The hit men snorted. Just a few days ago, Bartholomew
and Barnabas had seen the dreamseller disarm a man who was
going to shoot him at point-blank range. They now wondered
whether it as a fluke.

Still, Bartholomew took heart at seeing him challenge the
criminals to a fight.

"They're five losers." And turning his back on their leader,
he said provocatively, "And the little one there looks like a
pansy! Just 'cause he's got a machine gun he thinks he's a tough
guy." And he broke into laughter.

The executioners were used to killing but they had never

seen three people ready to meet their end so sarcastically, mocking them, even being abusive and cocky. The leader became embroiled in a fit of rage, ready to abandon his gun and use his fists. But he remained firm, determined to complete the mission.

As he was about to shoot, the Mayor shot first. Though fat and clumsy, he struck the leader and the other man, the two who were carrying machine guns.

"These guys are like little girls. If they didn't have guns, I'd make them drink out of the toilet." And he went into a disastrous boxing performance, challenging them to battle. "Get a taste of my fists, you wimps!"

The Mayor leaped around and punched the air. One of the assassins laughed at the sight. Encouraged, the Mayor continued to aim blows at the five killers. Suddenly, he turned to the side and unintentionally landed a punch on the chin of the dreamseller, who fell to the ground unconscious.

"I've killed the dreamseller!" he yelled. While trying to help him up, the Mayor couldn't bear the weight and fell on top of him, just as he'd done with Geronimo.

The hit men stifled their laughter. They saw they were dealing with bunglers, weaklings, poseurs capable of killing themselves all on their own.

"You're a disaster that walks like a man. A gutless wonder," Honeymouth told the Mayor. "You've never killed even a rat and now you want to take on these guys. This is a job for a real man." Turning toward the assassins, he said, "Use your fists first and then your bullets, you pansies."

The five men didn't hesitate. Before killing them they could vent their pent-up anger and have a little fun. They were dying to pummel these arrogant punks. And they proceeded to do so.

"Hold on! Let us get into position," said the dreamseller, trying to regain his composure.

The dreamseller and Honeymouth stood side by side. The cowardly Mayor hid behind them and, making the sign of the cross, told them, "You two start and I'll finish the job!"

It was a violent, totally uneven fight. The five criminals began beating the dreamseller and Bartholomew, first punching them and then throwing them to the ground and kicking them mercilessly.

Realizing he would die of internal bleeding, the dreamseller went back in time in his mind to see his children, and he hugged and kissed them. They seemed to be alive and implored him not to give up selling dreams, especially the dream of life. But his aggressors continued to beat him mercilessly. His fate was sealed. He was about to close the final chapter of his extraordinary history.

CHAPTER 19

At Risk of Dying

THE DREAMSELLER TRIED TO PROTECT HIMSELF, BUT IT WAS futile. His face was bleeding badly. His eyes were bruised and swollen. Sweat and blood flowing from the cut in his eyebrow blurred his vision. The trauma to his chest barely allowed him to breathe, while the blows to his skull affected his sense of balance. Bartholomew was also on the ground, bleeding from both lips. The Mayor, like a cornered animal, crouched down to protect his face, but it did no good; he was also taking a beating. They were going to die, the dreamseller thought, because of him. It was unfair.

In a fraction of a second the face of each disciple flashed through his mind. He loved them. When he seemed about to give up, the image of his children, of the wounded Bartholomew and the other disciples triggered in his brain an eruption like a volcano spewing indignation. He might die, but not without fighting for his life.

At that crucial moment, the dreamseller and Bartholomew looked at each other and gained new strength. When the attackers' leader and one of his henchmen kicked them in the stomachs, both reacted in a surprising way: they grabbed the aggressors' feet and twisted them, causing them to fall down.

The dreamseller and Bartholomew rose and assumed the

posture of martial arts experts. Although no one knew it, in reality both had been excellent fighters in the past. The dreamseller had been a black belt in karate in his youth, and Honeymouth was a specialist in jujitsu before succumbing to alcoholism.

The Mayor, though, was no fighter. His only specialty was talking. The dreamseller and Bartholomew had vowed to sell dreams in a violent society without resorting to force, but this was a special occasion. They had to choose between life and death, between the dream and the nightmare. Billions of neurons went into high gear, leading them to fight like warriors.

They pummeled the assassins masterfully, using their feet and fists. The criminals were stunned. They had never seen people so strong and determined. Now, they regretted not opening fire.

The leader aimed a kick at the neck of the Master, who skillfully deflected the blow and struck him in the chest. Gradually, the killer realized that his opponent was the better fighter. And the struggle continued. The attackers lost ground minute by minute. Two of them were almost unconscious.

In the confusion, the Mayor grabbed the guns and threw them over the wall. He never considered forcing the criminals to surrender, as he was afraid of guns and didn't even know how to pull a trigger. The leader, seeing the Mayor tossing the guns, punched him in the face, but he was quickly rescued by Honeymouth. A bit disoriented, he shouted to his friend, "Don't be a wimp, Honeymouth. Give that guy a beating he won't forget!"

The Master came to Honeymouth's aid, but a blow to the back from a henchman left him unprotected from an attack by the leader, who slammed him in the chest several times. But the dreamseller returned the blows, causing their leader to wonder,

"Where did he learn to fight like this? And how's he staying on his feet?"

The Mayor, seeing his two friends winning the battle, sat on a bench and began giving orders: "Hit him! Punch him in the face! Harder!"

A third attacker went down. Now the fight was two on two: the leader against the dreamseller, and a minion against Honeymouth. But seeing the Mayor's audacity in giving orders, the leader left the dreamseller and went after him. Running off in fright, the Mayor shouted: "Get him, Master! Get him!"

The dreamseller didn't attack him from behind. He tapped the leader on the shoulder and began displaying his full ability. He easily warded off the other's blows. And in a sudden move, hit him in the stomach and then on the right cheek. Their leader fell to the ground, and the dreamseller jumped on top of him. His eyes wide, the assassin waited for the fatal blow, but the dreamseller held up and went to help Bartholomew fight against his attacker. That was when they heard police sirens two or three blocks away.

Fearful, wounded and weakened, the attackers, as if having the victors' permission, helped one another to their feet and jumped over the high wall. They trotted away like stray dogs.

The police never arrived. They were on their way somewhere else, apparently. The three friends were left, each leaning on the other. Incredibly, Honeymouth hadn't lost his sense of humor. Just as he had done after being punched by Crusher at the independence monument, he asked, "Mayor, are we alive or in heaven?"

"I don't know about heaven, but we just left hell," he replied.

Though he was the least injured, the Mayor went limp. He was between the other two and threw his considerable weight on them to carry him.

Honeymouth asked the Master: "Boss, I never saw anybody so nimble. Where'd you learn to fight?"

"Here and there. But I'm out of shape. How about you?"

"I started in the orphanage, in classes with a Japanese man who volunteered there. Later, at a jujitsu school. But that was before I became an alcoholic and started living on the streets."

The Mayor, brazenly, didn't want to remain in the shadows. Despite being an unmitigated disaster in a fight, he still felt the need to brag. Staggering and leaning on the others, he said, "I used to teach boxing. But I'm hurt, Master."

"Why is that, Barnabas?"

"Honeymouth stood in my way and protected the bad guys. If he'd let me go, I would've made mincemeat of them." And then he winced, "Ooh, ooh! They stomped on my belly."

"You coward! If I'd let that guy get you, he would have pounded you into ground beef."

"Ha! Didn't you see what I did to their boss? I whirled in a pirouette and smacked him. I knocked him into next Tuesday," bragged the Mayor.

And they went on walking and joking, despite being beaten and injured. Since mankind first roamed the planet, pain has blocked rationality. But those two used levity to unblock it, mixing pain with laughter.

Then, in the distance, we saw three staggering men coming toward us and discovered they were the dreamseller, Bartholomew and Barnabas, leaning on one another. We couldn't believe they were alive. But at the same time, we were shaken. They were bleeding all over. Their eyes were swollen and their faces and chests were bruised, especially the dreamseller's. We needed to get them to the nearest hospital.

As soon as he saw us, the Mayor, overcome by his compulsive speech syndrome, started to brag. Although he was fatigued, his tongue was intact.

"People, I landed so many punches that the guys wet their pants." And, to demonstrate his bravery, he suddenly showed us his main blow. He raised his right fist and, not realizing that Bartholomew was beside him, hit him in the chin. Bartholomew went down in a heap. Frightened again, the Mayor said:

"Good Lord! I've killed Honeymouth!"

We had to carry him to a clearing. But we later learned the charlatan pretended to be unconscious just so we'd carry him. Such is life. Even heroes have their villainous side.

CHAPTER 20

Dangerous Association

L IVING WITH THE DREAMSELLER WAS BECOMING EXTREMELY complicated. We couldn't stop thinking about why anyone would want to kill him. Revenge? But what could he have done? To eliminate a witness? But what secrets could a man stripped of power be hiding? He denounced the madness of society but didn't name names. Was he considered a revolutionary, a threat to society? But if that were how they thought of him, why didn't they take him to court instead of eliminating him?

We had countless questions with but no answers. We didn't actually know the identity of the man we followed or what forces were conspiring against him. In the next several days, I began to become paranoid. I started shrinking from strangers, even generous people, who I thought of as potential assassins in disguise.

Bartholomew and Barnabas came to understand that following the dreamseller wasn't a bed of roses. The journey had four possible paths: praise for his brilliant ideas, ridicule and injury—or even death. Fearing for our safety, the dreamseller once again argued that it would be better for us to separate. We rejected the possibility. But how much longer and how far would we carry that torch? We didn't know.

We were not a religion, a sect or a secret society. And we

certainly didn't swear a blood oath. We were free to leave whenever we wanted. But our friendship was interwoven with a poetic kind of love. We were friends who were learning to listen to our minds, to debate the mysteries of existence and to revamp the idea of power. We were dreamers who wished to sell the dream of free emotion.

Crusher was ashamed of not having been with Bartholomew and Barnabas at the moment they most needed him. Once again the instinct for self-preservation overpowered the urge for solidarity. But they didn't hold a grudge against him. They had learned to give without expecting anything in return, a lesson I was still far from learning.

Of the three, the dreamseller was injured the worst. His right eye was bruised, and his left eyebrow and lip were split open.

Worried about blood loss, infection and possible fractures, we took him to the nearest hospital, the Mellon Lincoln Hospital. Though it was a large private facility, the most prestigious and best equipped in the city, it had a charity ward. And we were indigent.

I was uncomfortable with the hospital because it bore the name of the father of one of the nation's most important leaders, Mellon Lincoln Jr., a man I had never met personally but whose power and influence I had criticized in the classroom. He was a very wealthy businessman, and his reach extended even into my university. But his power was a thing of the past. The father, Mellon Lincoln Sr., was dead, and so was his son. Their lives were gone but their names remained.

At the entrance to the magnificent hospital, the dreamseller bumped into two men wearing impeccable suits—the director of the institution and the chief financial officer. Seeing that he had brushed against an injured beggar, the director experienced not compassion but disgust. He was starting to clean his

Valentino jacket when he noticed a bloodstain. He nervously removed the jacket and issued an abrupt order to a nearby cleaning woman, only recently hired:

"Burn it."

The woman asked, "I'm sorry, who are you?"

"What, you don't know me? I'm the director of this hospital!" he told her, dripping with arrogance.

At that moment, the director and the dreamseller made eye contact. For a few seconds the director stood there as if anesthetized. His pupils focused unblinkingly on the man he had bumped into, who was wearing an old blue jacket with three buttons missing and a bloodstained white shirt with a torn collar. The dreamseller's face seemed like a phantom to him, and not merely because of the injuries and the stained clothes he wore. Hesitantly, the director said, "Do I know you?"

"How can you know me if I don't even know myself?" the dreamseller replied.

"I once met a very important man who looked a lot like you," the director said.

"Every man is important."

The director looked the dreamseller up and down, saw his injuries, and said, "He had your courage. But fortunately, he's dead."

"There are many among the living who are also dead," the dreamseller responded.

With a haughty gaze, the director asked the dreamseller's name.

After a pause and a deep breath, the dreamseller told him, "I'm just a simple seller of dreams."

The director thought the reply bizarre. Then he saw the injured Bartholomew and the Mayor, ran his gaze over the rest of the group, and pronounced his conclusion.

"The psychiatric ward is in the rear, to the left, and the in-digents' ward is to the right."

The Mayor held out his hand to thank him, not having un-derstood the other man's arrogance. But the director turned his back, walking away without the slightest trace of sensitivity. To the man who ran the most important hospital in the city, we weren't humans but animals who needed veterinarians and a dosage of pity.

The dreamseller had always told us that most men are des-perate for any type of power. The director was one of them; he had become a god. When he was ten steps ahead of us, the dreamseller called out his name: "Lucio Lobo!"

The director turned suddenly and his eyes widened as if in a horror film.

"Lucio Lobo, humility is the foundation of the wise, and pride the sin of the weak," the dreamseller told him.

The director tried to rush ahead, but as he glanced back, he bumped into a cart carrying medications and various portable medical equipment. Everything fell to the floor. The great man got up and, as if fleeing from a bomb about to go off, moved away even faster.

His CFO asked, "What's going on?"

"Nothing. Let's get out of here. I think I'm seeing things."

None of the disciples understood the significance of that moment. "How did the dreamseller know the director's name?" I wondered. "Of course," I thought. "The dreamseller is very observant and must have seen his name on his badge." But I didn't recall seeing any badge. Since he read newspapers he found in the trash, he must have read something about the di-rector. Concerned about the dreamseller's, Bartholomew's and Barnabas's injuries, I put aside these questions and went look-ing for help.

After waiting in line for two hours, they were attended to without sympathy, without altruism, without kindness, like paupers who had to kneel down in gratitude for the privilege of being treated free of charge. The doctor didn't offer them a word of comfort or even ask what caused the traumas. He thought they were violent men suffering the consequences of their aggressiveness. The nurse who treated them was more generous.

After examining the dreamseller and putting in a few stitches even before the anesthesia had taken effect, the doctor took a look at Bartholomew's thorax. He seemed impatient, as if reluctantly doing us the greatest favor in the world. He made less money when he worked in the charity area than when treating private patients or those with insurance. Observing his lack of sensitivity, the dreamseller said:

"Why are you in such a rush? You're dealing with a fascinating human being."

"Right, I'm a movie star," said Honeymouth facetiously.

The doctor reacted aggressively to the dreamseller's subtle criticism. "Just who do you think you are, beggar, to address a doctor in that manner?" Then he whispered to the nurse, "I can't stand these homeless types. They've got no money but they demand everything."

"You're a doctor, you studied psychology, so why act as if you'd never heard of it?" said the dreamseller.

Loath to be confronted, the doctor again reacted, this time going further. "Look here, beggar, you people are a burden on society and on this hospital."

"Didn't the founder of this institution, Mellon Lincoln, provide conditions for doctors to treat the impoverished with the same care given to the wealthy? I guess he was wrong about a lot of things and not worthy of his power."

"What? Who are you to criticize the founder of this hospital? What gall! Just look at yourself."

After a sarcastic laugh, the doctor ended his hurried consultation and shooed them out of the examination room. He gave them a card to seek the services of a psychiatrist.

After leaving, we saw the nurse call the doctor aside and say, "Doctor, that's the man who's been stirring up the city."

"That's him? I can't believe it! We were talking about him just the other day. Why didn't you say anything?"

He felt he had missed a chance to explore the mind of a genius. Yes, he had let slip through his fingers the opportunity to buy some dreams. Instead, he would go on wallowing in his tiny world.

CHAPTER 21

Ten Minutes to Silence a Life

WE WERE CROSSING THE MAIN LOBBY OF THE HOSPITAL ON our way out. Suddenly, two men in white, with stethoscopes dangling from their necks, spoke to us very graciously, asking if we had been treated well and apologizing for any misunderstanding. They looked at the dreamseller and, without asking permission, began examining his lumbar region and listening to the left side of his chest. They decided he needed additional treatment. They examined Bartholomew and the Mayor as well but told them they were fine.

They insisted we go with them. The dreamseller wanted to leave, but Monica and Jurema asked them to complete the examination. He was determined to leave. Then the group glutton intervened. "I'm feeling weak," the Mayor said. "If I don't get something to eat I'm gonna faint." And he began exhibiting what he assumed were signs of dizziness.

"Of course, sir. We've prepared a meal for you and anyone else who cares to come," they said.

"You need to mind your health," said the Mayor as he and Bartholomew each took one of the dreamseller's arms and pushed him toward the new examination room and, obviously, toward their next meal.

Crusher and Edson joined them in the other room to eat. Ju-

rema and Monica stayed with me. After examining him, they
said the dreamseller needed medicine and asked me to wait
outside, but I refused. Monica and Jurema sat outside. They
located a vein and hooked up the IV, injecting some ten vials
of what they said was glucose and antibiotics. They said the
dreamseller would fall asleep briefly and that they would return in ten minutes.

I was suspicious and rummaged through the trash to see
what they had added to the serum. It was fentanyl, an anesthetic. "Anesthetic?" I thought. Despite not being a doctor, I
knew that in a few minutes he would be dead. The dreamseller
had also pinched shut the IV feed as soon as they left. He, too,
was suspicious.

We immediately removed the needle from his arm. I called
in Jurema and Monica to help me and we rushed out of there. I
asked them to call Bartholomew, Barnabas and the others, and
we quickly left the hospital.

Once we were outside, the dreamseller looked sadly at the
walls and the equally cold people who worked inside them. He
knew that inside those walls, money had become more important than life.

We went to our old home, Kennedy Bridge. Professor Jurema wanted us to go to her mansion, but the dreamseller declined because there were more risks to come, and he didn't
want to involve her or us. He asked Bartholomew and Barnabas
to go with her, but they refused to leave his side.

Jurema and Monica bought ice packs and medicine and
looked after him until nightfall. And before saying good-bye
to the women and Crusher, the dreamseller asked us to gather
in a circle.

"All of you have been a source of happiness. You've taught
me, each in your own way, that it is worthwhile to invest in
humanity. But it's time we parted ways."

"What are you saying?" asked Jurema. "We're a family!"

"My dear Jurema, we can no longer travel together. You're all too important to me to be put at risk. I don't know how much longer I have to live. Please, don't insist. Each of us must follow his own path."

"But, Master," said Monica, with tears in her eyes, "if we're in danger here, we can go to another city, another state, even another country."

"My enemies are powerful. They will pursue me to the ends of the earth."

When I heard that, I couldn't bear it anymore.

"Master, I know that you have never made us talk about our past unless it was of our own free will. So please forgive me for invading your privacy. Who are those enemies and why do they want to kill you?"

He looked into my eyes and apologized for not wishing to go into details about his background. "Whoever knows my secrets is at risk. Because of my love for all of you, there are certain secrets I cannot reveal."

He paused and showed us his chest and back, both of which bore large scars. And he told us as much as it was possible to tell:

"These scars are from a fire, the first time they tried to kill me. And they almost succeeded. A charred body was found, that of a good man without a family, who lived in the streets as we do. I hired him to be my gardener and had long conversations with him, came to know his traumas and his pain. I gave him a gift, a ring with an image of two children that symbolized my son and daughter, as thanks for listening to me and serving me. One day we were talking and there was an explosion. Flames spread rapidly through the house. My friend died, and they thought it was me. My enemies were quiet until they discovered I was still alive."

"But why do they want to kill you?" insisted Dimas.

He hesitated before replying. He wanted us to love him for what he was and not for what he possessed. He wanted us to sell dreams because it was the greatest project for a human being and not because of the influence of some powerful figure. All he said was this:

"Money attracts enemies and drives away friends. I have nothing, yet you insist on staying. I'm close to death, but you don't abandon me. You are truly my friends."

"If we're your friends, don't ask us to leave," said the Mayor, his voice choked with emotion.

The next day, the front page of the city's major newspapers carried headlines saying that the gentle, calm man who claimed to sell dreams and denounced violence had shown an aggressive side. Ignorant of the facts, they distorted the dreamseller's image, but because he was no slave to public opinion, he continued on his journey.

We said good-bye to Jurema, Monica and Crusher, and lay down to sleep. The night was touch and go. Sleep barely came. I can't say if the cold rattling my bones was caused by the weather or the anxiety reverberating in my body.

We woke up several times, frightened. Honeymouth was also experiencing an agitated sleep; three times he punched the air, feeling pains in his body. The Mayor woke up in the middle of the night and slipped away unnoticed. He came back at two in the morning with a few shots of vodka in him. It was his first relapse since joining the dreamseller.

The Master asked our patience as the Mayor tried to give another speech:

"On this glorious night, I would like to promise you that I'll send you to hell if you don't vote for me," he mumbled. But he was tired and quickly fell back to sleep. In half an hour he was snoring like a horse.

Finally, the sun woke us up to the sound of sparrows, pigeons and other birds, singing despite the storm the previous night. I thought to myself that we're the only species that thinks and that thinking is both a privilege and a curse.

Sitting on his worn mattress pad and inspired by the birdsong and the sunlight filtering through the bridge, the dreamseller, though injured and marked for death, began to sing:

I thought I couldn't lose.
But in the very core of my being,
My heroism crumbled,
My confidence was shattered.
And now that I've discovered myself,
I will not despair.
Until death finds me,
Like a bird I would take
From each day its greatest melody.

Dimas took out his harmonica and started playing along. We celebrated life in the early hours of dawn. We knew we were going to die, but in an all-too-brief existence we wanted to take from each day its greatest melody. Fear could not spoil our celebration.

We got up famished and quickly found Monica, Jurema and the other followers. We taught them our new song. It was seven o'clock on a sunny Saturday, and the sunrise was enchanting.

An hour later, we stopped by the bakery owned by Gutemberg, a seventy-year-old Portuguese man who was afraid people would eat and not pay their bill.

"Gutemberg, my good man," said Honeymouth, trying to butter up the baker, "you have the privilege of serving this notable group of hungry people."

"Man of bread and dough, when I assume the leadership of this nation, you will be my head chef," added the Mayor.

The baker twisted his mustache with his left hand and rubbed his right index finger and thumb together, indicating that he wanted money. The Mayor tried another tack.

"Then you can be my minister of industry!" Gutemberg continued to make the money-sign. "How about economics minister?" But still no bread was forthcoming. Then he appealed. "Invest in this man of the future!" he said, tapping his chest like the craziest politician I'd ever seen.

We got up a collection to buy our breakfast. Jurema and the other women who followed the dreamseller often supplied some of our necessities when they were present, but he discouraged them from bringing more money than they would need in a day.

But Jurema, who was in the beginning stages of Alzheimer's, forgot her purse at home. She didn't even have money for her own meal.

Gutemberg, though outwardly gruff, had saved us a dozen times with stale bread that he wouldn't be able to sell the next day. Milk, coffee and bread and butter brought joy to our taste buds, especially because we didn't always eat dinner, or at least not in an adequate fashion.

The night before, we ate the remains of spaghetti that a nearby Italian restaurant was about to throw out. Edson, the Miracle Worker, begged the cook and managed a small, cold plate of spaghetti that was scarcely enough to quiet their hunger pangs. Restaurants seldom gave leftovers to the homeless for fear of making them sick and becoming the target of lawsuits. One more way the system punished the poor.

CHAPTER 22

A Human Being's Worst Enemies

OUR BRIEF CAMARADERIE AT GUTEMBERG'S BAKERY allowed us to forget the recent dangers we had survived. Once again the Portuguese baker's stale bread saved the Mayor, though it took three helpings to line his stomach.

The dreamseller appeared concentrated but calm. He left after having breakfast. As always, he went off without telling us where he was headed. We quickly followed him, and after about twenty minutes arrived at a beautiful garden.

Multicolored butterflies floated everywhere, and hummingbirds hovered in the air, contemplating hibiscus flowers before extracting their nectar. At my university there was also an immense oval garden, but I had never spent any time learning its secrets. I thought life only pulsed in the classroom or in the professors' lounge.

Where there is only knowledge, anguish flourishes. Joyless thoughts are like an existence without flowers. In my department we overvalued reason and crushed emotion. We were unbalanced and specialists in conflict. It was a rare intellectual who hadn't made enemies.

The dreamseller taught me simple but fundamental things. To him, reason and emotion were never separate. He trained us in the art of internalizing, observing, reasoning through deduction and induction. He taught us to lose ourselves in the details before looking at the big picture. Our eyes were like a film director's, capturing tiny details imperceptible to someone who was inattentive. We experienced grand emotions over small events. We were envied even by celebrities who met us.

In a time when suicide rates were climbing a hundred percent each decade, especially in affluent nations, we were obsessed with life.

As soon as we entered the garden, a Muslim leader with a few of his followers approached the dreamseller and kissed him, eager to hear what he had to say. Just ahead, an Orthodox Jew, accompanied by several boys, did the same. They all wanted to listen to him. A group of twenty women from another institution were there to drink in droplets of his wisdom. And I asked myself, "What kind of man is this who attracts such different people?"

During the walk, the dreamseller asked us to observe the trees and imagine ourselves to be the dry leaves falling from the small branches, floating carefree until reaching the ground, where we would enrich the soil with their our bodies.

"In the end, a person's purpose is to enrich the society in which he lives. Living only for ourselves negates our existential role," he said.

Everything seemed perfect that morning. But traveling with the dreamseller was unpredictable. He slowed his pace and stood before the group, looking down in concentration. Everyone stopped and tried to see what he was seeing. Actually, he was absorbed in observing the small weeds growing in the cracked concrete. He was dazzled by the miniature round leaves that formed dark-green bouquets.

How can a wise man spend time on weeds that not even the most dedicated gardener would notice? It seemed like a waste of his intelligence. But he didn't care about public opinion or ours. He bent down and muttered a few almost inaudible words. But we read his lips.

"Heroic weeds. You are born in inhospitable places, without water and almost without soil, and you resist the indifference of passersby. You are like street children who stubbornly cling to life. I salute you."

What he said was passed from mouth to mouth, for all to hear. Seeing us watching him, he stood up and, without explanation, said:

"If the world were at war with you, the battle might be bearable, but if you're at war with yourself, it is unbearable. Without facing your internal enemies, it's almost impossible not to create mental wars—or to survive them."

"What war is he talking about?" I thought. While I was pondering the matter, Bartholomew, who specialized in reacting without thinking, said, "Boss, I'm a man of peace. I don't have any enemies."

"I wish that were so, Bartholomew, but we humans are experts in creating them, even the wisest among us. And the worst enemies are those we don't see or can't admit."

The Mayor insisted he, too, was a man without enemies. He had forgotten that the night before he had done battle with his own imagination.

"Dreamseller, I'm a conci—conci—" He stumbled over the words. Then, furious at himself, said, "Out, you blasted word!" Trying again, he succeeded: "I'm a conciliator of ideas. The problems I have come from conspiracy by the opposition." And he looked at me as if I were part of the group that opposed him.

The dreamseller must have thought, "What am I doing here with this band of incorrigibles?" But he said patiently:

"I'm speaking of a war fought by great and small, by rich and poor. A war that takes the shine from celebrities, sleep from the religious, serenity from intellectuals, and transforms the courageous into cowards. I'm speaking of a war that we have imported from society around us."

He continued. "I'm talking about the war concealed behind smiles, disguised by the culture, covered up by philanthropic gestures, hidden by the tyranny of fashion and dark glasses."

The dreamseller then spoke with an astuteness unlike any I had ever heard, about the setbacks suffered since man first acted out his existential play on the enigmatic stage of time.

"Some entrench themselves against their fears, others against an excess of euphoria. Some do battle with their worries, others with their alienation. Some are haunted by fixed ideas, others by morbid thoughts. Some are frightened of the future, others of the past. Some struggle against excessive saving, others against compulsive spending. Who is brought up to survive in this war? Who is trained to escape unharmed or with minimal trauma?"

No one, I thought. I had never seen the slightest mention of this subtle war within the human mind or how to equip oneself to survive it. Hundreds of billions of dollars were spent to train and equip soldiers for wars that drain blood, but no one was training us to combat what drains us of altruism, creativity and wisdom.

I knew that over seventy percent of students suffered from anxiety. The epidemic of anxiety was denied by academics. More and more I agreed with the dreamseller that the educational system was sick, producing sick people for a sick society.

I was sick. I had to admit I was tormented by worries, unresolved conflict, feelings of guilt and jealousy, a neurotic need to control others and many other demons. While I thought about my war, the dreamseller spoke of his:

"Today I'm a person in rags, but I was once a man envied and considered invincible. Everyone was familiar with my outward armor, but they didn't know I was unprotected in the one place where I should have been most secure. I was beaten, defeated. But, when everyone thought I would never recover from my irreparable losses, I reunited with myself. I rose from the ashes. I haven't destroyed the ghosts in my mind; my mission is to tame them, discipline them."

Many tried to hide their mistakes, but the dreamseller exuded sincerity in facing them. He didn't promote himself, didn't speak about his wealth, his academic background, his social status. He spoke only about what was essential. Then the philosophical prophet shocked us with these words:

"I have always told you that the weak attack, but the strong are tolerant. Now I ask you not to be tolerant with your ghosts. Fight with all your strength against everything that disturbs your mind. Either conquer your worries or they will conquer you. Tame your feelings of guilt or they will make you their slave. Shout, go into a rage against negative states of mind, fixed ideas, alienation, compulsion. There are no giants. Share your battles with your friends. And if you don't win, look for professional help. Existence is too precious to be confined in a cell."

It was the first time he told us to rage, not against others but against our phantoms. It was the first time he recommended we seek out a psychiatrist or psychologist if necessary. I thought he detested them. We plunged into a state of silence, broken suddenly by our resident psychologist:

"People, I've got experience! And I'm charging just fifty bucks a consult," said Bartholomew, evoking laughter from those present. Yes, he had "experience" all right—in complicating other people's problems.

"That man has already driven five psychologists nuts!" said Edson of Bartholomew. The Miracle Worker had always been religious but never recognized his fallacies.

"Slander! I'm a complex man in search of simplification,"

said Bartholomew effusively. "Whoever doesn't simplify me complicates me. I'm a genius!"

The Mayor, hearing this, felt obligated to outdo him. "Folks, although I'm more intelligent than this bigmouth, I charge only a sandwich for therapy."

"But, Mayor, you've already given three psychiatrists heart attacks," said Monica, needling him.

"Yes, but, but—" The Mayor couldn't think of anything to refute Monica. He called on Bartholomew for help. "I'll let my secretary of education answer."

"The Mayor gave psychiatrists heart attacks because his illness is inexplicable and untreatable."

Believing he had been praised, he kissed Bartholomew on his swollen eye. I never knew if the Mayor was naïve or the shrewdest of us all. Excited, he thanked Bartholomew for his words: "Great men need to be followed by stagnant minds."

"Stagnant?" said Honeymouth, neither understanding nor liking the term. But the group's politician explained without explaining:

"Stagnant with information. Having a brain impregnated and bewildered with old data." But now Bartholomew understood even less than before. He didn't know whether he was being insulted or commended.

I started thinking it was time for academic curriculums to undergo major surgery, and perhaps the dreamseller might one day be among the surgeons. Our students destroyed themselves, becoming sick, depressed, and we simply denied the psychic phenomena that assailed them. Whenever one of them committed suicide, we were stunned, secretly nursing our feelings of guilt.

We took refuge behind textbooks and exams, as if exams measured a true education. Often, exams were a cloak to hide the madness of an educational system and disguise our alienation.

CHAPTER 23

Women with Complex Minds

THE DREAMSELLER NEVER CHASTISED US. EVEN KNOWING we could be ridiculous sometimes, he encouraged us to debate. Simply walking among this group turned your world into a circus.

That's why, more and more, it wasn't just intellectuals who followed us but also groups of young people. We discovered that this was because certain psychiatrists and psychologists were advising some of their patients suffering from anxiety and depression to seek out others like them. It seemed that this unusual group had a potentiating effect on antidepressants and tranquilizers.

I suspected the dreamseller had chosen our group of misfits to help temper his ideas. He was serious and focused, but through us, he taught playfully. The problem was that my friends got carried away, putting him and other disciples in precarious situations.

I used to teach both students and university faculty. I never kidded around in the classroom, never used humor in my lessons. My classes were a restaurant where people ate out of obligation. And to think I was considered the most eloquent member of the faculty.

The dreamseller never set the locations of his open-air classroom, nor the hour when he was going to speak, much less the subject he would discuss. Nevertheless, people of all ages, cultures, and levels of education sought him out, eager to hear him. In contrast, I used to set a time, place and topic but people weren't excited to hear me. It's sad to say, but were it not for the tests, my classroom would have been empty.

While I was thinking about my past, the politician decided it was time to speak. The Mayor, elated at the number of women in the audience, which included a mix of Jews, Muslims, young people and other potential followers, started into his speech:

"Beloved voters of this generous city. As one of the leaders with the broadest vision of the future among this mass of mortals, I would like to tell you that women are more intelligent, gracious, sensible, wise and creative than men."

The dreamseller applauded. Monica, Professor Jurema and the other women also applauded enthusiastically. I thought to myself, "Here he goes again, trying to upstage the dreamseller." But to keep up appearances, I applauded as well.

Seeing the women applauding vigorously, he bellowed, "Buuut . . ."

Several of the women rolled their eyes, figuring the Mayor never dished out praise without strings attached.

Then he added playfully, "But they invented shopping centers!"

The women burst into laughter, and all the men, including me, joined them. They admitted that the compulsion to buy was one of their worst enemies. I couldn't understand how the guy managed to be so funny. Encouraged by his "truthful joke," I decided to risk being playful.

"From their hair to their toenails, women have something to spend money on. How did you manage that feat?" I asked.

Dimas, a con man who had stolen women's purses in the past, chimed in with this joke, stuttering only slightly:

"People, these days you d—don't need ultrasound to know the child's sex. You just run a credit card over the woman's belly. If it's a girl, the child starts kicking like crazy."

Everyone laughed and felt at ease. As always, Bartholomew couldn't keep his mouth shut. But he seemed quiet as if meditating. It was the first time he wasn't flamboyant.

"Are you sick, Bartholomew? Do you have a headache?" Monica asked.

Monica was naïve. Encouraged, he could cause the biggest headache of the morning. And he did. Clearing his throat, he said, "Beautiful Monica, most intelligent Jurema and all the other women hearing me. You are more magnanimous than men!"

"Magnanimous?" I thought. I wonder if he even knows the meaning of that word. As if reading my mind he continued:

"For those who don't know, 'magnanimous' means giving, benevolent, generous, charitable."

The women applauded. Seduced by this lunatic, they hung on every word. And he went on. "If not for a woman, my brain and I wouldn't be here." We laughed at that piece of foolishness.

"What about your father? Didn't he participate in your construction? Or were you by some chance cloned?" asked a Muslim man.

"Yes, Daddy spent nine minutes and Mom spent nine months in that construction. It's with good reason that Jews consider that only someone with a Jewish mother is genuinely Jewish." And imitating the dreamseller, he said, "I bow before you women!"

An Orthodox Jew applauded him spiritedly. And the women were won over, too. Extremely excited, Honeymouth continued his exaltation of women:

"Wandering through the labyrinths of my privileged mind,

I recall a story that demonstrates the superiority of women. I was once walking along a beautiful beach in Miami, thinking about the mysteries of life, when suddenly a dazzling bottle washed ashore from the far corners of the Atlantic. Like any curious person, I opened it. And do you know what was in it?" he asked the audience.

"Money!" the Mayor guessed.

"No, my friend. A genie! But a stressed, agitated, irritated genie like my friend the Mayor. The genie was so impatient that he hurriedly told me, 'You get three wishes, but I can only grant one. Hurry up, I have a therapy session I need to get to!' The genie's world had also turned into a giant mental institution, like ours. And this genie was brilliant and insane, like our Julio Cesar. I told him emphatically, 'I want to visit Cuba!'

"'Cuba? Is that all?' the genie asked, happy to get rid of me so easily.

"'Yes, I want to visit Cuba, *but* . . . I'm afraid of planes and boats. So I want you to build a bridge from Miami to Cuba!'

"'What? A bridge that long? Are you crazy?' And he grumbled, 'Gimme a break. Do you have any idea the amount of planning and engineering that goes into building a bridge? Much less one that long? Forget it, wish for something else.'

"So he asked me for my second wish, adding, 'Remember, money is tight, so I can only grant one wish.'"

Bartholomew paused before continuing with the craziest story ever.

"So then I asked him about the desire of every politician, executive and economist. I told him: 'I want to know how the world economy works, the logic behind it, and how to prevent new crises.' When he heard my second wish, the genie started panting and having stomach cramps. He grabbed his stomach and said, 'Tell me your third wish. And make it fast.'"

Bartholomew paused again. No one blinked.

"Then, people, in a stroke of extreme lucidity, I announced my third and final extraordinary wish. A wish that thinkers and philosophers of every era have dreamed of."

"Out with it!" we yelled, bursting with curiosity.

"That's what the genie said: 'Out with it! Out with it!' I looked him in the eye and said, 'Genie, my wish is simple. I want to understand the mind of women!'" When he heard my third wish, he groaned and asked almost breathlessly, 'So, do you want that bridge to Cuba to be two lanes or four?'"

People were falling over with laughter. The women in the crowd also laughed uncontrollably. But good-naturedly, they went after Bartholomew.

Professor Jurema hooked her cane around his neck. Surrounded by the women, she said, "Women really are complex. So complex that we were kept quiet for centuries for fear of our intelligence."

Once things calmed down, the dreamseller spoke.

"It's obvious that the socioeconomic system over the ages has been male-dominated and riddled with errors," he said. "Men's reckless ambition has generated wars, religious conflicts, discrimination, financial crises, predatory competition in international commerce. I would like to see women become heads of state across the world. If they act like their male counterparts, they will commit the same mistakes. But if they act along the lines of their intuition, femininity, generosity and sensitivity they will change history."

I remembered reading sociological texts about the behaviors of men and women. Men always committed more crimes, more acts of exclusion and were more violent and corrupt than women. Their instincts were different.

And just like that, just as the wind blows unexpectedly and without course, the dreamseller went on his way. Wandering was his fate, thinking was his commitment.

CHAPTER 24

The Greatest Inventory

VARIOUS INTERESTING EVENTS HAPPENED THAT WEEK. I took countless notes on scrap paper. One day I must compile them. Since I'm relating selected events, admitting that my criteria are fallible and distorted, I want to tell you about an incident that occurred the following Saturday, one that penetrated the depths of my mind. Something I never imagined could happen.

Our group was passing by the building that housed the city's most important civil registry. There was an enormous public square nearby, an isolated spot rarely bustling with people. But now, counting the closest disciples and casual followers, there were close to forty of us. In our group were five psychology students and six medical students in their last year of school. All of them had taken part in other meetings, so they were familiar with us.

As soon as we arrived, we saw two identical twins walking by us arguing about the inheritance they were to receive. Each of them had a lawyer at his side. They had spent hours trying in vain to reach an agreement about the estate. The twins had been the best of friends before the death of their father, apparently inseparable, but they became enemies after the reading of the will. One of them wanted to sue the other.

The dreamseller looked at them and suddenly asked us about the most important possessions of a human being. "Who among you has made an inventory of the most significant facts that constitute the quilt of your story?"

"Inventory? What do you mean?" Monica asked.

The dreamseller replied, "Making an inventory of our story is much more than just thinking about the past. Making an inventory is to describe the most relevant facts of one's own self. It's bringing together the pieces and reorganizing them. It's being an engineer of the mind who builds bridges between his experiences."

And, gazing at the students in the audience, he said, "We're a fragmented society made up of fragmented people. What is the relationship between losses and pleasure, between despair and peace? What is the bridge between fear and tranquillity? Are they irreconcilable? Is depression completely separate from joy, or can it provide us with a map for finding it?"

The psychology students looked at one another blankly. They had never studied anything about bridges between fear and tranquillity, between depression and joy. They were familiar with theories and diagnoses of mental disturbances but hadn't discussed the construct of a mental map capable of connecting different experiences to promote learning and maturity. The medical students were equally puzzled.

"Many thinkers have died without building bridges between the power of analysis and the power of happiness, between painstaking observation and the contemplation of existence, between internalization and socialization," the dreamseller said.

He managed to blend psychology, sociology, philosophy and pedagogy. Great men were fractured individuals. Newton was antisocial. Einstein had depressive traits. They were experts in some areas but fragile in others. Perhaps they never thought of building bridges between the elements of their past.

"Where are the celebrities who have managed to reconcile their inventory and established connections between social success and emotional success? And the great journalists? Who among them learned to erect bridges between criticism and relaxation? The great politicians of history—who among them built byways throughout their lives capable of connecting power and simplicity, between being constantly in the spotlight and an awareness of their vulnerability? Whoever doesn't construct mental bridges builds instead islands in the cerebral cortex. One moment he may be a lamb, the next moment a lion. At one moment calm, explosive at another. In these times of collective anxiety, youth the world over experience that drama," he said.

I sat down to reflect on this information. I didn't know if it was correct, but for the first time I heard coherent explanations for the contradictions in human behavior. I had never understood why the reactions of the great men of history fluctuated between extremes. Their cerebral cortexes weren't continents, rather, they were made up of islands.

"Caligula was insignificant but thought he was more beautiful than Rome," the Master continued. "He had outbursts of kindness and fits of fury. Nero was a young man given to the arts but became one of the most brutal men in history, never thinking twice about killing those who opposed him. Stalin ordered the murder of supposed enemies at night and the next morning had breakfast with their wives as if nothing had happened. Hitler patted and fed his dog, but starved and froze to death a million Jewish children."

The dreamseller paused to let us reflect critically on his ideas. But there wasn't time; the Mayor shattered the silence.

"My people, I'm a man of bridges," he said with a politician's pride. "If I come to power, I'll build bridges throughout the city. I'll be quicker than Honeymouth's genie. I'll build bridges between city hall and the shantytowns. I'll build bridges between Congress and the city's psych wards."

Encouraging his friend, Honeymouth said, "Very good, noble Mayor. I request you build bridges between the banks and the cemeteries."

"Why, Bartholomew?" asked Solomon.

"Because that's where my friends in debt are." And he took out a handkerchief to dry his crocodile tears.

"Wait, didn't you say they're buried in the banks themselves?" Crusher said, cutting in.

"Yes, but there's not enough room for so many bankrupt people."

This time they buried the dreamseller's ideas, mixing fractured minds with bankrupt people, politicians with insane asylums. A real jumble. But the dreamseller was happy to see his disciples reflect on these questions.

"When someone dies, an inventory is made of his goods. But which are the most relevant—jewels, cars, houses, stocks, farmland?" he asked. "None of these! It's the body of experiences that make us historical beings. A human being without history is a book without letters. We must make an inventory of the most frustrating and the most joyful experiences of our lives and give it out to those we love, while we're still alive."

And then he looked up at the tall buildings and began shouting like a madman.

"No pain should be borne without bridges of relief being built. No shortcoming should be corrected without a lesson learned. Otherwise, suffering is useless. There is no truth to the idea that pain serves to enrich character. Unless we make certain connections, pain worsens the human being, fear traumatizes him, guilt smothers him," he said.

These last words made me recall my several therapy sessions. My therapists urged me to stir up the innards of my past, agonize over my conflicts, but I couldn't recall them. I felt powerless.

I would walk the streets panting, gasping for air, my muscles aching, my memory failing, unable to remember everyday facts. My mental energy was exhausted. I felt like a hundred-year-old man in the body of someone in his forties.

When I was in crisis, I had no bridges to my successes. My crises lasted forever. When I was in anguish, I had no channels to wake me and make me see that my life wasn't a loss, that it was in fact bright with color and joy. The windows of my brain could shine into one another. I carried around a library in my head, but I was an isolated intellectual, lonely and miserable.

CHAPTER 25

The Inventory of Five Traumas and Their Bridges

OVERHEARING THE DREAMSELLER'S LECTURE TO THE psychology and medical students was Fernando Lataro, warden of the famous maximum security prison nicknamed "Demons Island." He was accompanied by two police officers and three educators from the prison. He was a weekend follower, as it was difficult for him to leave work, the comforts of home and his cars to become a wanderer with no place to live or anything to eat.

"Whoever doesn't learn to mine the gold in his own life will never be able to improve himself and overcome," the dreamseller had said.

Some of my students were cocaine or marijuana addicts, others were addicted to gambling and still others were compulsive spenders. When it came to relationships, some had fits of jealousy and became paranoid when rejected, while others changed partners the way you change clothes. Some lived in fear of not succeeding in life, while others were alienated as if there were no tomorrow. Neither of us had learned to sort out our history and bring together our extremes.

The dreamseller asked his listeners to sift through their past and reflect on the five most anguished moments of their lives, in descending order of suffering, from greatest to least. He also asked us to analyze the bridges we had built or should have built between these and other episodes of our story.

We remained silent for an hour, prospecting for anguishing facts that had marked us. Some sat on benches, others on the ground, and some remained standing. It was a fascinating experience.

After the exercise came the big revelation. The dreamseller had us sit in a circle and said that whoever felt free to do so could describe those five episodes and comment on one of them. He emphasized, "Don't talk unless you feel comfortable."

I thought no one was going to open up. We were all inhibited at first. After two long minutes, incredibly, Edson spoke up, and what he said surprised us. The man who loved to perform miracles for self-promotion had descended to the lowest level of the human condition. He took an inventory of his anguish, a declaration he had never made to anyone except his God.

He spoke of the five most painful episodes in his life starting with the most troubling. I never imagined anyone could dissect his soul so transparently.

"One: I was sexually abused as a child. Two: I lost my mother when I was a teenager. Three: I was publicly humiliated at work. Four: My father beat me when I was thirteen. Five: I lost my best friend to cancer when I was fifteen."

That scale of suffering demonstrated that the sexual abuse was more agonizing than the loss of his mother. While the loss of his mother was indescribable, the pain of sexual abuse was almost irreparable, at least for Edson. The sequence also showed that, to him, being humiliated publicly was more painful than losing his best friend to cancer. The public humiliation caused a rupture in his personality. That might explain why he was always trying to promote himself.

"I learned that to violate the intimacy of a child is a crime

that destroys the springtime of our history. I learned that behind the least suspicious people and the most innocent conversations can hide inhuman psychopaths who don't think about
the consequences of their actions and want only to satisfy their
instincts."

Edson said that before the abuse, he was extroverted, free
and outgoing, but after those episodes—there was more than
one—he lost his spontaneity, his sociability, and withdrew into
himself. He became dispirited, turned inward excessively. He
grew up feeling rage for the parents who hadn't protected him,
and hatred toward his aggressor. He dreamed every day of
strangling him or throwing him off a cliff. And, he said, in his
relationship with God he had found mechanisms of tolerance
and a brake to soften his instincts.

"But unfortunately I didn't build a bridge of dialogue. At
first I kept quiet because of the psychopath's blackmail. Later I
kept quiet out of shame. Finally, I kept quiet because I thought
I had overcome my conflict, but I was in denial that some of its
roots were still active in my personality."

He said that since joining the dreamseller he had begun to
see there are other ways of violating someone's trust, such as
blackmailing him or pressuring him to accept your ideas and
truths.

Some intellectuals commit that kind of abuse, I reflected.
They violate the mind of those who disagree with them and
who depend on them. I'm a socialist intellectual and supposedly a humanist, but I now see there's an animal in my intellect
eager to devour whatever defenseless minds dare to contradict
me.

Edson concluded his remarkable exposition by saying, "I
hope to grow to understand the difference between exposing
and imposing our thoughts."

It's a pity I had never asked my students to make an inventory of their histories. Of course, they wouldn't need to recount them in public, but today I think that if they had learned even the fundamentals of being prospectors of their minds, they'd run less risk of being slaves to their conflicts.

Edson's story moved me. I had considered him a charlatan, an egomaniac, a religious wastrel. But at that moment, I was ashamed of my shallowness. I didn't know him, even though we had spent months sleeping next to one another. Now I understand that behind his anxious drive to make his presence known is the vital need to be accepted. Am I any better than he? Not at all. My authoritarianism in the classroom stemmed from a sick need to be socially accepted. Behind every authoritarian is a child wanting to be loved.

We applauded Edson for having the courage to dissect his history and for the bridges he had built.

Monica gave him a long hug. "You're incredible! I believe in miracles. Especially the miracle of friendship. Anyone who has friends has a treasure," she told him.

The Mayor and Honeymouth lifted him onto their shoulders, singing and playfully joking with him. And they took advantage of the situation to tweak me: "For Edson's a jolly good fellow! For Edson's a jolly good fellow! Not annoying like Julio Cesaaaar! Which nobody can deny."

CHAPTER 26

Dammed-up Pain

SOLOMON WAS THE SECOND TO TELL US HIS INVENTORY. Though he had suffered some relapses, his tics and his hypochondria had lessened as he walked with the dreamseller. But as he began talking about himself, his compulsive behavior worsened. He began opening and closing his mouth repeatedly and putting his hand on his chest to see if his heart was still beating. He made the inventory of his five greatest dramas as follows.

"First, I was humiliated at school. Second, I lost my parents in an accident. Third, I went hungry as an adolescent. Fourth, I suffered burns as a child. Fifth, I was in a car accident."

I was surprised by the scale of his issues. I realized I understood very little about psycho-sociological matters. Solomon loved his parents. They were generous and sociable. Their loss when he was fourteen struck at the roots of his being, shook his structure, but, as incredible as it seems, that wasn't the worst crisis of his life—being publicly humiliated at school was his worst existential experience. Which indicates that there are episodes that go unnoticed by psychiatrists and psychologists but are more relevant than our science can imagine.

To clear away any doubts, Solomon described the apex of his drama:

"My obsessions always attracted the attention of my class-mates. And even as I would overcome one mania, another would appear. I used to jump up and down five times before entering the classroom so no one would die; I would slap my forehead; I would feel my neck constantly looking for signs of cancer; I coughed all the time; I would repeat the last five words someone said on the phone; count the windows in a building I passed; look for holes to stick my finger in."

We were all astonished at how the young man had suffered. After a pause to collect his thoughts, he continued.

"One day when I was thirteen my classmates held a surprise party for me," he said. "I was happy as could be. They brought out a cake, and the boys and girls started singing 'Happy Birth-day.' Then I saw the words they had written on the cake: Psy-cho Solomon. I ran away, crying. To this day, birthday parties make my skin crawl."

And he added that several times during recess, when his incessant hand gestures were out of control, students from all the other grades would form a circle around him and start to scream, "Crazy!" and hit him on the head. The principal, seeing Solomon's tics, tried to hide a smile. He never reprimanded the other students or helped to build any bridges between those whose behavior was different.

"Going to school became a torment. It was like being in the Coliseum in front of a bloodthirsty mob. I wanted to die, to disappear from the world. When my parents died, I went hungry for a year, but nothing was as severe as the hunger for understanding. I didn't want the other students to love me, but for them to treat me like a person and not like a circus animal."

After a brief pause considering this difficult chapter of his life, he continued.

"The years passed and I built bridges," he said. "A psychia-trist helped me. With her I learned that, despite being obsessive I wasn't a piece of trash, I was a human being. But I didn't learn certain fundamental bridges. I should have learned what the dreamseller has taught us, to not demand from others what they can't give, because those closest to us are the ones who cause us disappointment. How could I demand understanding from my colleagues if they were at war with themselves?"

Solomon took a breath, deeply relieved. He had lost the fear of being who he was. He slept under bridges but had learned to feel like a human being, a star in the theater of society. By making his inventory he let cool air into some of the suffocating corners of his mind. I stood up and embraced him as if he were my son.

"You're one of the anonymous heroes Hollywood never makes movies about," I told him. "A social actor more brilliant than the brightest stars. Congratulations!"

Bartholomew got up and also hugged Solomon. "Dude, you're beautiful! I'm obsessively crazy about you."

The Mayor, more unrestrained, said, "I'm going to cover you with kisses." And he moved toward him. But Solomon ducked his head and ran as we all laughed.

After applauding him, Professor Jurema also gave her powerful inventory. I never could have imagined that behind that remarkable woman, admired by the leading educational figures in the country, lay a tormented soul. I never guessed from reading her books and articles that behind them was a terribly wounded child. I have to revise my process of interpretation, build bridges in my mind to read between the lines.

"The mental illness of my father was the saddest chapter in my life. After that was the passing of my beloved twin brother when I was ten years old. My third dilemma came when I had breast cancer. Next was the loss of my husband. And the fifth was the battles I had against the educational system."

The loss of her brother, breast cancer, the loss of her be-

loved husband all shook her world, but nothing rocked that
solid professor as much as her father's mental illness at a time
when treatment was inadequate and prejudice was rife.

"My father," she said, taking a deep breath, "was my hero,
my friend, my support, my safe harbor. He was the person who
loved me most in this life and the one I loved most. He owned
a large grocery store. He was a brilliant and humane businessman. He was the oldest child and helped raise his six siblings.
He was so humane that he gave what he had to whomever
needed it, without receiving anything in return. My mother
detested that in him. My father couldn't see anyone going hungry without coming to their aid. Whenever he put together a
food basket for a needy family, he would take me with him.
To him, giving wasn't a burden but a celebration. Investing in
human beings was his joy."

"Walking with the Master," she said, turning to the dreamseller, "I see my father in him every day. And he was his age
when his world came apart."

Tears welled in her eyes. She choked back a sob before
speaking of the most anguished period of her life. All of us
have an inexpressible chapter in our story, one which words
fail to describe. Jurema's pain was unfathomable. She spoke of
how the calamity came about. Her father had cosigned a loan
for his youngest brother. When the brother defaulted, her father had to assume the debt. The country was in a period of
economic crisis, and he had no savings. In less than a year he
lost everything he had amassed in decades. And that was only
the beginning.

"Many lose and start over. My father would have, but in
the midst of the crisis he caught my mother in bed with my
youngest uncle, the one who had bankrupted him. Maybe because of me or because he loved her so much, I don't know, he
didn't leave her. Then some of the men he owed accused him of

trying to start a revolt. And that same uncle was in collusion
with them. My father was unjustly tried and humiliated. He
was imprisoned for a month."

Her father, shamed, withdrew into his quarters and began
to suffer panic attacks, screaming as if he were about to die.
The doctors couldn't find anything wrong. His insanity grew
deeper, and he lost the will to fight.

Her voice faltering, she said that none of his relatives ever
came to visit him. His own brothers wouldn't touch him for
fear of "catching" his mental illness.

"My hero had become a villain. Finally, something terrible
happened. My mother had him committed to an asylum. I was
ten years old. They had taken away my foundation, stolen my
innocence."

At that moment, Jurema collapsed in sobs. Monica lent her
a handkerchief. After regaining composure, Jurema spoke of
the core of her pain, the events that had hurt her the most.

"When they were taking him away to the asylum, I heard
my father calling my name: 'Juremita! Juremita! Don't let them
put me away! I'm not crazy. I love you, help me!' I ran to help
him, but my mother and my uncles stopped me. 'It's for his own
good, sweetheart,' my mother said, tired of the man she didn't
love and who could no longer work. I'm an elderly woman, but
to this day I dream about my father calling out to me and asking for help."

The episode had occurred over seventy years ago, but the
torment still raged in her mind. All of the dreamseller's followers were moved to learn once again that we didn't really know
one another. We discovered that without making an inventory
of our histories and sharing it with those we loved, our social
relationships were mere theater. We were a group of strangers
under the same roof.

Jurema begged her mother to let her visit her father but was told he needed to be isolated. That separation was against all the principles of psychiatry. Little Jurema sent letters almost daily to her father, but they never arrived. Her mother didn't mail them.

After so much pleading, two years, seven months, six days after the commitment, her mother finally gave in and took her to visit him. The girl was perplexed at seeing her father. He was completely different, both physically and intellectually from when he had been taken away. He had been disfigured by mistreatment and by countless electroshock therapies. Weeping, she ran to him and said, "Daddy, Daddy, it's me, your daughter, your Juremita." But he didn't recognize her.

Jurema stared at us and completed her inventory.

"I shouted my father's name, trying to wake him up from his sleep," she said. "Seeing my desperation, a cold, unfeeling, inhumane psychiatrist appeared and told my mother in front of me that my father's illness was genetic in nature and that I stood a good chance of ending up like him. He urged her to find a psychiatrist for me. That's how I grew up, with a ghost haunting me. I grew up thinking that sooner or later I would meet the same fate as my father."

A year later, her father died and was buried. She didn't go to see his body. Many years after she had become a university professor, she decided to study psychopathology and came to understand that her father's illness, panic syndrome, was perfectly treatable. But psychiatry, then in its infancy, committed atrocities.

"I've learned that throughout our lives we must build bridges of pardon, especially to pardon ourselves. Otherwise, we won't survive. I've learned that no mental illness diminishes a human being's dignity. I've learned that to exclude or isolate someone is to kill them emotionally, to murder them without stopping their heartbeats."

The dreamseller stood up and solemnly applauded her. With tears in his eyes, he told her in a soft voice, "You do more than I can ever do. You sell more dreams than I do."

"I need to look upon life as the show of shows and understand that both tears and laughter are privileges of the living," she said. "In the months or years I have left to live, I have to learn to remove the restraints from my mind. To be freer and more flexible, to live more gently and to be more wildly in love with life. And for that I need this band of misfits to help me." And she smiled.

We all ran to embrace her, as did the students of psychology and medicine.

The Mayor told Jurema, "Mommy, I'm going to kiss you. You're beautiful." And he kissed her several times on the forehead. She tried to escape, asking the others for help.

Once things had calmed down, Honeymouth added, "Mommy, if you become mentally ill, I want you to know that there are two perfectly healthy men here who invented the revolutionary scream therapy. No mental demon can withstand our technique."

"I'm going to scream, all right," she said. "But to get away from you, you scoundrel."

We all laughed. Then, we danced and sang, and made fun of one another. We have all experienced tragedy, but we have found shelter in each other.

CHAPTER 27

Ghosts That Must Be Tamed

PROFESSOR JUREMA'S INVENTORY WAS A BALM THAT salved our stories. We discovered that it is possible to transform our arid mental terrain into a blooming garden like the one we were in that day.

For years I studied the human condition in sociology books, but it never entered my mind that heaven and hell, comfort and pain, were very close at hand. I never imagined that it was so difficult, yet so easy, to share some of our secrets. I never realized that it was so complex, but at the same time so simple, to built bridges, to connect the islands in our minds.

After that solemn celebration we were at the height of joy. No one had gone to Disney World, yet none of us had ever had so much fun. No one had gone to the movies, yet we never experienced such emotion. No one went to a psychotherapy session, yet no psychotherapy ever had such an effect on us. No one went to school, yet we had never learned as much.

We sat in a circle, awaiting the dreamseller's latest words. He breathed several long, satisfied sighs. He sold dreams of a free history, one that reunites its fragments, binds up its wounds, breaks the chains, and lets air flow into every corner of its vaults. That was the dream of Buddha, Confucius,

Socrates, Plato and the other great thinkers. It was the dream of the teacher of teachers, the man born in Nazareth.

"It's refreshing to take off our makeup and be what we always were: human beings, silly and lucid, incoherent and wise, fragile and secure—in short, paradoxical. Whoever doesn't invent his story doesn't rewrite his texts. Remember, every human being either has his ghosts or constructs them.

"I cry when I think that from preschool to university we're creating children who don't know how to delve into their minds. They're like houses built on foundations of misinformation. When storms strike, they have no shutters to protect themselves, no emotional filter to help them survive."

Unlike many masters of past and present, the dreamseller was selling motivational words. He didn't talk about a victorious life crowned by success. For him, existence was a contract of risk. And the clauses in that contract contained every part of man's story: stress and peace of mind, tears and laughter, madness and sanity. It is in that whirlwind that his lessons emerge.

He was an honest man, more honest than any mental health professional I ever met. He sold dreams of a free mind, but that freedom had to be won amid our ghosts and through intellectual sweat. As if examining his own history and plunging into his own inventory, he told us a story.

"Even a well-to-do person without financial ghosts can be tormented by social ghosts: betrayal, disappointments, offenses, slander, loss. Even if he has no social ghosts, he can be disturbed by mental phantoms: guilt, anguish, an inferiority complex, shyness, obsessions, bitter mental images. And even if he has no mental phantoms he can be unnerved by existential ghosts: death, transcendence, the lack of meaning in life. And even if he has no existential ghosts he may worry about the frailty of his body, fatigue, headaches, muscular pains, sleeplessness, nightmares."

And, intently observing his listeners, he stated, "The great human challenge is not to eliminate the ghosts we have created but to tame them. I say this because we possess surprising creativity."

Yes, it's true, we see problems where none exist. His ideas, cutting but at the same time gentle, reverberated in the hundred billion neurons of our brains.

"I know my project of selling dreams generates both admiration and scandal," he said. "Some call me a lunatic, others an impostor, still others a heretic, a deceiver, an instigator. But when I look over the inventory of my ghosts, when I review the traumas I've been through, the monsters in the present shrink and those in the future no longer frighten me. The bridges between my past, my present and expectations for the future bring me peace."

The psychology students had the privilege of hearing ideas that would mark their story. They understood that if they didn't recognize their ghosts and their troubles, they would have limited ability to treat the ghosts of others. I saw that young Solomon was fascinated by what he had heard, but also tense.

"I have ghosts that terrify me, Julio Cesar," he told me.

"So do I, my young friend. But we can't give in to them."

Just when everything was flowing smoothly, once again the pair of agitators stepped in to stir things up. Barnabas said, "Voters of this great city: I pledge that if elected mayor I will put all the people's ghosts in jail. There won't be a single one left to haunt you."

"The Mayor is a demagogue. Look at me! I'm a professional ghost hunter. I have experience!" Bartholomew said, cutting in.

The Mayor reached into his pocket and took out a stuffed toy mouse that he'd found in the trash and kept for just such an occasion. Tying it onto a string, he dangled it in front of Bartholomew, and something incredible happened: Bartholomew, faced with that tiny animal, went into a panic. We couldn't believe that the invincible and unstoppable Honeymouth harbored a ghost we were unaware of: a phobia of rats.

Bartholomew squealed like a schoolgirl and jumped into Crusher's lap. The philosophic atmosphere of that great inventory came crashing down. But on the other hand, I loved seeing the egomaniacal Honeymouth humbled by a mouse. We never laughed so much. It was like getting our revenge.

The Mayor continued his joke, trying to place the small inanimate mouse in Honeymouth's hands. The dreamseller took advantage of that moment to teach us: "Ghosts appear when we fail to distinguish fantasy from reality."

We saw Bartholomew shivering and cringing. It wasn't appropriate to laugh; after all, it was one of his fears. But because he made fun of everyone, even at the most inopportune moments, we couldn't hold back our laughter. For the first time, I assisted in turning drama into comedy.

"The great orator, the dragon slayer, in panic over a little mouse," I said, getting even.

Embarrassed, but without losing his poise as a street philosopher, he climbed out of Crusher's arms, "dusted" his pants and shirt, and answered, "Julio Cesar, noted emperor of the madhouse of society, knows that every great man has his secrets."

CHAPTER 28

Demons Island

JUST AS WE WERE JOKING ABOUT BARTHOLOMEW'S GHOSTS, Fernando Lataro, the warden of the maximum security prison, came closer. He was astonished at what he had seen and heard. Before taking part in the experiment of the historical inventories, he had felt that his institution was society's sewer, the end of the line, a warehouse for brutal criminals and incorrigible sociopaths.

That institution was notorious for its violence and uprisings, its drug traffic and riots. It was on an island some thirty miles from the coast, nicknamed "Demons Island" because it housed the country's most dangerous men. Since he had taken over its administration two years earlier, five uprisings had occurred, resulting in the deaths of three guards, one administrator and ten prisoners.

Life had no value to the majority of those prisoners. They had committed unimaginable atrocities. Some had killed their wives, others their parents, and still others their children. Some were kidnappers, bank robbers and drug traffickers. Others were terrorists and Mafiosi who thought another person's life wasn't worth more than a bullet.

Working on Demons Island meant facing a different kind of ghost. The clergy wouldn't dare visit. Musicians wouldn't play there. Philanthropists pretended the institution didn't exist. No one would take a chance. The turnover of guards, social workers, psychologists and educators was staggering. Some fell ill the first month there. Every year, half the employees requested medical leave, with real justification.

I knew Demons Island and its reputation better than most. In the past, I had asked my students to do sociological research into the perspective of those criminals. They were unsuccessful. They were threatened and thrown out by the inmates, some of whom commanded gangs from inside. My students feared being threatened by their accomplices on the outside. Cocaine, heroin, pot and hallucinogens would frequently get past the institution's rigorous security checks.

The warden and his staff were desperate over the prisoners' recent actions. They suspected an escape was being planned. The warden himself, three guards and five educators had received death threats. They had to have bodyguards, even outside the prison. "Violence has reached unimaginable levels," the warden told us, concerned. "It's not just the socially underprivileged youths or ones with serious family problems who are perpetrating criminal acts. Now, young people from the middle class are committing atrocities against innocent people. In many schools, violence has become routine. I don't understand it." And, remembering the dreamseller's words from an earlier occasion, he added, "We've made breakthroughs in technology, but in terms of altruism and tolerance we're in our infancy."

Following his brief account, the dispirited warden made a request of the dreamseller that shook me:

"Master, I was moved by your technique of making an inventory of the five greatest dramas in our history. Do you think you and your disciples could teach it to the inmates in my institution? At least to some of them? Maybe they'd have a chance to develop some spark of sensitivity and social responsibility."

I thought, "Is that even possible? Who could make those psychopaths look inside themselves? It's an extremely risky, extremely dangerous experiment. How would we get them to see the importance of sharing their story with others, when they kill without hesitation?" One of the Demons Island staff was more incisive.

"Society treats our inmates like garbage," he said, "and those of us who work there have to endure them. Despite their crimes, they're human beings. Can't you please try to help us?"

Of course, I never expected the dreamseller to accept. For one thing, his life had already been in jeopardy recently. Surely he wouldn't want to expose himself to this kind of risk, much less expose his vulnerable disciples. But before he declined, Honeymouth answered for the dreamseller and the rest of us.

"Count us in! We'll teach those boys a lesson or two."

"A few raps on the knuckles and everything'll be fine," the Mayor joked.

They didn't know what they were talking about. But before I could contradict them, the warden and his workers applauded. "Bravo! Thank you so much!"

Bartholomew and Barnabas, naïve as they were, thought the institution was a public school with some unruly students. They had no idea what Demons Island was like. They'd be eaten alive the first time they opened their mouths to crack a joke.

"At last, noted thinkers are going to invest in Demons Island," an equally naïve guard said.

"Thinkers?" I asked myself silently. "They only think about nonsense."

"Educate the young and prisons will become museums," the Mayor said.

This time the dreamseller became very pensive, barely breathing. He knew the terrain he had been invited to tread.

"You've just accepted a mission to perform in a maximum security prison," the dreamseller told the two showoffs.

Honeymouth realized what he'd done. With a lump in his throat he asked, "Maximum security prison, master?"

"Yes, and if you really want to, this is an opportunity to sell dreams in a setting where it's almost impossible to dream," the dreamseller said calmly after a long pause.

Fernando Lataro brightened up.

"I'll provide all the security we have at our disposal," he told us.

Bartholomew, trying to come up with an excuse to get out of the mission, turned to Barnabas: "Mayor, I can see you look tired, unsteady on your feet. Maybe we should . . ."

"No, I'm fine. Ready for anything." Then he caught on and corrected himself, "Oh, I mean, uh . . . no, I'm not fine. I'm going through male menopause."

But it was too late. The dreamseller had taken a liking to the project.

"Why don't you put on a show about Bartholomew's rat phobia for those prisoners and use that to explain the formation of emotional phantoms?" he told them. "After all, we all have some rats in our mental cellars. Maybe Julio Cesar could direct the skit."

"Excellent idea! Maybe we can do some cleaning up in those criminals' lairs using the story of this complicated human being," the Mayor said, pointing to Honeymouth.

"My people, this man, alias the Mayor, is an example of a poor wretch who had every opportunity to turn down the wrong path. And in the end he did . . ," Honeymouth said. And he burst into laughter. Then, seeing the Mayor's reaction, he corrected himself. "But because he's learning to tame his unruly ghosts he's still got a chance." And he laughed again.

The pair joked about everything and everyone, and at the

most inappropriate times. But they were so amusing that it was virtually impossible not to laugh at them. Some smiled without having the slightest idea what awaited us. But I turned to Jurema and whispered, "Do you know what Demons Island is?"

"Yes. We'll be roasted on a spit," she hissed under her breath. "And anyone who gets out alive will probably have a target on his back!"

Monica overheard the conversation and shuddered. The professor was well acquainted with the notorious institution. She had sent some of her students to try to work with the inmates. But nothing was effective. Her students left there almost stripped bare.

Seeing how risky the mission was, I drew back: "Master, forgive me, but I'm out! It's too risky. Wandering about with Bartholomew and Barnabas is one thing, but working with them to educate the offenders on Demons Island is insanity."

"Well, look here, everyone. The great educator is scared of his students."

And to my amazement, a med student, John Vitor, a drug user who had cried on my shoulder several times in recent weeks, said, "Why not? I'm game to help them, too. I've been in jail myself."

John Vitor was nearly expelled from college. He had injected cocaine, and his veins had hardened from shooting up daily. In desperation, he started in on his hands and feet. I saw my son John Marcus in John Vitor. Similar names with similar stories. But after walking with the dreamseller the last two months, he had begun to reorganize his story.

I first met John Vitor when I found him convulsing from an overdose. I panicked, thinking he was going to die in my arms. I came to invest in the young man with every fiber of my being. We would meet under the bridges where he slept. Once we talked from eight at night until four in the morning.

I was happy to see him recover, and I began to dream that he might become one of the dreamseller's disciples. I knew it wouldn't erase his past as an addict, but it could help him form a new future. But this mission was very risky. And John Vitor's time in jail for small amounts of drug possession couldn't prepare him for the institution that Fernando Lataro ran.

There were other drugs users who followed the dreamseller. Little by little they learned it was possible to inject adventures into their veins without using drugs of any kind; walking with Bartholomew and Barnabas apparently was enough. But the adventure to Demons Island seemed destined to fail.

I didn't want to disappoint John Vitor, but I was reluctant, even after the warden's guarantees. I had to reveal that I cared about people's pain. I had to abandon my status as intellectual and show my humanity. But I hesitated.

I shook my head. Monica, Solomon, Dima and Edson, who were more daring than I, urged me on. Then, Bartholomew challenged me.

"If the great Julio Cesar directs the play, I'll give an unforgettable performance!"

"Yes! If the emperor of the theatrical arts directs me, I'll set that institution of pampered men on fire!" said the Mayor.

Still unsure, I decided to accept the challenge. And as soon as I did, I suddenly had a flash. I thought: "This is my great chance to get even with these miserable gasbags. They've put me down, made me the butt of jokes, but now they'll pay."

"Okay, I accept," I said, to the applause of the crowd. "I'll write the script and cast the characters in incredible roles."

They were all happy. They carried me off on their shoulders. They had fallen into my trap. But deep down, I was afraid of falling into a trap of my own.

CHAPTER 29

Threatened on Demons Island

TO WRITE THE SCRIPT FOR THE PLAY WE WOULD PUT ON AT Demons Island, I listened attentively to some of the periods in Bartholomew's life and the reason that rat trauma haunted him like a ghost. The loudmouth talked and exaggerated, and I furiously took notes. I had to have the patience of Job. As I was writing the script, I prepared small traps for both the street philosopher and the barroom politician.

As I structured their characters, I thought they'd be eaten alive by the audience of criminals. Of course, I didn't want things to get out of hand, but I confess I dreamed of teaching them an unforgettable lessons. It was my opportunity to take the place of the dreamseller and educate those insubordinate and uncontrollable disciples in my own way. I knew I committed many errors as an educator, but my authoritarian instinct was aroused, my claws emerged from my unconscious and came into play at the conscious level.

It was one thing to write the script; rehearsing was another. They wouldn't memorize the text, they improvised dialogue, and joked around too much. We rehearsed under bridges, in squares, on the streets.

"Director, I'm surprising myself," said Honeymouth, patting himself on the back. "I've discovered I'm a very talented actor."

"If directors in Hollywood discover me, I'll take my place alongside Tom Cruise and Chaplin," said the Mayor.

"Chaplin's been dead for a long time," Solomon said.

"Dead? Well, not in my heart, Solomon," he replied, craftily extricating himself.

After rehearsing for a week, we took a ferry to the infamous Demons Island. All the closest disciples were present, including the beautiful Monica. Although we recommended she stay behind because of the unforeseeable risks she would run from being exposed to those sexually deprived men, she insisted on going. The boat was an old modified ferry, a hundred feet long, with wooden seats. Its white paint was faded and its tired motors growled. There were five guards on board.

The wind swept our hair into our eyes, producing a pleasant sensation. The breeze from the sea perfumed our nostrils and cleared away the fetid odors of gloomy bridges. It was shaping up to be a memorable day. And it was. Unaware of what awaited him, Bartholomew said, "Ah! I love being pampered."

"I'm gonna make the audience cry," said the Mayor.

The helmsman, hearing this, shook his head and said, "Everybody leaving this damned island cries, my friends."

I had a lump in my throat. The grind of rehearsals clouded my consciousness, narrowing my perception: we were going not to a theater but to a slaughterhouse. My heart shuddered at seeing the island in the distance. I suspect tears actually rolled down my cheeks. I turned toward the small port from which we had departed and brushed the hair out of my eyes to see the continent to which we were saying farewell. I wondered if I would ever set foot there again.

I was never an optimistic man. Pessimism is in fact the favorite diet of most intellectuals. Optimism, we often think, is something for stupid people alienated from reality. But that day I had concrete reasons for wallowing. I had a feeling that my plans weren't going to work out. As we approached the island, my heart and lungs lost their serenity, accelerated, begging for a way out. I asked myself, "What was I thinking when I agreed to do this?"

There were no beaches on Demons Island, just cliffs rising more than thirty feet into the air. The waves crashed violently against the rocks, producing a deafening roar. That funereal landscape, devoid of life, revealed a devastated coastal vegetation like the souls on that rock.

The prison was surrounded by a stone wall forty-five feet high. At one time, this had been a holding area for political prisoners. Later, the imposing structure was turned into the most respected and feared maximum security facility in the country.

As we entered the prison, we were subjected to a thorough inspection. Five men searched us. We were racked with fear as we approached the inmate area. If the landscape outside the walls was unusual, the inside was caustic. Small gardens with badly tended grass. There were no flowers, no trees, no beauty. Worn walls, faded paint and holes in the narrow streets contributed to the image of punishment. It was one more sentence imposed on those dangerous offenders. Their dream was not to pay their debt to society but to flee the chaos. Atop the wall, men with machine guns patrolled, knowing that sooner or later another riot would break out.

Many of the prisoners were serving life sentences. Killing or dying made little difference to those whose hopes had been exhausted. As we headed to the amphitheater, we passed through an immense central courtyard with cells on both sides. Only a few criminals were "free" in the courtyard. Some were there for good behavior, others through bribery and still others to keep down internal tension. Those who were loose were exercising under strict supervision. I felt a chill from their hateful stares.

A criminal with tattoos on his shoulders and chest shouted to his comrades, "They're visiting us like you visit animals in the zoo." And he imitated various animals, from elephants to lions.

Professor Jurema lost her balance and became dizzy. Dimas, a specialist in petty theft, seemed like a defenseless infant compared to the capacity for evil of those men. Solomon was feverish and sweating. Edson's lips were trembling, and he was praying under his breath to ward off the specter of panic. Crusher was silent. John Vitor went pale and regretted having encouraged me to accept the challenge. I couldn't read Monica's reaction, for she had had to wear an unkempt wig and baggy clothes to conceal her curves.

Honeymouth and the Mayor were, as always, on another planet. They swaggered like a couple of playboys, as if commanding a battalion. They were ten yards ahead of the group, with three unarmed guards, as guns were forbidden in the courtyard. Wherever they went, they waved, greeted, said hello, exactly as they did with strangers when they were in the streets.

One psychopath, in a cell to the right some twelve yards away, seeing them moving so casually in his territory, became irritated. He spat on the ground toward them. The pair spat right back. I don't know whether they were trying to provoke him or to show they were his equal.

A murderer who had wiped out a family of five, seeing the Mayor blissfully gobbling down crackers, shouted, "Get ready to go on a diet, fatso. You're gonna lose a hundred pounds."

"Fantastic! That's my dream, big guy," the Mayor replied insolently.

But I sensed that he was starting to feel shaken. His politician's spirit began cooling off. Ten paces ahead, a kidnapper insulted Honeymouth. Amid laughter from his companions, he bellowed, "Where ya goin', baby? C'mere, sweetheart."

I thought that this time Honeymouth would keep quiet, but to our amazement he stole a glance at the guards walking beside him and reacted. "That's it! Hold me back!" And he raised his fists.

The prisoners went wild, trying to break through the bars. I froze and my lips started to quiver.

Tensely, the guard advised him, "Listen, anybody who can't take an insult in here ends up sleeping in the cemetery."

Honeymouth swallowed hard, and his bravado subsided. He and Barnabas opened up more space between us and them; fear quickens one's steps. The dreamseller was walking unconcerned at our side. I couldn't understand where that calm came from. But even calm men have a limit; the dreamseller was no different. It wouldn't be long before I saw him shaken.

CHAPTER 30

Conspiracy

A MAN NICKNAMED "EL DIABLO," WHO HAD A SHAVED HEAD and scars on both cheeks, was sitting on a bench in the courtyard, near another criminal nicknamed "Shrapnel." El Diablo and Shrapnel were dangerous terrorists, gang bosses and leaders at the prison. They were feared and dictated the "honor code," ordering hits on people inside and outside Demons Island. Each of them was serving several life sentences for their crimes, not to mention the crimes for which they were still waiting to be tried. They were in the courtyard because of their power. Fernando Lataro felt it best to allow them a few privileges rather than have them incite the beasts and start a rebellion—a dangerous tactic of dubious value.

El Diablo rose from the bench and stared at length at the dreamseller. Shrapnel did the same. Slowly, they approached. In addition to the guards accompanying Bartholomew and Barnabas, four more were at our side. The guards began to get nervous at their approach. If they gave the signal, an armed guard would lock his rifle on the courtyard. But the terrorists made no aggressive moves. El Diablo was astonished at the sight of the dreamseller. Like the director of the Mellon Lincoln Hospital, Lucio Lobo, he looked as if he'd seen a ghost.

When he was six feet away from the dreamseller, he said

vehemently, "It's not possible! You're alive! Are you here for revenge?"

For the first time, I saw the dreamseller puzzled. He didn't understand. Revenge was not a word in his dictionary. He lived the art of tolerance. Surely the criminal was confused, I thought.

"Revenge? The best revenge against an enemy is to forgive him," the dreamseller said.

"You're full of it! You wouldn't forgive your executioners. You came here for revenge. But you won't get out of here alive." And he threatened to lunge at the dreamseller. We were on edge. Fortunately, other guards with weapons showed up and calmed matters.

"Can't you see he's a beggar?" said one of the guards, trying to calm the aggressor's anger.

I was distressed. In recent weeks the dreamseller had faced two assassination attempts. For whom was he being mistaken? Every theater director has moments of insecurity when he begins a new season, but I would have given anything in my power to resign from the job.

We were quickly brought to the backstage area of the amphitheater. Bartholomew and Barnabas were already there. But no one was able to concentrate. This was going to be a fiasco. We wouldn't even be able to speak the lines, much less act them out. Worse, we would probably spark a riot. Later we learned that some of the leaders, including the members of the Chinese Mafia, were planning to use the event to attempt to escape in the boat in which we'd come.

The day of the event, Fernando Lataro got word of the escape plan and, instead of canceling it thought it best to make a show of force by setting up a comprehensive security plan. He didn't want to add to the prisoners' dissatisfaction since our performance had been announced for over a week. In addition, he wanted the worst criminals to be present in order to better keep an eye on them. And he dreamed that the technique of making a historical inventory might produce some effect on his "clientele."

Little by little, the amphitheater began to fill up. The criminals were grumbling. We could hear some of the cursing:

"Let's get this piece of crap started!"

"Theater is for little girls!"

"Open that goddamn curtain right now!"

Hearing the insults and knowing we were on a powder keg, I began having hot flashes like a woman in menopause; at the same time, my mind froze. I couldn't think. There were thirty heavily armed guards in the side hallways. The dreamseller, the warden, three staff members, two social workers and a psychologist were sitting in the front row, on the left side. El Diablo and Shrapnel, along with the other crime leaders, were in the front row on the right side.

The criminals began raising the level of their threats:

"If I don't like it, I'm gonna kill one of 'em," El Diablo shouted angrily, drawing applause from the audience.

"If I don't like it, I'm gonna eat all the actors' livers," snarled Shrapnel.

They were enraged because this play had foiled their initial plan to riot against the guards that day. As our play dealt with the construction of ghosts of the mind, I thought that the mere staging by the actors wouldn't be sufficient to explain the concept. I felt a narrator was necessary and cast myself in that role. I would therefore have to go onstage before the actors, pick up the microphone and give succinct explanations of the progress of the piece. I began to realize that I had been caught in my own trap.

Seeing my hesitation behind the curtain, the Mayor shoved

me through, and I suddenly found myself onstage. I dropped the cordless microphone. They started booing and shouting nonstop. "Get going, dumbass."

Trying to regain my composure, I remembered the days when my students, shivering in fear, would remain deadly silent. So I raised my voice and began the greetings. But the only authority these criminals respected were revolvers and machine guns.

"I'd like to thank Warden Fernando Lataro for the invitation."

As soon as I mentioned the warden's name, they roared like predators facing an easy prey. They seemed to have a Plan B. They would confront the guards, and even if some of them were shot, they would overpower them and take control of their weapons. It would be a disaster. They had committed serious crimes and possessed the biological tools for survival on that wretched island, but their intellectual, emotional and cultural tools were crushed. They were frayed, frustrated human beings who felt like rats in a sewer.

Terrified, I tried praising the participants in order to reduce the tension.

"Esteemed spectators, it is an honor—" Hearing this, they shouted:

"Enough of this garbage!"

Others yelled, "Lets trash the place."

Desperate, I immediately proceeded to the objective. "I'd like to tell you about this story."

But no one was interested in hearing about or seeing any play.

"Stupid intellectual. Kiss ass!"

In anguish, my voice catching in my throat, I looked to the dreamseller to see if I could borrow some of his energy. But I saw nothing. My heart was racing so fast that you could see it moving under my polo shirt. I wanted to be anywhere else in the world but there. All my knowledge of violence and criminality turned to dust. The worst criminals in the country were prisoners behind bars made of steel, and I was behind bars of panic. We were all prisoners, and all of us wanted to flee.

CHAPTER 31

Shocking the Psychopaths and Murderers

WORRIED ABOUT A PRISON RIOT, FERNANDO LATARO TRIED to assert his authority as warden. He climbed onto the stage and asked for respect. Instead of heeding him, the inmates rose and started toward the stage. The whole place was charged. I didn't know whether to run away or stand my ground. The uproar had become unsustainable. Just as the guards were about to attack the criminals, a phantom applied a 10,000 volt shock to all present: It was Bartholomew.

He came onto the stage so quickly and screamed so loud that I almost had a heart attack. The warden was startled. The audience, taken by surprise, took a second to process the hurricane that had just been unleashed.

He wore a wig whose strands stood straight up and out to the sides like something from a horror film. It was Monica's wig. He was dressed in a navy blue blouse, a skirt and jacket and high heels. The clothes were from another era, lent by Jurema. He, or rather "she," was so ugly that not even the most perverted men in the prison could be turned on by the sight. Then the Mayor came on stage wearing a blond wig, emitting primitive sounds along with Honeymouth and thrashing about. They were performing scream therapy onstage.

Witnessing the performance of those two, I was all but beside myself. What were they up to? If anything, I was sure
they'd fuel the riot. They had no idea what they were getting
into. I had visions of the predators in the audience tearing them
limb from limb.

El Diablo and Shrapnel, seeing their comrades distracted by
the two crazies, snorted in rage. They looked at all the posted
guards and, just as they were about to give the order to start
the uprising, Bartholomew and the Mayor went right up to
them. They removed their wigs, threw them onto the floor in
anger, and crossed their fingers. I thought they were making
the sign of the cross because they felt they were going to die.

El Diablo and Shrapnel, when they saw them, were stunned.
They immediately took a step back, confused. The criminals
seemed to be waiting for a cue from them for how to react.

Just then, someone turned down the house lights. Seeing that
calm was being reestablished, instead of also quieting down and
going backstage, Bartholomew and the Mayor donned their wigs
again and began to imitate various animals, from bears to di-
nosaurs. And they were actually good at it. They looked like a
couple of crazy people having a psychotic break.

Fernando Lataro sat down again. He was as lost as the prisoners. Maybe the play's already started, he thought. But all of
that had been improvised. Some of the prisoners began laughing at our misfits. Suddenly, the "loonies" stopped. An absolute
silence fell over the theater. Creepy music, like something out
of a Hitchcock film, began to play.

Honeymouth walked slowly to center stage, staring at the
audience in silence, as if about to devour them with his eyes.
He then emitted a sound as though his heart was exploding.
And he collapsed onto the floor. He hit his forehead against
the platform and lay there, still. The psychopaths, murderers,

kidnappers, terrorists and rapists looked at one another and wondered what it meant.

Then the Mayor, who had sneaked backstage, appeared with a coffin on his shoulders, material he had requested without my knowledge from one of the staff members. His appearance was horrifying. He placed Bartholomew in the coffin. Then he raised his head and, eyes wide as if he were the main character in a horror movie, said in a haunting voice: "I am death." And, pointing to the audience, shouted, "I'm going to eat your brain, rip apart your thoughts." With a terrifying laugh, he said, "I am death, hahahaha! I destroy the powerful, crush psychopaths, hahahaha!"

At that instant, the stage lights dimmed even further, imparting more tension to the scene. The Mayor took a knife from inside his shirt, kneeled beside the coffin and stabbed Honeymouth, moving as if he were cutting open his brain. I was truly frightened. It looked so real . . . Moments later, after smearing himself with "blood," he yanked something from his friend. I was close to four yards away and almost fainted when I saw what it was.

"I've got his braaaaaain!" he screamed, as if holding up a trophy. It looked like an actual brain. And, as incredible as it seems, he began to eat it and smear himself with blood.

"I love killers' brain," said the Mayor, howling with delight and fear.

I was so stunned by what I was seeing. While he spoke, strange sounds came from behind the scenes, making the horror scene seem more realistic.

I stole a glance at the audience, now in rapt attention. An instant earlier we were on the verge of being lynched; now the prisoners seemed like helpless little boys. Some had their hands on their head, trying to protect their skull. For the first time, the criminals felt like victims of fear. But I was afraid that if anything disturbed the atmosphere of tension, it would be shattered and the rebellion would begin.

The Mayor presented himself as the psychopath to end all psychopaths. He invaded the prisoners' minds uninvited. El Diablo was dismayed; he couldn't take his eyes off the old coffin. Reflecting, he understood that one day he would face a phantom from which he could not defend himself: his own death. Like virtually every violent man, he avoided thinking about it with all his might. But now he was forced to think that everything he loved, everything he had fought for, everything he had aspired to would crumble in a tiny tomb. He would become nothing, simply nothing.

The dreamseller watched a small sample of the revolution of the anonymous take shape on stage. The Mayor rose beside the coffin and proclaimed:

"Silence! I am going to speak of the most conspiratorial theory in existence. A theory that would baffle Einstein, destroy this prison and make agent 007 shudder!"

A theory? What did he have up his sleeve? Many of the prisoners didn't even know what a theory was. At most they'd had a few years of schooling. But none had ever cracked a book or learned even the simplest arithmetic. How could they understand a theory?

Then the Mayor approached the silent audience, which was intently following every move, and bellowed, "The theory of the flatus!"

"Flatus?" said warden Fernando Lataro, extremely concerned.

"Flatus?" the dreamseller wondered aloud.

"Theory of what?" everyone asked. No one laughed; the atmosphere they had created was so tense that no one imagined what that theory could mean. Perhaps it dealt with a chemical weapon, or a new rocket fuel. But suddenly, to our relief, Bartholomew got out of the coffin, the stage lights went up, and circus music began to play!

The general sentiment shifted from terror to comedy. My mind did flip-flops. So did the prisoners'. Even those men, accustomed to the risk of death, of being mutilated and imprisoned, weren't prepared for such an abrupt change. For several seconds they didn't know whether to laugh or cry.

Even the dreamseller appeared confused. All he knew was that those two irrepressible characters stunned this crowd. I began to imagine that maybe Bartholomew and Barnabas knew those criminals better than any policeman or forensic psychiatrist. Maybe they represented a greater danger to society than the offenders on Demons Island.

When the lights went up, the pair was wearing clown noses and top hats. The audience applauded them, and then the Mayor spoke of his "complex" theory. Once again, I nearly fainted.

The Mayor turned his considerable backside to the audience and said:

"Distinguished public, whoever understands the theory of the flatus will never again look upon his buttocks the same way." And the Mayor let loose a thunderclap that shook the amphitheater. At that moment everyone understood what the theory of the flatus was.

The audience erupted in laughter. Everyone went from experiencing the height of tension to the height of release. One moment their brains were swallowed up in a coffin, the next they were farting like school kids. My head started to hurt. Clinging to my theories, I asked myself: What happened to the pedagogical atmosphere? What about teaching the historical inventory?

The dreamseller brought his hands up to his face. I didn't know if he was enjoying himself or if he wanted to run away.

But he seemed to be smiling. I didn't know whether the pair had created this Plan B with his consent or whether everything was improvised, as always. I didn't know anything. I was totally uninformed, the last to know what was happening.

The warden was apprehensive, thinking that this time the circus really was about to catch on fire. The guards in the corridors were of two minds, some were relaxing and smiling, others were fearing the worst and grasping their weapons. Suddenly, another character appeared on stage to perform with the two buffoons and explain that wackiest of all theories: Professor Jurema. I couldn't imagine that a brilliant intellectual like her would get mixed up in this craziness.

"My children, the air is democratic. It belongs to all and must be cared for by all," she told the offenders. "Defendants release flatuses, policemen release flatuses and so do intellectuals. It's one way we're all the same. No one is exempt: babies, children, adults, the elderly, celebrities, the anonymous, rich, poor—in short, everyone farts. The only ones who don't are dead," and she pointed to the coffin.

"Every human being releases ten thousand flatuses during his lifetime, increasing the greenhouse effect. We are all 'farters,'" said Honeymouth and the Mayor in unison.

"There are several varieties of flatuses," said Professor Jurema.

And the two rowdies began explaining the famous types.

"There's the psychopathic farter," said the Mayor. "The psychopath comes along all sweet and light, nice as can be, and when everyone least expects it, it erupts like a silent torpedo that sinks the victim."

Next, Honeymouth explained the "Judas flatus."

"It's the most treacherous of them all. You trust that flatus, believe it's your best friend and think it'll never betray you. You take a deep breath, pray for it to come out quietly and

not give you away. But suddenly, when you least expect it, the
Judas comes out like screeching tires. And you innocently say
something like 'I think it's going to rain today,' but everybody
knows it was you who broke the thunder."

I looked at the prisoners and saw them cracking up. It was
hard to believe that those men were the most violent members
of society. I thought to myself, "Every human being, whether a
criminal or a victim, is hungry and thirsty for laughter." Freud
was right when he said that the pleasure principle rules the
human mind.

Honeymouth continued effusively:

"There's the socialite flatus. Imagine three high-society
women friends meeting. Each of them wearing dark glasses bigger than their heads. One of them looses a subtle flatus, inaudible. And has the gall to say, 'I think there's something rotten
in here.'"

"Dear listeners, there's also the intellectual flatus," bellowed the Mayor, looking at me. "That's the most shameless of
all. The guy knows the flatus is at the doorway of—of making
its escape." And he looked at Professor Jurema, who approved
the pedagogical language.

"Yes, the gases are at the doorway, and he releases them
without a second thought. The intellectual subtly goes on talking like nothing happened."

The inmates were enjoying themselves like children. They
didn't even seem to be aware that they were in a maximum
security prison. At that moment, I sidled over to Jurema and
whispered, "What about teaching them Piaget? And Vigotski?
And Morin?"

"My boy, what are we to do? Even Marx would be lost with
these lunatics," she said. "Educating isn't the art of transmit-
ting ideas, it's the art of making them understandable. Those
criminals are fed up with advice and sermons. Bartholomew

and Barnabas captivated them." And, criticizing me, she added, "Get out of your head, and let yourself go!"

I had a revelation. I had never succeed in reaching my students, never used their own language. I felt that descending from my pedestal and entering their world was too high a price. While I was pondering these things, the Mayor, seeing the crowd delirious with his teachings, went into a trance. His politician's spirit reemerged.

"Citizens of this great institution, hear my platform for the next election. It is based on a simple truth: *No one is worthy of his ass, unless he acknowledges his flatuses!* If every voter who breaks wind votes for me, it'll be the biggest landslide in history!"

After the presentation the three bowed before the audience, along with those who had been working behind the scenes. Later I found out it was John Vitor, Dimas, Solomon and Edson who were controlling the lighting and sound. They were part of Plan B, and I became a mere spectator.

It goes without saying that they brought down the house. For the first time in its centuries of existence, Demons Island became Angels Island, at least for a few hours.

The criminals remained on their feet, applauding the troupe. I stood awkwardly to one side and applauded them as well. They had managed to do what no psychiatrist, psychologist, educator or sociologist had ever done in that institution. When one has a free mind, it's possible to think about other ways of educating.

CHAPTER 32

My Script, Finally

AFTER RAISING A HULLABALOO, MY FRIENDS RETURNED TO their place behind the scenes and I took to the stage. It was my turn to act as narrator of the script I had originally written. A hellish task. But I was more relaxed now. I vowed not to remain indifferent to their misery.

Before beginning my narration, I looked at those men who behaved like teenagers and saw them as little boys whose childhoods had been stolen. Yes, they were responsible for their acts, guilty of their crimes, but they had shattered backgrounds. How could we expect serenity from them if aggression was the pen with which they wrote the fundamental chapters of their story?

I went to center stage. I didn't need to raise my voice or exert any kind of pressure. They had simply quieted down, awaiting my words. I quickly explained that I would be the narrator of the story. The curtains closed, and Bartholomew and the others began their preparations. I asked the spectators to pay close attention to the movements of the characters and to try to understand how easy it is to cause traumas. And I asked a question to wake them up.

"If overprotective parents can traumatize their children, can you imagine what the absence of parents or the presence of violent or neglectful parents can mean to a child? We're not trying to justify our mistakes but to show how our ghosts emerge."

The curtains opened and the spectators smiled in excitement. Bartholomew, dressed as a woman, was reading a magazine. His name was Clotilde. He was wearing a wig even weirder than the first. The Mayor, whose name in the play was Romeo, was Clotilde's spouse. That was my bit of revenge in the script. The two would be ridiculed mercilessly. Married for ten years, they were irritable, ill-tempered and highly critical of each other. They represented Bartholomew's parents in the first years of his life, before his father died and his mother left him in an orphanage.

Romeo was a TV addict, constantly complaining about the government. Jurema, Clotilde's mother, was perverse, slovenly and insane. Clotilde was a professional at embroidery—and gossip. Dimas and Solomon played the couple's two children, ages two and five. The rest of the team worked backstage managing the sound.

I began to narrate the story.

"Imagine that in the living room of a modern family, a wonderful, beautiful woman is reading a fashion magazine." The audience whistled at Clotilde. Excited, she leafed through the magazine from back to front and from bottom to top. And, ad-libbing, proclaimed loudly, "Lovely! Lovely! Ah, this model looks just like me!"

"Imagine," I said, continuing, "that the magazine shows nothing but photos of very thin models, undernourished and sick by medical standards. The more Clotilde reads the magazine, the 'smarter' she becomes," I joked.

I asked them to continue freeing their imagination.

"In that same living room, a father is watching a cop show." I pointed to Romeo. "The kind of crummy show where everybody knows ahead of time what's going to happen. There's a good guy and a bad guy. The good guy needs to somehow catch or kill the bad guy, a dishonest type like some people you know. But no one knows how or why he became a criminal. Often the movies treat criminals like scum, human garbage that has to be removed. It's as if they don't have dreams, don't cry or love."

The audience applauded, and I was surprised at their reaction. The criminals were beginning to identify with the scenario. Perhaps it was the first time they'd had the opportunity to look inside themselves and draw conclusions. Romeo, forgetting the script, was rooting for the bad guy, shouting, "Give it to him good!"

The Mayor and Bartholomew, because of their compulsive speech syndrome, continued to throw in dialogue that wasn't in the script. Clotilde, or rather Bartholomew, couldn't help himself. He put aside the fashion magazine, got up from his armchair, and went to Romeo.

"Sweetheart, my great frustrated politician. Just look at that awful man beating his wife. As a great leader, how can you condone such violence?"

Actually, Bartholomew was playing dirty, trying to incite the Mayor. And he did. The Mayor forgot his character and, assuming the role of protector of women, declared:

"As one of the leaders of this great nation, I proclaim that anyone who strikes a woman, even with a flower, is unworthy of being a man."

"You're the best man in the world," Clotilde said, extending her hand, but then slapping him so hard it sent Romeo reeling.

"What's going on, Honeymouth?" the Mayor raged. He

raised his fists, ready for battle. But Clotilde, batting her eye-lashes, said:

"Sweetheart! Not even with a flower!"

The Mayor bit his lips, held his breath, and saw that Honey-mouth was using the theater to square accounts. Still a bit dizzy from the slap, he looked at the audience, then at his "wife," and tried to maintain the pose of a man:

"Clo, dearest, you nearly sent me down for the count!"

Suddenly, another character ad-libbed. Jurema, playing the granny role, moved behind Romeo while he was arguing with Clotilde and gave him a swift kick in the pants. He jumped to face Granny.

"Get your butt out of that chair and do some work, you bum!"

Clotilde showered her with praise. "You're the best mom in the world."

"Thank you, dear. Oh, the zipper in the back of your dress is open, let me fix it for you."

"Of course, 'Momma,'" said Bartholomew naïvely.

When Clotilde turned around, Jurema gave her an even swifter boot to the backside. Honeymouth dashed away, look-ing back.

"Are you crazy, woman?"

Professor Jurema had been waiting a long time for her chance to settle accounts.

"I'm just beginning, you scoundrel—I mean, hussy," Ju-rema said.

"Nice one, Granny," Romeo said.

You can imagine how the audience of criminals reacted when they saw the two brain-eating theorists of the flatus taking a beating from an old lady. El Diablo, a scowling, ill-humored man who only smiled sarcastically, had never had so much fun. He was like a child.

"Give it to him, Granny," El Diablo yelled. "You deserve it, you drunk!"

Drunk? How did he know Bartholomew had been an alcoholic? Just a lucky guess, I supposed.

I had never been as happy as this in the last few months, finally being able to settle my debts with those two. The dreamseller must have been thinking: What are these people doing? Where are the lessons I taught them?

Heads cooled down, and the characters returned to following the script, at least for a while. Clotilde's mother went back to her sewing. Romeo concentrated on his TV and Clotilde on her fashion magazine. I gave a sigh of relief and returned to the narration.

"Suddenly, when everything seemed calm with this dysfunctional family, a threatening character entered their living room and sent everything off balance. Who was it?" Everyone pondered the question. "A brain-eater," yelled an older murderer who had served thirty-five years.

"Worse than that, sir," I replied. "A mouse!"

At first they were disappointed. They didn't know that Bartholomew was deathly afraid of mice, or that I had to replace the plush battery-powered toy mouse with a small plush bunny so that he, in the role of Clotilde, wouldn't have a panic attack.

But I didn't make the replacement. And still worse, the mouse in my pocket was not battery-powered—it was the real thing. My desire for revenge rose to the surface. I remembered the many times he had called me Superego and said that intellectuals were naïve imbeciles. This then was the moment to settle a few accounts of my own.

CHAPTER 33

The Greatest Crisis in History

THE MEN WATCHING OUR SHOW WOULD SOON LEARN HOW small acts can have rippling effects. They would see that earthquakes are born of small shifts in tectonic plates, a mountain is formed by minute grains of sand, and an ocean by tiny drops of water. The same thing happens in the human brain.

When no one was looking, I let the real mouse loose.

Clotilde's, or rather Bartholomew's, reaction to the tiny animal was dramatic. He screamed so loud he almost gave the Mayor a coronary. He went into a trance for thirty seconds, not knowing whether he was inside a prison or an earthquake.

Jurema, seeing the mouse was real, gasped. She, too, was terrified of rats. I started fanning her with one hand while grasping the microphone in the other to continue the narration. The audience was startled at Clotilde's panic, realizing that things were getting out of control. She was standing on top of a chair, screaming like mad, "Kill it, Mayor! Kill it!"

Unfazed, I continued to narrate.

"Then, inside Romeo's house, the movies came to life—in widescreen and in color. That man hadn't so much as killed a fly in years. Nevertheless he took off his shoe and threw it at the mouse, but he missed. Enraged, he took off his other shoe, aimed at the monster and missed again. He grabbed Clotilde's sandal and threw it as hard as he could at the mouse, which scampered from one side to the other. And he missed.

"Of course he missed, gentlemen! That mouse had a better quality of life than Romeo, who would plop down in his easy chair, do nothing but complain, and never exercise, while the mouse was running around all day long," I said, continuing to narrate the play.

Clotilde, seeing that the Mayor had terrible aim and trying to encourage him to keep after her enemy, threw gasoline on the fire of his feelings of impotence and anxiety. "Are you a man or a mouse? Even a tiny animal gets the better of you!"

"Ten years ago Clotilde and Romeo got married and promised to love each other in sickness and in health, for richer or for poorer," I said to the audience. "But now something as small as a mouse was causing a war in their home." I recalled my own broken marriage and improvised. "We don't trip over tall mountains but over small stones."

Bartholomew forgot he was playing the role of Clotilde and the Mayor forgot he was playing Romeo. Both were mixing their fictitious personalities with real life. Angry at being called a mouse, the Mayor grabbed Clotilde's magazine—"Not the magazine, Romeo!" she yelled—and threw it at the animal, but he missed again.

Romeo began snorting with rage. And despite his enormous weight, he leaped into the air trying to land on the mouse, emitting horrible grunts like an ape-man.

Suddenly, the mouse leaped off the stage and headed toward the audience. And something incredible occurred. Some of those brutes actually climbed onto their chairs. They weren't afraid of facing the police or the army, but they shook like leaves when confronted with a tiny rodent. The mouse set into motion the monsters lurking in the cellars of their minds. After two minutes, a prisoner with the scowling look of a hit man caught the mouse by the tail and returned it to the stage.

Back onstage, the mouse was more cunning than ever, scurrying from side to side. "Come over here, Mickey, come to Daddy Disney," the Mayor said, wishing he could stick the rodent in the microwave as a former mother-in-law had done to him. But the tiny animal outmaneuvered the Mayor and emerged behind him, as if laughing at his aggressor. Then, suddenly, the mouse ran up the back of the Mayor's pants. That wasn't in the script.

The Mayor let out a scream every bit as blood-curdling as Clotilde's: "Eee! Not there, little guy!"

He began shaking his butt, trying to dislodge the intruder. But the mouse scaled the heights with incredible tenacity. Unable to put an end to the wretched creature by himself, he asked the help of none other than Jurema.

"Granny, give this psychopath a good kick."

That was all Jurema needed to hear. She would help out her friend and at the same time get the privilege of once more planting her foot on the street politician's rear. As she paused for thirty seconds to line up the target, the Mayor lost his patience.

"Do it, old woman! He's in the western hemisphere. Careful . . ." As he tried to give away the enemy's position, he shook as if being tickled.

With total concentration, Professor Jurema approached the penalty-shot line, closed her right eye and, at the last moment, backed away, unsure. "Lower that gigantic rump of yours a little."

The Mayor had never been so vulnerable and humiliated, but he obeyed. Jurema took aim again, and this time . . . pow!

The Mayor howled, "Owww! What's the matter with you, old woman?"

"Did I get it?" Jurema asked anxiously.

"Nooooo! You couldn't hit the broad side of a barn, Granny."

Young John Vitor was laughing so hard behind the scenes it hurt. He experienced what crack, cocaine and hallucinogens had never given him.

Seeing Romeo rubbing himself and quivering from the misplaced kick, a prisoner inquired, "But where'd the mouse go?"

Romeo couldn't talk. The animal had invaded his modesty.

"Did he cross the street?" Clotilde ventured to ask her "husband."

The Mayor, almost in tears, confirmed, "Yes! He went to— to the other side," he said impatiently.

I was gasping for breath from laughing so hard. Then the "great politician" implored the elderly Jurema: "Try another kick, Granny. But carefully. Take good aim and let the little devil have it."

Professor Jurema was more than happy to oblige. But in order to avoid another out-of-bounds kick, the Mayor tried to describe the invader's location with pinpoint accuracy.

"He's on top of Sugar Loaf, the right side, two inches from the tunnel."

No way to go wrong, he thought. But Jurema wasn't much for navigation. Once again she requested, "Lower that fat posterior of yours more," causing him to shiver.

Reluctantly, the Mayor lowered his hindquarters. Because the mouse was in constant motion, he started contorting his body like someone on a dance floor. Jurema wanted to do the right thing but didn't know whether to laugh or cry. She looked downward, saw a bulge in the area of the Mayor's right pocket, concentrated, got ready and launched a vigorous kick.

"Owww! You're trying to kill me, Granny," he complained, not knowing whether the target had been hit.

And he reluctantly moved his hand to the spot where Jurema's kick had landed. He stuck his hand into the pocket and protested solemnly:

"You attacked my cheese sandwich, Granny." He took out the sandwich, whose cheese had been smashed from the impact. Instead of continuing the war, he paused, raised the sandwich to his nose, sniffed it as if he were a rat, found the smell reasonably acceptable, and stuck it in his mouth.

The Mayor suspected the mouse had climbed Sugar Loaf because it wanted his sandwich, but he wasn't about to hand it over. As he ate, he philosophized, "Every man needs a cease-fire from his battles. I'm not made of iron. Permit me a pause to eat," he said, chewing with pleasure.

Noticing the mouse moving at will about the Mayor's buttocks, Jurema said, "Now I see why you're so unhappy."

"Quiet, Granny," he said, trying to feel where the mouse was going. The animal had entered his undershorts; the unforeseeable, the unimaginable had unfortunately happened. The Mayor screamed, "Nooooo!"

No one understood anything. Prisoners and guards alike asked in unison, "Where is it?"

Clotilde, trying to pique the Mayor, said, "It's going into the tunnel, Romeo."

The Mayor, crying, turned to her and asked in distress, "How do you know?"

"Female intuition!"

The Mayor jumped around, howling.

"Not there, you little beast! Not there, you killer! You devil!"

The audience was nearly faint from laughing. El Diablo, remembering the theory of the flatus, yelled a recommendation: "Let out a psychopathic flatus."

In a state of shock, the Mayor said, "I'm trying, man. But the car's flooded, the tailpipe's clogged. Your suggestion has failed."

The dreamseller was reveling in watching his loony followers. The comical relationship between Bartholomew and Barnabas was a sociological and philosophical case not found in any textbook.

CHAPTER 34

The Greatest Squeeze in History

AFTER BEING INSULTED BY CLOTILDE, THE MAYOR FOUND HIM-self in a dilemma. He didn't know whether to punch her out or flop onto his butt, thus finally crushing his tiny tormentor. He opted for the latter. It was an act of courage, of valor.

He leaped almost a foot and a half in the air—not much, but enough to nearly kill himself. That was when the Mayor experienced the greatest squeeze in history. The suffering was too much for any man to bear.

When his buttocks collided violently with the floor, he thought he would never get up again. He was weak and demoralized.

He needed Clotilde, Granny and me to help him to his feet. Both sides of the Mayor's rear end ached badly. But at least he felt he had exterminated his enemy, as it had ceased moving about. When he examined his posterior, however, his expression changed; he turned white, purple, then red. Something terrible had happened.

The mouse was still alive. And it set off rapidly on an extremely dangerous course. So dangerous that this time the Mayor did a somersault without falling.

"Not there, you little creep!" he shouted. "Oh, God, don't go there, you skunk!"

No one understood a thing. "Clotilde bit her lip and asked, 'Did he, um, take the subway?'"

Almost sobbing, the Mayor confirmed: "Yes!"

"Subway?" we asked, confused. Seconds later, seeing his distress, we decoded his language. The mouse had snuck through space between his legs and onto the other side, the forbidden area.

Biting his lips, the Mayor said, in an almost inaudible voice, "Get away from there, you shameless little bastard! Oh, oh! He's playing basketball."

My friends, the theater rolled with breathless laughter. Psychopaths who had never let their guards down laughed like school children.

But that wasn't the worst of it for the Mayor. "He's climbing my Statue of Liberty!" he yelled.

Words fail me to describe the two combatants. The Mayor was like mythological fire-breathing dragon and the mouse was mocking him. That was when I realized my trap had exceeded my expectations. I pitied him. I felt he had paid for all the sins he had committed against me and the rest of the group—with interest. I wanted to help him. But how? Unfortunately, he had to suffer martyrdom alone.

As the dreamseller told us, "There are times when we are alone, profoundly alone, in the midst of the multitude. At such times, neither expect nor demand anything from anyone. You must stand by yourself." The Mayor was profoundly alone, in the middle of more than a hundred people who wanted to help him but couldn't. The prisoners wanted to rescue him; the guards, dying of laughter, wanted to set aside their weapons and offer moral support. Smiles and comedy had united criminals and policemen.

There was another option—to take off his pants and search

for the mouse in the cellars of his intimacy in that lair of men. But an experienced politician would never reveal his "sins" in front of others; it would be the end of his career, he thought. So he stuck with the alternative.

He would solve the problem on his own. A good swift blow at the correct angle and his enemy was a goner. But he was panting, and the immediate environs of the target were delicate. He might never have children if he missed. He held his breath, raised his right hand, took aim—and then Granny spoke, destroying his concentration.

"Leave it to me, my son. This time I'll get him." And she approached, ready to launch a kick.

"No! Not here, Granny. If you miss, a lifetime of Viagra wouldn't cure me. This is a job for a professional," he said with conviction.

He covered his eyes with his left hand, raised his right hand into the air like a general commanding his last battle, and prepared to strike. Everyone watching, including me, instinctively protected our own groins. Pitilessly, the Mayor pummeled himself.

The blow was so powerful that we all groaned in unison, as if experiencing the same pain.

"Aaaaaaaaiiiiiiiii!"

The Mayor was literally paralyzed. We didn't know if he was dead or alive. We held a minute of silence out of respect for his bravery. After that dramatic period when you could hear a pin drop, we all asked:

"Did you kill it? Did you kill it?" The Mayor didn't answer. The pain was so great that he couldn't form an utterance.

"Did you kill it?" we insisted. After two long minutes, he spoke, haltingly and slurring his words.

"I crushed my *bolitas*. I'm sterile. Oh, oh!" Unfortunately, the fleet-footed mouse had managed to escape the final battle and win the war. Great politicians, especially the shrewdest ones, are destroyed by tiny pests. Politicians create the rats and the rats corrupt the politicians.

He would have to leave the stage and drop his pants, totally humiliated, beaten, shattered. As if the humiliation and pain weren't enough, Clotilde added to his wounded pride: "No problem, Romeo, you haven't been up to it for a long time now."

Enraged and unrecognizable, the Mayor moved toward Bartholomew. But as he took the first steps, the mouse abandoned the Statue of Liberty, took the subway, went down Sugar Loaf, and slowly descended the Mayor's leg. When it reached the floor, it was staggering, dizzy, stunned.

"The Mayor's slap had no effect, gentlemen, but his primitive scream was the winning blow. He inflicted a mortal wound on the poor animal," I said.

They all watched the sluggish motions of the mouse. They liked him, as did I. The jaunty little animal moved uncertainly, listing first to the right, then to the left. Stopping then advancing with slow steps. Two yards further on, it raised its right paw, placed it on the left side of its chest, looked at the audience like some brilliant actor, and succumbed. It lay on the floor, its paws upward. It had suffered a heart attack.

"The poor thing kicked the bucket," said Honeymouth, who in all the confusion had overcome his phobia about rats and tamed that ghost. "For the first time, I fell in love with a rat."

"The mouse died of stress," I explained to the crowd. "Be careful that you do not suffer the same fate."

It was then that the greatest criminals in the country discovered they were dying like the mouse, through stress and anxiety. Because they were not productive, constructive, creative or contemplative in their cells, they lived tense, embittered, stressful lives. Ten criminals had already suffered heart attacks on Demons Island that year, twenty had cancer, and the majority had other stress-induced conditions. Which confirmed the idea that, imprisoned or free, human beings inhabited a huge madhouse.

The dreamseller always warned us that out in the global mental hospital in which we all lived, few of us free men and women had ever committed crimes against others. But we never failed to commit crimes against ourselves. I was one of those criminals, more machine than man, working and studying, irritable and impatient. I was incarcerated in my own private prison, although the professors and students of my university believed I was free. It was all an illusion.

Clotilde, seeing her enemy motionless on the carpet, rose from her chair, looked at Romeo and said affectionately, "Dear Romeo, you're my hero."

Romeo, feeling like the good guy in the film, the most fearless of men, inflated his chest, raised his voice, and declared his love.

"Clotilde! For you I flattened my basketballs, sacrificed the Statue of Liberty and leveled the Sugar Loaf. Thanks to that miserable rat, I'm not the same man anymore."

And they shared a Hollywood kiss.

Both had placed a small apple between their teeth and pretended they were kissing. Provocatively, Clotilde jumped into the arms of Romeo, who fell and choked on the apple. He had to be clapped on the back to expel the fruit. The Mayor, though lightheaded, still had the spirit to say, "Clotilde, the rat killed me . . . and you buried me."

At the end of the play, they both went to the center of the stage along with Professor Jurema. And even before they took a bow, these criminals—feared by judges, prosecutors, and the FBI—rose to their feet and gave them a standing ovation.

"The moral of the story," I said, after the applause had died down, "is that Clotilde and Romeo live happily ever after until—" And the prisoners responded as one:

"Another mouse comes into the picture!"

CHAPTER 35

Cellars of the Mind

THE INMATES BEGAN TO UNDERSTAND THAT RATS ON THE outside may die, but those scurrying around inside the secret spaces of our minds reproduce over time. They can't be exterminated, only tamed. They began to understand that it did no good to destroy external foes when their real enemies were inside them. It was a fantastic lesson.

I whistled, the mouse awoke, came running toward me, and I scooped it up. Everyone was astonished. That's when everyone discovered I had hired a trained mouse. He was a great actor. Everyone applauded for the tiny animal. Including Honeymouth. The Mayor put his hands on his head and whispered, "Vote for me, you little bugger, and I'll forgive you for all this humiliation."

I turned to the audience and asked, "Have we forgotten any characters?"

Everyone looked toward the stage and saw two actors with their hair standing up. Yes, we had forgotten to clap for the "children."

At that moment, I asked the dreamseller to come up to the stage. He protested, but I insisted. It wasn't planned, but those men with shattered histories needed to hear him as I had.

He agreed. The criminals had a hard time believing that a

homeless beggar could be the leader of the group. The dream-seller ran his eyes over the audience, waiting to start in.

He didn't want to give a lot of explanations, so he once again chose the Socratic method.

"Can a small mouse be transformed into a monster? Can a small stone become a wall in our minds?" Then he asked them to search their histories and try to find small issues that had been transformed into great conflicts.

Twenty people raised their hands. "Shotgun," a stone-cold killer, stood up in the second row and began telling his story.

"Every time I urinate I give a little jump. The reason is that when I was a child, a Doberman bit me at the exact moment I was urinating. From then on, I couldn't go without jumping," he said, laughing.

I was taken with his boldness. I would never have guessed that these men harbored such subtle thoughts. The dreamseller continued.

"In the play, the children registered both the image of the mouse and the image of their parents' reaction. The im-ages merged in their unconscious, becoming one and the same thing. That process increased the destructive power and the threat of that small animal. The mouse became a real monster, a ghost, a trauma."

The stage lights dimmed, soft music began to play. And, demonstrating that life is cyclical, that there is time to smile and time to cry, he urged those present to be wanderers in search of themselves.

"Travel within your story. Remember the tears that were dammed up inside you but were never seen on your cheeks. How many losses and acts of violence suffocated you when you were boys? How many hugs were denied? How many de-privations did you suffer? Many of you had your childhoods crushed when you should have been playing like children."

The inmates journeyed to the past and were moved. El Diablo and Shrapnel were puzzled by the dreamseller's generosity. The latter in particular had accused and threatened the dreamseller. He had offered them a shoulder to cry on as he helped them dissect their pasts. Terrorists, murderers, drug dealers and thieves were left defenseless by all they had just seen and heard. It was now the moment for them to go below the surface and penetrate into the deeper layers of their minds.

"Think now, without fear, of the childhood you destroyed, the lives you shattered and the dreams you crushed. So many traumas! So much anguish you caused! So many irreparable losses you brought about! There are many things that explain your traumas and your suffering, but none of them justifies inflicting suffering on others," he said without fear of retribution.

"Violence explains violence," he said, "but no act of violence justifies violence."

Hearing him, I remembered the professionals who had died there in the last two years during riots. I also remembered that Fernando Lataro and other prison workers were marked for death. And I recalled how my students had been run off the island without succeeding in interviewing even the least dangerous prisoners. Now, here—face to face—the dreamseller was speaking to the leaders of the penitentiary about their most grievous mistakes, and they were listening without resentment in their hearts.

Then he addressed one of the best known texts in history, and one of the least understood. He spoke of the ghosts of betrayal, denial, and guilt.

"At the Last Supper, Christ was deeply saddened by his disciples. The most intelligent of them, Judas Iscariot, would betray him, and the strongest, Peter, would deny him. Which of these crimes is the greater?"

I had never thought of those two famous historical mistakes from the standpoint of sociology. Where was the dreamseller heading?

"Both were extremely grave betrayals. Judas betrayed him once, Peter denied him three times, vehemently. But the lessons Jesus taught us are powerful. He did not punish his betrayer. Just the opposite; he broke bread with him, showing in a veiled manner that he had no fear of being betrayed. In this way, he revealed to us that our errors must be rectified with the nourishment of education, symbolized by the bread. Nor did Christ condemn his denier, Peter. He shouted silently to him: I understand! He gave Judas and Peter the tools to tame the ghost of guilt and thus gave them the chance to start over. Only Peter made use of them. Judas was torn apart by his demons. Will you be?"

The dreamseller pressed them further.

"Are you guilty? Yes. Whoever fears recognizing his mistakes will take the ghosts that haunted his mind to his grave. Face your ghosts and you will have some chance of taming them.

"More than eighty percent of you—the majority under forty years of age—will grow old in prison and rot in this place. Many others will leave here hunched over with age. And about half of you will only leave the island in a body bag, sentenced to life in prison. I know that every day, when you think about your hair turning white, your muscles losing their strength, and your eyesight failing in this cold and gloomy prison, you go into a state of panic. Can you tame those ghosts and survive with dignity? That's the biggest question. A crime takes place in minutes, but its consequences can last a lifetime."

And, in an inspired moment, the dreamseller breathed deeply and continued.

"I also committed crimes, but not those found in the criminal statutes. I have debts to my conscience that I know I'll never be able to repay." Hearing the leader of the group, without coat and tie, dressed worse than they, confess to unpayable debts reached them in the depths of their souls. None had ever opened the pages of his story in that maximum security prison.

At that exact moment, El Diablo whispered something to Shrapnel and other leaders of a faction who were sitting beside him. The dreamseller stripped himself bare before those fragmented men.

"My crime? Today I'm homeless. But, like some of you, I loved money more than people. Dollars were my god. I was a child in the theater of time and never marveled at the phenomenon of existence. I was dead even as I lived. I had never made an inventory of my life.

"I never spoke to my children about my tears so they could learn to cry theirs, never spoke to them about my fears so they could face theirs, never spoke about my mistakes so they could learn to overcome theirs. By the time I realized I should do things differently—when I dreamed of hugging them, asking their forgiveness, of leaving my mental prison—time betrayed me. My two children died in an airplane crash in the rainforest."

The dreamseller caught his breath.

"Who can settle that debt for me? What law? What prison? What psychiatrist? What friends? What amount of money? I'm to blame and can't hide from it. Every day, I have to tame the ghosts that point out my insanity and prevent me from starting over. I'm not looking for understanding, sympathy or reprieve. I'm looking to find myself. I'm a wanderer. There is no oasis in my desert. I must create one in order to survive and remake myself."

Then he asked the inmates to reflect on two important moments—one in which they had been injured and another in which they had injured someone else—and to make bridges between them. He wanted them to search for the only freedom that cannot be imprisoned behind iron bars. The only one that, if lost, can transform existence into the most unbearable of dungeons.

CHAPTER 36

Ripping the Soul

ITTLE BY LITTLE, MORE THAN TWO THIRDS OF THE IN-
mates, men who had never had the courage to talk about
themselves or listen to the misfortunes of another, crumbled.
They knew what crimes they had committed and the laws
under which they had been punished. They knew the weapons
they had used. But not the losses they had suffered or the tears
they had shed.

Some confessed that when they took drugs for the first time
they swore they'd never use them again. But then came the second time. And the third. Others talked about the first time they
stole, how they vowed never to do it again. But then came the
second time. And the third. Still others confessed they'd had
insomnia for many nights the first they shot a person. But other
crimes soon followed, finally annihilating their conscience.

Some of the criminals in the theater were weeping as they
spoke of the wounds they had suffered or caused. They were
irreparable errors. Lives had been lost, children had been injured. In making a brief inventory of their stories, they lac-
erated their mental core and seemed to return to the womb
in search of protection. After twenty minutes, we left quietly,
without saying good-bye. They were still talking about their
monsters, unrestrained, fearless.

As we left, Fernando Lataro and some of the staff, social workers and psychologists were beaming. They couldn't thank us enough. The warden felt that everything he had seen and heard had helped not only the inmates, but him, too. Seeing his enthusiasm, the dreamseller threw cold water on him.

"Everything that happened today is just a drop in the sea of their needs. No one changes anyone. There is no magic to overcoming conflicts. Memory isn't wiped out. No one leaves the hell of his mistakes unless he finds the door to paradise: compassion and education.

"Maybe there could be classes in theater," the dreamseller, added. "Maybe Demons Island could have elementary education. Trades and courses in technology could be taught via satellite. Maybe there could be music and art classes. Maybe there could be computers with access to limited areas of the Internet for their distraction and to expand their minds instead of allowing them to think about foolishness and feeding their ghosts and permitting their unchecked desire to flee."

Fernando Lataro gave a rather ironic smile. "Dreamseller, we have no money. The prisoners are treated like human beings in theory, but in practice they're treated worse than society's garbage."

One of the staff members added, "Even the federal government has abandoned the island."

"No business would ever invest a cent in this human sewer," a psychologist said.

The reality was raw, cruel and painful. Everything would go back to what it was in that factory of criminality. We had ideals but no money. The only one with resources was Professor Jurema, who had assets but no income. The dreamseller took Dimas aside, looked him in the eye, placed both hands on his shoulders, and almost inaudibly, gave him an order that made us laugh like crazy.

"Dimas, see to the resources."

"Dimas, go rob the Central Bank," Bartholomew said, laughing.

"You're looking at the next guest of Demons Island," said the Mayor, then apologized to the dreamseller. But since he too was laughing, we thought he was satirizing the financial crisis.

If even the two loonies thought the dreamseller's order was a joke, imagine how the rest of us felt.

"No need to protect your pockets, folks," Edson said. "We're all poor." And he broke into laughter along with the rest of us, including Fernando Lataro.

"Master, Dimas is going to need Edson to pull off the miracle of the loaves and fishes," I added.

"Look at that. The intellectual has a sense of humor, after all. Congratulations!" Honeymouth said.

I had seen Dimas hoodwink a lawyer who had just gotten him out of jail after a petty theft because he didn't have a penny on him. Dimas and the dreamseller were in the same boat. But, to our amazement, Dimas innocently thought the dreamseller was speaking in earnest. Like the chancellor to a king, he asked jubilantly, stuttering as always, "Are you sp-sp-speaking seriously?"

"Yes, Dimas, perform the miracle without Edson," said the Master, smiling.

Dimas hummed and danced like a child. He hugged the Master, kissed him on the cheek, and grabbed his right hand, raised it overhead and danced with him.

The team almost burst a seam laughing. Philosophy had taken on a sense of humor never seen before. The warden and his subordinates didn't take the dreamseller's proposal seriously. After all, dreams and delirium are close relatives.

Two days later, we were walking down a busy street when suddenly the wind blew a page from a big-city newspaper into my face. As I was about to put it in the trash, a headline caught my eye: "Mellon Lincoln Jr. may be alive."

"It can't be," I thought. Mellon Lincoln Jr. had been expected to be the presidential candidate of one of the major political parties. But since death doesn't discriminate, it had come knocking at his door. When he died, I was living in Russia, separated from my wife and far from John Marcus.

I was out of the country for a year, doing my postdoctoral, and knew no details about that powerful leader's misfortunes. He was such a celebrity that I thought the article about Mellon Lincoln was just another sensationalist effort to increase circulation.

The dreamseller was also an unrelenting critic of the man. I remembered that the first time we went to Jurema's house he made very unflattering comments about him.

I quickly handed the paper to the dreamseller. His expression changed. "They want to bring back the dead," he said, shaking his head. "Society stupidly looks to its past heroes. It doesn't invest in the revolution of the anonymous."

CHAPTER 37

Banning and Wounding the Man in Rags

I T WAS THREE IN THE AFTERNOON ON A WEDNESDAY. THE dreamseller had given us some pears and apples he had received from an admirer. We hadn't had lunch and were famished. While we ate the fruit, I glanced sideways and saw the dreamseller eating a near-rotten pear. It was always that way: he gave us the best he had.

As our hunger wasn't satisfied, we stopped in front of a fancy French restaurant to ask for any leftover food. I told the group, "This isn't our kind of place."

"O, ye of little faith. Let's give it a try, brother!" Edson replied.

Elegantly dressed people leaving the restaurant eyed us and gasped. The Mayor made a gesture indicating he was feeling faint from lack of food. And he was. If he went more than two hours without chewing on something, he would get dizzy. Fruit barely moved the needle.

The owner saw the rabble in front of his fine establishment and quickly directed us to the area in back, where he would serve us. We were pleased at the prospect of eating dishes from that famous restaurant. On a professor's salary I would have had to work for a week to spend an hour there.

Frowning, the owner appeared with two security guards

and placed the food on disposable plates. After serving the dreamseller, he became aggressive, animal-like. He spat into his food and ordered, "Don't ever come back unless you want to go to jail."

As the owner turned to enter the restaurant, the dreamseller pushed aside the part where the owner had spat, and told him, "Thank you, Jean-Pierre, for your kindness. The *rôti* sauce is delicious."

The restaurant owner's eyes widened, he started to pant, his voice caught in his throat. Like the director of Mellon Lincoln Hospital, he reacted as if he'd seen a ghost. Once again we didn't understand the significance of these events.

The next day, after a two-hour walk from the bridge where we slept, we came to an enormous building, forty stories high with a mirrored exterior, surrounded by a magnificent garden of tulips, multicolored daisies, and chrysanthemums: the headquarters of the powerful Megasoft group.

The dreamseller crouched down to observe a tulip. He asked us to breathe in its perfume and contemplate its anatomy. Immediately, a guard came to shoo us away. We were on the sidewalk, a public place. However, the guard didn't back down.

We were hungry again but decided to give French cuisine a wide berth. Monica had some change that at most would pay for her lunch. Professor Jurema had forgotten her purse. Crusher was broke. John Vitor barely had enough for a grilled ham and cheese sandwich.

We would sing, the dreamseller would recite poetry and give speeches and people would spontaneously donate whatever they felt like giving. That was our major source of income. We didn't ask for alms, we weren't professional beggars. We were poor by choice. The dreamseller never had us ask for money, and only rarely did we ask for leftovers at restaurants. But his disciples were always breaking the rules.

Four well dressed men who appeared to be Megasoft executives passed us on their way to the main building. The Mayor, overcome with hunger, asked them for change. "Most esteemed men of commerce. Could you finance lunch for this future leader of the nation and his advisers?" he said, pointing to us.

"Get out of here, you bum," the most senior among them said.

The Mayor scaled down his request: "A few coins will do."

To get rid of him, the guy took two dimes out of his pocket, and instead of placing them in the Mayor's hand, arrogantly threw them onto the sidewalk.

"These beggars ought to be sent off to Iraq," he said as he walked away.

The dreamseller was overcome with indignation.

"I remember a young man who in a speech as head of a corporation said: 'A great executive must value the human being more than the product he manufactures.'" He paused, then added, "But time belies speeches."

The businessman stopped and took a step back, startled. His eyes widened and, astonished, he asked, "Who are you?"

"That doesn't matter. What matters is, who are you?"

The dreamseller ran his eyes over the magnificent building that housed the Megasoft group and nodded. Then he spotted a lovely tree a few yards away and improvised a poem that disturbed the "gods" in ties and touched my very soul:

More generous than men are the trees that extend their
*   arms to travelers,*
inviting them to rest in their shade.
Once they have rested, they turn their back and leave
*   without a goodbye.*
The trees neither complain nor ask for anything in return.

More giving than men are the trees, which house the birds
    that flock to their branches.
The next day, they depart without paying rent or offering
    thanks.
But the trees say farewell by applauding with the
    movement of their leaves at the touch of a breeze.
They give of themselves with pleasure.

The four executives stood rooted to the spot, unable to explain the sensation overtaking them. Their legs wouldn't move. They were silent, speechless. Without another word, the dreamseller bent down, picked up the two coins and returned them. "What's not given freely offers no relief."

One of the executives, a man with white hair, apologized, but the man who had thrown the coins couldn't react. He had to be led away by the arm.

And as they left, the dreamseller applied the coup de grâce. They wouldn't sleep for nights on end.

"When I fall dead on the streets and you lie in a grand mausoleum, it will be the same thing. We will all be equal in our smallness."

Afterward, instead of leaving the scene, the dreamseller made an unusual decision. He decided to enter the headquarters of the Megasoft corporation.

Just then, we were blocked by three security guards. We were barred without even being asked our identity, based solely on our appearance. Appearances open doors, but it's intelligence that defines the journey. Doors never opened spontaneously for us.

"Leave immediately or we'll call the cops," they said, pushing us away.

"This is the legacy of Mellon Lincoln Jr., the billionaire who created the culture that expels people," the dreamseller said, finally losing his patience. "A sick legacy, exclusionary and elitist. Go ahead and call the 'gods' of this institution. I want to speak to them."

Other Megasoft executives passing by took offense at the criticisms of their great founder. The dreamseller had shaken the dogma of their religion, the temple of finance. He had attacked an untouchable guru. One of them looked at us from head to toe and said, "What asylum did this band of psychos break out of?"

We didn't exactly blend in. The dreamseller was wearing patched black pants and a white shirt with an ink stain in the pocket. I was wearing a white polo shirt and blue jeans. Solomon had on green denim pants and a yellow T-shirt. Bartholomew and Barnabas looked like something from another planet. Except for the two women, Jurema and Monica, we stood out for all the wrong reasons."

"No one is worthy of being a leader of business if he's not first a leader in the theater of the mind. And no one will be a leader in the theater of the mind unless he learns to see beyond the outward trappings," the dreamseller said, unnerving the young executives.

"Who's this beggar who memorizes sayings from philosophers and recites them to impress us?" one of them asked.

No one knew. Then they ordered their security officers, "What are you waiting for? Toss these buffoons out of here."

"We come in peace," Honeymouth said. And he told the Mayor, "Send in the heavy artillery."

"You mean," Barnabas asked, "the killer flatus?"

And the Mayor let loose a deadly burst of gas.

The executives beat a hasty retreat. On their way up in the elevator they contacted security, claiming that a band of terrorists were in the lobby. This caused a stampede. Immediately, two dozen guards carrying a wide variety of weapons, including AK-47 assault rifles, stormed the building, holding us at gunpoint.

They quickly overpowered us. They violently threw the dreamseller, Bartholomew, Barnabas and Solomon to the floor. The rest of us froze where we were. They searched us, humiliated us, insulted us. After determining that the dreamseller was the leader of the group, a guard put his foot on his neck and mercilessly twisted his right arm. He was being suffocated.

He shouted demands for the dreamseller to identify himself, but our leader remained silent. They fruitlessly looked for identification. They actually believed he was a terrorist disguised as a ragamuffin.

They lifted him up from the floor. Because one of the guards had pressed his foot against the dreamseller's trachea, he coughed violently. One of the guards slapped him in the face to make him stop faking. That violence was unimaginable in a democratic society. Being branded a terrorist is worse than being a leper. They are killed first and identified later.

Recovering from his coughing fit, the dreamseller still had enough breath to strike the only way he could.

"Who pays your salary?" he asked.

"None of your business," said the head of security.

"Does Mellon Lincoln or his estate pay your salary for you to be polite or aggressive, to prevent or to punish?"

The security chief punched him in the stomach and then in the face. He dropped him to the floor and stuck his pistol in the dreamseller's mouth, injuring his lips and teeth. The docile dreamseller was bleeding. The women cried and called the relentless guards murderers.

Bartholomew tried to come to his aid but took a blow to the chest and was knocked flat.

"What do you know about Mellon Lincoln?" the chief of security shouted. Taking the gun from the dreamseller's mouth, he bellowed, "Who are you? Identify yourself!"

The dreamseller was uncooperative.

"The ruthless billionaire who only cared about making money infused his cold inhumanity into this firm. Is this brutality his policy?"

The security chief pistol whipped the dreamseller on the head, tearing a gash into his scalp. Blood began to run down the dreamseller's face, creating a horrifying image even worse than the week before, when he had been attacked near Luiz Lemos's house.

This man of peace was attacked ruthlessly. We were all staring down the barrels of guns, unable to help him. Indifferent to the dreamseller's wounds, the security chief, who undoubtedly had killed people in the course of his profession, pressed the gun against his neck and yelled, "You're Al-Qaeda, aren't you?"

The revolver had become a god that could decide life or death. In the past, Mellon Lincoln Jr. had suffered a terrorist attack, after which his group, already concerned about his safety, had become paranoid. All of the company executives had bodyguards.

Watching this scene play out made me think about the dreamseller's criticism of the social system. And humans belonged to the system. Without a "reputation," it wasn't possible to exist or survive in our society. Rousseau would have to modify his motto: man is born with his instincts, and society educates or imprisons him. If the dreamseller continued to insist on his unusual way of life, it would soon cost him his life. The sociological experiment that had attracted me would end in disaster. Human beings had become their own predators.

Despite his dizziness and his bleeding, the dreamseller managed to turn his head slightly and face his aggressor. "Humberto," he said, "without mankind and its welfare as its focus, Megasoft practices its own form of terrorism."

The security chief's hands went limp, barely able to hold the revolver.

"How do you know my name?"

I looked to see if the security chief wore a name tag, but he didn't. Humberto repeated the question but was drowned out by the sound of ten police vehicles. Thirty heavily armed policemen swarmed in, handcuffed the supposed terrorists, and took us away like criminals to be interrogated. No one cared about the dreamseller's wounds. Hundreds of people approached. Some of them knew the dreamseller. They looked at his forehead and cheek covered with blood and became outraged at the cruelty with which he had been treated. They began to protest, shouting. But no one listened to them. Several journalists photographed him handcuffed. As we were about to get into the paddy wagon, the chief of police showed up. He approached the group and went straight to the dreamseller.

"You again?" he said, grimacing as he saw the dreamseller's bleeding wounds. "I've been following your work. And I fear for your life. Get out of this city and keep quiet, for your own good."

"If I keep quiet, the system wins," the dreamseller said.

"You can't change things. You have to see that," the police chief said.

"I'm a sower of ideas. My responsibility is to bury those seeds."

And the police chief just shook his head, knowing there was no silencing him. He told the guards to let us go, saying that he knew us, had already questioned us and that we represented no danger.

"You see, people? We beat the police. No one can shut us up," the Mayor said enthusiastically.

"Quiet, Mayor," said Monica.

The police chief wanted to take us to an emergency room to treat the dreamseller's cuts and bruises, but he refused. Several people wanted to hug him but kept their distance because of his hands, which were bloodied from wiping his face. Despite that, more than a few said, "Thank you very much for your words. You've changed our thinking." And they immediately dispersed.

Professor Jurema came forward, gave him her handkerchief, and told him, "My son, I'm proud of you. It's an honor to follow you."

"But it's not safe," the dreamseller said. "All of you must leave."

We knew he was right. But we looked at each other and knew we couldn't abandon him. An indescribable force united us. Staying near him was as dangerous as a desert and as refreshing as a mountain spring.

CHAPTER 38

The Pain of Slander

THE NEXT DAY'S HEADLINES WERE SENSATIONAL. SOME defended the dreamseller, saying that a prejudiced society doesn't tolerate people who are different. They stated that a gentle and intellectual man had been wronged. Another denounced him as a dangerous man. I had a fit of rage when I saw that headline. Honeymouth crumpled up the newspaper, and the Mayor started to chew it. But the dreamseller was calm and told them softly, "We are what we are. The dimension of our conviction about who we are determines the level of our protection or our vulnerability."

But nothing infuriated me as much as when I saw his picture with blood running down his face on the front page of the city's leading newspaper, which the Megasoft group owned. The headline read: "Seller of nightmares attacks again." And it stated that the dreamseller consorted with prostitutes, bums and alcoholics—in a word, the worst strain of society. People should avoid contact with him; the young should ignore him. The article went on to say that the great social phenomenon could be one of the biggest psychopaths the city had ever seen.

Even the dreamseller seemed disappointed. The newspaper had interviewed only one party in the story, namely the Megasoft executives who suspected he was a terrorist and the

security guards who had abused him at the corporate headquarters.

The article added that he was an atheist who believed only
in himself. He wanted to be a kind of Christ, a god in his own
century. Without ever investigating him, they had thrown his
inventory in the trash. The newspaper coverage influenced
some. One person who read the article slapped the dreamseller
and spat in his face. "You want to be Christ? You're an atheist,
a man not worth his own life," the stranger told him

Wiping his face, the dreamseller looked his aggressor in
the eye and said poetically and serenely, "Yes, I was an atheist among atheists. To me, God was the fruit of a diminished
mind, a superstitious and reductive mind. But, though I defend
no religion, when I analyzed the 'son of man,' and his ability to
shape generous human beings even when he was betrayed and
seen as social trash, I saw my own childishness. And you who
follow him, do you recognize your childishness before him?"

The man went away speechless.

As a sociologist, I pointed out to my students that a journalist who doesn't investigate both sides of a story equally is a
disgrace to his profession. It was almost unbelievable that the
newspaper had been so partial.

The story led to a biased and totally slanderous view. It proclaimed loudly on page one that the homeless man nicknamed
the dreamseller has caused an uproar at the stadium, had attacked the director of Mellon Lincoln Hospital and incited a
riot on Demons Island, slandered the founders of the Megasoft group and had instigated an unprovoked assault on that
group's security guards.

The article tried to destroy him as critical thinker. It called
him a scoundrel, a fraud, an impostor, a con man. He was violent, vengeful, and possibly a psychopath, it said. It recommended that people stay away from him.

I looked at the dreamseller and saw him saddened. The gentlest and wisest man I knew had been thrown into society's trash bin. Even worse, he had no way to defend himself. They might as well convict him in the court of public opinion and sentence him to Demons Island.

And speaking of that island, the same newspaper did run a story that filled us with joy. Two theater groups were beginning to function full-time in the institution. Music and art teachers had been hired. In addition, Demons Island was to receive a hundred computers. Word came to us unofficially that at last money from the government would be forthcoming.

We were happy for Demons Island but anguished over the slanders in the newspaper. I remembered what the dreamseller had said. He valued journalistic criticism but considered prejudice a cancer to society.

"Criticism acknowledges existence, while prejudice annuls it," he said. "In the land of the blind, a one-eyed man is a stranger, the object of scorn and rejection."

After reading the story, we began walking down one of the city's best-known streets. My friends and I were melancholy. A man who looked to be around seventy, wearing a dark suit, white shirt, and a striped yellow tie, rapidly came toward us. As he got within ten yards, he flashed an unforgettable smile. He spread his arms and with uncontained joy ran to greet the dreamseller. It was an encounter overflowing with jubilation. But we didn't understand a thing. Perhaps it was someone who admired him but didn't know him.

The stranger embraced him affectionately, talking nonstop.

"You're alive! I can't believe it!"

To our surprise, the dreamseller responded with tears in his eyes. One of the wounds from the beating of the night before had opened and begun to bleed.

"Forgive me, I've gotten blood on you," the dreamseller

started to say. But the man demonstrated that not only was he intelligent but a gentleman as well.

"It's an honor to be stained by the blood of the man I love and admire the most," the stranger said.

The dreamseller put his hands on the other man's shoulders and nodded in gratitude.

Then he greeted us all. But he greeted Dimas with more feeling and joked, "How's the kleptomania? Have you overcome it?"

"Still the joker," the dreamseller said.

I didn't understand anything. Ever since I began accompanying the dreamseller and started writing this manual of dreams, I've become more confused. The consolation is that ideas are born in the terrain of discomfort.

The stranger was astonished at the dreamseller's battered appearance. "Good Lord, you're injured! What did they do to you? Tell me, which hotel are you staying in?"

Bartholomew broke out laughing.

"The best hotels in the city: overpasses, bridges, park benches and homeless shelters."

"What? You're sleeping under bridges? At least stay at one of your hotels."

"My dear man, you're speaking to the wrong person. The dreamseller is as poor as a church mouse," said the Mayor.

All of us were closely following that unusual conversation. The dreamseller answered the stranger, ignoring the Mayor. "I rest in the bed of peace and make the stars my blanket. You don't know the sheer joy of being a simple human being."

"But you could get sick. You look destroyed! What restaurant have you been eating at?"

"At Mr. Gutemberg's bakery. Day-old bread and lots of leftovers," Edson said.

"What? No, I can't believe it! You used to eat in the best

restaurants. It was your favorite luxury. What restaurant do you want me to buy?"

The tenor of the conversation staggered me. We had to humiliate ourselves anytime we wanted to eat. We had to jump through hoops, sing, put on clown acts and depend on the kindness of others to eat. Now this man came along proposing to buy the dreamseller a restaurant? Honeymouth couldn't hold his tongue any longer.

"Hey, I know all about food. I'll pick the restaurant," Honeymouth said.

The man speaking to the dreamseller looked at the band of misfits who followed him, and found them odd company. And he had just met us. Imagine if he spent a day with us!

"You can't deny who you are!" he said emphatically.

The dreamseller gave a soft, ironic laugh and replied, "Who am I? Today I look at myself and I'm astounded to confirm that I only knew the superficial levels of my being."

"You can't deny your past. You were the greatest businessman of the last decade and became one of the richest men on earth, even with the stock market crisis."

"Rich, me? What riches can bring back what I love the most? What amount of money can buy the source of happiness, the fountain of hope and the wellspring of dreams? If you accuse me of being rich, I admit it: yes, I'm rich. I have what money can't buy."

He paused, and pointed to us.

"Look at my friends; they're my treasure. They love me for who I am. They love a ragged man, a man without glamour, status, money, a pauper. Yes, I'm rich. I have eyes to see the flowers, I have time for the things without names. I have the smiles of children to nourish me, the experience of the elderly to instruct me in serenity, and the madness of psychotics to make me see my own insanity. Yes, I'm rich. I have what's important.

I have what neither gold nor silver can buy. What about you? Do you have those things?"

The stranger stood there silently and gave a wan smile. He realized that the dreamseller still possessed a brilliant sense of reasoning, better even than the last time they'd seen each other.

"I can't say that I do," he said. But he didn't give up. "I'm not speaking of those solemn riches, Master," said the elderly man, calling him Master for the first time. "I'm talking about that which men covet."

"Did you know that money attracts enemies and drives away true friends?"

"Yes, I do know. It's the system."

Honeymouth, the street philosopher, affirmed, "Money is like a corpse that feeds bacteria and attracts hyenas." Then he again patted himself on the back: "Gee, what brain cell did I extract that from?"

"If you lose everything you have, even your children and your image in society, how many people will stand by you?" the dreamseller told the man.

After a warm silence, the stranger answered, "Maybe far fewer than I dare believe. But you can't deny your power. It extends to every continent. Kings admire you. Celebrities fade in your presence. Presidents court you."

"Power? What power do I have, Charles?" the dreamseller said, using his friend's name for the first time. "Every day I die a little. Every day trillions of cells that make up my fragile body need to be nourished to keep from collapsing. Every day time howls in my mind reminding me that life, however serious it is, is only a play in eternity. Every day, time shouts at me that soon I'll perform my final act. What power do I have, Charles? Tell me."

"Wake up, man!" said Bartholomew. "We're the poorest people in the city. Can't you see that?"

"Dear Mr. Charles, do you maybe have some spare change you can lend me?" the Mayor asked.

The stranger scrutinized the pair of compulsive talkers from top to bottom and minced no words.

"I don't think your disciples are kaleidoscopic."

The Mayor drew close to Honeymouth and whispered, "Did that guy just praise us or insult us?"

"Good question," he said.

"But I like the word," the Mayor said.

"Don't you think your followers should be a team of intellectuals?" Charles told him.

"Intellectuals? In the Master's school, intellectuals and crazies are on the same level," Honeymouth said. "What you need is experience!" And he looked at me provocatively. But I was pensive and deeply interested in the conversation between the dreamseller and the stranger.

The dreamseller looked the man in the eye.

"If you knew my followers, you'd discover they are coarse, honest, ingenuous—different from us," he said. "Their wisdom doesn't come from the academic world, their sensitivity isn't revealed in art exhibitions, their fame isn't made known by the media. They live in anonymity, away from the spotlight, as if they were without merit. But I guarantee they are fascinating human beings."

After this praise, Bartholomew and Barnabas went around greeting all the disciples, congratulating them on being fascinating.

"I pity Hollywood, pity TV, pity magazines that ignore us," said Honeymouth proudly, striking an actor's pose.

"Yes, we are the great ignorant ones," the Mayor said, and I just shook my head.

CHAPTER 39

The Great Revelation

THE STRANGER DIDN'T KNOW WHAT TO SAY. HE WAS SPEECH-
less in the face of the bizarre group that followed the
dreamseller. The dreamseller saw we were confused and felt
he should give us some information about his past. Instead of
denying that he had been courted by kings and celebrities, he
said, "Forget who I was. What matters is who I am."

Hearing this, I almost collapsed. If he was telling us to forget who he was, it was confirming that he was someone great. It
wasn't possible to rationalize that information. It didn't fit into
any logical framework.

My mind swarmed with questions. If the dreamseller had
been so extremely rich in the past, how did he end up with almost nothing? He was a generous homeless person who divided
what he had with those who had nothing. He would give up
eating to feed the hungriest.

Not even the most rabid socialists dispensed with the privileges of comfort. Some of them, like Stalin, Brezhnev, Ceau-
şescu, and Kim Jong-Il, loved luxury more than capitalists did,
even when their people went hungry. Marx wrote about the
government of the proletariat, but not even he relinquished his
comforts.

In Nietzsche's terms, the dreamseller was human, all too

human. It was impossible to imagine that he had abandoned everything. Yes, he denounced a social system that had become a factory for producing sick people. Yes, he desired to sell the dream of a free mind. But not because he was a spiritual prophet or a messiah, but because he was a prophet of philosophy. He denounced the barbarity of modern society because he had developed critical thinking.

But if he were rich, how could he disdain the privileges of his work and his success? Only if he was unbalanced, crazy, unhinged. But none of that matched the facts. His intelligence exposed my own stupidity, his wisdom dissected my madness, his maturity revealed my childishness.

I could only conclude that the stranger was just flat wrong. He was just one more admirer who exalted him as a social hero for trying to change the way of society. This dreamseller, who even frequently took the subway to save money for food, couldn't have been admired by kings.

While I was pondering these questions, the dreamseller replied to the elderly, serene man who begged him to give up his life as a homeless wanderer.

"I don't have a blanket to sleep under, but I have the mantle of tranquillity. I don't have money to throw extravagant parties, but I celebrate life every day. I'm penniless, but I own everything that enchants my eyes. I have nothing to buy, but I sell dreams."

Charles was motionless, paralyzed. The dreamseller always confused those who heard him. But his friend made one last effort.

"If you want to sell dreams, you at least need to treat your injuries. Go to the hospital that you established in honor of your father," Charles told him.

I flushed and gasped for breath. After recovering, I blurted out: "What hospital?"

The stranger was silent for a moment. He looked at the dreamseller and received his approval to speak.

"Mellon Lincoln."

"What? Mellon Lincoln? I can't believe it! That can't be right!" I said, almost speechless. "Then you're . . . Mellon Lincoln Jr. The powerful head of Megasoft! The man slated to lead this country."

The dreamseller said nothing, and I was dumbfounded. All my friends also stood mute—even the compulsive talkers. I stared at the dreamseller's bruised face and pulled out the newspaper with the old photo of the handsome Mellon Lincoln Jr. I compared them, and my blood froze.

The dreamseller could see it in my eyes. I couldn't think. From beneath the rubble of my thoughts, I stared at the man who had rescued me from jumping off the top of the San Pablo Building.

"I criticized you several times in the classroom. I thought you were despotic, cold, removed from the plight of society, alienated from human conflicts," I said. "But look at you now, a pauper, a pauper who became my master. I heard you tear into Mellon Lincoln Jr. several times. I heard you provoke the executives of the Megasoft group, denouncing the founder of the institution—you yourself. Why? Why, for God's sake?" I asked, stupefied and using the word "God," something I, an atheist in transformation, rarely did.

The dreamseller sighed deeply. A crucial moment in our relationship had arrived. He looked at each one of us.

"Are you astonished? The *Homo sapiens* incapable of criticizing his sapience is unworthy of being *sapiens*. How could I survive without destroying my mind? How could I rescue my lucidity without denouncing my acts of insanity? How could I move on without recognizing my austerity, my damages and my stupidity?"

CHAPTER 40

The Creature Devoured by Its Creator

ALL MY FRIENDS WERE AS PERPLEXED AS CHARLES—EXCEPT for Dimas, that is. We had branded him a con man and a swindler, but to our surprise he was the young assistant to Mellon Lincoln Jr.

Dimas suffered from kleptomania and a complicated past. As a kleptomaniac, when an object, often without monetary value, entered his field of vision it set off a mental trigger that aroused a compulsion to possess it.

As an adolescent, he had robbed Mellon Lincoln Jr., whose bodyguards had caught him in the act. Instead of punishing him, Mellon Lincoln Jr. protected and educated him. He paid for his studies and made him into a kind of secretary to his family. We found out later that the dreamseller's children loved him. But Dimas broke down after the children's death and the dreamseller's mental collapse. But we still didn't have all the details about this relationship. Jurema seemed to have a gut feeling about his identity, but I had thought she was senile. Now I believe she had just preferred to keep quiet.

Bartholomew, Barnabas, Edson, Solomon, Monica, Crusher and several others who followed the dreamseller were trying to digest all this new information. They couldn't believe he had given up his comfortable life, scorned his power and turned his back on his status and fame. They replayed the last few months in their minds and were more confused than ever. They launched a battery of rapid questions at him.

"*Master*," said Monica, "you were humiliated at the stadium by leaders of the worldwide chain of ladies' clothing La Femme, a subsidiary of your company. And you let it happen! Why?"

"You were blocked from the entrance of your corporation as if you were some criminal," Edson added.

"And you were beaten by security guards whose salary you pay," Bartholomew, said, adding, "That's it, I'm gonna take those guys down . . ."

"You were slandered, called a lunatic and even a psychopath by the newspaper that's owned by your Megasoft group," Solomon said, dumbfounded.

"And you were almost killed by lethal injections in your own hospital!" I reminded him, indignant.

The dreamseller raised his eyes and saw some sparrows chirping and dancing in the air. Breathing deeply, he returned his gaze to his group of friends.

"The creator carefully raised his creature only to have it grow and bare its teeth against its master. An animal that needs to be whipped to be tamed will never be your friend, will never let you sleep in peace," he said, deeply upset. He then added, "If the Megasoft group turned against its creator, imagine what it does to strangers."

"Well I don't have to imagine. I know. The friends you trusted have become vultures," Charles said angrily. "The men who injured you don't know you."

"You think they really don't know me? Perhaps those who injured me don't know my identity, but some of those who want to take my life know quite well."

"I'm at your service, Mr. Lincoln," Charles said. "Who are

these enemies of yours? Who do you want me to punish? Who should I fire or send to prison?" Heads would roll.

Before the Master could respond, Bartholomew and the Mayor had already made a list of the heads that should be severed.

"That no-good who runs the hospital. Send him to Iraq for a year. Two journalists, five security guards, four executives. Let's see, who else . . . Ah! Tulio de Campos, who never liked Julio Cesar."

But the dreamseller cut them off emphatically: "For now, no one is to be punished!"

"No one?" the Mayor replied, dissatisfied. "It's our grand chance to wipe out these bastards!"

Charles, also indignant, said, "What do you mean, no one? They almost killed you. They're not worthy of walking around free, much less working for your company!"

"There are no saints in this story. I was to blame for instilling a philosophy that crushes the humanitarianism of those I led. The lack of money impoverishes us, but its misuse makes us miserable," he said.

Hearing him, I thought, "I don't have his maturity and dignity. If it were up to me, heads would roll. I used to cut students and professors off at the knees in the sociology department I ran for much less."

The dreamseller was a billionaire who lived under bridges. He was enriched by that which can't be bought. Then he repeated what he had told El Diablo on Demons Island.

"Besides, Charles, the greatest revenge against an enemy is—" And before the dreamseller could finish the phrase, Charles completed it:

"I know, I know. It's to forgive him . . . Just like your father used to say. He died because of it, as you well know."

I realized that Charles had known the dreamseller intimately since childhood. And so he was naturally extremely concerned about the dreamseller's living conditions and about the premeditated attempt on his life at the hospital.

"Either you assume your power or you must leave the country and sell your ideas somewhere they can't find you. Maybe in one of your summer homes in the Greek isles, in Scandinavia or French Polynesia."

"My bags are packed!" the Mayor said.

I couldn't believe my ears. As a university professor I suffered to pay the mortgage on my small, modest house, and the Master had several summer homes he never used. What kind of self-denial was that? "I don't have any bags to pack," the dreamseller said, joking with the Mayor. He turned to answer Charles.

"I almost died of guilt, depression and anguish in one of those summer homes. Today, I say let each day bring its own problems and its own solutions. Maybe the homeless man will work things out and find a reason to be what he once was. Maybe the pauper speaking to you will one day find joy in assuming his miserable throne of gold."

Charles had admired Mellon Lincoln Jr. long before he had faced his demons, before losing his children. He knew him to be courageous and bold, with a rare creative spirit and an unshakable determination. Charles understood that no one could convince him to change his path, once he had made up his mind. "I promised your father on his deathbed that I would never abandon you. If you need me, you know where to find me. Oh, and that siren that scared away the five men who almost killed you wasn't just a stroke of luck. I tried to do what I could to protect you. An informant I had tail you said you still know how to handle yourself with martial arts, but we still haven't had any luck finding out who hired those assassins."

Charles sighed deeply and put his hands on the dream-seller's shoulders before leaving. "Mellon . . . son, you're very important to a lot of people, but you're putting your life at risk. Please be careful." He took out his wallet and tried to give him over a thousand dollars, but the dreamseller refused. With tears in his eyes, Charles left silently.

Bartholomew and the rest of us bit our fingers, wanting to grab the dough. The dreamseller had twenty bodyguards, five armored cars, two private jets, but he had preferred freedom, with all its dangers, to being kept in a dungeon illuminated only by the light of society's spotlight. Incomprehensible? Yes, the man we followed had a complex mind. And he tried to ex-plain himself.

"If I had a thousand years to live, maybe I would go back and spend time on what I consider secondary. But because our time on earth, from childhood to old age, disappears in an in-stant, I can't afford the luxury of living without freedom. I don't ask you to understand this, only to respect it."

CHAPTER 41

Great Men Also Weep

WE NOW KNEW WHO THE DREAMSELLER WAS AND WE were all stupefied. He had gone out into the world seeking to confront the conflicts that haunted him. He had been part of the very system he criticized. Now, it was time to be free.

He looked again at the swallows flying overhead and recited the wanderer's anthem, hoping his words would take flight and be as free as the birds.

"Who am I? Powerful? Famous? No! I'm just a wanderer who lost the fear of getting lost. You may call me crazy, you may mock my ideas. It doesn't matter. What matters is that I'm a wanderer who has learned to break out of the cell of routine."

An hour later, we found ourselves back in the courtyard of the federal courthouse. We were flying high, for now we felt we were following a powerful man. That made us ecstatic. Everything would be simpler, we thought. Our paths would be smoother, our days more at ease, our existence infused with more creature comforts. We should have known better.

A man with grayish hair, who looked to be around fifty, came quickly up to me and placed an envelope in my hands, then left without identifying himself. It was addressed care of the old friends Honeymouth and the Mayor and signed by none other than El Diablo.

I was startled at first. It was only then that I discovered my two companions had been longtime friends with the infamous Demons Island leaders. I handed the letter to them, and they glanced at each other before opening it. Bartholomew took the initiative and gave me a quick explanation.

"El Diablo and Shrapnel were friends of ours from the orphanage. We were lost to drinking and they were lost to a life of crime."

They opened the letter and began reading it together. I moved away to respect their privacy. As they read, their lips started to tremble for the first time. A sudden anguish overcame them. They were paralyzed. They dropped to their knees, tears covering their faces.

I had never seen those two jokers who always made light of even the most serious things, fall to pieces. But they did. They lost all their joy, their good spirits. Of course, I wanted to know what was in the letter. They handed it to me, nearly drained of all strength. It had been addressed to them but in reality it was intended for the dreamseller. I began reading the short letter and was as astonished as Bartholomew and Barnabas. I couldn't believe what I was reading. The dreamseller's enemies had beaten and slandered him and now they intended to bury him.

The last thing in the world I wanted was to hand that letter to the dreamseller. Everyone else wanted to read it, but I couldn't bring myself to show it to them. Short of breath, flushed, I walked tensely toward him. He saw my emotional state and, I instantly saw the tension build on his face.

The dreamseller took the letter. As soon as he read the opening lines, for the first time since we'd known him, we saw him break down. He was no longer the invincible, intrepid leader we had followed. Instead, he transformed and became a disturbed, shaken man.

After finishing the letter, he fell to his knees as Bartholomew and Barnabas had done. His heart had been ripped out mercilessly. He raised his hands to the heavens and shouted:

"Noooo! It can't be!" He screamed the names of his two children, Fernando and Julieta, over and over. He clenched his eyes closed and wept bitter tears.

Everyone in the square froze. It was as if the dreamseller were dying. And he was—inside. Expressing inexpressible pain, he began to sob and say repeatedly, "No! No! Because of me—no!"

The letter fell from his hands and the wind blew it to Professor Jurema. She caught it and read it to the other members of the group.

To the seller of dreams,

I was touched by your words on this miserable island, and I felt I should give you a piece of news— even though I know hearing this will be the worst nightmare of your life. You said the best revenge against an enemy is to forgive him. And now, I am asking for yours. I know that every man has his limits, especially where his children are concerned. You should know that two of your closest "friends" at Megasoft paid to hire a hit man. Your children didn't die in an accident. Everybody thought you would be on board flight JM 4477 on March 23. You were the target.

Signed,
El Diablo

The disciples stood silently in that immense courtyard. There were no birds singing, no caress of the breeze, no rustling leaves. A few passersby chuckled at seeing a man on his knees, weeping. That's the human story. Some are depressed while others smile, some shout while others remain silent.

We wanted to console the dreamseller, take him in our arms, say anything that might soften his pain, but it was impossible. His anguish was so deep that no words could lessen the blow.

In light of this information, a great dilemma would mark the dreamseller's story. As he had told us, enemies can frustrate, but only friends can truly betray us. The dreamseller has two false friends who committed the ultimate betrayal, men more violent and powerful than any criminal on Demons Island. Men who had probably dined, walked and laughed with the dreamseller but who sank to the lowest depths of crime. Who were these psychopaths? Why did they commit that unspeakable act? What would the dreamseller do? Would he continue to be homeless? Would he take up his seat as one of the most powerful men in the world? Would he run in fear of his pursuers or plot his revenge against those who killed his children? Consumed with hate, would he renounce his belief that violence does not justify violence? Would he be able to see the difference between vengeance and justice? Would he stop selling dreams and distill hatred instead?

And what would he do with us? We had built an altruistic unprecedented brotherhood. Given the risks he'll face from now on, would he abandon us? Would we be able to live apart from one another? Some of us might get by. I have my university, Jurema has her possessions, Solomon his house, Monica her apartment, Edson his religion. But what about Bartholomew and Barnabas? They have nothing. They're street wanderers with no address or protection. All they have is the dreamseller and their new family. They knelt and both wept for the dreamseller's children. They had adopted him as their father, a ragged father who didn't punish, exclude or shame

them, one who embraced them, loved them and invested everything he had in them. There was a completely unselfish, poetic,
serene and unexplainable love between them.

I remembered something the dreamseller had said: "You're
responsible for the consequences of your choices."

Every man has to make choices. The moment had come
for him to make his greatest choice. Would he continue to
explore his path or would he be afraid of losing himself?
Would he go back to the cult of celebrity, of which he had
been so critical?

Dozens of questions hurtled into my mind. And I didn't
have any answers. I only knew that he had managed to reorganize his fragmented history in masterly fashion, but now his
being had again been shattered into a thousand pieces. I had
seen him go off alone, night after night, talking to his children
in his imagination, begging their forgiveness for the time he
didn't spend with them, for trying to give them the world but
denying them his presence—which is all that really mattered.

This intriguing man taught us that the greatest test of all
was taming our ghosts. But now the ghosts of anger, pain, revenge and retaliation emerged like a sudden earthquake to
haunt him. Would he pass the greatest test of all?

As a philosophical thinker, he had solemnly defended the
thesis that existence is cyclical. Drama and comedy, tears and
joy, peace and anxiety are privileges of the living and inexora-
bly alternate for every human being.

What would he say now? Would he abandon his own belief?
How would he deal with the cycle of existence? I didn't know.
I only knew he would have to go from the seller of dreams to
buyer of dreams. He would need the most intelligent and lucid
to bear the full consequences of his own theory: "Life is like a
theatrical production, the show of shows. When we close the

curtain on the theater of time, the show doesn't end; the spectacle continues for the audience in tears."

At that moment I saw him on his knees, spent, simply a part of the sobbing audience.

Great men also weep, and when they fall, they shed inconsolable tears . . .

THE END

(of the second volume)

Acknowledgments

I have met countless sellers of dreams along the way. Through their intelligence and their generous acts they inspired me, taught me and made me see my own smallness. They paused in their journey on the paths of existence to think about others and give of themselves while asking nothing in return. They made of their dreams lifetime projects, and not desires that shatter in the heat of the tempest.

I dedicate this book to my dear Geraldo Pereira, the son of the great editor José Olympio. It has not been long since Geraldo closed his eyes forever. He was a poet of existence, a fine seller of dreams in the universe of literature, as well as in the theater of society. He was my friend and counselor. I offer him the most grateful homage.

I dedicate this book to my esteemed friend and reader Maria de Lourdes Abadia, ex-governor of Brasília. She sold many dreams in the Brazilian capital, of which I cite, especially her dreams for the underprivileged who live in and from the city's garbage. She gave back to them something fundamental to mental health: dignity.

To my esteemed friend Guilherme Hannud, an entrepreneur endowed with a noble sensitivity and a thirst for helping others. Through his social projects, he gave employment opportunities to hundreds of former offenders so they would have the strength to extricate themselves from the morass of rejection and achieve, despite the scars of the past, the inalienable status of human beings.

To my dear friend Henrique Prata and the excellent team of doctors of Pio XII Hospital, among whom I cite especially Dr. Silas and Dr. Paulo Prata (in memoriam) and my friend Dr. Edmundo Mauad. As compulsive sellers of dreams, this team transformed the small Barretos Cancer Hospital into one of the largest and best in the Americas by offering free treatment of the highest level to poor patients who would never have been able to pay for it. They proved that dreams prolong life and alleviate pain.

To my dear reader Marina Silva, who in childhood was punished by the vicissitudes of existence, but whose dreams of changing the world fed her courage and intellect and made her a senator and later an extraordinary minister of environment. Marina passionately yearns to preserve nature for future generations. Through her, I would like to dedicate this work to all the scientists of the Intergovernmental Panel on Climate Change who tirelessly battle to illuminate the mind of political leaders so they will take urgent measures to ameliorate the disaster of the greenhouse effect. Unfortunately, many of those leaders lie down in the bed of egocentrism and resist "buying" dreams.

To the beloved Catholic friends and leaders, of whom I cite as representatives the priests Jonas Abibe, Oscar Clemente and Salvador Renna. In them, love of one's fellow man and tolerance ceased to be theory and entered the pages of reality. With surpassing love, they have sown dreams of a society suffused with brotherhood and altruism. To the beloved Protestant friends and leaders, of whom I cite as representatives Marcelo Gualberto, Aguiar Valvassora and Márcio Valadão. The pleasure of giving of oneself found in them a fertile ground. Wherever they go, they have spread the perfume of love and greatness of soul. To my countless Buddhist, Muslim and spiritualist friends. They have enchanted me with their dreams. To my atheist and agnostic friends, I was part of that group and know that many of them are outstanding human beings, dear dreamers.

I dedicate this novel especially to society's greatest sellers of dreams, the educators. Even with low salaries, they insist on selling dreams in the microcosm of the classroom so that students may stretch the frontiers of their intellect and become agents of change in the world, at least in their world. I have numerous professor friends in all fields. To represent them, I cite Silas Barbosa Dias; Dr. José Fernando Macedo, president of the Medical Association of the state of Paraná, not only an excellent professor of vascular surgery but a seller of humanism in medicine; and Dr. Paulo Francischini. Dr. Francischini has used one of my programs to notable effect to guide thoughts and protect emotion in masters and doctoral courses in his discipline, with the aim of molding thinkers.

To Jesus Badenes, Laura Falcó and Francisco Solé, brilliant executives in the Planeta firm, one of the largest publishers in the world. They do more than publish books; they sell dreams to nurture creativity and the art of thinking in their readers. To dear friends César, Denis, Débora and all the other members of the Planeta Brasil team. They were so excited about *The Dreamseller* that they stimulated me to write the continuation of this work. I especially thank my friend and editor Pascoal Soto for his intelligence and serenity. His opinions were of extreme value to the present work.

To my inspiring father, Salomão, who from childhood I watched selling dreams by taking needy sick people to hospitals for the simple pleasure of helping. He was always an excellent storyteller and an exceptional human being. To my cultured father-in-law, Georges Farhate. As incredible as it seems, among the dreams he sold, he taught us that it is worthwhile to believe in life when, at the age of ninety, he again ran for public office, while many young people of twenty or thirty feel old and alienated. To dear Dirce and Áurea Cabrera for their affection for my works.

To my beloved wife, Suleima, and my daughters Camila, Carolina and Cláudia. They fascinate me with their astuteness, intelligence and generosity. I hope they will never come to love the worship of celebrity, that they will live the art of authenticity and understand that the most beautiful dreams are born in the terrain of humility and grow in the soil of nonconformity. I yearn for them not only to be in school, but for school to be in them, and for them to become dreamsellers until the last breath of life.

To my beloved patients. I not only taught them but also learned much from them. I learned much more from their deliriums, their crises of depression, their panic attacks and obsessive disturbances than from the restricted universe of scientific treatises. To all of them, my eternal gratitude. I found diamonds in the soil of suffering human beings. Whoever fails to recognize his conflicts will never be healthy, and whoever refuses to be taught by the conflicts of others will never be wise.

I have lived in a forest for close to twenty years, in a small and beautiful town that has no bookstore. In that unusual setting, I developed the psychological, sociological and philosophical ideas found in my books. I never expected that one day they would be read by millions of people, published in many countries and used in various universities. My dreams have taken me to unimaginable places.

About the Author

Augusto Cury is a psychiatrist, psychotherapist, scientist, and bestselling author. He has written more than twenty books that have been published in more than fifty countries. Through his work as a theorist in education and philosophy, he developed the Theory of Multifocal Intelligence, which presents a new approach to the logic of thinking, the process of interpretation, and the creation of thinkers. Cury created the School of Intelligence based on this theory.